Unbroken

Count On Me #6

Unbroken
(Count On Me #6)
By
Melyssa Winchester

To the woman that showed me what real love could be between two men. Cheryl, the Hummel to my Berry, this book and the love in the pages is dedicated to you. Thank you for continuing to inspire me daily just in being who you are.

"Being who you are is a lot easier than faking it." – Adam Lambert

Prologue

Ryder

"What's a sweet thing like you doing here drinking all alone?"

Sadly, this isn't the first time I've heard this line. I swear it's the go-to line for hookups, at least when they happen here.

Gretchen's Place. The piece of shit watering hole I go to when I need the escape from life's bullshit. Also where I go when the escape I need is more than just a mental one.

The body that's attached to the voice, it's older, more mature. Looking up and taking in her face, it's easy to see why I made that determination. There are creases in her forehead, bags under her eyes and all of that added to the sagging tits, it's enough to tell me that she's someone's mother, or at least old enough to be mine.

As much as I need the physical release right now, it's definitely not gonna happen with this chick.

"How many times have you used that line tonight?'

It's not what I wanna say, but telling her to fuck off seems mean. It's not her fault that her life has taken such a shitty turn that she's standing here now picking up guys half her age. It's pathetic, sure, but aren't we all?

I know I am.

"Would you believe me if I said you were the first?"

"No, not really." I laugh. "I get the feeling you've used that line a little more than you wanna admit. It's probably one of a dozen that gets you the result you're after."

Where I expect my truth to offend her, it has the opposite effect. She smiles first and then laughter spills out around us. Well, if I can't fix my own screwed up head, it's nice to know I can at least entertain hers.

"You might be right about that."

"I usually am."

"So since the line is an obvious fail," she concedes. "And you're not looking for a hookup like the rest of us; what brings you here?"

That's a good question. What am I doing here? It's probably the last place I need to be with what today is, yet here I am, same as always, drowning my shit and feeling less than satisfied with the results.

"Nowhere better to be."

"Somehow I doubt that."

"You'd be wrong."

"I'm pretty sure the last thing you wanna hear is what an old broad like me thinks, but I don't believe that. Guy comes in here looking like you, I have a hard time believing there isn't a pretty little thing waiting for you at home."

"Again," I repeat. "You'd be wrong."

"No one at home?"

"No one period."

"Excuse me while I call bullshit. I don't believe it."

It's not the first time I've had a conversation like this with a random stranger and had them come to the same conclusion. People think that because of the way I look; blue eyes and parted light brown hair along with my build from years of playing sports, that me being alone is an impossibility. I'm too good looking to be alone. They really don't know shit.

Being alone is my penance. It's what I deserve for the firestorm of shit I created two years ago and the damaged people I left behind when it was over.

"Well, if I'm too fake for you, there's about ten other guys here that I'm sure your tired old lines will work on."

Here we go. It's time for the venom to come out.

"Maybe I like fake."

"Or maybe you've tried everyone else and I'm what's left."

"It's not working."

"What's that?"

"I know the way you see me and I even know why you're saying the shit you are right now. You want me to hurt the same way you do. The thing is, you can't hurt what's already been destroyed."

That's the first thing she's said since she showed up that I can actually agree with. I'm just not about to admit it to her.

I *really* shouldn't have come here tonight. This will teach me the next time I need a tension release.

"The only thing hurting me sweetheart is the fact that you're still here."

She turns to leave and for the first time since I got here, I'm filled with relief, but it doesn't last because where I'm expecting her to go, she lingers and the next words she says are like a knife straight into my chest.

"What you're hoping to bury; the thing you don't wanna admit or focus on; kiddo, you ain't gonna find it here. This place don't serve your kind."

My kind.

"And what kind would that be?"

I need to get up and go. Get as far away as I can, as fast as I can until this place is completely in my rear view, but I'm stuck.

Even with as badly as I want to escape, I know I can't.

"The kind that turns down a real chance at escaping because deep down, it's not in the form he really wants."

"That's a whole lot of assumption for someone who knows nothing about me."

"I don't have to know you, sugar. It's written all over you. What you want, it's not here. So if nothing else sticks tonight, I hope this does." She pauses and I use the moment to slide off the stool, more than ready to get the hell out of here. "Stop running from it. You'll feel a whole lot better when you do."

Yeah right. The minute I stop running, I'll have to admit the truth. I'm determined to never go down that road again, even if I have to fuck my way through every female on and off campus in order to distance myself from it.

I'm never gonna admit that she's right. That what I want really isn't going to be found in this heterosexual hellhole.

I'm never going to admit I'm gay.

Chapter One

Ryder

"The game against Central, you're out, and if something doesn't change with you, getting cut from games is gonna be the least of your worries."

He doesn't have to say it. I know what he's getting at.

Academic Probation.

"You're a hell of a ball player, Kane, but when more than one of your professors comes to me about your performance in their class, what do expect me to do?"

He really doesn't expect me to answer that does he? He can't. What I expect him to do and what he's gonna do, is gonna be two different things. I'm not even gonna waste my breath.

"I get it, Coach."

"Son, I don't think you do. When you're out on the field, nothing can stop you. It's the way you are that wins us games, but it's gotta be about more than that. You gotta use that same tenacity in class or you're not gonna go anywhere."

That's the point. I don't wanna go anywhere. I'm only doing this college thing because it allows me to do what I love. Play football.

What he doesn't get is that when I'm on the field, it's the one place I can push everything else down. I don't have to focus on what a fucking mess I am. The deep dark secret that only me and a few other people back home know about. I can let it all go and be Ryder Kane, Wexfield Panthers Running Back.

"How do I fix it?"

There, that seems like the right question to ask. Let him believe I give a shit about my performance in class so he'll stop me from having to go home with my tail between my legs and admit what a complete waste of space I am.

"Put more of an effort into showing up for class. Past that, I think you need to look into getting yourself a tutor. If the reason you're pulling this crap is because you're not understanding the material, then get help until you do."

"I understand it all just fine."

"Kane, you wanna get back on the field?"

"Yeah, of course I do."

"Then stop lying."

"I'm not—"

"Denial only makes it true, son."

The way he calls me son pisses me off. I've already got a father. I don't need another one, especially when it's just more of the same disapproval I've been hearing all my life.

"Fine. I'm lying."

"That's better. If you wanna play ball again, and I know you do, I suggest you do what I said and look into getting help."

"How am I supposed to do that? I don't even know where to start."

"You show up. That's how. You show up and you keep showing up until your teachers are so damned annoyed they've got no other choice but help you. I guarantee, if you do that, you'll get where you need to be."

Where I need to be.

How can he know where that is when I don't even know anymore?

I lost the right to be anywhere the night I thought it was smart to take a pissed off attitude, add alcohol to it and wrap my car around a telephone pole.

Killing the only person that mattered.

Survivor's guilt. I can fill a 747 with the stuff. The wrong person died that night, and no matter how many days I get up and go through the motions, nothing's gonna change it. It's not gonna bring him back.

When Gavin died, I died too.

"Does my exile from the team extend to sitting on the bench for practice?"

"No, but are you sure you want to torture yourself that way?"

He has no idea the lengths I'm willing to go to torture myself.

"I can handle it."

"Ryder, I know how bad it looks, but it's not too late to turn things around."

It's not his intent, but those words, I've heard them before. It's what the first therapist said the minute I sat down in his chair about a week after I was released from the hospital. His attempt at trying to make me feel less responsible for the life I took that night. A useless attempt since it didn't sink in. The same way it's not sinking in now.

"You know what you gotta do?"

"Yeah, Coach."

"Good because two weeks from now, I want you back on the field. You hear me?"

"Loud and clear."

Conversation's over. Looks like I know what I gotta do now.

It's time to find myself a tutor.

*****

After the talk with my coach, I went to talk to two of my professors, who only confirmed everything he already went over. I was dangerously close to being thrown on probation without some serious intervention. I needed to start giving a shit if I ever wanted to play ball again.

If that wasn't enough to turn this already shitty day worse, the look on Dillon's face the minute I get home seals it.

"We need to talk."

"We do?"

"Yeah we do, Ry."

Dillon transferred in a few months before I did and being on the same team, we bonded over our love of the game. It didn't take long from there for the two of us to be friends, which after a couple of explosions in his personal life, ended with us living together.

It's been a pretty easy go of it considering my hatred of being around people, but something tells me from the look on his face, the fun ride is about to come to an end.

"What about?"

He sighs and what was left of my spirits, the hope I had that the day wouldn't be total shit, dies with the sound.

"Ry, did you really think he wouldn't come talk to me?"

Now I get it.

Coach came and talked to him about what he said to me earlier and Dillon being Dillon, is going to take his turn on the merry-go-round. I knew I was going to hate him taking the Assistant Coach position.

"Not in the mood, D."

"You know, I'm not exactly in the mood for this either, but sometimes you gotta do shit you don't like."

"I feel for you, bro. I do. I can see how horrible this is, having to call me out on my shit like you're my fucking father or something. How about I save us both the aggravation and leave?"

"Don't be like that."

"Like what? Not in the mood to hear another lecture? Offended that this is coming up in the one place it shouldn't?"

"Fine. You don't wanna talk about what Coach said, let's talk about last night."

From one annoying topic to another. It really is like he's the parent and I'm the child. I don't even need to ask what he's getting at. It's another screwed up reminder I don't need.

"Not going there either."

"When we made this plan to live together, I told you I didn't care what you did with your personal life and Ry, I meant it. I can't ignore last night though. It wasn't right. How many did you bring home this time? Three?"

It was two, but I'm not arguing semantics with him. It will just make it worse and I want this over with so I can go in my room and forget the day even exists.

"You just said that you didn't care, so you wanna tell me why this matters?"

"Because you weren't the only one they kept up all night with their screaming, that's why."

What he's referring to, it's how I cope. When going to the bar yields less than desirable results, I'll hop around to a club or two, find whatever willing participant I can and bring them home. Last night, it happened to be two of them. They did what I needed them to do and by morning, they were gone. Another notch in a bedpost I stopped giving a crap about a long time ago.

Women. I drown myself in them because I can't handle the way I feel normally. Being attracted to guys, it's what landed me in this messed up situation. Falling in love with one of them only made it worse. So if jamming my dick up in something I don't need to give a shit about in the morning is the only way I can get relief, so be it.

"Won't happen again."

"Somehow I doubt that."

"Of course you do."

"Ry," standing from the sofa, he makes his way over to where I'm leaning at the entryway to the kitchen. "Do you think I'm an idiot?"

"If I answer that truthfully, are you gonna hit me?"

"Maybe."

I debate whether or not to push it, but with the way this conversation is already going, decide against it.

"No, I don't think you're an idiot, but what does that have to do with this?"

"You saw what happened to me. You remember it right?"

"The shit a few months back?"

"Yeah."

"No offense, D, but if you don't get to the point soon, I'm going to bed."

For a few minutes, we're bathed in some pretty heavy silence and it's only when I go to move around him that he decides it's time to speak again.

"You're doing what I did. You can say it's none of my business, but take it from someone who's been there. You don't wanna go down that road."

"What road is that?"

This is starting to remind me of the other night with the random woman dishing out her advice even though I wanted no part of it. Something I'm definitely not in the mood to repeat.

"I got hurt on the field and instead of just admitting what that did to me, I turned to something else in order to take it away. You're doing the same damn thing and you need to stop before you lose everything."

"Losing everything implies having something to lose in the first place."

"So your position on the team; the one you're gunning for now that I'm not there; that doesn't mean shit to you?"

Damnit. He's got me. Running back was never my dream position, I wanted something bigger and with Dillon on the sidelines indefinitely, I was primed to take over as quarterback. I was until I screwed it all up anyway.

"What's your point?"

"You bringing home all these women, it's your drug." He says, referencing the amphetamines he was taking in order to continue playing after the injury to his knee. "And despite what you think, I give a shit and don't wanna see you become me."

The problem with his speech is, it's like the one I gave him when I caught on to what he was doing. Walking into the locker room, catching him swallowing pills, it didn't take a brain surgeon to see what was going on, especially with his mood changes. When nothing I said got through, I took it to the only other person that had half a chance of making him see the damage he was causing himself.

His girlfriend.

It's just too bad that like the night two years ago with Gavin, I was too late then too. Another failure I've gotta live down, despite the fact that Dillon seems happier than I've ever seen him.

"You're wrong."

"No, Ry, I'm not."

"Yeah okay, Dad. You're right. I'm so screwed up that I use women in order to feel better. Happy now?"

"Acting like a dickhead isn't gonna change the fact that I'm right. You forget that you're talking to the king of them. What's it gonna take for you to wake the fuck up?"

"Wide awake already, D."

My fake laugh or as he calls it—me being a total dickhead—is only making this entire thing worse. I can tell by the scowl on his face that it's not gonna be long now before I frustrate him enough to make him lose it.

Dillon Murphy is pretty damn scary when he's pissed.

"You live with me for a few months and suddenly you think you know me?"

"I do know you because I *was* you."

"You don't know shit."

Before I realize what's going on, I'm being pushed up against the wall and he's got a grip on my shirt, forcing the full weight of his own body into mine, keeping me locked in place.

"I know that you're holding on to something pretty damn heavy and it's changing you. I also know that the women you bring around here are only a smoke screen because you don't wanna face the truth."

"And that is?"

"You're gay, you idiot and before you try and deny it, since it's engrained in your god damned head to do it, let me remind you of what happened in the shower a couple of months ago."

Son of a bitch.

The truth I've been trying to bury about myself, most of the time I've got a grip on it, but sometimes, like what happened with Dillon, I slip and of course he caught me.

If it was just me looking, I could have easily blown it off, but it's the amount of time I spent watching him that blew my secret wide open. It's something I hoped he'd forgotten about with how I've acted since, but obviously that was too good to be true.

He knows and with the way he's smirking at me, I'm pretty sure any denial I mount is gonna fall on deaf ears.

Releasing the hold, he backs up and makes his way back across the room until he's throwing his body back down onto the sofa completely stretching out, his smirk now a full on grin.

I'm officially screwed.

"Now that I've shut you up, you wanna talk about what Coach said?"

He's giving me an out and I'll be damned if I'm not gonna take it. Maybe if we change the subject, he'll forget about everything he just said and I can go back to hiding the way I have been. It's the way it has to be.

"I need to get a tutor, get my grades back up in a couple classes and he'll let me play again. I got a few names from my Poly Sci professor and another one from English. I'm working on it."

"The names they gave you. Did a guy named Isaac come up at all?"

"Yeah, that's the one my English professor gave me. I'm supposed to text him. Why?"

"He helped me out when I got here. He's good. Use him."

I still can't believe how quickly the conversation changed. The only thing that hasn't is the smile lingering on his face and no matter how much I try and focus on something else, my mind won't let me.

What the hell does he have to smile about, and why does it bother me so much?

Isaac

"Mr. Crawford, may I steal a moment of your time?"

Nodding, I slide out of my seat and head to the front of the room, paper at the ready for whatever he's got waiting for me.

Being called out by my professor should scare me, but it doesn't. It's half the reason I take so much time getting my things together at the end of class. It makes it easier should they need to reach out. Considering my issues, it's the least I can do.

I'm what the world calls High Functioning Autistic but with a twist. I don't talk. I haven't spoken since I was two and no matter how many different therapies were tried, I still haven't. I've adapted to it, but the rest of the world, well, they need a little bit more of a push.

When I came here in September, finally ready to take the plunge and enter the world as a college student, I was surprised with how easily my professors seemed to adapt to the way I am. Where I expected looks and even total lack of acceptance, I didn't get it, at least not from them.

The students were another story, but it's just another thing I'm used to by now. No matter how much I wish it was another way, the world is always going to be filled with the ignorant. The only thing I can do is rise above it.

It's gotten a whole lot easier to do that since Isabelle Reagan showed up in my creative writing class. She's autistic too, but just like no two coins are the same, we aren't either. It's because of her that I'm still here and able to make my way around campus with a bit more confidence then I had before. She's shown me that just because no one else seems to see the best parts of me, it doesn't mean they aren't there.

Who am I tutoring this time? :)

When his laughter comes, I know I've hit the nail on the head. It's another thing that not a lot of people realized when I first showed up. I'm smarter than the average bear. It didn't take long for the professors to clue in and use it to their advantage. Though if I'm honest, with how much I get paid for helping a lot of the people that have been tossed my way, I'm using it to my advantage too.

It's nice having a side business when most people think I'm too stupid to do anything at all.

"Ryder Kane. His attendance alone speaks to his need for help, but the work he has submitted is also not at the level I was hoping he would be at by now."

When do you need me to start?

"As soon as possible. As with the other students you've helped, I've given him your number. It is my hope that over the next couple of days, he will reach out to you so we can help him."

If he doesn't reach out?

"Ryder isn't like the others. I can't go into details, but it's a safe assumption that if he does not reach out, it will cost him dearly."

He doesn't need to say anything else. I can read between the lines pretty easily. Ryder, even though I don't know much about him, is probably like Dillon was when he first transferred here. Sports oriented and not at all interested in the academics needed to have a fall back option if that road wasn't there anymore.

Dillon changed though, so I've got no doubt that with the right amount of work, Ryder can too.

Does he know that he has to text me?

"Yes. I've made him aware of what he needs to do."

Okay. Well, I'll do my best.

"I know you will, Isaac. I'm not concerned about that. I just hope that we're not doing this too late."

Does Ryder really need that much help?

"Ryder Kane needs a level of help that I'm not even sure your level of intellect can provide. It's my hope that curing one problem will help with the rest."

This is where things get uncomfortable. He's not giving me personal information, but what he is saying is enough to make me draw my own conclusions about what my professor believes is the issue here.

It's information I have no business knowing.

I'll do what I can for him.

It's the truth. I'll help Ryder in whatever way I can. I just hope that knowing what I do now, I don't live to regret it.

Chapter Two

Ryder

This has got to be someone's idea of a sick joke.

Considering who recommended this guy to me, there's no other way I can look at this. I'm the damn punchline in an elaborate joke put together by my annoying roommate.

Isaac Crawford.

I should have put two and two together when his name was given to me days ago, but of course, in another life I must have been a blonde because I didn't see this coming. The guy that's supposed to be helping me out of the mess I got myself into, my ticket to getting back on the team and not getting thrown out of school altogether, is the one guy on the entire campus that can't even talk to me.

Even on a campus this big people talk, and a lot of the time it's never anything good. It's even worse with the guys on the team. There's a lot of shit talking that goes on and I've heard a lot more than I want to admit about this guy. If I'm Dillon's punchline, than I'm pretty sure Isaac is everyone else's.

I should just bail out on this now that I know, but I don't. Choosing him the way I did, especially now that I know he's in every class I need help with most, I've got no other option.

Isaac it is.

"So how does this work? Do I just tell you everything I'm completely bombing in and you work some kind of magic until I'm back on top again?"

Way to go Kane. That didn't sound perverted at all.

He slides the paper across the table and despite not wanting to react, I laugh.

I already know what you're bombing in. It's everything.

"You caught me. I suck at everything that isn't football. So can you help or not?"

I can help.

Screw this. I can't sit here passing paper back and forth like this and not ask. I need to know if this is for real or not. To hear the guys on the team tell it, he does this in order to make girls feel sorry for him. If that's true, I'm gonna put an end to it. I'd much rather talk to my tutor if I'm gonna be spending the majority of my time with him.

"Man, I gotta know. This whole not talking bit, is it for real?"

No. It's all a lie. I enjoy making my hand hurt by writing to thoughtless meatheads all day. It completes me.

"Thoughtless meatheads? Is that the best you got?"

Calling you a brainless moron wasn't enough for you?

Well, when he puts it that way, maybe I need to quit while I'm ahead. With the way I've been treating my classes, I'm pretty sure the name is accurate.

"Point taken. So where do we start?"

I've put together a list of things I think we need to focus on. We'll tackle one subject every few days and then I'll test you on what we've gone over and go from there.

"What if I do all that, take your tests and it turns out I'm a lost cause?"

No one's a lost cause, Ryder. Some people just need a little more work than others.

Shit. Of all the ways I expected him to answer, especially with his earlier sarcasm, it definitely wasn't like that. I need to say something back, but I don't have the first clue what.

His earlier assessment is true. I am a brainless moron.

Is there somewhere more important you need to be right now?

Wow. Pulling away from the conversation with him, going inside my head like I always do, I didn't even realize how much time passed.

"Nah man. Why do you ask?"

You're fidgeting and you keep looking at the door.

Another thing I didn't notice I was doing. Shit. At the rate this is going, he's gonna be the one to bail. I need to turn this around or I'm never gonna get back on the team.

"I don't think I need the help, but I don't have anywhere to be."

He slides a set of papers across the table and when I look down, I see what he's done. He's taking what I've said and turned it around until it's glaring me in the face.

"You enjoy showing me what an idiot I am?"

His eyes move down between the papers in front of him and the table. Anywhere but at me, where for some weird reason I want them to be. Considering I just asked him a question, turning away and not responding, even though I shouldn't care, bothers the hell out of me.

"I guess that's a yes." I whisper under my breath and that's when I see the pen start moving across the paper. Pushing it across until it's bumping up against my tapping fingers, I see the reason for the speed. I've pissed him off.

I don't think you're an idiot. I'm pretty sure I know what your problem is and it's not that you're stupid. If this is going to work, I want you to see the reality of your situation, and what we've got to do in order to fix the mess you made to get you back where you need to be. That's all.

"Sorry."

It's okay, Ryder. I'm used to it.

I should just leave this alone, but the way his eyes go back down to the table, weakened from the way they were when I got here, I can't just let it sit. I need answers.

"Used to what?"

He taps the pen against his cheek before placing it on the paper and writing out his response. For whatever reason, this answer, unlike the other ones he's given me since I got here, is one he's taking his time with and if what he said earlier wasn't enough to intrigue me, this definitely is.

You're not the first stubborn football player I've had to tutor. I know what people think about me and what the guys on the team say. I went to high school with a lot of them and

it's been the same repeated stuff for years. **The way you are, I'm used to it. This is the last place you want to be and I get it because if I had a choice, I wouldn't be here either.**

Damn. He pretty much told me that I'm the last person he wants to be sitting here with. I should open my mouth and agree with everything he said because it's basically the truth, but I can't. I don't know what other people besides Dillon he's tutored from the team, but if this is gonna work, he needs to know that I'm not everyone else. Even if I've spent the last fifteen minutes proving otherwise.

"You wanna know the truth?"

Sure.

"When I got here today, I didn't realize you were the Isaac that was going to be tutoring me. You're right. The guys on the team talk a lot of shit about you. I wanted to bail out on this because I don't get how someone who can't even talk to me is supposed to be the one helping me. It's a dickhead thing to think and even say, but it's true."

Can I show you something?

"Yeah."

Sliding two separate pieces of paper across the table until they're resting against my fingers just like the paper he's writing on, I see what he's trying to show me.

This is Jamie's test before he was tutored and the other one is what he scored after it. It's the same test, just given at different times. Look at them and tell me if someone who can't speak to you can help or not.

The first test, it's even worse than some of mine. I thought it couldn't get worse than the way I was performing when I was in class, but apparently it can. I don't know the rules about showing me other peoples work, but looking at the other test and seeing the score in the high eighties, there's no doubt he's made his point.

Again.

He's also effectively shut me up, which judging by the grin on his face, is exactly what he was going for.

So Ryder Kane. Do you still want to bail?

This guy. Damnit. His grin is wearing me down because my answer to that question isn't even in the same ballpark as what I said before.

"No, I don't, but I do have one more question."

Shoot.

"Do you think you can help me beat his score?"

Isaac

I've helped a lot of people since I got here. It's one of the things that despite all of the other crap I get, I know I'm good at. There's nothing better for me then when someone I've tutored comes back and shows me how much sitting with me helped them. It gives me a purpose and for a really long time, I didn't have one.

When I got here this morning, that's what I was focused on. It's only when he entered the conference room, stopping at the door the minute he noticed it was me here that everything started to change.

When he finally threw his body into the seat across from me, I was on edge, prepared to run head first into the brick wall that is Ryder Kane's body because he looked like he wanted to be anywhere but here. It's a place I've been more than once, so I was ready for it.

What I wasn't ready for was what happened when he finally raised his head and looked at me for the first time.

The way people talk about me, they do the same thing with Ryder, but in a different way. The girls talk about how good he looks and the guys talk about what a force he is on the football field. Hanging around Belle and her friends, I've even heard Dillon say it a few times and no one knows football better than him.

I know nothing about sports, but the eyes I catch staring at me, I start to get what the girls are talking about. They're blue like Belle's, but a lot lighter. They're like the experiment in chemistry class my senior year of high school. Round pools of crystalized glass and hard as hell to break away from.

He's built the way I expect a football player to be, almost menacing as he leans across the table, but not so much that it's distracting. His eyes do that enough on their own. He shakes his head, bringing his hand up through his light brown hair and when it falls, it parts in a way that affectively breaks the staring contest I've had going on since he walked in.

Focusing my attention back on the reason we're here and putting my eyes down toward the papers in front of me, he sighs and I force myself not to look back up and acknowledge the sound.

There's no doubt about it. What the girls say about Ryder is all true and for the first time since I finally admitted I was gay, I'm physically reacting to someone. It just sucks that it's him.

Even though I don't have a lot of experience with dating, I can still appreciate a good looking guy. Until now, nothing has ever clicked past that and knowing what I do about Ryder, it clicking now is wrong.

Ryder Kane is straight and definitely the last person on the planet I need to be reacting to.

The bubble I put myself in when he arrived, it didn't take long to burst. The minute he opened his mouth and the first question out of it was about my inability to speak, whatever I thought was going on when he looked at me, vanished completely.

He was finally the way I should have seen him from the beginning. A certifiable jackass.

The more we went back and forth, my annoyance at having to deal with yet another football jerk vanished and it quickly started appearing the way it should of from the start.

Ryder may be a player for the Wexfield Panthers and he might even be a bit of a tool, but he's definitely not like the others. Realizing that, knowing the way I judged him based on the question he asked in the beginning, sets the tone for the internal tongue lashing I give myself.

"So can you do it?"

You want me to help you beat Jamie's score?

"No, not really. I just want to know if you think I can."

He's looking at me again and just like every other time he's done it in the last few minutes, I'm having a hard time focusing on much else.

What is this? Why is it happening now? Of all of the people for me to feel some sort of connection to, I really don't need it being Ryder. He's out of my league.

It's not about whether or not I think you can do it.

"Then what's it about?"

It's about you believing you can do it. Do you think you can?

If I thought my reaction to his eyes was strong, it's nothing at all compared to the way I react when he smiles. It's not a big one, just a cocky smirk, but it's the way it seems to pull at his entire face that changes everything.

God, I'm pathetic. I'm starting to act as bad as the girls that drool over him. I need to get over this quick before he catches on and he makes good on his promise of bailing.

"You know, I think I can. There's no way in hell I can let Jamie Marsden beat me in anything."

Then let's get started.

There it is again. The smile that in the moment feels like it's only for me. A smile that only makes what he says next that much harder to ignore.

"I'm completely at your mercy, Isaac. Let's do this."

Chapter Three

Ryder

I'm not sure how he did it, but I'm pretty damn sure Isaac is a miracle worker.

It had taken three hours, but by the time I finally slid my body out of the chair, I could admit that what hadn't sunk in before, was starting to make a lot more sense and it had nothing to do with me. It was all him.

When you're in class and you're taking notes, listening to the professors drone on about things you're pretty sure you'll never use in everyday life, it all just runs together. It's a struggle at any given moment to make sure you stay awake. It wasn't like that at all with Isaac and it has nothing to do with the fact that he can't speak.

It's because when he's teaching you something, he has a way of dumbing it down so even the biggest idiot in the world can get it. I understood him easily and where I expected there to be moments where it became frustrating and I would want to give up, it never happened.

The conversation wasn't one sided even if I was the only one talking and now that I'm in another class and away from him, I'm starting to see just how fucked up that is. How impossible.

Not being surrounded by him also means I can focus on other shit I noticed during our time together. I can freely admit that I looked at him a lot more than he knew about and that for the first time in what feels like forever, it didn't feel like I was committing some federal offense doing it.

For the first time in two fucking years, I didn't hear the sound of glass shattering or the smell of blood. It was peaceful, calm and a sensation so foreign yet so enticing, I never wanted to let it go.

Shit. I can't think about this crap. Isaac isn't Gavin.

Those eyes though.

Pools of darkness filled with a ring of sadness and despair. They aren't gonna be so easy to forget about. Especially when I'm pretty damn sure if anyone saw us side by side, they'd see the same damn thing in mine.

He shouldn't look like me. A couple hours around him and I already get the sense that he's a lot better of a person than I can ever be. No one should have this look unless they've done something to deserve it.

Isaac doesn't need to pay the way I do.

Fuck. Thinking about Isaac is bringing all this Gavin shit back up and I swore when I came here that it wouldn't happen again. I left it behind for a reason and it needs to stay as dead as he is.

I need a distraction.

It's not gonna stop until I put an end to it myself. Coming to class was a mistake. I should have gone with my first option.

Picking up the first girl stupid enough to come on to me and bringing her back to my place. Pulling her to me the minute we're away from everyone's prying eyes, tangling my fingers up in her hair, breathing in her deep scent of desperation while whispering every preprogrammed sexual innuendo I know until she's creaming in her fucking panties. Ending this completely and burying myself so deep in her that it takes me away from this hellhole entirely.

I really need to get out of here. My need for release is mixing with my desire to forget and that never ends well. It's even worse because it's not the idea of taking a woman that's creating the level of need I'm dealing with. I could care less about whoever the unlucky girl is gonna be.

No, this is all about one person. Isaac.

The untouchable one.

If I hadn't gone there and spent the last three hours with him I wouldn't be dealing with all of this shit right now. I wouldn't have noticed his eyes, the way the build of his body is similar to

Gavin's and everything would have been fine. Instead I'm sitting in the back of some class I don't give a crap about, my hand over my crotch in order to conceal my reaction to the way he looked and how much he reminds me of a past better left forgotten.

Concealing a need I'm not allowed to feel because it's the reason for the implosion that leveled what was supposed to be a pretty awesome life.

That's what no one gets. What I don't let anyone even try to understand.

The accident and what happened to Gavin that night, it's all my fault and not because I was behind the wheel drunk and pissed off at my parents. It's because I told them I was gay. I came out of the fucking closet and because their reaction was less than stellar, I lost the only person in the world capable of loving me.

My devout Christian parents couldn't handle the fact that their progeny wasn't as pure and plain as them and wanted to throw me into some program designed to kill the gay inside of me, and I rebelled.

I swore on Gavin's memory that the moment he died was the last time I would ever look at another guy again and so far, I've done well other than my slip with Dillon. At least, it was good until I walked into that conference room and saw Isaac.

Now it's all blown to shit and it's only a matter of time before my carefully constructed walls come crashing down and I'm right back where I started.

All because I couldn't keep who I am buried in the closet where it belongs. Gavin dying wasn't because I was wasted. It's because I loved him and loving him was wrong.

I see that now, and no matter what I felt seeing Isaac, the way I walked out of that conference room less haunted then when I walked in, I can't be wrong again.

Screwing random women and shutting myself off, consumed by the utterly devastating shell of emptiness that comes when you're numb to everyone and everything, it's the way I have to do things. It's the only way I can make sure that what happened to Gavin never happens again.

Isaac

I should have seen this coming.

My professor warned me that working with Ryder wasn't going to be easy, but with the way our first session went, I figured we'd gotten past the worst of it.

Showing up is half the battle.

Nice G.I. Joe reference. Might go over better if it wasn't in your head.

Glancing down at my watch again—the tenth time I've done it in the last ten minutes—and seeing that the hands haven't even ticked by a full minute since the last time I looked, I go over the way everything was the last time I stood here.

For three hours yesterday, Ryder Kane seemed different than the other meatheads I've had to tutor. He showed promise quicker, seemed to grasp the material and had a willingness to learn, something the rest of his teammates just didn't have until much later in our sessions. By the time it ended, I was pretty confident that this would be the easiest job I'd ever taken on.

Shows how much I know. It's obvious with him not being here that he didn't feel the same and just proves that I'm as big an idiot as everyone seems to think.

No. That's not right. I'm not gonna let him and his lack of caring turn me inside out. He's not going to make me doubt the good I do here when I help people that genuinely want it. He's the idiot, not me.

The empowering feeling I get admitting that lasts for a few minutes, doing such a good job of distracting me that I don't even bother looking at my watch the entire time. The problem with speeches is, with me they don't last. I start feeling good and then the high ends and I'm right back at the start again.

Doubting myself; my worthiness of even standing here and breathing air. It's only going to eat away at me until I start feeling like the piece of gum stuck under someone's running shoe.

Screw Ryder Kane. His cocky attitude, the stupid smirk he wears that gets him anything he wants. The way his hips melt into his jeans so flawlessly, and his stupid crystal eyes. I'm done. I'm not going to let him waste another second of my time.

He can figure out the mess he got into on his own.

"Crawford!"

Turning at the sound of my voice, my body tensed and ready for a fight the same way it's been since the altercation with Randy and Bryan, I relax the minute I see it's not someone I have to fear.

It's another meat headed jock, but at least this time, it's one I can stand.

Tossing my bag onto the ground while he makes his way over and grabbing out the notebook and pen, readying myself for the inevitable conversation that's sure to follow, I stand back up and bridge the gap between us.

"You and Ryder finished already?"

Scribbling across the page, I hold the book out and watch as he reads what I've written.

"Son of a bitch!"

You don't have to be such a jerk. My mom's not a bitch ;)

His shoulders, which had been almost as tense as I was when he first called out, visibly relax and he smiles.

He was supposed to be here an hour ago. I waited around hoping he was just running late, but I'm pretty sure he's not coming.

"I was there when he left this morning. He said he had to run an errand, grab some Monster at the store because he slept like shit, but that he was going to meet up with you right after."

Looks like he lied.

"Yeah, no shit. I'm sorry."

What do you have to be sorry about?

"When he told me that he had a list of tutors, I pushed him in your direction. I know what kind of help he needs and trust me, no one else would be able to do it."

It's not often that people go out of their way to compliment me and definitely not guys like Dillon. Sure, I help a lot of them out, but getting something as simple as a thank you when it's over is like getting a root canal. It's painful and in the end you wish you'd never gotten it done at all.

What are you doing here?

"I was coming to see if I could talk you into giving him a break. We've got a practice coming up and I wanted to go over some plays with him even though he won't be playing."

Understanding but choosing to ignore it, I ask the only question that's been on my mind since I caught his surprise at Ryder not being here.

Does he do this kind of thing a lot?

"Honestly, he's never bailed out on a commitment before and he knows what doing this means. It's big Isaac. It's not just football, ya know?"

Yeah I do know. That's the problem. I know a lot more than I should about Ryder and the others. I just wish I didn't because even though I'm helping them out, I still don't think it's any of my business.

Tutoring is business, plain and simple. The minute it gets personal, its trouble.

For me, Ryder Kane is trouble.

I give up, Dillon. When you see him, you can tell him that I'm not wasting my time with someone who doesn't care whether he gets thrown out of school or not. I've got more important things to do.

"I get it. For what it's worth, he's never been like this and I'm sorry that the first time he is, it's with you. I know that we're not exactly friends, but you deserve better than this."

You're right, I do, but with as many times as I've been through this, I should be used to it by now.

"On a good day, I'm a first class prick, but even I know that being treated like you're disposable is something no one should ever be used to."

You're not as big a prick as you think you are. Thanks, Dillon. :)

Picking up my backpack, unzipping it enough to toss my notebook and pen inside before closing it, I repeat the same action I did on the page before I took it back and give him a genuine smile.

I'm pretty sure he doesn't realize he's done it, but standing here and talking to me, has given me the distraction I was looking for but couldn't give myself. The way he seemed to be genuinely upset that his friend completely bailed is comforting.

It validates the anger I have over being treated like I'm less by someone I deluded myself into believing wouldn't treat me that way. No matter how much proof I have in my history that should make me believe otherwise.

"Yo, Isaac!" Dillon calls out. When I turn, praying when I do that he asks me something I can give a nonverbal answer to, I catch his grin first and with a movement of his hand toward the parking lot, he jogs over to me. "You've got some time before your next class right?"

Nodding, his smile lifts even higher.

"Wanna go for a ride?"

Ryder

"Yes, Ryder! Just like that, squeeze them harder, make me feel it, baby! Make me scream."

How about what I want?

Closing my eyes, blocking out the sight of her while she continues to moan her pleasure in the sound of my name and a whole lot of screaming for Jesus, I focus my attention on anything that will take me away from what I'm actually doing.

It always happens this way, even if the timing this time around is different than I'm used to. Normally when I need to forget, I can push it down, head out to Gretchen's and pick up the first available piece of ass and indulge. With the way last night went though, it called for a bit of a routine change.

"More! God, Ry, give...me...more!"

God she's demanding. Maybe I need to start being more selective. Wouldn't be a bad idea to invest in someone a little quieter either. She's fucking distracting, and not in the way I need her to be.

Keeping one hand gripped tightly around her bony waist, averting my gaze and focusing on the peeling wallpaper we still haven't gotten fixed, I slide my other hand down until my fingers are grazing over the one place I know will get her off faster. Rubbing each finger in succession over her heat while at the same time picking up speed and pounding my dick in and out at a pace I don't think I've ever done before, I finally stop once my thumb finds the perfect spot. Rubbing furiously, I feel her body start to quake from the pleasure she's experiencing and a flood of satisfaction rolls through me at the same moment she coats my dick in her juices.

Thank fucking Christ! It's over. I can finally stop pretending.

Sliding in and out a few more times, digging my teeth into my bottom lip as I wait impatiently for the quaking of her body to stop so I can pull out, I close my eyes and like always, picture Gavin the first time we were together.

The way it felt having his tongue running up and down my cock, watching him take me deeper into himself. Within a few seconds of the image coming alive in my mind, she's not the only one releasing. Only with me, it's not her name that pours from my lips. It's his.

Isaac.

No! That's not right. It's Gavin. It's always been Gavin.

"What the fuck was that?" she shrieks, the sound of her voice as shrill as nails on a chalkboard, causing my body to shiver and my dick to twitch inside her, making the moment even more uncomfortable. I pull out quickly and ignore her completely.

There's no way in hell I can acknowledge her question. It's only going to lead to even more questions I can't give her answers for.

"Did you really just call out a guy's name when you came?"

"Nah babe," The lie spilling effortlessly. "Maybe you just wish I did."

"Ryder, I'm not deaf. You clearly called me Isaac."

Damnit, I need to do some serious fucking damage control. She's not gonna let it go.

Sliding my hand down, I roll the condom off, but before I can move in order to get rid of it and then dispose of her, I hear the key sliding into the lock and two people making their way into the apartment.

Shit! I knew bringing her back here was gonna end up biting me in the ass.

Locking eyes with Dillon, his face quickly turning into a disapproving scowl, I turn away, the look too much for my guilty conscience to take. Focusing my attention on the person standing beside him, expecting to land on Cadence, I'm shocked when I see it's not her.

It's the last person I expected to be here. The last person I ever wanted to see me like this.

Isaac is here, and his widened eyes along with the surprise written all over his face, makes my already shriveled dick climb even more into itself until I'm pretty sure it's not even there at all.

Fuck.

What the hell am I supposed to do now?

Chapter Four

Ryder

"Don't, alright? I know what you're gonna say and I just…"

My voice trails off, my train of thought sounding ridiculous even to my own ears. Dillon can and will say whatever the fuck he wants and he should. What I did bringing that girl back here and fucking her was stupid.

Beyond stupid. Wrong. Mortifying. Disgusting.

That's the real reason I don't want him to say anything because nothing he could come up with would be near as bad as the shit kicking I've been giving myself for the last couple of hours since he got Isaac out of here.

His face. I can still see it so clearly that it's like he's in the room with us. He was mortified by what he walked in on and he should be.

Why it matters is beyond me. Why I'm reacting at all when I know next to nothing about him, even more so. It shouldn't matter what some mute guy thinks about what I do with my off time. It's not even like we're friends.

He's my tutor, that's it.

Apparently now I'm not only the king of screw-ups, but also of lying too.

The way I reacted when I was screwing the girl I can't even remember the name of, proves that Isaac is a little bit more than just my tutor. I mean shit, he's the reason I even had the girl here at all.

"You have no clue what I'm thinking right now, let alone what I'm gonna say, so don't even start with me."

"You're gonna tell me that I screwed up, right? That what I did bringing her here was wrong and you're disappointed."

"Not even close."

Now he's got my interest. I would have expected with the way he ushered Isaac out and leveled me with the purest look of hatred and disgust that I've ever seen, he was going to lay the disappointment on thick. It's what I would have done if the roles were reversed.

"That guy stood outside waiting for you for hours, Ry. Hours! Even though it was pretty damn obvious after about fifteen minutes that you weren't gonna show, he still stood there waiting."

Damn. I don't wanna hear that. Knowing that Isaac stood around waiting for me, ties my damn insides up. I didn't think it was possible to hate myself more, but apparently I was wrong.

"You wanna know why he did that? Because despite knowing that the majority of the people we're on the team with are total fucking douchebags, he still has hope there might be someone decent in the bunch."

"What the hell do you want me to say? I screwed up!"

"You're damn right you did and considering the way you treated him, I'm pretty damn sure you can kiss any chance of getting back on the team goodbye. They don't make tutors better than Isaac and once word gets around about what a flake you are, no one is gonna wanna take the chance!"

Here he is. My roommate slash father. I wondered when he was gonna make an appearance.

"I'm a fuck up. Got it, Dad."

"Ryder, would you pull your head out of your ass for five fucking seconds?"

Ignoring the question, I focus on the one thing I still don't know. I fully expected when I took the risk to have Dillon walk in on me, but what the hell was Isaac doing with him?

"Why did you bring him here?"

"When I caught him waiting around, I felt bad. You bailed on him and he looked upset. Pissed off, hurt most definitely, but even worse, he looked lost. I was looking for you anyway, so I figured I'd bring him along."

"Guess you learned your lesson, didn't you?"

"Yeah, because he never should have walked in on that. What the fuck were you thinking?"

I can't go there with him. He might think he knows shit about me because he knows a part of me that I don't share with the rest of the world, but that doesn't mean I gotta sit here and open up about it even more.

"I was horny."

"Bullshit. Try again."

"It's not bullshit."

"Ry, I've known you awhile now and I know the way you operate. You don't get horny, at least not with the random bar whores you bring back here every other night. So try again."

I let the room fall silent because there's no way I'm answering his question. I can come up with any amount of lies, but with the way he's looking at me, I'm pretty sure he'd see right through them all. And there's no way in hell I'm telling him the truth. That I brought the girl back here because I spent the entire night drowning in memories of Gavin, twisted together with ones I haven't even created yet with my tutor.

The same damn tutor he just brought into my nightmare.

"Fine. You wanna evade that question, then answer another one. Do you wanna get back on the team?"

"You know I do."

"Then how are you gonna fix this?"

"I don't follow."

"This! Isaac! You heard what I said a few minutes ago, right? No other tutor is going to look twice at you after what you just pulled."

Isaac just walked in on me fucking some random girl. I'm pretty sure there are no collection of words alive that can make up for that. I wouldn't even know where to start if there was.

"Maybe I'm not meant to fix this."

"Spoken like a true idiot."

"Coming from you, that's a compliment."

"Deflect your shit back on me all you want, but it's the truth."

"Are we done? I'm getting tired of this." I sigh, motioning between the two of us.

"No, we're not done. This isn't over by a long shot."

"Dill, this is my shit, not yours. You need to back off."

"I should do that, you're right. The problem is, if I do, you're just gonna keep on spiraling until there's nothing left. Been there, done that and I'm not looking to repeat it. You need to get your shit straight, Ryder."

"I don't know how."

This entire conversation and that's the first truthful thing I've said and the way his face relaxes, I can tell Dillon sees it too.

"Now we're getting somewhere. Now that you've pulled your head out a little bit, you wanna tell me what the hell you were thinking bailing on him today?"

Well, since I've already been honest once, I can't see how it could get any worse. I might as well admit everything and let it go where it goes. It's not like there's much left to lose anyway. I've officially destroyed the only thing that ever meant anything.

"It's complicated."

"So simplify it."

"Isaac reminds me of someone. I can't say who, so before you ask, you won't get an answer. I just couldn't go there today."

"Even though bailing means losing your one chance at doing what you love?"

Nodding my head, he sighs.

"Is this like what happened in the shower a few months back?"

"No—yes. I don't know, maybe, but it doesn't matter because even if it was, Isaac isn't like that. I can tell."

Dillon scoffs, but says nothing to give me any insight into why he did it. It's obvious he has an opinion on the subject and him not vocalizing it when I know he's probably dying to is strange.

He isn't known for keeping his mouth shut about anything, especially when it's something like this.

"Why didn't you just tell me that before?"

"It's complicated."

"Yeah, I can see that. Everything with you seems complicated."

"I'm a gigantic ball of complicated, with a side order of gigantic mess. Figured you of all people would have been able to tell that, all things considered."

"Oh, I see it. I just thought if I got you around the right kind of people it would help. Not make things worse."

"You didn't make it worse, Dill. It's always been this bad."

"I've got a question for you."

"Ask, but I can't promise you'll get an answer."

"Fucking that girl, did it help?"

The truth is, it didn't. As hard as I've been trying to block everything out, it hasn't been helping for a while. I'm starting to think that I'm burned out on that particular brand of therapy.

"No."

"So why do it if it's not giving you what you need?"

"Because it's the only thing I know."

"Then you need to learn another way."

"Don't you think I would if I could?"

"No, because you can and you're still doing the same tired things. You're hitting your version of rock bottom here, Ry."

Is that what today was? My rock bottom? Is it this moment that's supposed to make a light bulb go off above my head and clue me in to just how screwed up I really am? Force me to acknowledge it and make a change?

"I don't know what you expect me to say."

"This has nothing to do with what I want, man. This is about you. How it felt when we walked in on you today and whether or not it was enough of a shock to wake you the hell up."

Dillon walking in, it wasn't enough. Maybe it's because we live together and I knew the risk I was taking before we even took our clothes off that doesn't change anything for me, but him alone isn't enough to do it.

Isaac though, even knowing he's not like me, sure has me twisted up enough inside to make me think it's a wakeup call.

"Did he say anything to you before he left?"

"Not really. He wrote that he was glad you were alright and not off lying in a ditch somewhere, but he was pretty quiet otherwise."

"I'm not gonna be able to fix this, am I?"

"I don't know, Ry. Do you want to fix it?"

I figured the answer to that would be obvious, but apparently not.

"Yeah. I mean, you said it. He's my only shot at getting back on the team and other then the way I reacted to him, the way I think I'm always going to react because of what he represents...he was helping."

"Alright, well you know what you gotta do now, don't you?"

"No, but I'm sure with the smirk on your face, you're gonna waste no time telling me."

"Apologize. Make it right and for fuck sakes, Ry, don't screw it up again. If it happens again, I'll hit first and question you later."

"Gee, thanks."

"It's not a joke. When I got here, I didn't know my ass from my face with the classes I was putting myself through. Isaac helped me and for that, he earned my respect. Not only as a tutor, but as a human being. I want you back on the team where you belong because it's shit without you, but if you screw up again, I won't hesitate to take you out."

Message received loud and clear. I need to make this right.

I need to find Isaac and beg him to take me back, even if it throws my whole world into a tailspin in the process.

Isaac

I'm losing my mind, I'm sure of it.

Dillon walked me out of his apartment hours ago and not once in the time since I've been out have I been able to get the image of a very naked Ryder out of my head. I'd like to be able to say that I can't let it go because it's a nice image to have, but that would be a lie.

Ryder having sex isn't a surprise. It's not even a surprise knowing he's doing it with a bunch of different girls. I've known all about that watching him since he got here and ended up in a lot of my classes. What is a surprise is the way he treats it.

I imagine sex to be something private between two people. When you think about why bedrooms were created, being intimate with someone in that way is the perfect example of why it happened. It's something that you just don't expect to be shared with the entire world.

I'm not as naïve as people think. I know all about pornography and how open sex is to the world, but that doesn't make it right for me. In a way I figured he might have thought the same way.

I was so unbelievably wrong.

Ryder obviously looks at sex the way ninety percent of the campus does. They'll do it wherever and whenever they want and not give a crap who knows or sees it. Where if it ever happens to me, I will care who sees and knows. It will only be me and the person I end up choosing to be with.

It's just another way I assumed things about him and had to be shown up and close and personal just how wrong I am.

When Dillon asked me to go with him, I didn't really understand why at first. Outside of the times when he's around me because of Belle, we don't make a habit of hanging out together. It all started to make sense once I got in his car. We weren't really hanging out, he just wanted to find Ryder.

Getting to their place off campus, Dillon going through the normal routine of getting us into the building and then the long wait for the elevator that would take us up where he lived, he was in complete control of the situation. He turned his key in the lock and walked through without a care in the world.

Not being able to speak, I pick up on body language and atmospheric changes faster than most. I felt Dillon's body go hard, his feet stopping the minute he walked through. I also caught the loud exhale of breath before I ended up making my way around him and inside.

I should have known off that reaction that something I wouldn't want to see was waiting for me, but I'd just kept moving forward until all I could see was Ryder, completely naked, his face nothing but a mask of shock and annoyance, along with the bare leg of a giggling female coming up and over the back end view of the sofa.

Dillon's arm wasn't long coming out, the strength of it pushing me backwards, his intent obviously to block me from what he was now also getting a full view of, but he wasn't fast enough.

Ryder's hand, sliding off the very real latex evidence of what had been going on before we got there, his eyes meeting mine in one brief moment, looking sadder than I've ever seen him.

He looked haunted and ashamed.

This is where things are confusing because never being in a position like that before, I have no idea if that's the way a normal person acts when they've been caught. All I know is that no matter what I do in order to forget about this, turn the movie in my brain off, nothing works. It just keeps playing on until I can start to feel my own body reacting to it.

It's wrong, reacting to what I saw. It was a private moment between two people, not something I'm supposed to sit here and glorify, but it's happening despite it.

The way he looked when I walked in, if I take his facial expressions out of it entirely, it makes my heart race in a way I'm not familiar with, and the very real part of my anatomy that until now I've been able to placate and ignore, stand at attention.

Seeing him naked is turning me on.

What is it about Ryder Kane that I can't seem to let go of?

I know the way I reacted to him yesterday when he walked into the conference room. Sitting here now though, alone in my bedroom stroking my pants because of the intense visual playing over in my head, filled with a need I've never felt before? I don't understand why it's happening.

I'm as messed up as everyone thinks. Reacting to this at all proves there's something seriously wrong with me. I need to stop thinking this way. I need to stop thinking about Ryder.

Shifting my body on the bed, turning over and grabbing the book on the bedside table, I settle in with it until I'm caught up in a world that's not my own. After a few minutes pass, I hear my mom's voice calling from downstairs.

Slipping off the bed, I cast one final look toward my pants, hoping to god that my earlier thoughts have receded so I don't give her the surprise of her life when I get to the top of the stairs. Content that the small amount of reading I did tamed me, I head through the door and am nailed right away as her smile greets me.

"I was wondering if you heard me or not. Someone's here to see you."

Lifting my hands in lieu of not having paper to write the words out, I ask the question and motion with my head towards the door.

Who?

"He didn't tell me his name, honey. Only asked if you were home."

The last person to show up on my doorstep like this had been Kayden after Isabelle's accident and since she'd met him that day same as I did, I know for a fact it's not him, which means whoever's waiting for me could be just about anyone.

Jackass meatheads from school included.

"Isaac, is everything okay?"

Signing out the word yes, I walk around her and make my way down the stairs until I'm standing on the other side of the door. Sucking in a deep breath, willing my now pounding heart to cease, I grip my hand around the handle and pull, not looking up until its open and I'm able to see exactly who's standing on the other side.

Standing on my doorstep, looking like he walked straight out of a designer clothing catalog is none other than the very person that caused me to react so strongly before.

Ryder's here.

Chapter Five

Ryder

This is a fucking mistake.

I can't believe I'm standing on this doorstep, praying that when he gets to the door he'll see the effort I'm making and not slam it back in my face the way I deserve.

Dillon was right. Nothing is gonna change until I pull my head out of my ass and do something about it. He was also right about anyone else taking me on so I can get back on the team. I've been written off by loads of people for a long time now, so it's not any different in this case.

I can't let it happen with Isaac, and that's the most bizarre part of this. Even after what happened back at the apartment and the sense that my roommate slapped into me, I still wanted to fix it the second after it happened.

Reacting to Isaac, calling out his name in the throes of an orgasm, I can write it off as similarity to Gavin all I want, but even someone as idiotic as me knows it's about more than that.

Isaac isn't like anyone else I've interacted with and it was evident five minutes into our first conversation. He wasn't shy about his dislike at helping me and even let me have it more than once when I said something he found to be out of line.

I'm not used to that, which means it's appealing to me. I just wasn't expecting how appealing it would be. Everything that's happened since yesterday morning, it's probably the most I've felt in over two years and instead of running from it like a complete pussy, I need to face it head on and deal with it.

His face filters through a myriad of emotions in a matter of seconds. First he registers shock at me standing here, then they lower just a little, sadness evident and when he looks back up again, they're filled with annoyance.

He doesn't want me here.

If I wanted to turn this thing around, the right thing to do would have been to talk to him outside one of the classes we share, but no, of course I have to go and do it the wrong way.

Shit, it's getting worse now.

I should be happy that his look has changed from annoyance, but considering his empty hands and his inability to speak, the way he looks now, his eyes almost bulging out of his head, is worse than the annoyance ever was.

Isaac is frantic. He needs answers and can't get them. I need to end this shit.

"I know I'm probably the last person you wanna see, but can I get five minutes to try and explain what you walked in on earlier?"

Moving back from the door with a tight nod, he motions me into the house and when I'm completely inside, he kicks it shut behind him before pointing down the hall.

Once I've made my way into what looks like a family room, he holds a finger up in the air and heads back the way he came until he's diving around a corner and out of my view entirely.

After a few minutes of him being gone and no sign of coming back, I start to think he bailed out and left me here. As I'm about to get out of the chair, he enters again and I start to relax.

I need to chill out. I'm here to get him to agree to tutor me again, not ask the guy on a date. Reacting this way, it's only going to make everything worse. I've already screwed up enough, I'm not looking to do it more.

Passing the notebook over and taking his own spot on the sofa to the left of me, I look down and for the first time since I made the stupid plan to come here earlier, I finally shut my mind off and just read.

There's nothing you need to explain. I know what I walked in on and what you do with your time is your own business.

"That's not true, Isaac."

What do you mean?

"What you walked in on—what I was doing, it wasn't happening on my time. It was happening on yours."

He nods and his agreement is enough to push me forward.

"You're my last hope here, man. You know it and now, after having the point slammed home, I know it. What happened earlier never should have happened because I should have been at the center with you."

You're right. You should have been.

"I know it's asking a lot, but can we just forget about earlier? I know I fucked up, but I swear, if you say you still want to help me, I'll make sure it doesn't happen again."

Those are really nice words Ryder, but I don't believe them. I can't be the only one taking this seriously. As nice as your words are and how sincere you're making them sound right now, I have a hard time believing them. I don't believe in you.

I figured that would be his response. With how erratic I've been acting since Coach talked to me, I have a hard time believing in me too. I wasted Isaac's time and burned a bridge with my roommate all because I couldn't handle the firestorm going on in my head and needed to act out in order to cope.

This is exactly what I deserve.

"I understand."

I don't think you do.

"I'm lost."

That's the first thing you've said since you showed up that I actually believe. :)

The guy I met in the conference room yesterday, he's back now and the smile on the page proves it. He's doing it now just like he did then and it's affecting me in a way I have no familiarity with, but one I know I like.

"You think me admitting I'm lost is truthful?"

Yes.

"You gotta give me more than that."

The reason you're not on the team. Why you need to come and sit with me every day, and the reason what

happened earlier took place at all. It's because of what you just told me. You're lost.

I came here to get my tutor back, not be psychoanalyzed. If he's gonna sit here and try and get inside my head in order to figure me out, he's shit out of luck.

"You're wrong."

That's where you're wrong, Ryder. I'm right.

This guy is unbelievable. I knew coming here was a mistake.

Sliding out of the chair, I only make it a step away before his arm reaches out, his hand coming to rest on mine, stopping me.

Holding out the paper with his free hand, I take it and read.

The sooner you admit it, the sooner we can get past all of this and get you back where you belong.

"And where's that?"

Back on the team, off the probation list and maybe if it's possible, happy.

Am I really that transparent to this guy? Is it that obvious I'm not happy and I haven't been in a long time?

How easily he just seems to know me, it's crazy, yet at the same time the most natural thing in the world. Maybe it's because he can't speak, but him knowing this much about me, I don't hate it as much as I should.

Starting on a new piece of paper, finally releasing the hold around my wrist, he runs the pen across the page and in a few seconds, another one is coming out in front of him just waiting for me to grab it.

Please sit back down so we can talk.

"Did you mean it?" I ask the minute my ass is firmly planted back in the chair. "Do you still want to help me?"

I wouldn't have let you in the house if I didn't. I don't waste my words or paper on people that don't deserve it.

"After what you saw today, how can you think I deserve anything?"

That's easy. We all deserve something. For some, even more than something.

"And you believe I deserve something?"

No. Not exactly.

"You're doing it again, Isaac. I'm lost."

You're not lost, Ryder. You're right here with me.

"Really? You're the Riddler now?"

As cool as that would be, no. I'm not the Riddler. I was just trying to make a point, but since it went over your head, forget I said anything.

"Too late. I don't forget anything, ever. So just do us both a favor and explain the point I'm not getting."

You asked me earlier if I believed you deserved something and I said no.

"Yeah, I know. I was there remember? I asked it like two seconds ago."

I said not exactly because I don't believe you deserve something.

"Then what do I deserve?"

Everything. And if I give up and walk away now, I'll never see if you get it.

Isaac

"Uh—I should probably go."

Way to go, Isaac. Now you've gone and freaked him out.

I can't let him leave like this or let that be the last thing I say to him. I don't even know what I was thinking saying it to begin with. I just hate how deflated he looked. How I made him so upset that he almost walked out before we could set things right. I needed to fix it despite not really understanding why.

You know why you did it.

No. I can't go there right now. I can't focus on that or I'm going to get so caught up in it, when I finally do pull away, he'll be long gone. He's still here now and I need to keep my mind focused on the reason why.

He needs my help.

You don't have to go. I'm sorry if what I said made you uncomfortable. I do that a lot. Words fall out before I really think them through.

"Did you mean them?"

Yes. I mean everything I say.

He laughs lightly before clearing his throat in an effort to cover it up and it's like we're back in the conference room all over again and he's smiling at me. It throws my center of gravity completely off course.

Why did you laugh and try to cover it up?

"You caught me?"

When I nod, he smiles before rubbing his hand over his face, again in an effort to hide his natural reaction, almost as if in some way it's wrong for him to even be doing it.

"I laughed because even though I don't exactly know you, I can believe that about you easily."

I understand. So why did you try and cover it up?

"Force of habit, I guess."

You should probably break that habit.

"Why's that?"

I expected what I said to upset him again so before the words even fell, I braced myself for the reaction that comes second nature to him. Fight and flight. When he doesn't even budge from his spot in the chair, I'm more than a little surprised.

Maybe I can't pick up on him as easily as I thought.

It doesn't suit you. I'm not sure it would suit anyone. It's unnatural.

"That sums me up pretty well."

After staring at the blank paper for a few seconds, unsure how to respond to what he said, I give up and just decide to go with brutal honesty.

You believing that's what you are is what's unnatural.

"Anyone ever tell you that you're too nice for your own good?"

Yeah. It's a good thing I don't listen very well. :)

His blue eyes soften and the simple response along with the knowledge that he's not even attempting to hide it, warms me in a way I don't expect. It's a good look for him.

Breathe, Isaac. You can't keep looking at everything he does like this, especially with what happened earlier. What you know about him.

Most people when their inner voice kicks in, listen to it because it's telling them something that in the end will protect them, but that's not how it's working for me right now. All the voice in my head is doing is annoying me and I just want it to hush.

"I'm glad you don't listen to it. If you did, I'd be on the lookout for a new tutor."

You might be right about that.

The words going back and forth between us every time he passes the paper back, I'm seeing them in a different light then I did when I wrote them. Things I'm saying, they're borderline flirting. Something I have no experience with whatsoever. Unless you count the one time I told Gregory Williams I thought his hair looked pretty.

I don't have the first clue how to do any of this, yet with the way he's reacting to it all, it seems like I do.

"So, what you said earlier—uh, if you meant it, you shouldn't apologize for it."

Maybe I have a force of habit too.

He laughs and this time makes no move to cover his mouth or mask it with a cough or clearing of his throat.

"If I've gotta break mine, you might want to look into breaking yours too."

I bet I could break mine before you do.

"Are you suggesting a wager, Isaac? Maybe I need to rethink what I said about you being too nice."

I never said I was nice. You only asked if I had been told that before. ;)

The way I'm acting, winking at him, even on a piece of paper, this isn't me. I'm not sure who's taken over my body, but it's most definitely not being controlled by me anymore.

Running a hand through his hair, his eyes taking in the room and avoiding any and all contact with me, I see the uncomfortable feeling from earlier returning.

I knew it couldn't last.

"I really should go, but before I do, I want to be sure about something."

What's that? I write even though it's not at all what I want to say. My mind is overflowing with other questions I can ask that will keep him here longer, the need to not have this night end right now stronger than anything I've ever felt.

"We're on for tomorrow morning right?"

Yes, if you're serious about it.

"Since I've never been more serious about anything in my life, I guess that means it's a date. I'll see you in the morning." He slips his body out of the chair again and this time I let him walk away. Before I can stand to follow him to the door in order to see him out though, he stops and turns back to face me.

"We'll iron out the details of the bet in the morning."

He turns and starts to walk, but not so quickly that I don't catch the deliberate reaction he leveled me with, making my heart flip the minute I catch it.

Ryder's entire face just lit up in front of me and he didn't do a damn thing to hide it, which just makes his final words even more significant.

I'm going to lose the bet.

Chapter Six

Ryder

"Ry, you need to stop and think about this."

I don't want to stop and think. Thinking is what got me into this mess to begin with. I spent so much time thinking about when the right time would be to come out to my parents and look where it got me.

They want to brainwash me in order to wipe out the fact that I'm gay. Put me back together until I'm as pure as the driven snow.

No thanks. I'm tired of thinking. It's time to act.

"Are you gonna come with me or not?"

"You know I will, but are you sure you're okay to drive?"

"Course I am, why?"

"I can smell the whiskey, Ry."

"If you're worried I'm gonna drive us over a cliff, don't bother coming with. I can leave just as easily on my own."

"Babe, you know I'm with you. It's us against the world remember?"

Proving his point, he backs away from the window and slides his body into the car, flashing the smile I love so much and putting my mind at ease.

The truth is, as much as I want to get out of here and am determined to do it with or without Gavin by my side, I'm glad he's here. I don't want to do this alone. It really is me and him against the world. I can't imagine going anywhere in my life without him.

I need him as much as I need air to breathe.

"Will you at least tell me what they said?" He asks as I pull the car away from curb, peeling out so quickly, I'm pretty sure I'm leaving tire impressions in the ground.

"No son of theirs is gay. I'm just confused and they had the answer to all of it."

"What was the answer?"

"You know when you're fucking obese, you get these moronic parents that will send you away to fat camp?" When Gavin nods I keep going. "Well they wanna send me away to a camp that wipes out the gay."

He exhales heavily and whistles under his breath, echoing my sentiments exactly. It's utter bullshit what my parents offered me and I'm not the only one who sees it.

When I texted him after it happened, before I jumped in my car and headed into the nearest bar that would serve me without use of the fake ID, I'd left all of this out. Telling him now, getting it out of my head, it's a relief. If anyone would understand my reaction, it's Gavin.

Even if his parents had been accepting when he came out.

"So where we are going?"

"Anywhere that isn't here?"

"That's not much of an answer."

"Are you sure you wanna do this, Gav? Your parents are cool with you and with us. You don't have to come with me."

"Do I really need to repeat myself? I meant what I said, Ryder. It's us against the world. If you need to get out of here, then so do I. I'm not letting you go through this alone."

Ryder?

Feeling the paper scrape against my arm, I shake off the memory and remember exactly where the hell I am and with who.

Shit. I can't believe I zoned out like that.

"Yeah?"

Looking up and catching his concerned eyes a whole lot closer than when he gave me the practice test, something about them completely undoes me.

Remembering Gavin and the last conversation we had before I took my attention off the fucking road and ran us straight into the telephone pole, it's never happened like this before. I don't have to worry about him haunting me when I'm in class, or like right now in tutoring sessions with Isaac.

So much for having a specific place and time for this shit.

Are you having trouble with the material?

That's laughable. I am having trouble with it, which is what allowed my mind to start fading into the walk down memory lane in the first place, but I don't want admit it. When he was explaining it to me, it was sinking in. Admitting that I can't do the simplest thing, he's gonna think I'm flaking again.

"This is really supposed to be a pre-college placement test?"

He nods and I sigh heavily. If I can't even get through the math that high school seniors can complete, I don't see myself ever pulling my marks out of the toilet. I'm pathetic.

"When you explain it to me, it sinks in, I swear. I can easily see what you're saying in my head and work it out. You saw how I did those other two problems, but looking at this test, it's like it completely drains out of my brain and I can't do shit."

Putting his hand on my shoulder, the tension that's been building since he put the test in front of me starts to break up, but the concerned look in his eyes doesn't. I need to wipe that look away. I hate having his eyes look so pitied. I know how pathetic I am, I don't need anyone else feeding into it.

We'll go a little slower.

"I don't think you can get any slower than what we've been doing, Isaac."

I watch as his eyes sink in and his lips raise and the sight of a different look on his face makes me want to cry out in joy. It's like he heard my thoughts and is changing things up.

There are 35 questions on that test. We can definitely go slower. I'm sorry.

"What did we say about that?"

A reminder of what happened the night before lightens my mood even more. This is exactly what I need. Who knew that

Isaac apologizing when he doesn't have to would be the thing to turn everything around?

So

Laughing the second I see the two letters come across the page and his rapid attempt to scratch them out, I reach out and rest my hand on his wrist. A natural move with anyone else, but one that the minute our skin makes contact makes me flinch from the shock that occurs.

"This is gonna be the easiest bet I've ever won." I admit, lowering my face away from his in an attempt to hide my very intense response to what happened when I touched him.

You haven't won yet. I just need to get used to it.

"You keep telling yourself that." Laughing again, I lower my gaze to the way our hands are and I realize something I didn't catch before. "Did you just write with your left hand?"

There's no missing the grin on his face or the way his entire face lightens the second he does it. Even with the short amount of time we've spent with each other, I can tell it's not something he does often, but whether he's aware of it or not, it suits him.

The only person that needs to have the clouded, dark and depressed eyes is me.

I'm actually left handed, but when I was younger I had a teacher that thought it was wrong and forced me to learn with my right.

"They forced it on you?"

Yeah. It's okay though. I actually prefer using my right hand now. As you can see, being able to do both comes in handy when special people grab my wrist before I can finish my thought. ;)

Motioning with his head toward our hands, I immediately slide my hand away, feeling the separation the minute we're no longer touching, but pushing it down where it belongs.

I can't let Isaac catch on to what's happening to me. If he does that, it won't take long before he's got me spilling out what I was really thinking about a few minutes ago.

"I'm sorry. I did it without thinking."

It's okay, Ryder. :) I

The pen stops moving and when I catch his unfinished sentence on the paper, it takes everything in me not to beg him to finish it.

This shit is crazy. I knew coming into this that I was going to react to him. He reminds me a lot of Gavin and the past I'm trying to run from, but I was determined not to let that win out again. I meant what I told him yesterday. I want to make this right, but the way I'm reacting now, the tightness in my chest at seeing his eyes a few seconds ago and the way it felt when he smiled, it's obvious I'm losing the damn fight.

"You what?"

If I wasn't seeing it with my eyes, I wouldn't believe it. His cheeks flush until they're tinging his skin pink and just like every other time anything's gotten remotely awkward with us, his head is starting to lower toward the floor and our feet.

Holy shit! He's embarrassed.

"Isaac, what were you gonna say?"

Starting at a new line, he begins writing and I resist the urge to lean over in order to catch what he's telling me. Drumming my fingers on the table, I lose all sense of space and time, focusing on the noise until the paper is again digging at my hand.

You don't want to know what I was about to say, trust me.

"Wouldn't have asked if I didn't."

He blushes again and it's more than I can take. With the way my thoughts were going when I should have been focused on the math, and how amazing it felt reaching out and touching him a minute ago, I need to close myself off. I can't let it continue.

I'm not gay. I repeat over in my head. *I do not find Isaac Crawford attractive and I can't wait to hit the bar later and pick up another girl so she can remind of who I really am.*

Straight. Into girls. Normal.

We need to focus on the math, Ryder. What I wanted to say doesn't matter.

God, he's so fucking wrong. It does matter. I don't want it to, but denying it isn't worth the fight. I need to know what he was going to say because if we leave it the way it is now I'll never be able to focus and his help will be for nothing.

"If you want me to focus on this, you need to answer my question."

"Why is it so important to you? They're just words."

"Humor me. I don't like leaving anything unfinished, even conversations that mean nothing with words that mean even less."

I liked it. Happy now? Can we get back to work?

"Well that wasn't so hard." Laughing, I put the paper with our conversation on the other side of the table closest to my bag. "We definitely need to start small."

Grabbing another piece of paper from the notebook without even a look back in the direction where I placed the last one, he fills out a few lines on the paper and rests it in front of me.

You did alright with the first five questions, which tells me that what you said earlier about grasping what I taught you was true. It's when things get a little more complicated that you seem to shut down. So we'll stick to basic algebra for now and move on to the other questions later. Does that sound okay?

The last thing I want to focus on right now is algebra, but if I want to extend our time together, it's what I've gotta do. I might even be able to twist the conversation around again until we can go over the terms of our imaginary bet.

With the way he sucks on his bottom lip nervously while he waits for me to respond, I know exactly what I want if I win. It's just too bad that no matter how convincing I can be in an argument or debate, what I want in this case is definitely something I'll never get.

I want to taste him.

Isaac

"Yeah, that sounds okay."

Wiping my hands on my jeans, attempting to get rid of all the sweat that's been pooling there since Ryder slipped his hand over my wrist, I do my best to focus my mind on the papers in front of me. The work that we're here to do and not everything else that's been filtering through both my mind and body since we got here this morning.

When I was eight, even though both of my parents knew at the time that it didn't matter, they sat me down and had a conversation with me that they labelled **the birds and bees discussion.**

They didn't talk about birds or bees, but I figured out pretty quickly what they were getting at. They were explaining the basics of love, attraction and sex even though at eight years old it was the last thing I wanted to hear, much less talk about.

It matters right now because everything they told me I would experience with someone, is happening exactly the way they described even though it shouldn't be.

Sweaty palms and underarms, hitched breathing, rapid heartbeat, inability to think clearly even though the math I'm teaching is so vivid in my head. Adding all of that to the very real ache in my pants, how uncomfortable I'm starting to become every time he so much as says a word or smiles in my direction and there's no doubt about what's going on here.

I'm beyond attracted to Ryder Kane and it's so strong that it's hard to think and focus on much else. His hand resting on my wrist burned me and even though it's no longer there, I'm pretty sure if I look down, I'll see his hand print left behind. It ignited something and as confusing as it all is, it owns me.

"Now who's the one spacing out?" his voice breaks through and despite the embarrassment I feel at being caught, I shake it off enough to raise my head and smile, which only serves to make his brow furrow and his head dip back down.

What is going on here? Why do I care? What is it going to take for me to shut off whatever this is and focus on what's really important?

Sorry. I was just trying to figure out where to go with you next.

What I really want to say and can't, stays lodged in my mind. *I want him to put his hand back.* I imagine him realizing what my earlier words meant, reaching out and joining our fingers together until we're completely connected.

I want him to lean across the table and tell me that he gets what I mean and he feels the same. It's only made worse when I bite into my bottom lip again in an effort to push the images away and I see his body tense.

Continuing to do things this way is only going to show that I'm into him and with the way I walked in on him, will send him running from the room.

I can't let that happen. I need to help him and somehow push down and ignore everything else that seems to come alive being this close. The way every look is heightened until I feel it searing into my skin. The need inside of me to break out of my silent shell and lean across the table and place my lips on his because I just *have* to know what he tastes like.

"Please continue saying sorry."

Yeah I bet you would love that. In your dreams, Ryder. You will not win this bet.

"Isaac, you've said sorry three times already today. I've got this thing in the bag."

That's not true. I've watched you bottle down your responses about the same amount of times, so it seems we're even.

"Shit."

At least you didn't hide that. :)

"I'll never hide my filthy mouth."

Turning to my bag, hoping that in the time it takes me to grab the algebra work and turn back around, the deep shade of red I'm sporting will be gone, his hand resting on mine stops me.

"Can we take a break?"

About to grab for the pen, but thinking better of it, I just nod. A break from him and the inside out way he makes me feel is the best thing I've heard all day. I hear the chair scrape back on the floor and turning toward it, watch as he rises to his feet, our eyes connecting again only when he's done wiping at some imaginary mark on his knees.

"Are you coming?"

I don't understand. Coming where?

"I wanted to prove to you that I was into making this right, so I didn't eat this morning. I know you're gonna throw more questions at me and I'm ready for them, but I need to eat first."

So go get something to eat. I'll be here when you get back.

"I was kind of hoping you'd eat with me."

Afraid of the crazy mob of girls you'll get the minute you leave here?

His laughter rolls over me and I silently thank myself for not saying something upsetting. With the up and down responses rolling off Ryder today, the last thing I want to do is make it worse.

"Yeah, that's it exactly. So on top of being my tutor, do you think you can be my bodyguard?"

Ignoring the fact that the word bodyguard and me in the same sentence is absolutely preposterous, the softened look on his face and the lightened way his eyes are as he waits for me to respond determines what my answer is going to be.

You can count on me. I'll protect you. Even if I did leave my cape and tights at home.

"Why do I get the feeling that you actually have a cape and tights?"

Because I do. They don't call me Superman for nothing.

"Hmm. I figured you more for Batman."

Is this really happening to me right now? Is Ryder really standing there talking to me about DC Comic superheroes?

Why Batman?

He starts to lower his head, hiding yet another reaction, but seems to think better of it because his head flies up and whatever he was hiding is now on full display.

His blush.

Ryder is blushing.

Holy crap.

"You're gonna think it's as stupid as I am."

The first time Ryder walked into one of my classes and I caught sight of him and who he hung around with, the name I called him during our first session was pretty accurate. The more time I spend with him, I'm starting to see that he's not as brainless as I accused him of being. Hearing that he thinks he is bothers me because I'm doing exactly what other people do to me.

Judging and making assumptions that aren't true.

I'm as big a meathead as the football players that harass me.

You're not stupid, Ryder. Why did you figure me for Batman?

"I'm pretty stupid, Isaac. There's a lot you don't know about me, but the reason I thought you'd be Batman is because he was quieter than the other guys. He thinks more. Internalizes. In a lot of ways, you're the same way even if yours aren't by choice."

I was definitely wrong about Ryder, but right with what I just said. He's not stupid. He's as far from stupid as you can get.

You sure you can handle going to lunch with Batman?

"Yeah." He laughs easily. "You know, I think I can, but only if you promise me a ride in the Batmobile."

Grabbing my bag, there's only one thought floating around in my head.

It's going to be a *very* long break.

Chapter Seven

Ryder

Normalcy. Business as usual. Normality.

I haven't known what those words are for two years. My version of normal changed back then and somewhere along the way I created a new way of being. One that no one else in the world is experiencing.

It's been three days since that break with Isaac and the new normal isn't quite as normal as it was when I created it. It's like I've gone back in time and I'm this walking combination of the old and the new.

Most days when I wake up I'm coming off a nightmare or three, so my ability to breathe is difficult and the last thing I want to do is get myself out of bed in order to appear like the ever studious college student. What usually gets me out is Dillon yelling about a practice. It's the one thing that always gets me pumped up no matter what.

Not having them to rely on anymore, I half expect the same result every day I wake up now that my one place to go is a conference room, but that's not at all what I'm getting.

This is where my new normal twists into the old one.

I've been waking up the last three days and haven't had that struggle to breathe. I can make my way out of my room and make coffee before heading over to the campus and waiting Isaac out. Purposely ignoring the need for breakfast fuel because taking a break with my tutor is a lot more fun than I realized and starving is the one way I can make it happen.

I feel alive for the first time in two years and as much as it scares me, I grip on to it as tightly as I can because I didn't realize how much I missed it.

Spending an hour of free time in the morning before people start arriving and the world starts moving should be a bad thing, but it's turning out to be the opposite. Where I expect the memories to overload me, create so much havoc I have no other choice but deal with it, it doesn't happen. I enjoy the silence.

I also enjoy seeing his face light up when he gets here and sees me waiting.

Sure, he gets this excited look in his eye when he talks shop with me, but past that, it's not often I see him brighten. There's this moment when he sees me every morning, when I can feel his eyes studying me that makes me want to find even more ways to make it happen.

So here I am. Third day in a row, the fourth since Dillon kicked my head in, sitting on the steps, tapping my foot in an effort to distract me from my anxiety. Watching professors drive in and make their way into the various buildings, prepared to hang out and wait for those bedroom eyes and lopsided smirk to arrive.

To get him before he gets me.

I think it's working to, until I see the shadow looming over me.

You're making me look bad showing up this early. I've got a reputation to maintain.

Handing it back, about to respond, I see it. Pulling the paper back and reading the words over again, my gaze slides down a few empty lines until I see it clearly.

There's a wink on the paper.

His innocent attempt at being funny should mean nothing. I'm sure this is how Isaac communicates with everyone he writes to, but there's something about the amount of times he does it and when that make it so much more than nothing to me.

His similarities to my past, what most of time scares the living shit out of me, it's not having that effect now. I don't want to run. I want to figure out if the winks, the smiles and the flushed pink cheeks are something more than what they appear to be.

Could I be wrong about Isaac? Am I the only one so wrapped up and twisted in knots whenever we're together, or is he feeling it too?

You're overthinking it, Ryder. Don't read so much into a stupid face on a page. He's not like you. He's not pretending to be something he's not.

There it is. My voice of reason. Knocking sense into me before I go and do something to make a total jackass of myself because there's something going on with me that I can't seem to fight anymore.

"Your rep is safe. I just can't stand hanging around the apartment doing nothing."

He moves from his standing position and doesn't stop until his ass is firmly planted on the step beside me. Placing his backpack on the ground, he opens it long enough to grab out a pen and before I know it, it's moving rapidly across the paper and then being handed across to me.

So getting to school early and doing nothing until I show up seems better?

Unable to control it, I let the laugh spill out and I'm rewarded when his lips lift into a smile. Our bet, what we're trying to do. I might have a chance at taking this after all.

"As usual, your ability to state the obvious is perfectly timed."

I aim to please.

Wrong choice of words, Crawford.

His words are dripping in innocence. He means nothing remotely dirty by them, but this is just another way I'm starting to see that I'm losing the fight between who I need to be and who I really am.

I react even though they're just written words. A heat builds in me until I have to shift my entire body in order to mask the very real and rising reaction.

He can't catch on to this or it will blow everything to shit.

Isaac must catch something though, because he writes across the paper again and passes it over before I can even collect myself enough to respond.

Are you okay?

Y-Yeah," I push out forcefully. "Why do you ask?"

You look uncomfortable.

Oh man, you have no idea.

"Just thinking about the work you're gonna force on me today. Any time I think about math it makes me look like this."

On the list of stupidest things to come up with, this has got to be at the top. I've never wanted to kick myself in the ass as bad as I do right now.

So math makes you look like you need to use the bathroom?

There it is again. His humor and my laughter, the latter even louder this time than it was a few minutes ago. Damn, what is it about this guy that makes everything just feel so easy? Natural? Right?

"Exactly."

Before we go in, did you eat this morning?

"No, why?"

My friend Belle wants me to meet her around eleven, so I thought if you were up for it, you could come along.

"Is this you taking pity on me?"

No.

Shit, I said the wrong thing. In the five days since we came across each other, he's never answered me with one word.

Seeing it on the paper, it's not right. I need to flip this around. Who knew reading full sentences from someone was actually fun?

I've lost what was left of my mind, obviously.

"If you're not taking pity, then is this where you finally take me for a ride in the Batmobile?"

Even to my own ears I trail off in sound after mentioning the word ride. Fuck. At this rate, I'm gonna have to use our break later in order to release a little tension. Between his eyes, the way he smells, the smile he always wears and the words on the paper between us that look suspiciously like flirting, it's gonna be pretty hard to hide what's going on with me soon.

The whole damn world is gonna know that Isaac Crawford is turning me on.

If by Batmobile, you mean using your legs and walking across campus to meet Belle, then yes, that's exactly what I'm doing. ;)

A wink. Closer on the page this time, forcing a tingle of heat straight down from my head all the way to my feet, with a short pitstop in between to the one place that Isaac really shouldn't be able to touch considering it's been dead to every male within spitting distance for two years. The place he touches without even trying.

My body and mind are fighting so fiercely against each other that it's manifesting itself with the wrong guy.

Fantastic. On top of being a complete idiot school wise, I'm also a freak outside of it.

Forcing my eyes shut in order to block it out, rubbing at my temples in an effort to deflect from my inability to stop what's happening, I focus on the one thing that is sure to bring me out of this so that I can answer him without giving myself away.

My father. Nothing can ruin a buzz of any kind, sexual or otherwise, better than Richard Kane. His words to me whenever we're together are like throwing a bucket of ice water on a person who's burning alive.

"God was trying to tell you the night of the accident that the way you've been living your life is wrong. I am pleased to see that you have also taken his message at face value and realized your true place."

Yeah, there it is. Instant buzzkill. Exactly what I need even though his words are still as wrong today as they were the day he said them.

Ryder, you're doing it again.

Fuck. He's right. I'm completely ignoring him.

"Sorry."

It's okay. Are you sure you're alright?

"Never better." My response coming a whole lot quicker then I intend it to. "So Belle, is she your girlfriend?"

Isaac's cheeks flush red and he lowers his head, but not before shaking it vehemently. Whoever Belle is, whether she's a friend or something more, it's obvious that any mention of them being together is a definite no-no.

"What did I say?"

Nothing. It's just, Belle and me, we aren't like that. I'm not really like that with anyone.

That explains the blushing then. What it doesn't explain is why the last thing he said is even on the page at all. It only took a few days around him for me to get what a decent guy he is. Why someone wouldn't want to grab onto that and keep it is beyond me.

If I'm honest, the way he is at times makes me want to grab him and not let go, and we don't even run in the same circles. We're two completely different sides of the coin, but it doesn't change the fact that he's someone people should die to be with.

"For what it's worth, people not wanting to be with you, it's their loss, not yours. They obviously have no clue what they're missing."

So much for taking it slow.

Isaac

Thank you. So will you come with me?

I want to say more. Tell him that what he just said is the nicest thing anyone's ever said to me before, but of course I can't. My head won't let me which means the pen won't write the words. Even if I could, I'm not sure letting that spill out is smart.

It's hard enough dealing with the way I react to Ryder. Admitting that his words are important or that they might have taken my breath away because of how sweet they were, it's sure to make things uncomfortable.

Hiding the way I am and pretending that I'm not attracted to this guy, is so hard. I can't speak, but that doesn't mean I can't wear the person I am on my sleeve easily for the rest of the world to see. I haven't been able to do that lately. I've been keeping it buried even though I've never wanted to scream it out more.

As wrong as it is, I'm attracted to Ryder. I can admit that and not experience a whole bunch of confusion about it. It is what it is. I just wish I didn't have to bottle it every single time we're within a foot of each other. I hate having to look away, not connect because getting too close will give away something I'm pretty sure he's not designed to handle.

Having a girl attracted to you or throwing herself at you, it's easier somehow. For a guy like me to do it, I can't see it ending well. He's strong and the last thing I want is to come on to him when I know it's not what he's after and have it turn violent.

I've had enough of that dealing with Bryan and Randy. High school may have only been taunts and some pushing around, but ever since I became friends with Belle and they realized how hot she is, it's turned into a whole lot more. Violence is something I'm not itching to repeat.

Ryder believing that Belle and I are dating, it's expected. With as deep as I'm pushing down my obvious attraction to him and her being my best friend, it's only natural people would make assumptions that we're together. Her boyfriend even believed it at one point, that's how close we are.

She's engaged to Kayden though and more than that, she's definitely not my type, so perpetuating the myth that we're somehow together, I won't let it happen. It also helps that I don't want to give Kayden another reason to kick my ass.

"Yeah. A break with you and a pretty girl? I'd be stupid not to say yes."

Now that's an expected response. Ryder calling Belle pretty. No matter how affected I am by his words, I need to remind myself that we're not alike, at least not in the way my responses to him want us to be.

Wiping my knees and standing up from the stairs, I motion toward the door. The reason we're here, we've gotta get on with it, no matter how nice it is sitting out here like this and talking while the rest of the world moves on without us.

Following behind until we're both in the building, he stops at the elevator and turns into me, his hair brushing across my face and sending a shiver straight through my spine before speaking and warming me with his breath.

"The questions you gave me last night, I think you're gonna be in for a surprise." When I turn and look up, he's grinning, making me wonder if this is something he's doing on purpose. It's confirmed when he leans in again, this time his voice lower than before, but the smile still firmly in place. "No red pen needed."

This is crazy. I can't keep swallowing this down. It's physically starting to hurt me to do it. He's trying to be funny, talking to me this way when the only way I can respond is with body language. It's just not the language he's going to want to hear.

Searing heat, tingles, and an itch that no matter how much I pull at my clothes I just can't scratch. That's what's happening now. My mind is completely dismantled and fuzzy whenever his breath grazes my skin.

If he doesn't stop, I'm going to melt into him. His low tone, the smile he's wearing, the way it all combines to make those crystal eyes glow. I'm going to liquefy right here in front of him and be the science lesson we haven't even gotten to yet.

The elevator doors open and I don't think my feet have ever moved so fast. Distance. I need it. If I'm going to focus on anything today, I need to make sure we're never that close again.

If we are, I'm going to end up doing something I can't take back. I will make a fool of myself and no matter how open he seems when we're together, how contented his eyes are when I catch them resting on me, it can't happen.

I cannot give in and make a move on Ryder Kane.

Chapter Eight

Ryder

"The professor asked us to write a flash fiction story about cats in fifty words or less. I go home and struggle with it all night and when I get to class and Isaac shows me his, I feel like an idiot."

The girl that Isaac wanted to have lunch with, I'm jealous of her. We've only been sitting here for about fifteen minutes and she's already made him smile at least thirty times. I thought that he didn't do it often, but with the way she brings it out of him, I'm starting to see that he just doesn't do it often with me.

The minute we caught up to her and picked a spot on the grass to sit, they gravitated toward each other and have been attached at the hip the entire time. I've even watched as she reached out and squeezed his hand a couple of times.

What I don't expect is the anger and jealousy I feel every time she touches him.

I want him to do that with me.

Shit. What the fuck is wrong with me? He's my tutor. I can't react like this, especially with someone I barely know. No matter how much time we've spent together over the last three and a half days.

"Why would what he wrote make you feel like an idiot?" I question, attempting to bring myself back into the conversation so I don't have Isaac's concerned eyes on me anymore.

"He wrote a poem. A silly poem that made me laugh so hard my stomach hurt. Here I was taking this thing seriously and he went home and made it into a joke."

"Did you hand it in?" Focusing on him, I watch as he blushes at the question before burying his face in his hands and nodding his head.

"You wanna know what his mark was?" Belle cuts in, breaking my focus away from how cute I find his embarrassment to be and reminding me again that there's someone else here besides two of us.

Someone that I'm the first to admit I haven't really been focused on because my attention has been diverted to the quiet guy beside her a little more than it should be.

"Damn right I do. You should tell me yours too."

"I marked a seventy. His poem? Eighty-Five."

"You're joking."

"I wish!" She says, patting Isaac on the knee and making my blood pressure spike. "I'm never taking creative writing seriously again."

After a few minutes of his head being buried in his hands, Isaac sits up again, this time reaching over to the notebook and writing before handing it over to Belle.

"What's he saying to you?"

She hands the paper over, Isaac's smile carrying over as she does. The only difference between the two of them is that hers seems a lot more devious than his.

There's something about the way she's looking at me now that makes me think I've seen it before. That I know her from somewhere.

You're not supposed to take creative writing seriously. It's supposed to be creative. He said write about cats, so I did. It's not my fault I did it in a funny way. Thanks for embarrassing me though. :P

This is the first time I'm getting to see how he reacts to people he cares about. The tongue face on the page, it's a first for me. It's something he's never done, but now that I know he does, I can't wait to get out of him myself.

Fighting this is pointless. I'm acting like a twelve year old boy with a crush and no amount of swallowing it pushes it down completely. The way the two of them are touching right now for instance. I want to reach across and pull her hand off his leg, make her understand that the only hand that should be there is mine.

Fuck.

I've got it bad for him.

"It was funny, Isaac. You shouldn't be embarrassed. Ryder isn't laughing at you, he's laughing with me."

I can't help it. She's got a point. The way I've been smiling since she started, the laugh I let escape when she finally told me what he scored combined with the way he's reacting to it all, I am laughing with her, but definitely not *at* him.

I'm laughing because it's cute. He's cute.

"Belle's right. You shouldn't be embarrassed." Reaching across the grass, I let my hand fall on his arm, gently squeezing before realizing my mistake and pulling back quickly. "It's a funny story. Nice job on the mark."

All traces of his embarrassment are gone when I finally look up and our eyes meet. It's been replaced by a whole other experience for us, but one I'm used to with as often as I see it when we're working together.

His head is dipped to the side, his eyes are making no move to break away from mine and he looks like he's searching me for answers. Isaac is confused and considering the stunt I just pulled, reaching out and touching him, he's not the only one.

Belle chooses that moment to lean into him and I immediately look away. Their closeness, the way it all comes so damn easily, I hate it. I can't keep looking because I'm so fucking jealous of it that I'm seeing red.

They can interact effortlessly without questioning every single move before they do it. The complete opposite of what it's like for me.

I want that kind of ease with someone. It doesn't even have to be Isaac. As hard as I've been pushing down who I really am, I managed to push everyone away at the same time, so having that type of intimacy with someone, even if it's just friends, is too much to take because it forces the real problem to the surface.

I'm lonely.

Being surrounded by people every day doesn't lessen it because the guys on the team and the girls I hook up with, they all mean nothing to me. They're just place holders on the map of my life, bringing nothing of substance.

I want substance. I want what Belle and Isaac have.

"Ryder?"

There's two things I notice when I look up. Belle's concerned expression as her eyes pass back and forth between Isaac and me, but more than that, the paper sitting directly in my lap and this time, the person responsible for it is smiling weakly, but not feeling it all the way through because it doesn't make his brown eyes light up like usual.

"Yeah?" Choosing to answer her instead of look down at the words waiting in front of me, she motions toward the paper and flashes me the same damn smile as the guy beside her.

Do you want to leave? I want to ask if you're alright, but knowing you, the answer you'd give me would be the one you think I want to hear and not the one that's truthful. I won't ask it, but if you want to go, it's okay.

His concern makes sense now. The way I'm reacting, he's catching on to it. Admitting things in my head, focusing on the way being here right now makes me feel, the best thing would be to take off. Get out of here, fall right back into my old routine and forget any of this exists.

If you walk away now, don't expect to come back.

"Can I have your pen?"

Passing it over, I smile a weak thank you and focus on what I need to say in order to respond. Words that even though she seems to get it, I just don't want to say out loud and let Belle hear.

I can't even make sense of what's going on with me, there's no way I'm putting it out there for anyone else to try and make sense of. Or even worse, judge me on.

I don't want to leave, but if you two want to be alone, I can make myself scarce.

He can say what he wants about the two of them being friends, but I've never seen friends that act the way they do.

Sure, I want that same thing for myself, but I've never reached across while me and Dill are having a conversation and touched him the way they do. I've never held his hand and he's my best friend, same as Isaac claims him and Belle are.

I'm definitely a third wheel in this scenario, no matter how much he wants to deny it.

Ryder. You're wrong.

Staring at the words, soaking them in, I don't realize that it's not just the three of us sitting around anymore. It's only when the new addition to the triangle we're making speaks that I finally look up and take in the changes.

"Hey man, how's the tutoring going?"

Seeing the guy standing there, really studying him as he asks me the question, I realize where I know these two from. Trixie's. They were there the night Dillon lost it and went off on his mom and her dealer.

"Good, I guess."

"You guess?"

Shrugging, the guy laughs and I shoot another look at Isaac, hoping that he'll meet my eyes and give me some unspoken answer to the questions now flooding through me.

He doesn't disappoint.

Reaching over and grabbing the paper from my hands, he starts writing across it and instead of staring a hole into him while I wait, I decide on another tactic.

Focusing my attention on the only person around me that can give me what I need, I really look at Belle. The way her hair moves as she swipes her hand up every few seconds in order to tame it. Her blue eyes that look a hell of a lot like mine. The way she turns to the guy beside her and they seem to brighten and glow all at the same time.

Her body is thin, but not sickeningly so. The way her breasts fill out her tank top, serves as the distraction I need from the real problem I have. I lower my gaze even further until I'm locked on the one spot she has that would take all of this twisted up agony away. The place I could bury my dick in and forget I exist, even if it wouldn't last forever.

The way she looks does absolutely nothing for me physically, but focusing my attention on her the way I am, it's alleviating the need I have to flip my head around and do the same thing to the one person here that will give me the physical reaction and release I crave.

It's only when a throat clears and I look up to see the scowl on the guys face that I realize what the fuck is going on.

"You mind not eye fucking my fiancée?"

Holy shit.

"That's not—"

"Yeah man, that's exactly what you were doing and you need to stop."

Belle's hand squeezes his and the same way it was when she did it with Isaac a few minutes ago, it's happening again now. I look away, ashamed that I was caught looking at her at all, but affected more than I want to be by the intimacy of the gesture.

I should have fucking known that they were together. Dillon's mentioned his friend and his girlfriend before, but for some reason her name never came up or I didn't care enough to register what it was. I should have known it was Belle.

God fucking damnit. I'm an idiot.

Isaac

It was only a matter of time before this happened.

Ryder can't help himself and even though I'm not attracted to her, I can't exactly blame him.

Belle is beautiful and I don't just mean that because I've gotten to know what a great person she is. I mean it because of the way she looks too. If I had to come up with a visual for what every guy on campus would want in terms of their dream girl, I'd look no further than her.

She has blonde hair and a lot of girls have that, but when you add the lightness of it to the bright blue of her eyes, it's a heart stopping combination. It's made even worse by the way she carries herself. When I first met her, she was a lot like me, but ever since Kayden came home, she holds herself differently. She's more confident, and when you put it together with the litheness of her body, she's pretty much the straight guy's version of perfection.

It also means that Kayden is the luckiest guy in the world because she only has eyes for him. Well, when I think about the way she looks, maybe he's not the luckiest guy because it means her lack of understanding of her beauty means he's gonna be beating the crap out of guys left, right and center.

I definitely don't envy him. Especially since I've been on the receiving end of how he reacts to it.

When Kayden catches what I've already been spending the last few minutes watching, I can already tell where it's going to go. I want to head it off, stop it and make up an excuse to get Ryder out of there before Kayden's anger gets the better of him, but he beats me to the punch.

"I guess that's my cue to leave."

What is going on here? What am I missing? Why does getting caught make him look so twisted?

Grabbing a piece of paper the minute I see his body stand and his backpack come up off the ground and over his shoulder, I start scribbling across the page faster than I ever have before, wanting Belle to know that I need to stop him before he completely bails again.

Clicking the pen closed, sliding it into my pants pocket the minute I stand, I grab my bag the same way Ryder did and passing the paper to her, squeeze her shoulder gently in my own version of goodbye and start running to catch up with him.

It's easy to see after a few minutes that he's doing whatever it takes to get the hell out of here quickly and it still makes no sense. Was it really so bad getting caught looking at a girl that he needs to completely bail?

This is one of those times I really wish I could speak. Call out and make him stop so I can catch up before he's separated from me completely. I don't want him to do that. I can't let him do that.

Picking up my speed, desperate to get to him before the light he's stopped at changes, I feel the burn in my throat the minute I do. I've never run this fast or been this determined and my body is screaming at me in protest, but I can't stop and listen to it.

I've got to get to Ryder. Make him tell me the truth and there's only one reason for it.

I like him and I'm getting tired of denying it.

Chapter Nine

Ryder

What a stupid move. Brainless. Wrong.

It's bad enough that I didn't put two and two together before I did it, but to actually use Isaac's friend in order to block everything out just wedges the knife of stupidity in deeper.

On top of being stupid, I'm also acting like a total dickhead right now because I can tell he's trying to catch up with me and I'm moving even faster so that he can't.

I've turned what should have been a nice break into something disgusting and I've never been more ashamed or felt dirtier than I do right now, which of course means I've gotta be flooded with memories of Gavin. Of things better left buried.

~*~*~

"Gav, can you stop doing that?"

Lifting his eyes, and catching the laughter dancing in them, I frown. He knows what he's doing. In fact, the way I'm reacting is exactly what he wants.

"Stop doing what, babe? This?" He slides his tongue over his bottom lip before biting down into it with his teeth and my dick twitches its unspoken reaction, which only causes me to groan.

"Son of a bitch."

"No actually, my mom's not a bitch. She's amazing. Try again, Ry."

"Really Gav? You're gonna twist my words now?"

"Until you admit what it is I'm doing that you can't handle, yes I am."

He grins and it's more than I can take. If he really wants an answer, he's damn well gonna get one. It's just not gonna be a verbal one the way he expects.

Sliding to my knees and crawling across the floor, I slip my hand around his head and pull it to mine until my lips are crashing down hard on his. Parting them, giving me the access I need to taste even more, I slip my tongue into his mouth probing until he brings his own forward and we're tangled up in each other.

Pushing him further, intensifying the kiss the minute he leans his body completely back against the carpet under us, I press my body to his and feel his hard reaction to our kiss press into my leg before he moans into my mouth.

"Fuck." I bark out as the heat that was pooling in my head shoots straight to my dick. "You drive me crazy, you know that?"

"Mhmm." He moans against my lips, shooting another bolt straight through and making my head even hazier. "I want your kind of crazy."

Running my hand down his body, rubbing it against his chest before sliding down until I'm massaging the inside of his thigh, he moans again and I'm completely lost. I press my lips to his, pushing my tongue roughly into his mouth until it's as deep as possible in his throat.

He growls and pushes back against me, as desperate as me to probe deeper, to feel more until the wave we're both experiencing crashes completely.

I've never wanted someone the way I want Gavin.

Pulling back, aware of where my thoughts are heading, what my dick wants, I search his eyes. I need to know if he feels the same. If what's happening, where it's leading, is where he wants it to go.

I need to know if he wants me inside him as badly as I want to be.

"Gav," I choke out, my voice hoarse, my mind pushing me to press my lips back on his again and just lose myself. "Tell me to stop because I don't think I'm going to be able to."

I expect him to put the brakes on the way we have in the past, but his eyes alone tell me that what I want to hear and what he's going to say are going to be two different things.

"I'm ready, Ry. Don't stop."

~*~*~

No. This is not happening right now.

I need to get the fuck out of here before the world gets a view of how easily I react to any memory of Gavin and they come up with some new and even more inventive names.

Being the campus whore has to be the worst of it.

Running the minute the light changes, I don't stop until I'm completely across and even further away from the reason all of this is happening.

If I could just shut down whatever this stupid reaction is to Isaac, I wouldn't be going through this shit. I would still have had the nightmares, still need to get completely blitzed in order to forget, but it wouldn't be hitting in the middle of a college campus in broad daylight.

It's all Isaac's fault.

Content that I'm far enough away that no one can catch me, I allow myself to slow down. Before my body can reach the place of calm I need it to go though, I feel the touch on my shoulder and spinning around quickly, my arm makes contact with a body and before I know it the person is on the ground.

Son of a bitch.

"No actually, my mom's not a bitch. She's amazing."

These memories; the flashes I get without even trying, I need to make them stop. I need to let Gavin and everything I felt with him go before it kills me.

Watching the person I hit get to their feet again, wiping at their knees and shaking at their head in order to get the dirt off, I swallow the huge lump in my throat and really focus on him.

Isaac.

Damn he moves faster than I thought.

"Are you okay?"

His nod doesn't do shit for me. He's lying. There's no way that with the pressure I put in that it didn't hurt. I know how hard I can be and now Isaac does too.

"I think you're lying."

He shakes his head and sighing, I go completely against the way my body and mind want me to flee and reach out to him. If I'm going to bail on him again, the least I can do is make sure he's alright before I go.

Flinching the second my hand comes in contact with his face, my body goes rigid. Shit. This is even worse than I thought. He's scared of me now. I'm fucking this entire thing up because I can't contain my 747 of crap.

"I'm not going to hurt you, Isaac. I just want to make sure you didn't hit your head." I whisper as I completely obliterate the remaining distance between us, like my calming tone is magically going to make everything alright again.

His hands start moving quickly and it doesn't take me long to figure out what he's doing. He's signing even though I have no idea what the words are because he's moving too fast.

"I know what you're doing—even why you're doing it, but I don't know what you're trying to say. Let me get paper, okay?"

His eyes drop and he exhales even though no sound comes out, but he makes no attempt to stop me as I reach around and unzip his backpack, grabbing what I need.

"Thank you—here." I say when I've got what I need and it's held out in front of me. His hand grips the notebook, but not before grazing across my fingers, causing me to flinch and back up the minute the shock hits. His brow furrows, but before I can question it, he leans down and places the notebook on his knee.

I'm fine. I just didn't expect you to spin around that fast. No need to check me out.

He has no fucking idea how badly I want to react to his words. Show him what checking him out really means.

"You're not just saying that so I don't feel bad, are you?"

He shakes his head ignoring the paper altogether.

"Why are you following me?"

We still have work to do.

"You ran that entire way because I'm bailing on our session?"

He shakes his head, but the pen hits the paper and he starts writing again, the simple no obviously not enough for him.

You weren't bailing, Ryder. You were running. I couldn't let you do that. Not when you swore to me four days ago that you wouldn't do it again.

Time for him to learn that I'm the king of broken promises. The king of broken everything.

You don't want to break him or be broken when you're around him. .

My voice of reason really needs to learn when to fuck off.

"I can't do this with you right now, okay? I need to go. I'm sorry. I'll be there tomorrow, but right now it's best if I just go."

Best for who?

With the time it takes him to write me, I could easily just turn and bail, but my feet are like lead. They're not gonna move so I'm not going anywhere. Another way I react to this guy that I can't stand.

"Best for me. You. Everyone." I sigh and he shakes his head, lifting it until its facing straight at me, his eyes on mine with no sign of breaking away. For whatever reason, he disagrees with me so completely, it's made him strong and stubborn at the same time.

It's not a way he wants to be with me right now because he's not going to like my reaction to it. The way it drives the heat level up until I'm damn near smothering. I definitely prefer it when he's weak and timid. This side of him is nothing but trouble.

Talk to me.

"That's a joke right?" I laugh, but his face remains completely expressionless, as if my dickhead comment doesn't even get through.

His lips start moving and despite the knowledge I have about him, what he's doing, I can't look away. He might not be able to make the sound, but he can definitely mouth the words.

Not a joke. Talk to me Ryder.

He just spoke to me and I heard him loud and clear. The way my chest expands painfully as I exhale, the ache at knowing that he's so serious about what he wants from me that he's willing to go to this length to prove it, is almost too much to bear. Talking is the last thing I want to do with him.

Moving in and closing the gap I created when I backed away, I grab his face hard, no longer giving a shit about words, reactions and the way he's going to feel about this when it's over. I can't handle any of that anymore. Running my tongue across my lip, my brain screaming at me, trying to talk me out of what I'm about to do, I completely block it out and push my lips down on his, feeling his entire body freeze the second I make contact. The paper and pen falling to the ground the only proof that he's as alive in the moment as I am.

The dampness of my lips connecting to the dryness of his, it's the perfect mixture and added to the way he smells, some body spray mixed with the scent of his sweat, it's my undoing.

I'm doing something so wrong, but it feels so fucking right.

Isaac feels right.

Fuck, I need to stop. I can't do this.

Pushing off him and avoiding his eyes completely, I turn, but not before saying one final thing. The only thing I have left that hopefully will stop him from following me.

"I can't—I need to go. I'm sorry, Isaac."

Chapter Ten

Isaac

Rough. Salty. Pushy. Wrong.

Passionate. Sweet. Deep. Right.

Right or wrong, it doesn't change what happened. He kissed me.

Ryder's lips for a split second were pressed to mine, the two of us in perfect sync.

My heart, the way it reacts when I'm excited or worked up about something, the rapid beat that's so strong it threatens to punch a hole straight through me, it wasn't there when his lips pushed down on mine. My heart didn't beat at all.

Everything was still.

Time ceased to exist, all sound dulled until all that remained was a hum in the background. Light from the sun was dim. The heat that appears whenever you're in direct contact with its rays was transferred completely until the only heat source around for miles is our bodies as they're pressed together.

When Ryder's lips touched mine, I burned hotter than the sun.

I'm still burning and the kiss happened three days ago.

Being kissed. I had all but given up on ever experiencing it, so when Ryder pressed his lips to mine and I reacted despite not knowing what any of it meant, I didn't know what to do next. What to say when he finally pulled away, what to do in order to make him see that kissing me wasn't a bad thing.

With as quickly as he took off when he pulled away, it looks like he was choosing what had to happen next for the both of us. Three days have passed and what he thought about the kiss is obvious as he's nowhere to be found.

When he didn't show up for our session the next day, I should have seen it for what it was, but I still held out hope. The second day, the hope drained away until there was nothing left. I didn't even bother showing up this morning because I just knew it would be a waste of time.

The difference between the ways I reacted the first time he bailed and this time, is that I searched for him. I went to our classes, hoping that he would at least show up for those, but he didn't. It wasn't just me he was avoiding. It was everything even remotely attached to me.

He wasn't at home when I went by or if he was, he didn't make a point of answering the door. Pulling information out of Dillon about what he does when he's not in class, I even went by the bars he frequents and there was no sign of him there either. It's like Ryder walked away from me and straight into the abyss.

I need to find him. Make him see that the kiss doesn't have to change anything.

He got caught by Kayden and he reacted in the wrong way, that's all. All it takes is bringing the image of his face that day up in my mind to know it was all just a big misunderstanding.

Our professor was right the first day. There is definitely more going on with Ryder then academic problems. He's conflicted. Bruised deep inside and when things happen that he can't handle, he reacts in ways others wouldn't. He responds to it wrong.

His lips pressed to yours didn't feel wrong.

No it didn't feel wrong. Ryder kissing me, it's the first time in years that everything just felt right. My mind, body and maybe even my soul were finally at peace.

This is crazy. I need to give up on him. He took off, left me alone and didn't even bother coming around to get the help he needs in order to get back on the team. I can't keep caring about this. Ryder made his choice and now it's time I make mine.

When you think about something and decide on a course of action, it should be easy to put in motion. It's not. I don't do so well walking away from things, throwing in the towel and giving up. It's about more than that with Ryder though. I don't want to give up because I get the feeling that's all anyone in his life has ever done and I refuse to be the same as anyone else.

Ryder deserves one person to be different from the rest.

It has nothing to do with the salty taste of his lips and how when I run my tongue over, I swear I can still taste it. Intoxicated again by a scent I can't place, consumed by the dampness of his lips and the taste that lingers long after its absence.

Thinking about this is going to shatter me all over again.

Ryder, where the hell are you? What are you running from? Why did you kiss me and then apologize? Why can't I forget you?

This is going to drive me insane. I can't get the words out like every other person and my heart is screaming at me to do that. Let it out before it breaks me. Why does one kiss, even if it is a first for me, have to hurt this bad? Why do I have to hurt at all?

I shouldn't be surprised with the way things happened. Ignoring the fact that the tension has been building between us for days, it was only a matter of time before everything came to a head. As deserving as I believe myself to be of the same things as everybody else, I realized a long time ago that it didn't work that way.

I could believe whatever the heck I wanted about what I deserved or didn't, but it didn't mean it would happen for me and this is the perfect example of that. The one person I feel more than a passing attraction for and it's the unattainable one.

He's not unattainable if he kissed you.

That's another thing I've been doing with the unlimited time on my hands. Overthinking every minute we spent together and the way Ryder looked, reacted or didn't react. What his smiles really meant, what keeping the paper I wrote on the other day is about and why he looked the way he did when we had lunch with Belle.

The feeling I had that something was off, it was my mind doing what it's good at. Filtering out all the other crap in order to get to the reality of the situation so I can make sense of it.

I know what I've managed to put together about Ryder, but I can't be sure if what I think is actually the way it is or is me wishing for something that can never be.

I want the kiss we shared, the looks he gives me, his words when no one else is around and the way my body reacts when I see him smile, to mean one thing and only thing only.

That I'm not alone and that he's gay too.

Ryder

This is all wrong. It's not supposed to look like this.

Dropping my knees to the ground and running my hand slowly across the name etched into the large gray stone, I feel the moisture building in the corners of my eyes.

I might not come here often anymore, but the lack of flowers is upsetting. Gavin touched so many lives for the eighteen years he was allowed to be a part of the world and there should be something here to show for it.

Not this flat, grass covered plot, the stone marker with his name on it the only proof that he even existed at all.

I need to do something about this. I need to make a plan to come back here more often even if it's the last thing his family wants, and when I do, fill the place with proof that he mattered to someone because he did.

He mattered to me.

Leaning my back into the gravestone, attempting to tame the wild beat of my heart and the screaming voice inside my head that's pleading with me to get as close as possible, it happens. I finally let the tears fall.

The pent up hurt, anger and overall disgust I have with myself for being the reason my life is this way right now, it all comes pouring out until I can physically see droplets hitting the grass.

"Gav," Swiping at my eyes, I run my fingers one by one along the stone in the same way I did to his face when he was alive. "I fucked up again."

Closing my eyes, I try to reflect on why I'm here, but the scent of the grass mixing with the willow trees and flowers from other gravestones combines until it's all I can focus on. My words and thoughts all fading off until they're nothing but dust in the wind passing around me. For the first time since I left, the emptiness in my chest, the ache that feels like a knife being repeatedly stabbed into me, it's dulled and I'm at peace.

The only time I've ever felt anything remotely close to this is when I was with him, which can only mean one thing.

Gavin is showing me that he's here.

"My promise. The one I swore to you I would keep when I left, I'm failing, Gav. I really tried, but I can't keep it. The harder I fight, the deeper I push it down, the more it comes back stronger and I'm so fucking tired that I can't do it anymore."

It should have been easy. With Gavin dead and buried, feeling the way I did for him with someone else should have been an impossibility, but that's not what's happening. It had taken two years, but someone is breaking through the wall I built and shredding it, piece by piece.

I'm letting Gavin down because it won't be long now before the final bit crumbles and I'm laid open and bare. Doing the one thing I swore I never would again.

Feel.

Isaac Crawford is twisting me up, breaking me down and making me feel.

One kiss and everything I worked so hard to build, the persona I've spent the last two years presenting to the world, while at the same time accepting for myself, is being blown apart.

A kiss that I initiated. I made happen.

This is my fucking fault. All of it. I'm to blame for everything. I did the right thing taking off and coming back here, walking out on Dillon before he could change my mind and talk me into staying and fighting for something that can never be mine. Someone.

Someone that deserves better than me.

~*~*~

Hearing the front door open and close but not wanting to stop, I keep my focus on the task in front of me. Pick up clothes, put them into the duffel bag until it's so full I can sling it over my shoulder and get the fuck out of here.

Go back where I belong. Where I should have been this entire time. The place where I will get everything I deserve.

"I wondered how long it was gonna take before I walked in on something like this." Dillon muses, the open bedroom door banging against the wall as I turn and see him leaning into it, his face expressionless.

The perfect visual image of what I feel inside. Empty. Devoid of everything that makes a person feel alive.

Exactly the way it should be.

"You gonna just stand there staring or tell me what happened?"

"Nothing happened. I just need to get out of here."

"Try again, Ry. That's a load of shit."

"Whatever. It's the fucking truth, but you'll believe whatever you want, so not even gonna waste my breath."

"Let me ask again, since apparently someone pressed pretty hard on your douche button and it's clouding the road to your brain. What happened?"

Turning back to the bed, more than ready to tune him out so I can get this over with, I'm not ready for what happens until it's too late and I'm caught in his grip.

Releasing the hold on the back of my neck, he grabs me up with both hands and shoves me away from the bed, stepping in front of my place near the wall, his face no longer expressionless.

Annoyance. Maybe even anger. I can't tell the difference with him anymore. It's becoming too frequent a look. I'm always making him look like this.

"Dill, don't fucking start with me. I'm not in the mood."

"You're slinging clothes in a bag, a lot of them from the way that bag looks ready to burst. If nothing happened, why would you need to try and pack your entire life up and split?"

"I just need to get away." The bullshit starts flowing and I hope by the time it stops, he's backed off completely. "Not being on the team, it's screwing with my head. I need to get away for a bit. Clear my head."

"You wanna leave because you can't handle not being on the team?"

"That's what I said."

"The team you could easily be put back on if you show coach that your grades are rising?"

"Yes." I moan, the sound of my voice a lot whinier than I was expecting. Another thing I hate about having to stand here right now. I'm so fucking screwed up, I'm starting to sound like a whiny bitch.

"You do realize how fucked up that sounds."

Pushing off the wall, more than done with this, I attempt to step out around him and he pushes me back. If there's one thing that hasn't changed about Dillon since his injury, it's his upper body strength. There's no way I'm getting off this wall until he lets me. I'm strong, but definitely not worth shit against him.

"You sure this doesn't have something to do with a certain tutor you've been spending every waking minute with?"

I am not going there with him about Isaac. No way in hell.

My lips pressed to his, the burning I felt head to toe the minute we connected, my aching need to push for more, it's all still crystal clear in my head. If I react to Dillon, I'm going to be powerless in the fight to keep the truth buried. It will come out and make everything even worse than it already is.

It cannot come out.

"Sorry to disappoint you, Dill, but pretty pictures like the one you've got in your head about me and Isaac, they don't exist."

He laughs and I want to wipe the fucking grin off his face because there's nothing about this that's funny, but he speaks before I can come up with a way to do it.

"Thinking about what you and your tutor do when you're together is low on my list of priorities, I can promise you that."

"So why even ask?"

"Ryder," he sighs and I just know with the way the knot in my stomach twists tighter that I'm not going to like what he says. "You talk in your sleep, bro."

Fuck. One time I fall asleep in the living room and now he's going to take anything I said and twist it around.

"So now my dreams are being held against me?"

"Ryder, that's not what I'm doing. I just want you to see sense."

"Why-do-you-care-what-I-do?" Spelling it out slowly, putting emphasis on every word, wanting a real answer to why me packing up and getting out of here for a few days is such a big fucking deal to him.

"Gee man, I don't know. Maybe because we're friends and I give a shit about you?"

"Love you too man." I laugh breaking up the serious tone of his words and the uncomfortable way they make me feel.

"I'm also doing it because you doing this, it's not because you can't handle not playing. It's because something happened with the guy tutoring you and for whatever reason, you can't deal so you're doing what you always do."

"What's that?"

"You're in flight mode. Running. Escaping."

"That's not what this is." I motion toward the clothes and he rolls his eyes at me, not believing it for a second and I can't blame him. I don't believe myself either.

"That is exactly what this is and I can't let you do it." He pauses, his eyes lowering to the ground before his hand raises and he starts rubbing at his chin. "Not when you don't know everything."

"If I let you tell me whatever it is you think I don't know, will you let me finish packing? I wanna get on the road before rush hour."

"What you need to know, if I'm right about what's happening here, should stop this trip altogether."

"Just spit it out."

"I will, but answer something for me and for god sakes Ryder, answer it honestly."

"Fine, what?"

"You and Isaac, what you said made you bail out the first time, is it worse?"

Son of a bitch. I should have known this is where he was gonna take it, but trying to end the conversation made me focus less on what I was agreeing to answer truthfully. I'm screwed.

"It's worse."

"What if I told you that it didn't have to be?"

"Being cryptic right now isn't helping, man."

"Humor me. What would it mean if I told you that what you're feeling when you're around the guy could be erased?"

"Everything."

It's the truth. If Dillon has some magic cure that can take away everything I've been experiencing with Isaac and set me right again, I'll do whatever it takes to get it. Even if it means forgetting about the kiss and how alive it made me feel.

"You gonna tell me what you mean by that or just keep me standing here all day?"

"Torturing you does hold a certain appeal." He laughs and despite the fact that my clothes are still thrown all over the bed, the bag in the middle calling to me to finish, I laugh with him.

"Isaac. He's not who you think he is."

"You mean he's not a super smart guy at the top of his class that uses his spare time to tutor idiots like us?"

Dillon rolls his eyes but nods his head at the same time.

"When you say it like that, yeah, that's who he is when he's here, but I'm talking about the type of guy he is."

"So if he's not the way you assume I think he is, how is he?"

"Ry, Isaac is gay."

I hear what he's saying but I don't believe it. I've spent enough time around him by now to be able to tell and there's never been one moment in that time I've ever questioned his sexuality. He's never given me a reason to. He's worn it for the world to see.

What Dillon's doing, I get why he's doing it. Telling me Isaac is gay is supposed to be the thing that makes me stay. What he doesn't get is that it wouldn't do that for me even if it was real.

I still fucked up and I'm determined not to let it happen again. Gavin's memory depends on it.

~*~*~

I can't believe I'm doing this. Thinking about Isaac and what Dillon told me before I bolted from the apartment, it's so fucking wrong.

The memory of Gavin that I want to keep alive, the way we were together, I'm tainting it by giving anyone else a second thought. I'm taking the natural high that he gave me whenever I was within ten feet of him and twisting it until it's not his face I see in the periphery.

It's Isaac's.

"Why were you the one taken? Why couldn't the impact have been worse on my side? What kind of sick bastard takes someone as amazing as you when there's a perfectly acceptable waste of space more than willing to go in his place?"

My answer is in the wind around me. It's no answer at all. The silence is deafening and smothering at the same time. The all-consuming guilt I feel at being the one left behind is my only comfort.

When we were together, even if we were separated, I could always feel Gavin. He was always with me, but now there's nothing there but an overwhelming need to lash out and join him the way I should have the night I plowed our car into the telephone pole.

"It should have been me. My broken, rotting corpse in a pine box six feet under."

Fucking tears. No matter what I do, they won't go away. They just keep coming and with each one, the knife that's been buried in my chest for so long just twists and plunges deeper. The pain is so intense it takes every bit of willpower I have not to scream out in agony.

"Answer me!" I yell, pounding my fist on the gravestone, feeling my knuckles cracking under the pressure but not giving enough of a shit to stop and check out the damage. "Tell me you forgive me for fucking everything up! Tell me I can make this right again!"

Moving as closely into the stone as I can, my voice continuing to plead and repeatedly beg for his forgiveness, I hug my body to it, letting the force of the tears crash to the surface and overflow, needing the release. The relief that comes from letting out something I've spent way too long bottling up.

My breathing is erratic, my head is pounding and I'm so weighed down by the self-hatred and loathing I have for myself that my body is breaking down from the weight of it all until I'm shaking. But there in the physical release is relief and falling completely to the ground, shutting my eyes and forcing everything else away, I reach out to it, craving it almost as much as I do the one that's holding on to it.

Isaac.

No. Gavin.

Shit, it's like I'm screwing that loud bitch all over again. Even thousands of miles away from him, he's still invading my thoughts.

"Gavin, please! I need you to answer me. Give me a sign that you hear me and I can fix this. I'll do anything to make it—make us, right again."

Yelling earlier has made my throat raw, the words falling out hoarse and dry, which just makes me unload another wave of tears, my eyes showing no sign of drying anytime soon. It's only when I finally lift my hands up to wipe at them again, trying to make them disappear that I hear it.

It's so quiet that it doesn't seem like I'm hearing it at all, but the second I hear the buzzing and feel the vibration against the side of my leg, I can't deny it anymore.

He did it. Gavin answered me.

He gave me a sign.

Chapter Eleven

Isaac

Come home.

Despite the way it looks to most people, I know how to use a phone. Just because I suffer from a disability that impairs my ability to speak, it doesn't mean it transfers over to everything else. I do own a phone and I've even been known to use it a time or two for something other than tutoring.

When Dillon found me after class and told me that he knew where Ryder was, explaining in the same breath why he believed I was the only one that could break though and get him to come home, it didn't take long to figure out that this was going to be one of the times I would have to use it.

Asking me for it, programming Ryder's number into the contact list, he hands it back over and waits while I shoot off the text. Two short words that I don't have the heart to admit won't work. Dillon believing that because I tutor his friend, it means we're close is a joke.

If anyone is going to bring Ryder back home, it will be him or one of the girls he's brought home. Not a guy who can't even breathe whenever we're together, let alone speak to him.

After a few minutes with no reply, I level him with a look. It's out of character for me to do it, rolling my eyes and pointing to my phone in an '*I told you so*' way, but considering this is turning out exactly the way I thought, there's no other look I can give.

Laughing once he catches it, he motions to the phone and smirks knowingly. Like he's aware of something I'm not and it's a secret. All I know is that it's annoying.

Picking up the notebook from the ground, I scrawl out a message and hand it over, which when he reads what I've said, only makes the smirk that much bigger.

He's not going to text. I told you that what you thought about us was wrong. We're not close. You want to tell me why you're smirking at me?

"You really don't know?"

He seems surprised by this. I know I've helped him out with classes in the past and because of that he knows I'm smart, but he has to realize that it doesn't extend to mind reading. This is real life and I'm definitely not a superhero.

"I figured you more for Batman."

Oh no. *No, No, No.* I'm not gonna go there right now. I finally managed to clear my head of all things Ryder Kane before Dillon showed up and now that I've texted the way he asked me to, I'm gonna go right back to doing it again.

Know what?

"Holy shit!" he laughs before slapping his hand over his mouth. "You really have no clue! I thought you were the smart one."

I'm going way past annoyance with the way he's acting right now. If he doesn't spit out what it is that I don't know, I'm going to turn around and go find Belle. He'll fit in with the others if I did that. His laughter would be aimed at my back instead of my face the way it is now.

"I can't believe I've actually got to spell something out for you. Usually it's the other way around, but here goes." He smirks again and with a quick eye roll, I wait for him to get on with it. "When you're with Ry, has he ever done anything that seemed weird to you, like out of character for him?"

The question is too vague. I didn't really know Ryder before a week ago. Sure, there are things he's done when we've been together that don't seem right, but I have no idea if they're out of character for him or not.

Not sure. Can you give me an example?

I can't believe I'm standing here entertaining this. Dillon obviously finds whatever he knows to be hilarious, so it's the last thing I should be buying into. Especially when it's about Ryder. There's nothing funny about the way we left things.

"I don't know," he admits before shaking his head, like he can't believe he's even having this conversation. "Does he ever look at you the way Kayden looks at Belle?"

Of all the examples he could have come up with to get his point across, I really wasn't expecting it to be that. Why would he ask me that? Doesn't he know his roommate is straight? That it's only my clichéd wishful thinking that wants that to be real?

No. Why would he?

"Jesus Christ. I can't believe he's gonna make me do this."

Who is going to make you do what? Dillon, can you please start making sense? I'm really confused and it's starting to make my head hurt.

"Sorry. Shit. Okay, I'm just gonna spit this out."

Before he can speak again, I scribble across the paper quickly and hand it over.

Please do.

"The reason I think Ryder will answer you back, it's not because you're helping get him back on the team. Isaac," he sighs before looking me straight in the eye again. "I wanted you to text Ryder because he likes you."

Ryder likes me.

Dillon doesn't get it, but he's being vague again. Liking me could mean just about anything, which doesn't explain away why it had to be me that texted. Anyone that likes Ryder could have easily done what I did. Thinking about how many people I've seen him around since he got here, I'd say that's about half the campus.

That doesn't explain anything. Ryder likes a lot of people. Some of them, like the girl we walked in and caught him with, he likes more than others.

"When he comes back, I'm gonna make him explain that night to you because holy shit, you've got the wrong idea about it, but I don't mean he likes you as a friend. It's more than that, you follow?"

What version of Ryder does Dillon know? The one that I've been spending time with is nothing like the one he's trying to get me to believe in. He tolerates me sure, we might even be friends, but anything past that, no way. He's just telling me what I want to hear. There's no proof. No tangible evidence that what he says is the truth.

You do have proof. He kissed you three days ago.

Are you trying to tell me Ryder's gay?

"Ding, Ding, Ding! We have a winner!"

No way. I know what I thought, but that was just me wanting to believe in something so badly because of the way I was reacting to him that I latched on and didn't want to let go. It wasn't supposed to be real. It isn't real.

No way.

"You really had no clue?"

Starting to shake my head, I think better of it and stop. Telling Dillon that I had no clue is a lie because deep down, I knew. I just didn't want to believe it because of what I'd been shown.

I had an idea, but I thought it was just my mind playing tricks on me.

Ryder with girls hanging all over him. Walking in on him after he had just finished having sex with one, appearing to be anything other then what Dillon is saying he is.

I need answers for all of that even though the haunted look he wore when we walked in on him is still burned in my brain.

I don't understand the girls.

"That makes two of us. Look, for whatever reason he feels like he needs to hide it. The whole thing confuses the fuck out of me honestly, but it's his thing and I don't want to change him. I thought coming to you, if you knew, maybe you could."

You want me to change him?

"No! You've met him right? No one can change that. I just thought you could get through to him. Make him see that he doesn't have to hide. I know you're not exactly happy that Kayden told me about you, but I'm glad he did because I could use the help."

You want me to help you with Ryder?

"Yeah. It wasn't all that long ago that there wasn't a person on the planet that gave two fucks whether I lived or died. I get the feeling it's the same with him, only he's in on it too. I want to help him before he hits rock bottom."

Understanding what he's getting at even though I don't know the specifics, there's only one thing left for me to do now. I've got to reach out again and this time make it count.

Handing over the notebook and reaching for the phone the minute Dillon takes it from me, I pull up the text window again and try one more time, only this time, it's not only as a friend.

It's as a lifeline.

Ryder, I understand now. Please come back. Come home.

Ryder

Unbelievable.

I always knew Gavin had a twisted sense of humor. He dragged me into it more times than I can count, but it's never been quite this crazy.

Ryder, I understand now. Please come back. Come home.

My sign from Gavin is Isaac.

Getting a text from him should surprise me, but it doesn't. It's the kind of guy he is. I should have known when I bailed that it was only a matter of time before he came around again. I just thought I would have a little more time.

Who the fuck are you kidding? Even running two hours away did nothing to stop what you're feeling for him. He's been with you the entire time.

As hard as it is to admit, it's true. He's still breaking down my walls from miles away. It makes everything that's happened between us clear.

The way I've reacted to Isaac, physically and emotionally, the way the memories of the past flood me every single time we're together, even kissing him, it's all Gavin's doing.

It's been Gavin the entire time.

He told me as much before he died.

~*~*~

"All of those people crying, Ry. It was like I was a bull in a china shop. One movement and they'd all collapse around me."

"I knew I should have gone with you, but I didn't want to push it."

Gavin hasn't been right since he got home from the funeral. It wasn't like I expected him to walk in and be his normal upbeat self, but whatever happened there, it's changed him somehow.

"Wanting to be with me, it's not pushing. It's sweet. I just—it was something I had to do on my own."

Gavin and his cousin Mike were close. Best friends more than family. They did everything together. When I first started hanging around with him, Mike was all he would talk about. Sometimes I wondered if they were the same person, that's how close Gavin showed me they were.

Having to attend the funeral, see Mike that way, I can only imagine what it's doing to him. The guy was only a year older than us for fuck sakes. It wasn't right that he had to die. God screwed up. He took the wrong person and now my boyfriend is left paying the price for his mistake.

"I don't—want to cry, but it hurts." *He sobs into my chest and I squeeze him tighter into me. He needs to know he doesn't have to be strong right now or ever. I'm never going anywhere.*

Us against the world.

"Promise me something, Ryder, and I don't want you to just say you promise and then not keep it. I really want you to mean it."

When anyone else says the word promise, it's in one ear and out the other and I'll say whatever I have to in order for them to shut the hell up, but by now Gavin has to know the same rules don't apply to him.

If I promise him the world, I'm damn sure gonna make good on it.

"Anything, Gav. You know that."

"If something ever happens to me, we're split apart or I die or something—"

"Gavin, look at me." Lifting his head from my chest and meeting my eyes, I push down the overwhelming urge I have to make this right for him even though I can't and focus on what I need him to hear. "You're not gonna die. We're not going to get split apart. It's us against the world forever. Please don't talk like you're going to disappear."

Reaching his hand up and stroking my cheek softly, he sighs and smiles weakly.

"I love you, Ryder Kane, do you know that?"

"Hmm, no, I don't think I do. Why don't you tell me again?"

"I love you, even if you're a gigantic ass."

"Pretty sure you mean smartass."

"No, I mean ass."

My laughs filters through at the same moment as his lighter one and they mix together into the perfect song. A sound that's ours alone and one strong enough to break through even the hardest felt grief.

"If for some reason I'm taken away from you." He holds up his hand to silence me the minute he sees me ready to argue. "Promise me you'll move on, Ry. That you won't feel the way I do right now. Mike not being here feels like someone has ripped a part of me away. I don't want that for you, so promise me."

"I promise, but Gav, I'm never going to let anyone take you from me."

"Tara said the same thing to Mike and you see how well that worked out."

"We're not them. What happened, I know how bad it hurts, I can see it every single time I look at you, but we're not them."

"I know." He whispers before collapsing back into my arms again..

"Ry?"

"Yeah babe?"

"If it ever seems like I'm not with you, I swear to you that I am. I'll always find a way to come back. I'll never leave you alone."

~*~*~

Two years ago I made a promise. A promise after death and one that up until a few days ago I took as seriously as breathing. Forgetting all about the original promise I made when he was still alive.

Coming out to my parents, getting pissed off when they didn't take it well and wanting to puke when they told me they wanted to kill the gay inside me, I've been using that for years as the reason for what happened to Gavin that night on the road.

It became less about me being drunk and more about me feeling the way I did about Gavin. It was me being gay that put it in motion and it was that thinking that made the promise I made him after he died spring to life.

Somewhere along the way that promise overrode the one I made to him after Mike's funeral and the sick feeling I had before, needing his forgiveness for screwing up with Isaac and breaking my promise, its worse now.

I've been focusing on the wrong promise the entire time and Gavin, he finally found a way to make me see it. He found a way to reach me and it was through the one person I've done nothing but swallow down, push away and run from for the last week.

Isaac.

The relief he brought me even when I was sitting here falling apart. So twisted and broken inside that I could see my life ending so clear that it almost became reality, it means something. It's not bad the way I've been making it out to be. It's not something a person runs from.

It's something they run toward.

His text coming through right when I needed it most, its Gavin's way of keeping his own promise to me and making me focus on the one I made him. The right one.

Gavin and Isaac, they're right. I need to go home. **I'm coming back now. Can I see you?** I just hope I'm not too late.

Chapter Twelve

Isaac

This is nerve-racking.

Ever since I got the text from Ryder, I've somehow gone through two classes unable to remember anything about them and made my way home on the bus with no memory of even getting on it to begin with. I've paced my living room about fifteen times, changed twice because I keep sweating through every shirt I own, and I'm driving myself so crazy waiting for the knock on my door that I'm pretty sure I'm going to pass out any minute.

Ryder isn't who I thought he was. I've been swallowing the way I react to him and I didn't have to be. This is nuts. If I had just seen the way he was acting for what it was, I could have opened up and he wouldn't have run from school or from me the way he did.

The strangest thing about all of this is the physical response I'm having and I don't mean my body shaking or sweating. It's my lips. About thirty seconds after his text came through, the tingling that I've been feeling since he kissed me, but that stopped after my conversation with Dillon, it came back and it just kept growing until it felt like they were on fire. It makes no sense, but we connected somehow and the closer he gets, it just gets stronger.

Yeah, this is definitely crazy. I'm crazy.

I'm not connected to Ryder. My thoughts are just moving so quickly that it's making my body appear that I am.

"Isaac, are you sure you're alright?"

I love my mom, I do, but she's asked me that almost as many times as I've paced the living room floor and the answer hasn't changed. By now she should realize it won't and stop asking, but that won't ever happen. She cares too much to drop it.

I'm okay, just nervous.

This makes her back down. I've given her a little more than I did the last time she asked. Backing down doesn't mean backing off though because now I've given her more to question me about.

"Are you nervous because of what this boy showing up here means or is there more going on?"

My mom knows everything. She knows I'm gay, she knows I get bullied for being mute, all of it. Her question, the concern I see in her eyes, it's because even though she's met Ryder already, she doesn't know if his intentions are to hurt me the way the others did or if it's about me liking him.

I tell her a lot, but I never opened up about that.

Until earlier today I thought there was something wrong with me, being attracted to a straight guy. It happens all over the world, but it doesn't to me.

Telling a guy that I think his hair is pretty is tame compared to the physical and emotional reaction I had to Ryder Kane almost a week ago.

He's not like the others, Mom. He's not going to hurt me. Pausing the pen on the paper, I wonder if I should just tell her everything. Maybe getting it out can make me see this with different eyes then I have been. If there's anyone in the world that will give it to me straight, it's my mom.

I like him and I don't know what to do with it. I've never felt anything like this before.

"What exactly are you feeling?"

Everything is more intense when he's around. All of the stuff you and Dad told me about, it's all there, but heightened. It's stupid, but when he smiles at me, it's like the Green Arrow is standing behind him shooting nonstop arrows into my chest. Does that make sense?

"Perfect sense, even the comic reference."

Telling her was the right thing. She knows absolutely nothing about comics or the heroes in them so responding the way she did, it's enough to break up the nervousness and make me laugh at the same moment she does.

I really need to stop bottling all of this up.

He scares me, Mom.

"What do you mean by scared? Are the feelings you're experiencing scary or do you mean he's done something that frightens you?"

Shaking my head, I start writing again, wanting to make sure that by the end of it, she understands that Ryder hasn't done anything to me. It's the thought of him now that I've learned the truth that's frightening because I don't know what it means.

He's not scary that way. I don't feel scared when I'm with him. I'm scared of what I feel when we're together. What I've spent a week burying down and hiding so he wouldn't think I was a freak. He's a really intense guy.

"You're not a freak."

I should have known that was going to be the one thing she pulled from everything I wrote. She's got a radar for that kind of stuff. She hates when I say anything bad about myself because she loves me and she just doesn't see it.

In other words, she's bias. I love her for it, but right now, I want her to talk about everything else I said, not the one thing that doesn't matter.

Not helping.

"This is a first for me too, Isaac. I always knew the day would come, but I don't think there's a parent alive that's prepared for when it does."

This would be so much easier if I was straight.

"Attraction, desire and everything that comes along with those things is tough no matter what your sexual orientation is. I don't have the answers that will make this easier for you because I haven't been nineteen in a very long time. It has nothing to do with you being gay."

Yeah, I forgot. You're really old. :)

"Very funny."

I know. I'm hilarious. I don't need you to solve this or make it right, Mom. I'll figure it out on my own. I just wanted

to know that what's going on is normal. As normal as it can be considering it's happening to me anyway.

"I could easily sit here and tell you every single thing I felt when I saw your father for the first time, but I'm pretty sure you're not looking to be grossed out before your friend gets here. What I will say is that everything you're going through, it's as normal as it gets. It would be strange if this didn't scare you."

Thanks for sparing me details on you and Dad. I really wasn't looking to be traumatized.

Smiling as she reads, she laughs before handing the paper back to me.

"It's going to be fine, Isaac. I promise you that. Even if this boy you like is as intense and scary as you say, it will all work itself out. If there's anyone that can handle that, it's you."

I don't understand.

"You've been handling scary situations and intense people from the moment you were born. This might be different, but you survived it before, so I know you can do it again."

She's right. What I feel with Ryder, the way he is, especially with everything Dillon admitted about him, I've handled worse. I can do this even if seeing him again still scares the hell out of me.

Putting the pen to the paper, about to tell her the same thing I just told myself, the doorbell rings and the grip I had on the pen, the strength I was just starting to build, it crashes around me and the pen falls to the floor.

"Stay put." She says, leaning over and picking the pen up. "I don't need any more lines in my carpet."

Squeezing my arm gently as she gets to her feet, she turns toward the door as the bell goes off a second time, but instead of moving forward the way I expect her to, she turns back to me again.

"You're gonna be fine, Isaac and if you're not, I'm only a few feet away."

Ryder

Yes you can.

Three words I never expected to see with the mammoth amount of shit I caused before I left, but ones that steady me the minute they come through.

Standing on his doorstep after what felt like the longest drive in history, I'm noticing things I didn't the first time I showed up here.

There is a whole lot of color surrounding this house. It starts with the two large green trees off to the side and continues on with the flowers that line both sides of the very front, with only the stone steps in the middle separating them. An assortment of a lot of different types, a bunch of different colors and absolutely impossible to ignore.

It's obvious that Isaac's mom has a green thumb and judging from how well taken care of they are, she cares a lot about them. From the small bit I've seen and know about her, I'm pretty sure the way she takes care of her garden is how she takes care of her family. Flawlessly. The complete opposite of my mom.

Diane Kane has a garden too, but the thing would die a million times over if she didn't have staff taking care of it. The same way I would have.

I used to spend a lot of time in the greenhouse when I was younger and not once did she step into it, unless you count the times she wanted to show it off to other people. She showed off those flowers and plants the same way she did with me and remembering that now, I can't help feeling jealous of Isaac.

I wish my mom was more like his.

I just wish my mom gave a shit period.

Out of the corner of my eye, I see movement and turning, I catch what caused it. In the far right corner, the wind is moving a yellow rose. There are a dozen different flowers around it, but it's the only one moved by the force of the breeze.

Stepping down off the step and making my way over, I pluck it out of the ground, swallowing down the guilt that rises the minute it's out and in my hand.

It's wrong, but with him agreeing to see me after everything that happened between us, I need to give him something. Show him what taking this chance again means to me. He could have easily texted me back and told me to fuck off and never contact him again, but he didn't.

This flower in my hand, it's another sign. I need to do it this way, even if it's wrong.

Sliding the stem into my back pocket and raising my shirt up enough to slide it back down over it, keeping it hidden until I'm ready to use it, I roll back and forth on my feet until the door swings open.

It's his mom again and if it's possible, she's smiling even brighter than she did the first time I showed up here unannounced. A smile I know for a fact I would lose completely if she knew what I just did to her mini flower garden.

"Ryder, come on in! Isaac's waiting in the family room."

Swallowing the last bit of guilt I feel and praying that when I do finally walk past her she doesn't catch the bulge in the back of my pants, I step in and start making my way down the familiar hallway, taking in everything around me.

Pictures line the walls all the way down. Portraits of what I'm starting to think is the picture perfect family. There are pictures of Isaac alone, and then a bunch with all three, but in every single one, they're smiling. Everything is right, which makes me being here feel so wrong.

What the fuck was I thinking? What am I expecting to happen with Isaac when I finally get in the same room with him? Am I going to beg him not to give up on tutoring me again or does the flower I grabbed make this something more?

Should I even be here? After everything I caused before I met him, do I really deserve to stand here with his mom smiling and him being nice to me?

The knife is twisting with each step forward. Can I really impose the way I am on these people? When they learn what I've done, will I even be welcome here?

Locking eyes with Isaac when I get to the end of the hall, his hand raised and moving back and forth in a wave, a smile on his face, I get my answer.

He wants me here. I can do this. I'm not gonna screw it up again.

Moving closer, but making no attempt to sit down, more than a little aware of the rose in my back pocket and the thorns now digging into my ass, Isaac looks at me confused and pats the cushion beside him.

Sit. He mouths and I shake my head which only confuses him more.

Making sure that his mom didn't follow me in, I slip my hand around, lifting my shirt up in order to get the flower out. Isaac's eyes are trained on my every movement, which forces me to stop and explain.

"It's not what you think. I need to grab something." I offer up before wrapping my hand around the thorny stem, slipping it out of my pocket and bringing it around until it's held out between us.

The pen hits the paper and I watch as he writes, stopping every few seconds to look between me and the flower. Finally finished with what he wants to say after a few more looks in my direction, he hands the paper over and I slide myself down on the sofa before I read it.

Why are you walking around with a rose in your back pocket? Don't you know those things hurt when they stab you?

"I do now. Don't think I'm gonna try that again anytime soon." I admit, laughing awkwardly. "The reason I did it is because I wanted you to have it."

Why would you want me to have a flower?

"My parents have a greenhouse, and when I was a kid, I used to spend a lot of time there hanging out with our gardener. He used to tell me about flowers. I saw this one outside, so I grabbed it."

Does a yellow rose mean something?

"Yeah." I blush, embarrassed that I even know this. "It's supposed to mean friendship."

Do you give flowers to all your friends?

"No."

Shit this is awkward. I should've just left the damn flower alone. I screwed up Mrs. Crawford's garden for nothing. I'm such an idiot.

You should. I'm sure Dillon would love to get a flower from you ;)

Laughing after the day I've had, it's strange yet at the same time relieving. I needed it a lot more then I wanted to admit and I'm glad that it's him bringing it out of me.

"I'm sure he'd love that." Holding the flower out again now that I'm sitting closer, he reaches out to take it and the second his fingers brush mine, the familiar shock shoots straight through me. "He's gonna have to get his own though. This one is for you."

Thank you. Did you say you saw this outside?

Shit, he doesn't miss anything.

"Yeah," I start, feeling the heat in my cheeks again and lowering my head in order to hide it. "I was looking at all the flowers, admiring them because they reminded me of the way things used to be when I was living at home. I saw that one move so I grabbed it. How mad is your mom gonna be when she finds out?"

She's gonna kill you.

"Fuck."

Glad you didn't hide your filthy mouth the way you hid your blush.

He smiles and even though the heat trailing across my face is threatening to burn me alive, I smile back.

"I'll tell her I did it. I'll even replant one if she wants me to. I just..."

You just what?

"I wanted to give it to you because of what it meant. What you saying you would see me meant."

I was only kidding earlier. She won't kill you. She probably won't even notice. I'm the one that planted them out there.

"Really?"

Yeah. I like the way they smell. Some things are harsh for me, but flowers are subtle. It's silly, but I get overwhelmed a lot and I wanted something softer to come home to everyday.

I know absolutely nothing about this guy.

I've kissed him, thought about him in some not so innocent ways, physically reacted to those thoughts, even had an orgasm with his name attached and I know absolutely nothing about him.

That needs to change. I want it to change. I want to know everything there is to know even if he's better off.

"That's not silly. Wanna know a secret?"

Sure, but once you say it out loud it's not a secret anymore.

"I think I can handle that." Laughing, I pull up the memory I want to share and seeing it clear as day, share a part of me that no one else knows. "I used to pick dandelions on the way home from school. I'd grab so many of them my hands were packed and I'd keep them by my bed in one of my dad's old beer mugs because I liked the way they smelled."

I used to pick those too, but they died too quick. :(

"Wow."

It slips out before I realize I've done it, but he catches it and starts writing. I've seen him draw happy faces before, but seeing the sad one, it's wrong. I don't know why, but I hate seeing it there.

Isaac should never frown, not on paper or for real.

What?

"I've never seen you make a sad face before."

I'm sorry.

"It's still a force of habit?"

The minute he smiles, the unsettled feeling I had when he frowned lifts and everything feels okay again.

No one was here to bust my balls about it.

"Bust your balls? Really? Is that what you think I was doing?"

He blushes and just like I did when I reacted to his touch a few minutes ago, he starts to lower his head. Reaching out until my hand rests on his chin, I stop him. I'm starting to see what he means by me hiding my natural responses now. I hate when he does it to me.

"Please don't turn into me."

Lifting his gaze until it meets mine, his lips lift into a smile and I bring my hand down until it's back in my lap and I'm leaning away from him. As comfortable as the moment is, it's not going to be much longer before we get into the real reason I'm here. If I'm gonna get through it, I need to separate myself, even if I liked the way it felt when my hand was resting on his face.

Are you gonna bust my balls if I do?

"Yes and I won't go easy on you either. I'll bust you so hard you'll break."

Holy fuck. Open mouth insert foot, Ryder.

That sounds bad.

Opening my mouth, prepared to tell him I didn't mean it, the pen starts moving on the paper again. When I finally look down, what I find knocks me on my ass.

In a good way.

Fuck. This can't happen right now. It's not what I want at all. They're just words on a paper for fuck sakes. I shouldn't be reacting to them this way. I shouldn't react at all, but least of all like this.

Heat, along with an intense pressure in my chest, mixes with my dicks response, as my mind intertwines the words good and bad together visualizing the way I could make them come to life with him.

Isaac deserves better than this. Responding this way to innocent words written by an even more innocent guy, I feel like a pervert. I'm disgusting.

He can't figure out what his words do to me. How it feels the way it did when we were on the side of the road. Him urging me to talk, wanting it so bad he was willing to mouth the words to make it happen and my desire to capture those lips until I was drowning in the feel and taste of them.

With everything I know about him, he might be okay with the way I'm reacting, could even be feeling some of the same shit I am, but it doesn't make it right.

Responding like this makes it look like I'm just here to get in his pants and that's not even remotely right. I want more then something physical here. I want the entire fucking thing, even though the last time I had something like it, I caused it to be ripped away from me.

Breathe, Ryder. Deep breath in, deeper one out. You need to get control.

No longer caring how it looks to the guy sitting beside me, I close my eyes and continue breathing, focusing my mind on just about anything that will tame the beast that's coming alive inside me. After a few seconds of deep concentration, my reaction to him finally starting to fade, I feel a light brush against my hand and my eyes jump open, my hand coming out and gripping tightly.

Isaac's fingers are trapped in mine. His eyes are wide, shock reverberating through them, which the second I catch finally makes me lessen the hold.

Fuck. I'm scaring the shit out of him.

His body twists to the side and when he turns back toward me, there's a paper in his other hand. Dropping it into my lap, I look down and read the words, releasing the hold completely.

Ryder, I understand. I feel it too. Please stop trying to hide it.

"You feel—this too?"

The struggle inside me to get those words out, how choppy they still manage to sound when they finally are out, I'm starting to understand Isaac more than I ever did before. If it feels half as brutal as that for him, why he doesn't speak makes sense.

He nods his head and in an effort to help him, I slide the paper over, but instead of grabbing it the way I expect him to, he shakes his head and brings his hand up to his lips, touching them before reaching over and doing the same thing to my ear.

Reaching up and sliding my hand around his arm while his touch continues to linger on my ear, I lean my head into him and sigh.

"Say what you need to say. I'm listening."

His lips curve into a smile and as they separate, parting just enough for him to silently speak to me, they start forming words and when he's done, he leans back and waits for me to respond.

I want you too.

"Isaac," His name a whisper, his words repeating on a loop in my head until they consume me, I give up the fight to complete a coherent thought. I can't think anymore. I just need to act.

Moving forward, pushing him back into the sofa before climbing on top of him, his body resting snugly between my legs, I lower my lips onto his while sliding my hands over his head, gripping onto the miniscule pieces of growth the deeper the kiss goes.

Pushing my tongue into his mouth, running it over his teeth and around the sides, playing with him while drowning in the minty flavor I'm met with the second he granted me entrance, a moan escapes from somewhere deep inside him. It's the first sound I've ever heard him make and unable to control my response to it, I answer it back with a possessive growl.

Fuck this feels amazing. He feels amazing. I should go slower, but I can't. I want more.

When his tongue finds mine, running circles around it, hesitant at first but growing more confident, the small string holding what was left of my restraint completely snaps. I push deeper, retracting enough to catch his tongue and suck on it, surrendering to its taste. Releasing the hold, needing more, I push my tongue forward until it's wrapped up in his, our tastes finally mingling together the way I want and that's when it happens.

I give in completely.

Chapter Thirteen

Isaac

I've thought a lot about what it would be like the first time I kissed someone. The awkward hands everywhere, biting when I should have been sucking, drowning the other person in saliva because there's no control whatsoever on how much wetness one can produce in a moment like that. I thought about everything.

Everything that would seem wrong or bad, but really isn't because a first kiss is supposed to be that weird and awkward. It was what I always knew would happen when I experienced it. If I ever did.

It was nothing at all like what's happening right now. There's no awkwardness at all.

Sure, this isn't exactly my first kiss. I experienced that three days ago on the side of the road when emotions were running high, but it wasn't awkward or weird then either.

It's because of him.

I have no idea how it feels for Ryder, our lips together like this, tongues joining, teasing and tasting the way we are. Is his head fuzzy? Is he sweating from the heat radiating off our bodies being pressed together the same way I am? Does the feel of my hands in his hair, the way I grip and tug whenever his growl vibrates up through his chest, make him want to get even closer to me the way I want to with him?

The way I feel, wanting to crawl out of my own skin and into his, it is so intense, it's scary. All sense of time is obliterated. I have no idea how long we've been like this and I don't even care. All I care about is making sure that this—us, right here in this moment, never ends.

God help me. I have no idea what I'm doing, but the way he's making me feel, I'm losing control. The way he sucks on my tongue repeatedly, before retracting and pushing his forward and tangling it up in mine again makes me want to do the same thing to him.

I'm so caught up in the way this feels that I'm just now realizing his hands aren't on my head anymore. They're on my back, under my shirt, searing my skin with their warmth. He's gripping me with one and rubbing with the other and my body is responding by arching into him, my own hands coming around until he's not the only one feeling skin.

This is so much more than a kiss.

Kisses are wet and awkward. The complete opposite of what is happening between us now.

Ryder Kane doesn't kiss. He makes love with his mouth. It's why I'm no longer solid because he's not just kissing me. We passed simple kissing a long time ago.

Shifting my body, not wanting to stop, but unable to ignore the pressure from the cushion digging into my back, Ryder shifts with me. His movement is enough to break the spell of the kiss, but not the rest of us as his face lingers only a hairs breath away from mine. His blue eyes staring intently back at me.

"Wow."

I want to scream out and tell him that what just happened is so much more than wow, but of course, the words, and the sound it takes to vocalize them, doesn't come. His body still lingering close, I ignore the urge to speak and focus on his scent. It's not an artificial one. It's all natural, all male and one hundred percent Ryder.

Exhaling deeply, he slides his body back until he's resting where he was earlier and I swallow down the urge inside to cry at the distance between us.

One moment in time, a simple kiss that turned into more and the second he moves away he destroys me.

Breathe. He's doing the right thing moving away unless you really want your mom to walk in and catch the show.

My earlier joke about her traumatizing me comes back and the hurt I felt at him backing away starts to fade. This needs to happen. Somewhere in the midst of us kissing, I forgot all about her and I really don't want her first experience with Ryder to be walking in on whatever that was.

Sliding back up until I'm recreating the way we were when he got here, I look down and grab onto the paper the minute I feel it brush against the side of my pants.

Staring at it, the multiple lines on the page running together into one big one because of blurriness in my eyes, I try to force down and stop what I know is about to happen.

I can't cry right now. No way.

"Isaac, what's wrong?"

I'm such a social virgin, it's disgusting. I can't admit that kissing him and the way we separated is turning me into an emotional basket case. He's going to think I'm pathetic.

"Please tell me."

Forcing my mind to focus on the lines, wiping at my eyes in order to keep them clear so I can get this out, I start writing, no longer caring if it's even across the line or not, just desperate to get it out.

I'm sorry. I've never kissed anyone like that before. I'm not very good at it. I understand why you stopped, but it still hurt when you moved away. I'm so sorry. It won't happen again.

Handing over the paper is a struggle. I didn't think I could sound any more pathetic then I do in my head, but the words I've written, they really slam it home. There's no way he's going to look at them and not regret kissing me altogether.

"Isaac," He says softly, pausing before sighing and running a hand through his hair. "Are you fucking kidding me?"

I don't get it. Why is he asking me that?

"You have no clue why I stopped."

He's wrong. I do. He stopped because I moved wrong, reminded him somehow of who it was he was kissing and he couldn't get away from me fast enough.

He didn't move away fast. He stayed close.

This is crazy. Nothing makes sense. I know he lingered for a while after the kiss ended, but he could have been doing that because he felt bad. All of this could have just been some crazy experiment to give the little gay virgin something he's never had.

"Tell me what you're thinking, yell at me for taking advantage of you or kick my ass straight out of your house. Whatever you need to, just please end this silence. I can't take it."

Why did you kiss me?

"I couldn't stand staring at your lips and not tasting them?"

Why are you answering a question with a question?

"Because I'm an idiot and I need to be taught how to answer properly? Do you think as my tutor that's something you can help me with?"

Despite how serious I am, the way he answers breaks through enough to make me smile and the minute it happens, Ryder reacts.

"That's better."

Why did you really kiss me?

"I wanted to. No, scratch that. I *needed* to kiss you."

You didn't do it because you feel sorry for me?

"You're joking right?" he laughs, but it's different than his other ones. He's forcing himself to laugh this time. "The last thing I felt kissing you was sorry."

Then why did you stop? Was it because I wasn't doing it right?

Reaching over toward me, he wraps one hand around my back and pulls me closer to him. Releasing his hold, smiling as he takes in just how close he brought us, he grabs my hand and before I can question why he's doing it, he motions down with his head and following along, I see why.

His hand is resting comfortably on top of mine, but it's not on his knee or another part of his leg the way I expect. He's got my hand resting on his crotch.

Oh God.

"You can feel it the exact same way I can. Ask me again if you did it wrong."

Sensing my discomfort, he lifts my hand, but where I expect him to let go, he does the opposite. He locks our fingers together.

"I stopped because if I didn't, I was going to combust *or* things were going to lead to a place I don't think either one of us is ready for. Kissing you, as amazing as it felt; and trust me Isaac, it felt fucking amazing, is not the reason I came here."

Most of the time when people talk to me, the things they say aren't so nice, so I do my best not to react or be affected one way or the other. Hearing Ryder explain why he stopped, why he had to back away and knowing deep down that he's telling the truth, I'm affected by it all and I have no idea what to say next.

"No response to any of that, huh?"

I shake my head and the room fills with his laughter.

"That's a good thing right?"

Nodding my head quickly, he laughs quietly.

"The reason I came here, it's because I wanted to tell you the truth about me. I needed you to know. It didn't exactly go down the way I thought it would in my head, but what I wanted to say, I'm pretty sure you know it now."

I'm pretty sure you know the truth about me too.

"I do, but to be fair, I knew about you before I got here."

Me too.

"Let me guess," he says and writing quickly across the page, I lift it up in the air at the same moment the name falls from his lips.

"Dillon."

Ryder

The first time I ever held hands with someone, I was six years old.

Katie Francis was a girl that moved in down the road from me and after about two weeks of us meeting in the middle and hanging out together, I finally worked up the courage to slip my fingers through hers.

I expected there to be this moment where our hair stood on end because of the electric pull between us, or even a fireworks explosion in the sky, but it didn't happen. Nothing happened. The way I felt before our fingers even connected was exactly how I felt after it.

At the time, I just thought it was because I wasn't all that into her. That I'd meet another girl; a better one and everything that should have happened when I held hands with Katie would happen then. Everything would make sense.

I should've known that it was never going to happen with a girl, but I was a little kid and a pretty dumb one at that, so I never even thought to question it.

It wasn't until I met Gavin and our hands accidentally brushed against each other that the payoff I'd been waiting for happened. There were sparks. I'm pretty damn sure the entire sky blew up in the few seconds it took for us to touch that way. It was in that moment I knew Gavin was it for me.

Holding Isaac's hand now, it's like that moment with Gavin all over again except different because I willingly joined our hands. There was nothing accidental about it. It's also different because I have no plans of breaking it. I like the way it feels too much to stop. It was the same damn way when we were kissing. I never wanted it to end. As long as I was wrapped up in him, I didn't have to think about how far off course I drove this thing.

I could experience what it feels like to be with someone and not have to pretend to be someone I'm not. I could enjoy it.

Finding out that Dillon went to him about me should piss me off, but it doesn't. If he was willing to tell me about Isaac, I had to figure he would take his meddling a step further and tell Isaac about me too. I'm glad he did because if he hadn't done it, with the way I was feeling at Gavin's grave, I might not be experiencing the moment I'm in.

I might not be experiencing life at all.

"Can we start over?"

Yes, but how?

"I'm not sure." I admit before an idea comes to me. Questions. We can ask each other things in order to get back to the real reason I showed up here. I can get to know him so I can figure out once and for all what it is about him that I can't seem to let go of.

"When did you know?"

Know what?

"When did you know you were into guys?"

I've never been into girls, so I guess I've always known. I came out to my parents when I was twelve though.

Twelve. A number pretty significant to me.

When did you know?

The answer to this question is easy, but if I want to keep this dialogue going with him and not have it turn back into what it was earlier, I'm pretty sure I need to keep my mouth shut.

"When I met my boyfriend in high school."

His nose scrunches up and ignoring the fact that it's kind of a cute look for him, I focus on whatever it is he's writing.

I don't believe that. Try again, Ryder.

How the hell does he do that?

"Twelve, maybe thirteen, not exactly sure. It's been a while since I thought about it."

What happened?

"I saw Robert Downey, Jr. in an Iron Man suit."

There's a hell of a lot more to the story then that, like how quick my hand slid into my boxers and started rubbing, but Isaac definitely doesn't need to know it. With the way he reacted to our kiss and me pulling away, I know for a fact he doesn't have a whole lot of experience with this. The last thing I want to do is give the guy a crash course.

My mom took me to the mall to get some new clothes. There was a new security guard on duty and when he was doing his rounds I saw him. He was so pretty I ended up making my mom follow him around the store because I couldn't stop staring.

"He was pretty?"

Isaac turns a deep shade of crimson and nods, and despite knowing that I've embarrassed him, I can't stop. I need to push it.

"Am I pretty?"

No.

"Ouch. That hurts."

If you need an ego boost that badly, try coming to class. There's a lot of girls there willing to give it to you.

When he said no and I responded, it was a joke. I didn't actually take what he said seriously, but what's on the page now, it's as serious as it gets. It means the mess of shit that I created and made him a part of, I now have to start to clean up.

"Isaac, I don't need an ego boost and even if I did, it wouldn't be from a bunch of girls I could care less about."

Is the reason you're flunking out of all your classes because you're confused?

Holy shit. It's worse than I thought.

"No. I know exactly who I am and I thought after the way you kissed me back, you were pretty damn sure of it too."

Nothing makes sense, Ryder. You confuse me.

"I confuse myself."

That's not helpful.

"I didn't grow up in a house with two loving parents the way you did, Isaac. I don't even know what the fuck that is. They cared about two things. Making money and church. I spent more time with the staff they employed then with them unless they needed to show me off at some function. That's when I was important."

I can't believe I have to go there right now. No one knows half of the shit I'm telling him, and until now it's exactly how I wanted it. There's no way in hell that when I get through telling him all of this he's gonna look at me the same. It's impossible. He's going to see me the exact same way I've been seeing myself. He'll be disgusted.

"I knew I was gay, but I kept it hidden. Whenever someone or something turned me on and I was around my parents, I'd find the nearest bathroom and fuck myself until it was gone and I could be presentable again. I even went and did it in the bushes at the back of the church a couple of times, that's how badly I needed to keep it hidden. I met my ex-boyfriend in junior year and that's when everything changed."

Changed how?

"I didn't want to hide it away anymore. I knew deep down how they were going to react when it came out, but there was this small part of me that wished they would react the way your parents obviously have. Pull me closer instead of pushing me away. I finally worked up the nerve to tell them and you wanna know what happened?" Pausing even though it's not a question I want an answer to, I take a deep breath and prepare myself for the worst of it. The one thing that's haunted me for the past two years.

"They told me there were places that could fix my problem. They even did charity work with a couple of them. They could kill the homosexuality. They didn't want to embrace the way I was the way parents should. They wanted to erase it. They wanted to erase me."

I can't look at him. I want to, but I can't because I'm too much of a fucking pussy to confront his reaction head on. I'm afraid of it. I don't want to see those bright brown eyes turn dark and distant.

He can't turn into me.

"What you walked in on the other day with me and that girl, it was me trying to force it down. I was fucking her to forget. I wanted to be someone else."

What's so bad about you that you think you need to be someone else?

I can't go there. I can't explain Gavin, the accident and why I did the things I did. It's too much and even with the chance I took coming here and reaching out, I can't ruin it.

When I tell Isaac everything; if I tell him, it will ruin it. There's no way it can't.

"I let their shit get to me. I swallowed who I was in order to make them happy."

The knife in my chest, the one that twists me up in knots and has been dormant since I got here, it's back again. Lying to him, twisting the truth, it's plunging it deeper than it's ever gone before.

I don't want to lie, he deserves better, but the truth, it's worse than a lie.

You really don't like girls?

Everything I've said to him and that's what his first question is.

God he's amazing.

"Not even a little."

You're into guys.

"Yes—No, not exactly."

What does that mean?

"I'm gay, so I'm attracted to guys, yes, but the way you said it isn't right."

So enlighten me.

"I'm not into *guys* plural. I'm into one guy, Isaac. You."

Chapter Fourteen

Isaac

"This is frustrating! I'm not a writer." Ryder moans as he drags his hand through his hair for what feels like the fiftieth time since we got here. "You want me to take down some guy and score a touchdown, I'm definitely your man. Stringing at least a thousand words together for a research paper? No way. I'm not gonna be able to do this."

He said the same thing about the math test I gave him yesterday and despite the litany of complaints, the doubt he had in his ability to grasp the material, he'd done better than I expected him to.

Ryder is a lot smarter than he thinks he is, but getting through to him, making him see that; it's impossible. I get the feeling that the only way he'll ever see himself the way I do is when the professors prove it to him.

Squeezing his shoulder before rubbing his back, doing the only thing I can in the moment to alleviate the tension in his body, he leans into the touch and sighs.

"I'm doing it again. I'm sorry."

It's okay. I'm getting used to it.

"You shouldn't have to get used to it. I'm being an idiot."

Please don't do that. You're not an idiot, Ryder. You're just taking too much on at once and it's stressing you out.

"Coach wants a detailed report from you and my professors by the end of the week. So far the only thing we've got to show for all the time we've spent here is a decent pre-college math placement test."

It's more than we had three days ago.

"Yeah, I guess."

Three days ago you weren't even here. You're back now and for the last two days you've been doing nothing but hardcore studying. It's a lot, even if you don't think so.

Putting the focus on the way things were, a time when not even his roommate knew if he was even alive or dead, I hate it, but he needs to see how far he's come since then.

"I've done more than just study the last two days."

Catching his smirk and the way his eyes glow, it doesn't take long to figure out what he's getting at.

Us.

Being here alone, calling for breaks every fifteen minutes because the need inside of us to connect is impossible to ignore. Ryder overriding my trepidation and nervousness with his raw intensity and making me forget the minute his lips touched mine what the real reason we were here even was.

Everything about our time together is intense and scary. It's obvious from the way he touches me that he's knowledgeable. A lot more than I am in knowing what to do or how to act. Considering he had an ex-boyfriend and I've had no one but myself since I came out to my parents, it makes sense, but it still leaves me feeling like I'm less.

Like I'm not going to be enough for him.

Write the paper, Ryder. When it's done, we can take a break. ;)

"Are you suggesting a reward system, Isaac?"

Does that appeal to you?

"Mhmm, it does actually." He murmurs before catching my bottom lip with his teeth and biting down with a possessive growl. "If I write this paper, what's my reward?"

What do you think you should get?

"You don't want me to answer that with the way you look right now."

What does he mean by that? I'm in jeans and a t-shirt, same as I always am. There's nothing about the way I look that should stop him from telling me what he wants. Unless there's something wrong with the way I'm dressed.

Maybe I don't want him to answer after all.

How do I look right now?

"You *really* don't want to know."

Ryder, please.

My plea even though it's on paper and not out loud must give something away because he grabs my face and lifts and turns it until all I can see is him staring back at me.

"Shit! You think it's bad. Isaac, no!"

Shifting my eyes toward the paper, wanting to reach out for the pen in order to respond, but his grip on my face making it impossible, he catches on and releases me.

"Can I ask you something?"

You can ask me anything.

"When we're together like this, especially now that everything's out in the open, how do you feel?"

I'm not sure what you mean.

"Hmm, let me try and explain it another way."

Okay.

"When we're here like this, even when I'm focused on the work, my body is fully charged. There's this low hum, like every nerve ending is ignited and alive. When you lean in, touch me—fuck, even breathe on me, it takes some serious willpower not to lean you back in the chair and just act on what I feel."

I understand his question now. He wants to know if he's alone in what's happening here. He's not, but I'm not sure how to explain everything I experience during our time together.

This is new to me. I always thought that when this happened finally, it would be different somehow.

"Is this too much for you?"

No. Maybe. I don't know.

I'm not making any sense. The confusion I feel, I'm now pushing it off on him. My inexperience is ruining everything.

"Try something with me?"

Forgoing the use of the paper, I nod my agreement and he smiles softly before squeezing my hand.

"What I asked you earlier that you weren't sure about, I want to try and get an answer. So I'm going to do some things and then I want you to write down what you feel. Can you do that?"

Yes.

"This first one, it's easy. I want you to tell me what you feel when you look at me."

He's right. This isn't hard. What I experience when he looks at me, it's the one thing about this that's never changed since it started happening.

When I look at you all I see is your eyes. The rest of your face ceases to exist because I'm stuck staring into eyes that look like crystalized glass. The longer I look, the faster my heart beats and the harder it becomes to breathe.

"Are you saying that looking at me takes your breath away?"

Yes.

"Wow. Uh—okay." He stammers as his cheeks flush. Catching himself, he pushes forward. "Tell me how this feels."

Moving his hand until it's resting on my shoulder, he starts sliding his fingers down my arm slowly, each passing second like torture until he finally stops moving the minute his hand is resting with mine in his lap.

Your hand on my shoulder because of the pressure, warmed my entire body. When you started moving, it felt like sparks popping in every spot you touched and the slower you moved, the more the sparks started to burn.

His eyes are softer now, but otherwise his expression remains the same. If the way I explained got to him in any way, he's not showing it. Instead he scoots his chair closer until our faces are so close together I can feel the breath from his nose grazing my face.

"I'm going to kiss you now."

Nodding slowly, I inhale a breath and wait for him to make his move.

The minute our lips make contact and he pushes deeper, slipping his tongue inside, the explanation of what I feel when he does this matches so perfectly to the one he gave me before he started his experiment.

Every nerve ending is alive, ignited and popping. My need mixing with his desire until it's not just my skin that's burning.

Pulling away and leaning back in his chair, he shifts his body and it doesn't take long to see why. One kiss and his arousal is undeniable. He's reacting to me physically and now has to adjust himself.

Caught up so completely watching him and the way the simple movement of his hand over his pants drives my body temperature higher than I think it's ever been, I don't realize how much time has passed until he chuckles and clears his throat, bringing my attention back up to his eyes.

"I want to ask you how that made you feel, but I think I already have my answer."

It's only when I follow his eyes down that I see what he's getting at. Ryder isn't the only one that needs to adjust because of his arousal.

I do too.

Ryder

What the fuck is wrong with me?

I know the way I am and instead of trying to tame it so I don't end up scaring the living shit out of this guy before I've gotten the chance to get to know him, I do the complete fucking opposite.

For as long as I can remember I've been an intense guy. It started off small; me taking all the pent up aggression and anger I had because of everything happening at home and throwing it all into fights against people in the neighborhood and at school. It carried on the same way until high school.

That's when I found a release for all of the intense and overpowering shit going on inside of me. I found an outlet.

Football was the perfect escape. I could take everything that up until that point I'd been bottling inside and unleashing on anyone stupid enough to cross me, and turn it around into something useful. Having a place to put it, a place where it was accepted, should have toned it down whenever I was off the field, but it never did.

It was still there, an engrained part of my personality that no matter how much I ignored it was just waiting to explode at any given moment. The worst of it might have been during my time with Gavin.

I wanna be able to say that the first time I saw him, I knew it was love, but it wasn't anything close to that. It definitely became that pretty quickly after we got together, the intensity of my feelings pushing us in that direction, but before that, it was as far from love as you can get, yet just as intense.

He walked into the hall after coming out of the office on his first day and all I could think was how badly I wanted to push him up against the wall and fuck him with my mouth until I had him screaming.

It was a raw physical reaction, the same way they've always been with me even when I was hiding it. It's never been some soft, tender and slow thing. It's hard and fast, rough and raw and completely fucking impossible to control.

The way it happened with him, it's happening now with Isaac. Instead of thinking with my head the way I should be and want to, I'm thinking with my dick and it's going to ruin everything.

Which makes me a sleazebag.

Even now, when I can sense his embarrassment at me calling attention to how turned on our kiss made him, I can't turn off the need inside me to react. To grab his shirt and yank it over his head until his chest is laid bare for me to completely devour with my tongue, lips and even the slight graze of my teeth.

Chill the fuck out, Kane. This isn't one of your fuck and forgets.

Being able to chill out and get myself out of this headspace becomes even harder to do once I feel the paper brushing against my arm and look down to see the words waiting for me.

I feel like I'm burning. Like every part of me is on fire and you're the only one that can put it out. I need to have your lips on me because when they're not I feel like I can't

breathe and I really need to breathe again. Please say you'll help me breathe, Ryder.

Son of a bitch. I was wrong.

What's happening between me and Isaac, it's not like Gavin and me at all. It's worse, because with Gavin even though we moved fast and were as close as two people can get within a few days of being around one another, I was at least able to resist for a little while.

I can't do that with Isaac.

Resistance is futile. I want him too damn bad and it's making any form of denying it impossible. I'm going to stop fighting against whatever this is between us. Finally stop trying to tame the way I am and give into it completely, no matter how scary it is.

If what he needs to breathe is me, then he's got it. He's got all of me.

"What you want...are you sure? If you're not, it won't change anything, but you need to tell me because once we go there, I don't think I'll be able to stop. I already don't want to stop and we haven't even started."

The time it takes for him to respond is agonizing. I know what I told him and in the moment, I meant it, but if he tells me that what he said isn't what he wants anymore, it's going to kill me and not because of some stupid physical reaction.

The physical might be the thing that drives me, but it's the emotional that's going to be the thing that brings me to my knees.

Isaac isn't the only one who needs to breathe again and I want him to be the one to make me do it.

I'm sure.

Unable to waste another second not giving him what he wants, I slide my body out of the chair until I'm standing over him, my hands pushing down on the arms of the chair so heavily, I can feel their edges marking me the same way the timid guy sitting in it already has.

Leaning my body down until he's resting all the way back and I've got an unobstructed view of his lips and neck, I rest my face directly on top of his and bring our lips together again. Our connection is softer this time, our pace slower, both of us content to just feel each other in the moment and not be guided by the hunger I know is just lying in wait.

This kiss is different than any other we've shared between us. It's different than any kiss I've ever had because this time, it's not just my body that's involved in it.

It's my heart too.

Once the kiss ends and the room stops spinning, the conversation from earlier that started all of this floods my mind and the answer to Isaac's question, it's clear. I know what I want.

Moving in again, this time resting my face against his and bringing my lips to his ear, I sigh deeply before stealing a taste of the guy I can't seem to get enough of, sucking on his ear before pulling back long enough to whisper the only thing left to say.

"When I write the paper and hand it in, I know what I want as a reward."

Pulling back, expecting to find him confused or maybe even a little frantic at not being able to respond, I'm met with his smile as he mouths the one word guaranteed to get him an answer.

What?

"A date. No studying or tests. Just you and me alone. So tutor boy, think you can handle that?"

Chapter Fifteen

Ryder

"Ry, pull over."

"I've got this, Gav. See?"

Lifting my hands off the wheel, the car veers left and I can see Gavin saying something, but the sound of my laughter drowns him out.

He's freaking out for no reason. I've got control of the entire situation. Nothing is going to happen that I don't want.

"Not funny. Pull over please."

"I thought you liked it when I went fast, Gav?"

"When we're screwing around, Ry. Not when you're behind the wheel of a ten ton machine."

Reaching over, I grip the inside of his thigh and despite the desperation in his voice and his need to get me to focus on the road and pull over, he moans. It's always the same with him. He's powerless against me.

"Ry, please." He pleads, his voice quivering and calling my attention completely away from the road.

Inching my hand up his leg, his breath hitches sharply before my name falls ragged from his lips, all concern at the way I'm driving gone.

"You're safe with me, baby, but maybe I should pull over so I can do this properly."

"Please pull over."

The sound of him begging is more than I can handle. My body comes alive and just like every other time, I've got to react. Keeping my one hand on the wheel, I take the hand that's been moving slowly up his thigh and grip it around his neck, yanking him to me until his lips are on mine and he's whimpering his pleasure into my mouth.

The car moves first, but this time my body doesn't slide with it the way I expect. I hear the honking next, like someone laying on a horn and that's when I feel Gavin break away, his lips moving but no sound coming out.

Turning back to the road, I see what he's trying to tell me but that I can't hear. I'm in the oncoming lane and there's a tractor trailer coming at us. Swerving the car a split second before the impact, I try to set the car straight, but it won't budge.

Slamming on the breaks, the car skids and just as I'm about to take a deep breath, thankful I was able to save us from a serious head on collision, my body slams forward forcefully, my head colliding with the windshield.

The world starts to spin and I hear glass shatter. My vision is blurred and my head begins to pound which only confuses me. Before I can turn and ask Gavin what's going on, the spinning turns to dark splotches and everything goes dark.

~*~*~

"*Ryder, wake up.*"

"Come on man! Wake up!"

Pressure, my body being shaken, what I can now feel are hands moving across a chest drenched in sweat. I feel it all but have no idea how it's possible. Finally becoming aware of the voice and what it wants me to do, I slide my eyes open and the minute it happens, I hear the person sigh.

"Finally!"

"Dill?"

Bringing my hand up over my eyes as they adjust, taking in the room complete with his shadow standing off to the side, I close my eyes and attempt to calm my racing heart.

I'm okay. I'm at home. I fell asleep on the sofa and Dillon is trying to wake me up.

I'm not in the car despite the sound of shattering glass playing repeatedly on a loop inside my head. The smell of the blood is gone. None of it is real.

It was just a dream.

"What's going on?"

"I was about to ask you the same thing. I was sleeping and you started screaming. By the time I got out here and realized you weren't being murdered by some psycho, you were banging your head on the sofa."

Son of a bitch.

I've had the nightmares for a while, but they've gotten hazier over time. Laying here now, completely awake, I can still see every scene of that dream like I'm experiencing it for the first time. It was crystal fucking clear and the way my head is pounding is just another reminder.

My head hitting the windshield—no. Hitting the sofa.

"Bad dream. Sorry I woke you."

"That was more than a bad fucking dream, Ry. It was like you were possessed."

That's because I was.

I don't just dream. Even when I was a kid and I would have a nightmare, it was hell trying to get me to go back to sleep. They were always so vivid and real that it would keep me up for hours, sometimes even days afterward. They completely owned me. I was possessed by them.

I didn't need Fred Kruger to make my nightmares come to life. I did it easily all on my own.

"It's nothing. I'm used to it. Sorry you got dragged in."

"You wanna talk about it?"

Is he serious? I think he's been spending too much time with his girlfriend watching chick flicks or something. I don't do feelings and especially not with him.

"Have you been binge watching Lifetime again?"

"Ha-ha man, real funny, but your attempt at deflecting sucks. Whatever that was, it wasn't just a nightmare and we both know it. You need to talk about that shit."

"No actually, *I* don't. I'd rather drop this entire conversation in favor of getting up and ingesting insane amounts of caffeine."

He wants to argue, I can see the conflict in his eyes, but he remains silent and nods, dragging himself into the kitchen and out of my view while I throw my legs over the side of the sofa and stand, preparing to follow.

I don't want to let on to Dillon, but last night is a complete fucking blur.

When I got home from classes, I remember throwing myself down on my bed, my thoughts as per their usual going straight to my tutor and everything that's happening between us. It's everything that came after I can't remember.

How did I end up on the sofa? Did I sleepwalk or did something else go down that for whatever reason the nightmare seems to be blocking out?

Picking my jeans up off the floor, I slide my legs in and pull them all the way up, following it up by slipping myself back into my shirt from last night before stumbling my way into the kitchen.

The way my body aches when I move, it's like I spent the entire night out drinking. Drowning the way I have in the past, but I know for a fact that I didn't do any of it. I haven't had a drink since I got back.

After using alcohol and meaningless sex for months to swallow down who I am, going without it is strange. I didn't really think I was an addict, but the struggle inside me going without, the way the nightmares are back and completely dominating my subconscious, it's obvious that I am.

I'm an addict in the withdrawal stage and I need answers for the time that's missing. Answers I'm hoping I can get from Dillon while we stand around waiting for our morning coffee fix.

"What time did you get in last night?"

"Eleven. Why?"

"Just wondering."

"I dropped Caddy at home, talked to her mom for a bit and came back here. I played a little GTA on the PlayStation and went to bed."

He's giving me answers without even realizing it. When he got home, I wasn't on the sofa, which means that happened sometime during the night. Sleepwalking is definitely something I've gotta look into. I've got no other reason for how I ended up where I did.

"You didn't see me at all?"

"No, and as much as I love repeating myself, please don't make me ask again."

"I can't remember how I ended up in the living room."

"That happen a lot?"

"Not when I'm sober."

"When's the last time you drank?"

"Before I left."

"You mean before you left yesterday or before you took off?"

"Before I took off."

"Hmm." He muses. "Weird."

"No kidding."

"So you and Isaac. You get your shit worked out?"

"We did, no thanks to you."

Laughing before turning back to the coffee maker, he doesn't even try to hide the smirk on his face.

"You got something you wanna say, Dill?"

"Since you asked so nicely. I do actually."

Of course he does. I'm starting to learn the more time I spend with him that he has an opinion about everything. Sometimes, it's a miracle you can get a word in edgewise.

"Well don't keep me in suspense."

"When I got here and everything went down, you and me bonded. You did things for me that at the time I fucking hated you for, but that needed to be done because I was acting like a complete tool. I saw a chance to return the favor so I did it."

"Don't you mean you meddled in shit that's none of your business?"

"Says the guy that tattled on me to my girlfriend?"

Shit. He's got a point. I can't exactly go off on him for getting involved when I did the exact same thing with him a few months ago. I pushed the boundaries of a pretty new friendship when I could have easily left well enough alone. It makes sense that he pays me back the same way.

"You really think telling Isaac I'm gay is returning the favor?"

"Pretty much. You weren't gonna do it. Seems like I did the right thing if you being non-existent here for the past three days means anything."

"Aww, Dill. I didn't know you cared so much."

I pucker my lips and lean in, fully prepared to give him a kiss on the cheek and just the way I expect, he catches on and shoves me away laughing.

"You're an asshole, you know that?"

"Takes one to know one."

Grabbing the pot and pouring coffee into both mugs, his laughter still hanging in the air, he pushes mine toward me before leveling me with a look that's no longer amusing.

"You not being around, is it because of Isaac or are you trolling again?"

"Isaac." The ease at which his names comes out astounds me. It also feels pretty damn good to be able to say that it's something other than my urge to forget that's going on.

"Figured as much."

"So why even bother asking?"

"What I walked in on this morning." He admits and the memory of the way I woke up comes flooding back. Gavin. The accident. My stupidity. Hurting everyone I touch. Shit. I need to turn this conversation around before I end up spilling my guts.

"I wanna be pissed at you for going to him, but I can't because it was the right move."

"You like him."

Like doesn't seem like the right word, but since I know what love feels like and I'm definitely not there, it's going to have to do.

"You make it sound like we're little kids. Yes, Dill, I like him. He's pretty hard not to like."

"Can I give you some advice?"

"I know that you hang around with a lot of girls and you're all in touch with your feelings and shit, but some of us can't handle the touchy feely crap man."

Shoving me in the shoulder, he laughs again.

"Whatever it is that caused that shit this morning, you need to get straight with it. Deal or whatever."

"I'll get right on that, Dad."

"I'm not saying this to be a dick, Ry. I'm saying it because when I said you liked the guy, your entire face changed. It's obvious you care about him, so get your shit straight. If you don't, you're gonna end up fucking up something that could be pretty damn epic."

"Is this you speaking from experience?"

"Damn right. I almost lost Caddy twice because I couldn't pull my head out of my ass and let shit from my past go. I joke around a lot, but I give a shit about you and I really don't want to see what happened to me, happen to you."

"You think Isaac is my Caddy."

"Are you gonna tell me he's not?"

The words are there, but they don't come and after a few minutes of waiting me out, he cracks another grin before grabbing his mug and making his way around me, slapping me on the back.

"Exactly. He's a good guy, same as you. You deserve that, but you can't get it and write a new beginning if you're still stuck at the end."

Chapter Sixteen

Isaac

"Isaac, it pains me to have to ask you this, but did Ryder write this paper or are you covering for him?"

If the question wasn't expected, I would be offended. After waking up and having my dad hand over the envelope with Ryder's finished paper in it this morning, I'd actually wondered the same thing.

For all of his claims that he wasn't a writer and that anything he did produce would end up flunking him out of the course completely, the quality work on the paper made me believe that he had gone to someone else for help in writing it.

It's not unheard of around here, especially with the athletes, to outsource their classwork. I've even heard of some tutors being paid to write the papers for them instead of just guiding them along the way I've been doing. When I saw his paper, that's the first place my mind went, but it didn't take long for the overwhelming feeling of guilt to kick in once it did.

"When I write the paper and hand it in, I know what I want as a reward."

Ryder wrote every word on the paper. This is his way of making good on the reward system we joked about yesterday. This is what Ryder is like when he's motivated.

He wrote the paper. I gave him the list of topics the way you and I discussed and this is what he chose. I did not help him in any way.

"I didn't believe that you did, but the quality of what he's written here, it's not what he's done in the past."

Of course not. He didn't want to go on a date in the past.

When he applies himself, Ryder is exceptionally bright.

"Spoken like a true future college professor."

I did learn from the best. :)

Returning the smile with one of his own, he turns his attention back to the paper, his eyes running over the lines at a painstakingly slow pace that just serves to make me even more nervous than I was when I got here.

I've got no reason to be this nervous considering I'm not the one that wrote it, but I am. I read what he wrote and it's obvious that he put a lot of thought into it, along with references in all the right places and proof that he actually did the research on the subject he wrote about. My nervousness isn't about what's written. It's about what it's going to mean when the professor is done grading it.

There's no way he's not going to get a passing grade, which means I'm going to have to make good on the reward. I'm going to have to step completely out of my comfort zone, forget about the material, tests and research and do something I've never done.

Go on a date.

Oh god, I'm going to be sick.

"This paper does not let him off the hook for his poor attendance and attitude, but if he continues to present work of this caliber, I have no doubt that he will complete the course with the passing grade he needs."

Held out in front of him is Ryder's paper and when I catch sight of the mark at the top, it does my heart good. I knew when we started working together that he was smart. That all he needed was to apply himself and the proof is sitting in front of me.

"I would still like you to work with him as you both see fit outside of class."

Of course. I'll help as much as I can.

Nothing would make me happier than working with Ryder. I'm just not sure my professor wants to know that writing papers and researching topics isn't the kind of working I mean.

"Thank you for bringing this to me, Isaac. I've kept you long enough. I'll see you both bright and early tomorrow."

See you tomorrow.

Smiling one final time before turning and making my way up the stairs as quickly as possible, amazed that the paper in my hands hasn't completely shredded with the death grip I've got on it, I push my way through the doors, looking down at my watch and trying to calculate how late I'm gonna be with how long I was in the room.

Completely unaware of anything going on around me, moving purely out of memory of the building and the routine of the steps I'm taking, I turn to head for the building exit and instead of catching air the way I expect with how fast I'm moving, I hit a brick wall instead.

A brick wall that once I get my bearings and look up, I see is a person. One whose eyes and smile I've been unable to get out of my head since they walked away from me yesterday afternoon.

My heart races as he smiles, his grip on my arm releasing but not pulling away completely.

"Hey."

Lifting my free hand, I twist it in a small wave before bringing it back down, my brain screaming at me to make contact with his body the way he has with mine.

"Aren't you supposed to be in class right now?"

Nodding and motioning with my head toward the glass door he's blocking me from getting out of, he nods in understanding, but makes no motion to get out of the way.

"Did you get my paper? Is that why you're here?"

When I nod again, he smiles even brighter and I will the rapid drumming in my chest to cease before it reaches my head and makes me completely unable to form a thought. His smile is heart stopping.

"So what's the verdict, tutor boy? Are we going on a date?"

Breathing is difficult with him leaning in like this and the strength I need in order to make my head move up and down in a nod is non-existent. All it would take is one slight movement of my body for us to completely connect. My lips pressing to his and the rest of the world ceasing to exist.

"Cat got your tongue, Isaac?" he teases as he runs his lips over my jawline and I gulp down the nervous knot lodged in my throat and the need inside me to beg him not to stop.

Whoa. I need to back up and get some space between us. This isn't like me. I don't act like this.

Meeting his eyes, wondering if the look I see in them mirrors what I'm sure is a dead giveaway in mine, they start to close and before I can make sense of why he's doing it, they're open again and the intensity I see gives me all the answer I need.

"Answer me, Isaac. Do I get you alone or not? It's *killing me* not knowing."

Raising my head up and pausing momentarily, I start to bring it down giving him his answer. In seconds I feel the tight grip of his hands on my waist and I'm being swung around until my back is pressed up hard against the wall and his lips are on mine.

Ryder is reading my mind. Giving me what I don't even realize I'm craving so badly until it's happening and its complete ecstasy.

After a few minutes of us kissing, he releases me and steps back. It's only when I finally allow myself to breathe that the reality of what just happened hits. He grabbed me in the middle of a hallway where anyone could have seen us and did what he always does when we kiss. Ryder made love to me with his mouth, and judging from the cocky smile playing on his lips, getting caught is the least of his concerns.

A point that's driven home when he holds his hand out to me, waiting patiently for me to take it. Sliding my hand into his, he raises it to his lips the moment we connect and kisses it softly.

It's a move so unlike him that I have no idea how to react.

"Come on, tutor boy. The sooner we get these classes over with, the sooner I can cash in on my reward for writing such an amazingly boring paper. And I fully intend on cashing in. Tonight, you're all mine."

Ryder

The more things change, the more they stay the same.

Of course this is what I'm thinking about. Two hours away from my first date in two years and I'm sitting in a bar remembering French proverbs.

I'm seriously fucked.

Spending all this time with Isaac and having my head stuck in a book has obviously screwed with my brain in more ways than one.

I should be back at the apartment, my head stuck under a shower nozzle, making myself presentable, so that I can head over to his house and pick him up, but that's too sensible. Too right.

So totally not me.

The proverb is true though. I can change all I want, come out and live my life the way I should be, but I'm still the same fucker underneath. I have to sit here and drink because when I collect my reward from Isaac, I'm going to do it completely numb.

Change for me is an illusion. It won't ever make it all the way through. I'm not sure I want it to.

Signaling to the bartender, more than ready for another shot of liquid courage, a hand brushes the back my neck, causing my body to tense. The touch is not one I enjoy, which means it's got to be female.

Fuck.

I knew coming here was going to be a mistake. It was only a matter of time before my nightly fuck and forgets came back to haunt me.

"I was wondering if I would ever see you again."

Her breath on the back of my neck, her inability to lay the fuck off and come around to face me is having the opposite effect of what she's obviously after. It's not turning me on, it's turning my stomach.

"That makes one of us."

Ignoring me completely, choosing instead to run her horribly manicured nails across my shoulder blade, she practically purrs into my ear before finally making her way around and sliding onto the stool beside me.

"I haven't been able to get it out of my head."

Jesus Christ. If I'm gonna deal with this shit, I need to do a hell of a lot more drinking. I'm definitely not drunk enough for this conversation.

Tipping the shot glass back, I pour it down my throat, the burn of the whiskey so harsh it blocks out the girl and her need to be fucked by me entirely. Placing the glass back down on the bar and turning my body inward, I run circles over the rim of the glass with my fingers until I feel her hand brush my knee.

It doesn't take long before the slight touch is moving up my leg, the alcohol in my system numbing me just enough to be unable to react the way I want to.

I don't hit women. I use them as a reason to forget, disrespecting them even, but I've never physically laid my hands on one in a way that was violent.

With the way her hand is moving up my leg though, any second about to run her fingers over my dick, I'm giving serious thought to changing it. If she doesn't knock it off, I'm gonna have no problem making her.

"God, I want you so bad right now."

"If you're looking for God, I think you're in the wrong place, sweetheart." I quip before lifting her hand off my leg and resting it back on her own before putting both hands back up on the bar again.

This girl needs to get a fucking clue and screw off before my lowered inhibitions make me do something I'm gonna end up regretting.

"Tell me you haven't thought about that night."

"Can't say I've thought about you at all."

"Maybe you just need a reminder."

I don't know if it's the alcohol or what, but I don't catch her next move until it's already too late and her fingers are brushing against the side of my face. There's something so wrong about the way her hand feels there that I've got no control over what happens next.

Grabbing her wrist, I finally turn and look at her. It doesn't take long once my eyes land on her that I realize who she is.

I go to school with her. She's in a few of my classes and the night I fucked her, she was with a group of her friends. On pitcher refill duty, we'd started talking at the bar and it wasn't long before I was bringing her and two of her friends back to the apartment and burying myself inside of them repeatedly until my reason for being there had been blocked out completely.

Not my finest moment. Also not an experience I'm itching to repeat considering where I want to be in less than two hours. Whatever she's looking for, she might find it here, but she definitely won't be finding it with me.

"What is it about me saying you're basically an afterthought that's not getting through? Get lost."

"You weren't saying get lost when you had your dick buried inside me."

"The way I remember it, I wasn't saying much at all."

"You're a prick."

"Yeah, I am and a pretty good one with the way you can't seem to keep your hands off it."

I need to get the fuck out of here. I don't even know what possessed me to come in the first place. Habit, needing to numb myself with a drink, I could have done that shit anywhere.

Gretchen's Place is for meaningless hookups I don't have to think about in the morning because they did their job during the night. It's a symbol of what I don't want or need anymore.

Not when what I do want is waiting on the other side of town for me to pick him up so we can go on our first official date. Someone that because of how screwed in the head I am, I lost sight of because I have no idea how to fucking do any of this. It's been too long.

Pulling out my wallet, ignoring the girl and everyone else around me, I slide the money out and slam it down on the bar before sliding of the stool and heading for the door.

The proverb from earlier, it doesn't have to be true. Things don't have to be the same. Sometimes when things change, you can change with them.

It's about damn time I did that.

Chapter Seventeen

Isaac

Tonight is a big deal for me.

This being my first date isn't what makes this night such a big deal. It's what going out means. We're going to be out in public together, where anyone and everyone can see. A first for me.

Wexfield is a lot like any other city on the planet. We've got our share of judgmental people who like to spew their hate about things they don't understand or don't even wanna try and accept, but because it's a smaller town and there are a lot less people, the hate is less in your face.

Going on a first date, being part of a couple, especially one made up of two guys, it's scary. Nerve racking. It scares the hell out of me because with as much attention as I get for my inability to speak, the last thing I want is to be flooded with more because of who I choose to date.

I'm not ashamed of who I am and who I'm attracted to, but there's only so much a person can take before they have to draw the line and admit that it's too much to handle.

It doesn't help that I also get the feeling I'm going to do something awkward, write something even worse and ruin the whole night.

Maybe I can text him and tell him not to come. There's still a few minutes before he shows up. If I explain that I've come down with some seriously horrible illness, maybe I can keep this from happening for a little while longer.

Fifty or sixty years ought to cover it.

Suck it up, buttercup. You're going to do this. You are not going to bail on him.

If I don't get a handle on this soon, it's going to be like the night he drove back from Toronto all over again. I'm going to sweat through every piece of clothing I own until it's either go out naked or not go out at all.

Naked. Ryder seeing it. Being naked with Ryder.

Breathe Isaac.

Right as I'm about to listen to my inner voice and do exactly what it asked, the doorbell rings and any hope I had of not being a complete freak of nature is thrown out the window.

Definitely can't text and cancel now.

"Isaac, you gonna get the door?" My mom calls out at the exact second the doorbell goes off a second time.

Okay, this is it. All you need to do is put one foot directly in front of the other until you reach the door and everything will be fine.

Yeah, fat chance of that happening anytime soon. I haven't even gotten there yet and I can already feel the constriction in my chest, making breathing, thinking, moving or anything that requires even the slightest bit of brain power impossible.

When the doorbell goes off for a third time, I hear my mom's feet moving quickly on the stairs and before I even have a chance to blink, she's at the door and even from here I can see she's giving me the worlds more sympathetic look.

I told her that Ryder wanted to go out with me and after using about two pieces of paper in order to reassure her I would be safe and that if things didn't feel right I would come home, she'd relented. So right now, the sympathetic look she's giving me, it's because she understands what the entire thing means and she's gonna do her part to get me through it.

I can't believe I'm acting like this. I'm nineteen for crying out loud. I haven't had a full blown meltdown for months and I shouldn't be having one now. It's just Ryder. I'm safe with him, so reacting this way is nuts. You'd think with the deep seeded fear inside me that it was Randy waiting on the other side of the door.

"Ryder. It's nice to see you again. Please come in. Isaac's waiting in the family room."

Responding back in some way that I can't make out because I'm just too far away, I avert my eyes once I see their bodies start to move so they don't catch on and think I've been sitting here listening in the entire time.

"Hey."

The hammering of my heart when he was on the other side of the door is worse now. One word and with the quickened pace, I'm expecting that any second I'm going to pass out.

I really need to get control of this.

"I hope it's okay, but I got you a couple of things."

Once I think I've got my heart under control, I look up and as he takes a seat beside me, see what he means by a couple of things. Not only does he have another single rose in his hand, but he's also got what looks like a diary and two silver pens.

Taking them from his outstretched hands, captivated as I always am with the smile that's now tugging at his lips, our eyes finally meet and that's when I see that something's not right.

Normally when I look in Ryder's eyes, they're crystal clear. It's one of the things I find so fascinating about them. I like that they remind me of glass. Even when they're intense and dark, I can always count on being able to see myself in them because of their clarity.

They're not clear at all right now. There's a film over them, and leaning closer in an effort to test my suspicion, my heart sinks into my stomach. His eyes aren't clear because he's drunk.

Not only is he standing here smiling at me after obviously spending time drinking, but he's also here with gifts that aren't cheap little things you can get in the dollar store. They're seriously expensive and way too much.

Using the key and twisting the lock on the diary open, I click the pen and start writing. If we're going on a date tonight, I'm getting answers first. All signs of fear and nervousness are gone now and all that's left is disappointment.

Tonight was supposed to be special.

Hi.

"Hey."

The softness in his tone, it's threatening to break my resolve. He speaks and all I want to do is lean over on the sofa and melt into him.

Why did you buy me these things?

"I wanted to?"

Don't answer questions with a question. It makes you seem less sincere or unsure of your answer.

"Is that your way of saying that I'm lying?"

If the shoe fits.

He sucks in a breath and dips his head down for a split second before bringing it back up and staring intently at me. I'm used to this with him. He's trying to get a read on me because the way I'm responding right now is confusing.

"Wow. Okay. You want a final answer like we're on some fucking game show, fine. I bought them for you because the second I saw them, I thought they were perfect."

Was this before or after you drank your body weight in alcohol?

"So that's what this is about." He sighs. "I had time to kill after my last class, was feeling like crap and didn't want to drown you in it, so I went and had a couple drinks."

Did you drive here?

"No. I left my car there. I don't drink and drive."

His eyes look pained and it makes my heart hurt. It's obvious from the haunted look he's wearing that whatever I said is bringing something up that he wants to keep buried. As disappointed as I am that he drank before coming here, something tells me that I need to take a step back and not push this anymore than I have.

Ryder's already run off twice. I don't want him to do it again.

Do you still want to go out with me?

"More than anything, but it doesn't really matter what I want."

That's not true. What you want matters.

His eyes soften, all traces of his earlier anguish gone and I'm glad. It might not be the ideal situation for a first date, but it's what I've got. Ryder never claimed to be perfect and if he was, I'm not sure I'd feel the same way I do about him.

Neither one of us is what the rest of the world would call ideal, but maybe if we're both willing, we can be ideal for each other.

"Did I screw this up?"

No, but the night's still young. ;)

Please laugh. I need to hear you laugh.

As he slides his body toward me he laughs. Coming to a stop the minute his leg brushes lightly against mine, his arm comes up and around until it's resting on my shoulder. He wastes no time pulling me into his chest, his body relaxing the minute I curve into him.

You spent too much on these things. They're amazing, but it's not something you have to do.

"I know I don't have to. I wanted to make tonight perfect for you. If it's too much, I can take them back."

The way his voice changes, the determination there to do right by me, it's doing what his eyes and voice have been doing to me for over a week now. Melting me, warming me and making me do the one thing I never thought in a million years would be possible because of the way I am.

Ryder is making me fall for him.

Chapter Eighteen

Ryder

One of the worst things about drinking is the smell. I could have had one beer earlier and Isaac still would have smelled it on me.

If I wasn't such a screw-up, I would have called him and made plans to meet up with him early, but no. I had to resort to the way I've always been and do the most selfish thing imaginable.

It's a fucking miracle he hasn't kicked me out of the house by now. I definitely deserve to be, but just like Dillon told me, Isaac is a good guy. Telling me the night isn't ruined and even making a joke of it, he's proving that he's not like everyone else and when push comes to shove, I don't ever want him to be.

Which brings us to the gifts.

After leaving the bar, the feel of the girl's hands on my body still twisting me up inside, I knew I had to do something. Wanted to do something. Getting him a gift, it wasn't about taking the attention off the way I smelled. It was about making him feel special.

The diary was the first thing I saw when I walked into the shop boasting handmade one of a kind items. I didn't even hesitate because it was just that perfect. The two silver pens were definitely a risk, but considering they had his name carved into them, it was a risk I had to take.

I spent a lot of money, but considering that ever since I came here I haven't spent a dime of what's been sitting in my account, I didn't care. If my parents are gonna be stupid enough to continue filling my account with it, I might as well use it on something great instead of pissing it away in every watering hole in town.

Besides, the look on their face when they realize what the money was for will be worth it. Screw them and their need to make me straight. The way it's felt since I showed up here a few minutes ago, I'm pretty damn sure I never want to cave in and be what they want me to be again.

"Do you want me to take it back?"

No one's ever given me a gift before. Well, besides my parents. I think it's too much, but I don't want you to return them.

That's another thing I've got to make right. The way he's been treated is fucking disgusting and it needs to stop.

His inability to talk isn't the problem. It's everyone's inability to hear and I've been one of the worst offenders because I judged him before he even said a word to me.

I need to change that and there's no better time to start then tonight.

"Do you want to know why I bought the diary?"

Yes, but can you tell me why you bought the rose first?

"Didn't we already talk about what the flower means?"

The yellow flower, yes. This one is red.

"The last flower meant friendship and at the time, that's exactly what I wanted with you, even if my body was at odds with it. I got you the red one because it's not just friendship I want with you now."

What do you want? What does the red mean?

"What it means and what I want are the same thing. I want something more with you. I want to take the next step."

Our date.

"In a way, yeah, but it's also the way we are right now too. The way you're resting into me, the way we're talking to each other. It's the little things."

I'm only good at doing things one way. I don't talk about my feelings, I fucking hate talking about myself at all, but the one thing I can do is react. I can experience things emotionally and manifest them in physical ways and get my point across. Isaac, he's not like that, even if I can get him to react to me the same way because of how intense I am.

The next step here, it's not about my physical reaction. It's about tuning myself in to his more emotional one. He's been my tutor for subjects that don't really matter to me. Maybe if I spend enough time with him, he can be my tutor for the things that do.

Why did you buy the diary, Ryder? Do I remind you of a girl?

Feeling the urge to laugh bubbling to the surface, but not wanting to do it, I swallow it down in favor of ignoring his question altogether and telling him the truth.

Burying it down might lose me the bet, but it's not going to lose me the guy.

"I bought the diary because of the way it looked," I motion with my hand toward the blue stitching around the side, running my fingers over the softness before focusing in again on the rest of my answer. "But the real reason is because I wanted you to have one place, where when things are too much, you can speak freely and not have to worry about what anyone else is going to think."

I feel his body lift and his eyes on me, but I make no move to meet them, at least not yet. There's still one more part of this that I need to say before I can risk turning and seeing whatever is there waiting for me.

"I did it for a selfish reason too."

How so?

"I'm pretty fucking intense and I get the feeling that you're spending a lot of our time together trying to catch up to that, match me somehow. It's stupid, but our first date, I don't want it to be our last date, so this book, it's what you can use when the way I am is too much."

I don't do this shit with people. I'm the king of bottling, not pouring, and right now, with him so close, I'm pouring out a lot. Admitting things to him that I haven't admitted to myself and I'm scared about how it's going to be taken.

It's not stupid, Ryder. This date started out as a joke, but it's a lot more than that now. I don't want this to be our only date. I want whatever the next step is, but I'm scared.

"Scared of what?"

Doing or saying something to screw it up. You leaving again and this time not being able to put together the right combination of words to get you back. Being hurt. Not being enough. You name it, I'm probably scared of it.

"You're not the only one scared."

The way he looks when I finally meet his eyes, it's obvious he's surprised by what I admitted, but I can't let him sit there and think he's the only one. Everything about this is scary to me and if the way I arrived here is any indication, I'll be the one to screw it up, not him.

I'm definitely scared, maybe even more then him, but I can't run from it. The next step for us, I need to see it through because I want what he's offering me so fucking badly.

I want Isaac to teach me how to feel again. How to breathe and how to just be. I want to feel alive because I've spent too long already knowing what it truly means to be dead inside. It's time for the Ryder Kane that was packed up and put away two years ago to make his return, but not for everyone else.

Only for him.

Isaac

After the way he spent his time before picking me up, the last place I expected him to take me was another bar.

To its credit, it's a lot more than a bar. There are at least a dozen flat screen televisions throughout the place, each one showing a different sport and further in the back, there are lines of pool tables. It's also the last place someone like me should be.

It's loud, which on its own isn't enough to set me completely off, but it's smoky. People are walking around or seated, cigarettes hanging from their mouths without a care in the world even though I know for a fact they're breaking the law.

I hate the way my mind works. Instead of focusing my attention on Ryder, I'm caught up in everything going on around me and how I don't fit in. As much as I want to go with the flow because the smile on Ryder's face shows how much he enjoys being here, I can't do it.

What I said before we left my house is true. I'm not going to be enough and I am going to be the one to screw this up. Our first date will end up being our last because I'm nothing like him and I don't think I ever will be.

A sports bar is not my idea of a good time.

Looking up as he nudges my arm, I catch his smile first and then lowering my eyes, I see the phone outstretched in front of him.

"Instead of a pen and paper, I thought we could try this."

Taking the phone and typing across the lined yellow page on the screen, he moves around me, slipping his arms over mine, reading my words over my shoulder innocently, but making it extremely hard to type from the breath now filtering across the back of my neck.

If his goal is to completely train my focus on him, he's accomplishing it. The smokiness is dulled, the noise from the televisions and the people surrounding us blocked out until all that's left is the hum I experience whenever he's connected to me this way.

Isn't it the same thing?

"Yeah, but with what I have in mind, we can have the phone closer to us and both be able to see it without passing it back and forth."

What exactly do you have in mind?

"Pool."

I should have known.

I've never played pool.

"Good. I was hoping you would say that. It means I'm going to enjoy this even more."

What do you mean?

Running his fingers up my arm, starting at my hand until he's stroking just past my elbow, he leans his head against my ear and with his breath exhaling, he chuckles lightly.

"Tonight I get to be the tutor."

Sliding my fingers across the screen and typing faster then I think I ever have, I finish and hold it up for him to see.

You're going to be my teacher?

His eyes are teasingly seductive, like there's more than one answer he wants to give to my question. It's only heightened with the delicious looking grin that crosses his face.

"In every way imaginable, tutor boy, but for tonight we're going to take it slow and stick to pool."

How is it possible that he makes even the nicest thing sound so incredibly enticing? Why does my body tremble with every breath he makes and the proximity of his body to mine make the heat level rise?

Taking his phone back and slipping it into his pocket, he takes me by the hand and guides me all the way to the back to the lone pool table in the corner. The space surrounding us completely empty, giving us the privacy that I crave.

With the way I am reacting to even the smallest touch from him, the last thing I want is an audience.

"Why don't you grab a stick off the wall while I rack the balls?"

That seems easy enough. I can do that. Turning toward the wall where a straight line of five sticks are held and waiting, what seems easy turns extremely hard. There are two sticks that are smaller than the other three and also different in color. Are they colorful for a reason? Do I need to get the smaller one or will it be easier with the one that seems as long as I am?

Crap. I have no idea what I'm doing. It's not gonna be long now before I completely lose it.

Twisting my body, willing myself to move back over to where I left Ryder standing, I feel his arms come around me, stroking my back, reacting to my obvious discomfort.

"It's okay, Isaac. I know it's confusing. I'll do it."

Grabbing one off the wall and doing some strange rubbing action with his hand over the tip, he squeezes my arm before he moves his body around me. Leaning over the table, he sets his body up and with my eyes moving between the way his body is leaning and the movement of the stick on the table, I watch as he slams a white ball into the eight colorful ones.

"Come here." he demands, motioning with his hands while keeping his smile firmly in place. When I finally force my legs to move and end up beside him, he moves his body in closer. "Did you see the way I was holding the cue? Do you think you can do that?"

Nodding, sure that I can recreate the same stance he had before he bent over the table and made his first shot, he grins and hands me the stick. Once it's secure in my hands I repeat his movements step by step and that's when the atmosphere of the room changes.

He's behind me now instead of beside me and his body is curving in the same way as mine, but instead of leaning over the table, he's leaning into me. I can feel his legs against mine, sending tiny shock waves of pleasurable heat through me. Moving in even more, his breath again hot against me as I hear him exhale, my body takes on a mind of its own and leans even more over the table, my backside now pushing directly into his crotch.

Sucking in sharply, Ryder pushes his body forward, the heat now pooling between my legs mirroring itself in the hardness coming at me from his.

"I think—you've got it." Removing his hands, he backs away, creating a distance I should be thankful for, but that I hate. "Take your shot."

Focus my attention and do what he says. It sounds easy enough, but I stand frozen, not sure in the moment if I'm even still breathing. I want to do it, but I want his body back on mine more.

What is going on with me? Why am I turning something so innocent into something tawdry and wrong?

Seeing the phone on the edge of the table, I grab it and running my fingers across the screen, twist my body just enough to hand it over to him.

I can't take the shot. I can't focus. Why did you move away?

"Isaac," he barks out, his voice hoarse. "If I stay that close, pool won't be what I'm teaching you tonight."

I like having you that close.

My cheeks flush and his body moves in on mine again, this time his hands embracing me, but not in the way he has since we got here. This time they've got purpose and when he uses his strength to turn me around until my backside is leaning hard into the table, the fiery look in his eyes explains everything.

Exhaling softly, he moans against my lips as his entire body presses against me, his grip around my arms loosening until they're resting around my back, keeping me steady as he finally crashes his lips down on mine hungrily.

The pool stick. I'm hyper aware of it resting between our tangled legs, pressing against the inside of my thigh and making the heat filled ache that was present before, even stronger and impossible to manage.

With one hand on my back, keeping my body secure, his other hand slips down and it isn't long before I feel it gripping my thigh, extending the level of pleasure until it's exploding through every pore of my skin.

Pushing his tongue against my lips after nipping them with his teeth, begging for entrance with the whiney growl that escapes, I give him what he wants until the only thing I'm aware of around us is the feel of our tongues pushing and tasting.

Hands no longer gripping onto the stick, one now resting on his back and the other in his hair tugging, I apprehensively grab his tongue and start sucking, the sound of his pleasure so loud it causes both of our bodies to vibrate from the force.

This is crazy. We need to slow down, take a breather and get back to the real reason Ryder brought me here, but I can't be the one to do it. Not when every nerve ending in my body is screaming to take this even further.

I've got the wooden table pressing into my backside, the pool cue leaning heavily into my leg and all I want is more. More pressure, more heat, more Ryder.

"Fuck." He barks out when I finally release the hold on his tongue and his lips completely break away from mine. Both of our breathing is labored, weighed down by the intoxicating and mind numbing desire of the moment.

His salty taste lingering on my tongue, across my lips and his unique scent erasing all others until it's the only thing I'm able to ingest through my nose.

"Slow is not an option with you."

Grabbing the phone, I type out a response and the minute he sees it, his eyes lighten and his hand comes up and rubs across the bridge of his nose, resting over his cheeks and the flush that's evident in them.

Cold showers are though, right?

He presses his lips back on mine, gentler this time, but not before I experience the way his grin against them feels. It's no longer awkward, reacting this way when Ryder and I get close, but it's still going to take some getting used to. I've never responded to anyone this way before, so I'm not sure if how overwhelmed I feel at times is natural.

"Yes. With the way I feel right now, I should probably make sure you don't expect me for our sessions next week. It's going to take about that long for me to cool off."

What I needed to know, it's there in his answer. He's as caught up in me as I am in him, which makes this the most natural thing in the world.

The only question lingering now is, how soon is my next pool lesson?

Ryder

Get the guy to bend over the table so I could reach around and help situate his body right and not expect my dick to respond to the way he feels pressed into me?

That's a first.

All thoughts of keeping this night pure and strictly on teaching him how to play pool flew out the fucking window the minute his body connected to mine. Heat came first, quickly followed by need and after that everything came together and exploded until I was powerless to fight against it.

His willingness, the need of his own to have me close, it broke me. I stopped caring about being pure and innocent and doing right by this guy. I just wanted to bend him over the table and do him period.

The way it feels whenever my lips are on his, his tongue doing these swirl like motions, it's like I'm drunk. It's so overpowering and all-consuming that I lose track of anything else my body might be doing.

My hands were on his thigh, squeezing, stroking, rubbing in motion under the pool cue and I have no fucking idea how they got there. All I could focus on was the high of our mouths together and the raw need it spread to every part of my body.

I don't kiss. It's intimate and needy and with the way I've spent the last two years, intimacy was never part of the agenda. I needed to fuck them, not desire them, or the way it is with Isaac; crave them. Not kissing makes it extremely impersonal, but at the same time completely silent.

The entire time my body is connected to his, the brush of his leg against mine shooting fireworks off in my brain, my dick throbbing and screaming at me to be released from the confines of my jeans, all I'm doing is making sounds.

I'm growling, moaning and even at one point, I could have sworn I screamed. All experiences I haven't had in two years. Some of them never. I'm doing things for the first time, which means that Isaac isn't the only virgin here. I am too.

When I finally come up for air, all I'm thinking is that I need to put a lid on this because I'm pushing this guy too far, but with the look of want in his eyes, all thought of slowing down obliterates into oblivion.

I'm so fucking turned on by him and crave him so fucking badly that going slow is impossible, just like I told him.

I want to separate him from his clothes, leaning him back so far on the table that his naked body is spread open and ready for me. I want to be on top of him, yet on my knees in front of him at the same time, touching and tasting until he crumbles under my mouth and hands, my name a soundless whisper that I somehow hear loud and clear.

This is so wrong.

One minute, I'm buying the guy gifts so I can break down walls I'm sure he's built over the years, and with the flip of a switch, I'm aching to bury myself inside of him until the need, passion and desire are dulled and we're both naked, covered in sweat and sated.

I don't think I even wanted Gavin this bad and I know the way I was with him. How often we found ourselves in situations just like this and how often the need to come up for air was non-existent.

It's not like that with Isaac. It's more and for the first time in two years, I want more.

God, do I want more.

We've been separated a few minutes, both of us needing to unwind from the spell, though with me it's more about simmering the heat threatening to burn me alive. I'm still acutely aware of how close he is, how easy it would be to start again and not stop until we get what we need.

The need for him is insatiable. I take a bit and then I want a bit more. Taking a bit more turns into me wanting to taste the whole fucking buffet.

Isaac is driving me insane and with the way he's biting his lip right now, I don't think I'm ever going to recover.

I need to turn this around, get my thoughts out of the fucking gutter and teach the guy how to shoot pool so we can do this again in the future. I haven't had a game since Gavin and I used to go around hustling people and I've missed it.

I'm not gonna use Isaac to recreate that time in my life, but there's no denying the enjoyment I get from playing with someone. If what I told him earlier is supposed to happen and this leads into something more serious, I want to share things I enjoy so that he can enjoy them too.

Whoa. If I need to slow down on the physical shit, I definitely need to do it with this too. Thinking past this one date, seeing us doing this again in the future, it's premature. I can't even picture my own future, there's no way I'm gonna see one with us together.

"Do you think if I just sit for a minute, you can take the shot on your own?"

I motion to the chairs behind me and he nods, all traces of nervousness gone and security back in its place now that I've spoken again. The way he bases his movements around the things I say, it feels good.

It's been a long fucking time since I could be around someone and have them react this way. Premature or not, I want him to always be that way with me.

Watching as he leans over the table, I have to turn away, the burn inside me ready to rise again even though it's the last thing I want. If we touch again before I can get a handle on this, it's going to end up with me bringing him back to the apartment so we can have privacy and it's not a place I think Isaac's ready for.

Brakes. I need to slam them on.

When he's taken the shot, he comes and sits beside me and the energy between our bodies is so alive that I swear as he leans in to hand me the phone, I can see sparks flickering in the air.

I'm past the point of no return now. Despite the way I started the night, the liquid courage I needed to drown myself in, I don't think I'm ever going to want another drink again.

I'm addicted all right. Driven to my knees from the intensity of the craving inside me, but it's not for liquor. It's not an addiction to something driving me now, it's an addiction to someone.

One someone in particular.

Isaac Crawford.

Chapter Nineteen

Isaac

Being here feels right.

I've been following along with a set routine for so long now that I forgot what it feels like to step out and try something new. The last time I stepped out of my comfort zone before I met Ryder was when I sat my parents down in the summer and told them I wanted to go to college.

I suppose meeting Belle could also be a step outside of my safe little box, but I don't look at it that way. She guided that first conversation and pretty much every one we had after, taking the pressure away. If it wasn't for me choosing to come here and going through all of that with her though, I wouldn't be sitting where I am now.

Winning a game of pool against Ryder.

Making sure to keep a safe distance between us, he attempted to teach me as much as possible and by the end of it, I think he was more surprised than I was that I picked up on it so quickly I was able to win.

The way he kept his distance, jumping back every time his body brushed against me was entertaining to watch.

From what I've seen of him before we began the tutoring sessions, he always appeared to be an extremely confident guy. Self-assured with a wall of confidence around him so tall, no one could penetrate it. But watching him in the moment, confident is the last thing he was.

I was getting to see a completely different side to the cocky footballer, but instead of being turned off by it, I never wanted it to end. When he was unsure, it took the pressure off of me. It made me feel less like a freak and more like an equal.

Ryder gave me a sense of belonging, like I had finally found the one place I fit and he has no idea he's even done it because until a few minutes after the game ended and he went off to order something for us to eat, I didn't know he'd done it either.

Watching him up at the bar, talking so easily with the female bartender, smiling at all of the right times, but his posture rigid and straight, it gives me a feeling of security.

I've felt secure with him before, but there's something about the way he speaks to the woman before turning his head back in my direction and smiling that heightens it even more. What he told me about his experiences with girls, what he used them for, he's proving to me now in his actions just how true they were.

He's also proving that at least for tonight, he only has eyes for me.

"I get up there, she asks me what I want and it occurs to me that I have no idea what you even like to eat. So I hope this is okay."

Setting the wicker basket of fries on the table as he pulls his chair out and throws his body down into it, I choose to answer him the only way I know how.

Slipping a fry from the basket and smothering it in ketchup, I smile as I open my mouth wide enough to drop the entire thing in before closing it, chewing silently and reaching out for another.

"I guess that means it's okay." He laughs and I grin again before repeating the same motion as before and swallowing another fry.

Pulling his phone and tossing it on the table, I reach across and grab it at the same moment as he leans in to push it toward me and our fingers connect, the lightning shock from earlier making us both jump back before I smile and he breaks the silence by laughing.

Unlocking the screen and typing while ignoring the tingle that's left from the shock we just experienced, I slide the phone across the table for him to read.

Who doesn't like fries?

Grinning before releasing a short chuckle, he slides it back to me.

"That's a good point. It's probably the one thing on the menu here that's safe." He pauses for a minute before grabbing a few fries and forcing them all in his mouth at once, his cheeks puffing out like a hamster, my eyes completely locked on what he's doing, fascinated by the things about him that I seem to find cute.

It's another first for me. I had no idea watching someone eat could be so appealing.

So now that the student has surpassed the master, what's next on the agenda?

"I still wanna know how you managed to kick my ass, having never picked up a pool stick before, but until you tell me your secret, I guess we can just hang out here and talk."

Hanging out here is fine as long as you don't suggest another game of pool. I don't want to embarrass you any more than I already have ;)

"Nice, Isaac. Rub salt in the open wound."

Better salt than alcohol.

"Smartass."

I'd rather my ass be smart. It matches up with the rest of me.

I've noticed one thing that hasn't changed during our entire exchange. He's been smiling and there's something about it that makes me happy. It always does that when he smiles, but the amount of times he's done it tonight alone means more.

"Even if it didn't, you can't have dumbass. I already claimed it and I don't share well with others."

He's doing it again. Ryder's not so different from me after all. The way he makes fun of himself, it's the same way I am, or at least the way I was before I met him. If I make fun of myself first, calling attention to my differences, when other people do it, the response isn't the same. It's me getting them before they can get me and it's another thing that I'm no longer alone in.

You not sharing well with others, is it just for dumbass or is it the same for everything?

I know what I'm hinting at, but I'm not sure he's gonna be able to tell, so before his eyes can even rest on the screen, I slide it back and add the one thing I'm sure will make him understand.

The minute his eyes catch the wink, my heart rate picks up. He definitely gets it and the way his eyes smolder and the blue in them grows darker, I know whatever his answer is going to be, it's definitely going to be one I want to hear.

"I don't share anything that's important."

Anything? ;)

Rising from his seat and leaning over the table, he grabs my face and pulls my lips to his forcefully, getting his point across before leaning back and sitting again.

"Anything or anyone. If it's important, it's mine." I can feel the heat rising and before I get a handle on it, he starts talking again. "And just in case it's not already clear, I don't plan on sharing you either. You're mine, tutor boy."

Ryder

I get all possessive, claiming him like he's an object that can be owned, and instead of getting offended, kicking me in the nuts and telling to screw the hell off, he blushes and smiles.

Isaac isn't like any other person on the planet.

No lie, if someone said what I just did, I would have gone off on them. There's no way in hell someone's ever claiming me like some prize in the lottery. I've never liked that shit and I see it a lot with the guys on the team and their girlfriends.

I'm not exactly one to talk considering I used a lot of those same girls in some pretty awful ways, but at least I didn't claim them, get all territorial and act like a Neanderthal. The only thing missing with some of these guys is the smashing of their fists on their chest and I swear they could be in the ape exhibit at the Toronto Zoo.

With what I just said, I'm well on my way to ending up there too, but I don't care because I meant it. I'm not going to share him.

The way we interact is a walking contradiction. I can breathe easier when we're together, yet lose my breath whenever our bodies are close. I get so hot around him that my body quivers and shakes as if I'm cold.

We're like fire and ice.

Do I have to share you?

"Do you want to share me?"

It's not what I wanted to say, but it's still a valid question. I've got no problem embracing the way I am with him even if it scares the fucking hell out of me, but I have no idea if he feels the same.

No.

"Then you've got your answer. You're it for me, Isaac."

There it is again. His face is a giant flush of red and it's so fucking amazing to see, I have to use all of my restraint to keep my body in the chair so I don't jump over the table and attack him.

The way we are, it's only a matter of time before we lose control of the situation and we take the physical to the next level. It's hardwired in my brain to be that way, but I'm dead serious about doing things right. As badly as my body wants to do what it was imagining earlier, I can't give in.

Whenever we get to that point, it's going to be because Isaac is ready for it. He's not Gavin. We're not going to collide in a hallway and a week later be buried deep inside each other. It worked in the past because of who I was doing it with and the feelings that developed, but it's not at all the same with Isaac.

Evenly paced; focusing on every single sensation, feeling, emotion and more. That's the way I want this with Isaac. When I do taste his body for the first time, it's going to be because he's begging me to do it and not a second before.

Hearing a tapping noise against the table and pulling myself out of my thoughts, I look down and see his hand tapping the phone, a new message waiting.

Why did you drink before you came to my house?

"If I told you I was nervous, would you believe me?"

A little, but I don't think that's the only reason.

"It's been awhile since I've been on a date with someone. I can fuck them and forget them, but do what it takes to go on a date? It's too much."

I was nervous too. When you showed up, I was ready to answer the door, but froze. I couldn't move and my mom had to come all the way down from her room to help.

I wondered why it had taken so long for someone to come to the door, but by the time his mom answered, it all faded away. I was just so happy to see the door open nothing else mattered.

Knowing he was that nervous, I'm not sure how to feel. I know I'm intense and too much to handle at times, but I never want him to be that scared. It's wrong.

"Does going out with me scare you that much?"

Going out period. I don't do it a lot.

"Is that because of your issues?"

In a way, yeah.

"What's the other reason?"

I'm afraid of seeing the guys I went to school with. They've said and done some stuff a few times when I've tried to go out. It's just easier when I'm home. It's safe there.

The guys he went to school with. The same ones that I'm on the team with, or I will be whenever I pull my grades up out of the gutter and Coach lets me back on. I know who he means and exactly what he's getting at. The way they talk about him and treat him is fucked up.

It's also something I never gave two shits about until now, so I'm no better than the ones that were doing it.

"Do you feel safe right now?"

Such a selfish thing to ask, but since that's another thing engrained in my DNA, it makes perfect sense that I'm asking it.

Yes.

The one word on the screen is enough to make me wanna smash my fist into my chest, but not in the animalistic way I was focused on before. This time I need to do it in order to kick start my now stopped heart.

Being here like this and knowing how honest and open he is, his answers to my questions never about telling me what I want to hear, but showing me what I need to see, it makes me want to do something I've never done. Open myself up. Be honest with him in return, even if there's a risk that when I do, he'll ask me to take him home and I'll never see him again.

It's so completely fucked considering the way I've spent the last two years, but I want him to know the real me. Not the person I became after Gavin died and my heart died with him, but the version that appeared when someone actually gave a damn.

I want Isaac to know the truth and there's no time like the present to make that happen. It's time for me to stop running and closing myself off from the world because of some misguided notion in my head.

I was worthy before. Maybe with him I can be worthy again.

"The real reason I went drinking tonight wasn't because I was nervous. It wasn't even because this is the first date I've been on in two years. It's because I'm a fucking mess and it's only a matter of time before you realize it and get the fuck out of dodge."

What makes you think you're a mess?

The way his face doesn't change, it's exactly what I need to continue talking. This is another new thing. Opening up and letting someone see inside and I'm expecting it to physically hurt, but with Isaac it's not like that at all. It's as easy as breathing.

Considering he helped me do that for the first time too, it's the perfect statement.

"I've only ever cared about one person. Loved one person in my life. He saw the ugliest parts of me and never left. He owned me. When it ended, all that was left behind was the ugly. The broken mess you're dealing with now."

Even in the midst of the truth there's a lie, but no matter how open I want to be, it's not enough to get me to admit that things didn't just end with Gavin.

I killed them when I killed him.

I don't see a mess.

There goes my heart again. It's completely stopped.

"What do you see?"

A person that loved someone so deeply that when it ended, it broke his heart and he hasn't been able to figure out how to recover.

He's right, at least partially. I did love Gavin, but what he's wrong about is the last part. It's not that I haven't figured out how to recover, it's that I never wanted to.

Until now.

"What if I said I didn't want to recover?"

I would be sad because it means you're lying to me.

"How do you figure I'm lying?"

It's a lie because you do want to get past this. You do want to recover.

"How do you know that?"

Because you're here. If you wanted things to stay the same, you never would have showed up in that conference room. You certainly wouldn't have come back after you ran away to Toronto, and you wouldn't be sitting here with me now. If you didn't want to get past what happened with your ex, you would just continue running.

He's right. It's wanting to change that got me off that barstool hours ago and brought to me where I am now.

Can I ask you something personal?

This is dangerous territory. When it's me controlling what is said and how much I admit, it's not a struggle, but if he's going to ask questions, I'm not going to have the control and I'm afraid it's going to make me do the two things I'm the master of.

Shutting down and running.

"Ask away."

Sleeping with girls. I know you said that you're not attracted to them and that they mean nothing to you, but is it something you need to do?

When I finally read the question on the screen, I'm pretty damn sure I release the biggest sigh of relief in the world. When he mentioned it being a personal question, my mind instantly went to Gavin. This though. This is fucking easy. He's asking a question that he already knows the answer to because he's embarrassed to ask what he really wants to know.

"I told you what that was about already. You know I don't need it, so why don't you ask me what it is you really want to know?"

You said you didn't want to share me. It's pretty obvious that we have something physical between us, but what happens when you get tired of that? What happens when I want something more? Am I going to be enough for you?

Holy fuck.

I knew I was screwing this up. I knew the way I react and push myself on him was too much, but I didn't realize it was this bad. He actually thinks that because of the way he is, combined with the fact that he might develop real feelings and want something more than just sex isn't going to be enough. I've made him believe that we're not on the same page.

I seriously need to fix this. It stopped being a physical reaction the day I got his text and showed up on his doorstep and it's about damn time he knows it, or at the very least is reminded.

"Isaac," I sigh heavily. "I'm sorry."

Shit. Fuck. That's not what I wanted to say at all. Ugh. I was right earlier. I am a fucking mess.

Sorry for what?

"For giving you the wrong idea."

I don't understand.

Reaching across the table, slipping his fingers from their tight grip around the phone and placing them in mine, I squeeze gently, careful to keep my eyes trained completely on him so he knows that what I'm about to say now, I've never been more serious about.

"I want you physically, it's not a secret. I wanted nothing more than to bend you over the pool table and bury myself inside you earlier. I'm never gonna lie to you about that, but it's not all I want. I apologized because me forcing myself on you, thinking with my dick instead of my head, it's made you believe that all you are is a fuck and forget and you're so much more than that."

Using his other hand on the phone, the one in mine not even making so much as a twitch to signal that he wants me to release it, he focuses his attention fully on the message he's writing until minutes have passed and he's sliding it slowly toward me.

If I'm not a fuck and forget, what am I?

"You're everything." I respond easily, not even having to give it any thought. He needs to know what he's become to me since I walked into that conference room for tutoring. I'm not going to be able to settle this shit inside me until he does. "I want you, Isaac. All of you. In every way I can have you, for as long as I can have it before I completely fuck it up. It's not a question of whether you're enough. You already are. I'm just not sure I'm going to be enough for you."

You already are.

What we have, it's fast and it's messy, but I mean every word I'm saying. He's enough for me and he doesn't have to worry about what happens if he wants more because I already do.

I want it all and if the way he's looking at me now means anything, I'm not the only one.

Chapter Twenty

Isaac

"Penny for your thoughts."

Oh man. I'm doing it again. I didn't even realize she was here.

As she makes herself comfortable on the grass, proceeding to grab her lunch from her bag, I grab the notebook and start writing. It's time for me to pay attention even if the way I was when she walked up holds more appeal.

The penny has been discontinued, Belle. You're just trying to get something for free.

She laughs when she finally pulls her attention away from her bag and reads what I've written. Leaning across and grabbing my hand and laying it out flat, she takes me by surprise when she places a nickel in the middle before closing my fingers around it.

"I figured that would be your response, so I came prepared. Now you owe me five thoughts mister."

The easy way she just answers my smartass comments back reminds me how glad I am that she reached out to me that day in the fall. If she hadn't done that, I know for a fact I wouldn't be where I am now.

"Wait! Before you tell me what you were thinking about, let me see if I can guess."

Did you develop mind reading abilities overnight?

"With all the movies Eric makes me watch, I've probably had them for years. I just waited for the right time to give them a test run."

Winking before breaking into a fit of giggles, she taps her finger on her chin and proves she's not just a pretty face.

"Staring off into space with a playful smile and this glossed over look in your eye. I do believe my genius bestie was thinking about someone special."

You might be right, but that doesn't prove anything.

"I see how you're gonna be. Fine. You were thinking about Ryder naked."

With how quickly the heat rises and spreads out over my face, I know there's no way I can deny it. She's not entirely right, but she's close enough that any effort to deflect off of it is pointless.

I'll have you know he's fully clothed. Not all of us are perv's like you, Belle. ;)

She claps her hands together gleefully before flashing her familiar smile, her acknowledgement and understanding of my situation evident in the way her eyes soften and the corner of her eyes crinkle.

If anyone is going to understand what I'm going through right now, it's her. I spent enough time around her before Kayden transferred back to know she feels the same way about him.

"I've seen the way he looks at you, remember? Maybe he's fully clothed in your fantasies, but I'm pretty sure you're not in his."

Thinking about what happened when we played pool two nights ago and the way it felt having his body pressed into the back of mine, it makes the flush in my cheeks that much worse. She has no clue how right she is.

Someone's been taking creative writing class too seriously. You're seeing stories where there are none.

At least none that I'm willing to admit to.

After admitting what I meant to him and having him tell me what he wanted with me, I didn't think the night could get any better. As I'm starting to learn the more time I spend with him is what I think can't be any better, he will find a way to make phenomenal.

Focusing back on our food after his admission, we sat in comfortable silence until he mentioned needing to get me home.

As much as I didn't want the night to end, his concern at making sure I was back before my mom decided to send out a search party, intensified what I was already feeling for him.

Choosing to walk the distance back to my house instead of wasting money on the bus, he slipped his hand through mine and didn't let go until we found ourselves standing on my doorstep about twenty minutes later.

~*~*~

"Hmm." Ryder muses and instead of reaching for the phone, I just squeeze his hand, hoping he gets the meaning and explains.

We've been on my front step for about five minutes and neither one of us has moved or said a word since we got here. Where the walk home had been relaxing, the conversation flowing easily between us, it's the opposite now.

It's not bad. It's just different.

"Doing this seemed a lot easier when it was just a thought in my head."

Proving how in sync he seems to be with me and what I need, he hands the phone over after unlocking the screen.

What seemed easier?

"Saying goodnight. I had it all worked out and now that we're here and I gotta do it, I can't."

I could always invite you in and tell my mom we're having a sleepover.

"Not helping, Isaac." He attempts to answer seriously before the smile breaks through and gives him away.

I think it is helping. You're having trouble saying goodnight, so doing things my way means you won't have to. ;)

Resting one hand on the back of my neck, making goose bumps appear on my arms as he rests the other on my face, he uses his body to push me back up against the door and presses his lips to mine, effectively shutting me up and making me focus strictly on the hum now vibrating through my body.

"If you let me in right now, a sleepover will be the last thing that happens."

The way I'm acting, the way I always seem to act whenever we're together, it's dangerous. It's so unlike me, but even knowing that, I can't stop because I like the way it feels. For the first time in months, I feel wanted, accepted and more than all of that, desired.

I said that I would tell my mom it was a sleepover. I didn't say that I thought it would be.

Flirting is foreign to me. Even typing the words, knowing what they're going to cause, it's strange, but with the way Ryder's eyes go cloudy as he's reading and his body gravitates even more into mine, it also feels right.

He sucks in a breath and steps back, his conflict evident in his eyes, but one I understand and wish he didn't have.

"You're killing me here, Isaac."

Why?

"I want to take what you're saying seriously, even knowing you're only teasing."

He has no idea that it's not teasing. No clue that the more I mention him coming in and staying the night, the more I want to have it happen for real.

I'm sorry.

He moves in again and runs his fingers slowly across my jawline before lifting his eyes and meeting mine straight on, his expression playful instead of serious the way I expect.

"Don't apologize for making me react. I like it. No—scratch that. I love it. I didn't know you had it in you to be so naughty, but now that I do, sorry is the last thing I want to hear you say."

What do you want to hear me say?

"You can start by saying that we can do this again soon." Pausing before running his index finger across my lip, he smiles sweetly, a version of his smile I've never seen but definitely like. "Please tell me I can take my boyfriend out again."

Boyfriend.

Holy moly. I'm Ryder Kane's boyfriend.

His words from earlier in the night filter through my head and even though I should have seen what it meant at the time, I didn't.

Ryder wanting to explore things between us, wanting to be with me in more than just a physical way, it actually has a name and for the first time in my life, I'm getting to experience it firsthand.

I'm someone's boyfriend.

"Isaac?"

Not speaking for a while, caught up in the way I was focusing on one word even though he'd said a lot more than that, I've worried him. The playful look in his eyes is replaced with concern.

Do you mean it?

"Mean what?"

You called me your boyfriend. Did you mean it?

"Mhmm." *He murmurs.* "I meant every word. I can't promise I'll be any good at it, but I want to try. I want to be with you."

I want to try with you too.

"Good." *he announces with a smile.* "That means there's only one thing left to do."

What's that?

"Kiss on it."

Don't you mean shake?

"Do you really think with what we're talking about, a handshake is the way to go?"

Shaking my head, he laughs and the second I hear it, I do something I've never done before. Something that I've thought about a lot since he showed up here tonight, but could never summon the courage to do.

I give him his goodnight kiss.

"Isaac and Ryder sitting in a tree…K-I-S-S-I-N-G."

Rolling my eyes but making no movement for the paper in order to respond, she smiles before turning her body the minute the shadow falls over us.

Turning and expecting to see Kayden, it's not his eyes I meet when I finally land on the person. It's Ryder and from the smirk on his face, he's heard every word of Belle's song.

"Never gave a shit about climbing trees before, but if that's what happens when I do, I might need to give it a try."

Lowering his body to the ground, making sure it's is as close as possible to mine, I lift my hand to block the red flush now covering my face as the embarrassment sets in.

"Who's giving what a try now?" Kayden says as he appears on the other side of Belle, leaning down and placing a kiss on the top of her head before doing the same as Ryder and sitting beside her.

"Ryder's going to climb a tree so he can kiss Isaac." Belle explains and that's when Kayden's eyes fall to Ryder and I remember what happened the last time were together like this.

Please don't let him run off again.

Feeling the brush of his hand across my arm, I raise my head and the minute our eyes connect, I see that I'm not the only one that's thinking about the past. The only difference between us is that there's reassurance in his touch and gaze and there's only nervousness in mine.

"Word of advice." Kayden says, his focus still completely trained on Ryder. "Practice safe kissing when you're up there. If you don't, you'll skip a bunch of parts and be saddled with a baby carriage."

His humor mixed with Ryder's reassuring squeeze breaks up the conflict, and while they all laugh, I smile and do the one thing I haven't been able to since he showed up behind me a few minutes ago.

I lean my body into his and allow myself to relax as he meets my movement with one of his own. Sliding his hand down until it's resting over mine, our fingers connecting, he leans his head comfortably on top of mine, a contented sigh from him a sign that I'm not the only one craving the connection.

Belle and Kayden cease to exist as I close my eyes and enjoy the way it feels being this close after spending the morning without him. It seems quick, but being apart after the way our date ended, it's hard for me. When I'm not with him, I'm thinking about him and when that happens, there's an ache in my chest that I've never experienced before, but seem to understand easily.

The ache is me missing him and having him here now, it takes it away and everything is right again.

"I missed our session this morning." He whispers and I squeeze his hand twice, letting him know the only way I can that I did too.

With only two classes being focused on for tutoring, we made the decision to ease back on the sessions, spanning them out over the week instead of every day. Today is only the first day and I already miss the routine of it.

"So that shit the other day." Kayden interrupts, causing my heart to speed up, afraid of what he's about to say next. "I overreacted."

"Nah man, you didn't overreact." Ryder admits. "I deserved it. I was eye fucking your girlfriend just like you said."

Kayden's eyes go wide, surprised by Ryder's admission. "You wanna tell me why?"

"Not really. It was a mistake." He says in way of explanation before turning his head toward Belle and looking her straight in the eye. "What I did was wrong. I'm sorry."

"It's okay." She smiles. "I know I'm not the one you really wanted to look at."

Leaning across the grass she slips her hand over his and just like she's done with me a million times, she squeezes tight before moving her body back into Kayden's.

Watching their movements, first with Kayden uncrossing his legs and opening them and Belle sliding so effortlessly into them, the two of them coming together like perfect puzzle pieces, it twists me up inside.

I want what they have.

Sitting here with them, I want Ryder to be like Kayden and let me slide into his arms. I want him to hold me, kiss the top of my head and keep me as close as possible. I want to be able to lean my head on his heart and listen to its steady rhythm, but I can't do any of it because I'm too afraid of what it's going to look like to everyone else around me.

I've never been ashamed of who I am or who I'm attracted to, but I've never had to worry about the way the rest of the world is going to react to it before. Ryder is my first real experience with being with someone, so I have no idea how much is too much.

Picking up on the tension, his arms come around until they're resting on my shoulders and he's rubbing gently. His head leans in until it's resting comfortably on top of his hand, his lips dangerously close to my ear. His even breathing the only thing I can feel and the second he speaks, all tension releases and I lean even more into him.

"What's wrong?"

Reaching across the grass to grab the notebook, his hands come out and holds me in place. Holding up a finger, he turns and when he faces me again, it all makes sense. His phone is in his hand and watching as he unlocks it, I see the notepad load and a blank page staring me straight in the face just waiting to fill it.

Nothing.

"I think someone's lying to me."

I'm not lying.

"Then why do you look so sad?"

Can I really tell him the truth? It's only been two days since he referred to me as his boyfriend. The last thing I want to do right now is blurt out all of my insecurities and make him feel bad for me.

"Isaac, please tell me what you're thinking."

I want what they have, but I feel horrible admitting it, so please forget I said anything. It's nothing really. No big deal.

"You're not the only one." He admits. "The last time we were like this, the reason I looked at Belle at all was because the way you and her were, I wanted it. When Kayden showed up, it just made me want what they had too."

Does that mean you wanted it with me?

"Yes." He nods and despite how torn up I still feel, my lips curve up into a smile.

"At the time, I didn't know...I thought, fuck, I don't know what I was thinking, but you and me ever being like them wasn't possible so I focused my attention on the way Belle looked in order to forget."

It all makes sense now. The reason Kayden caught him. Why he looked so haunted and the reason everything happened afterwards. I knew from things he'd said before that he was fighting a war against himself, but now I also know what part I played in it. What Ryder doesn't realize is that it's not just about wanting what they have. It's about something more, and it's that I'm having a hard time with.

How do you go from admitting that you want to be closer to someone, be more intimate and then switch it around and say that you don't want that closeness because you're scared of the way it's going to be looked at when other people see it?

It's confusing and messy and there's no way with as torn up as it makes me that it won't do the same thing to him.

I'm scared.

Two little words on the screen and I already feel like I'm going to hyperventilate. The way I feel about his eyes, how badly I want to look up until I'm completely lost in them, I can't do because I'm afraid of what I'll see when it happens. With the way things are going it looks like I'm scared of everything.

"Of what? Us?"

No. It's a good day if I don't hear someone refer to me as the mute kid. It gets even better when I can make it through an entire day without seeing Randy, Bryan and the others, because it's a day I don't have to worry about my issues getting the better of me. I can own them. Not talking, not having friends, it's made it easier to be who I am without calling attention to it. No one knows I'm gay unless I tell them...

My fingers are still sliding across the screen, the words pouring out in a jumble that I'm not even sure makes sense, but before I can finish it, get it all out so I can take a breath, he lays his hand across mine and stops me.

"You're afraid that when people find out we're together, it's another thing they're going to use against you?"

I nod weakly. I don't have the strength to type it out anymore. What's on the screen hurts enough as it is.

"I never thought about that. I'm sorry."

Don't be sorry. You didn't do anything. I like the way it feels having you this close, the way it felt hearing you refer to me as your boyfriend. Please don't think that I don't.

He sighs as he runs his fingers across the side of my face, his touch doing the same as it always does, calming the rapid and unsteady beating of my heart.

"I don't think that. If you didn't react to me at all, I'd wonder, but just a simple touch and you lean straight into me. It's not obvious to most people because you're not moving your entire body or anything, but it's there. It's subtle, just like you are."

Looking around us, I can see Belle and Kayden in a world of their own, caught up in each other the same way that I seem to be with Ryder, and instead of being afraid of what they're going to say or do once they see us, I just feel right. Comfortable.

My fear of discrimination, it doesn't extend to them. I'm safe here.

"I've spent over two years pretending to be someone I'm not. Now that I don't have to do that, I can switch gears easily. Do things the way I want and not give a shit who sees or cares or whatever. I didn't think about what it would be like for you. I get it now."

What does that mean?

"This is new for both of us and we're coming at it in different ways, but that doesn't mean we have to go through those different ways alone. If you need me to slow down when we're in public, I'll try, but I don't want to do it. I don't want to hide you, us or me ever again."

Is that what I want? Do I want to go on the way we have been and just be together in private so I don't have to worry about what other people will do or say? With as comfortable as I feel with my sexuality, do I really want to keep us a secret?

No, and I don't want that for him either.

I don't want to hide or be a secret. I just don't want to be hurt anymore.

"I won't let anyone hurt you, Isaac. No one touches what's mine."

No one touches what's his.

Me.

The feeling I get from hearing those words, it's like nothing I've ever felt before. It may be a physical reaction in the literal sense, but it's more than that. It's not a racing heart this time. It's a feeling of security.

His words are true. Now that he's no longer running from himself, from me and from everything else that haunts him, he's determined to make sure nothing happens. He's doing the right thing for both of us.

There's only one problem. If he sticks to what he says, I'm in danger.

Danger of giving up the one thing I've safely held onto for the last nineteen years.

My heart.

Chapter Twenty-One

Ryder

About a week after Gavin and I got together, shit started happening and it didn't take long to figure out the reason why.

Anyone that says coming out in high school is easy, is seriously screwed in the head. It's not easy and even with years passing, it still isn't. People can be ignorant fucks when presented with something they don't understand and in my high school, our relationship was definitely not accepted or understood.

It started out small. Little notes appearing in our lockers, a lot of them drawings of a cartoon character sucking off a pathetic attempt at a dick, that kind of thing. It used to annoy Gavin seeing them, but not enough for us to do something about it. It didn't stop there though. I wish it did.

We would hear names like faggot a lot, a few guys on the team even asking me if I liked it up the ass and if I enjoyed being shit on. It was some vulgar shit, but still not the worst of it. That came later and that's when I snapped.

One of the days I had to stay behind for practice, a few guys on the basketball team cornered him outside of school and beat the living hell out of him. Something they wouldn't have done if I had been around because I'd already made my position on the whole thing known. Taking out guys on both teams because of the hate they threw our way.

I'd gotten tired of being hazed about it. Having my clothes ripped and shredded during a practice so that I had to wear my gear home. Having my car keyed and spray painted with their ignorance, along with the notes and under the breath names in the hallway, and I made sure everyone knew that I wasn't gonna take it anymore. Until they grabbed Gavin and broke him down, I thought I'd gotten us past the worst of it.

Seeing him that night after the beating, something snapped inside me and leaving his house, I went in search of the assholes that hurt him. I couldn't find the others, but I did come across one and he was never the same after it. I know violence isn't the answer, but if they wanted to do it to someone I loved just because he loved me back, in my head at the time, they earned it.

I beat that asshole within an inch of his life and no one even so much as looked as us crooked again. My message was received loud and clear. I wasn't going to lie down and take the bullshit they wanted to dish out.

What I told Isaac, it's the way I'm always going to be. He means something to me, so I don't care if these are friends of mine or we've gotta play together on the team. If they make a move on him, say something about us that hurts him in any way, I will take them out.

I want to get back on the team, but not so badly that I'll tolerate this bullshit happening again. Once was enough.

It becomes obvious when I make my way into the locker room, heading for the coach's office that what I want and what's actually gonna happen are two different things.

"I'm not fucking with you, man. I saw the shit go down. He had his tongue rammed down Crawford's throat. He's a fucking queer."

"Bullshit. Ryder's nailed half the chicks on campus, including your girlfriend. No way is what you're saying true."

He's not wrong about that. If there's anyone on campus that would go under the radar, it's me. I've made quite a name for myself. At least Bryan didn't call me a whore the way he has in the past.

I could easily let this go, walk through and pretend I didn't hear the shit they're spouting off, but that isn't what's gonna happen. I've fucked up enough over the last two years, dragging Gavin's memory in the shitter with me. I'm not gonna do the same thing to Isaac.

"Bry, think about it. He lives with Murphy. They're close. With what I saw with him and Crawford, you gotta admit it looks weird."

"It's called roommates, jackass and when Kane gets here, I'll ask him and you'll see."

"Ask me what?" I ask, coming around the lockers and heading straight for them, secure in the fact that my face is giving away nothing.

"Nothing man. Just Randy being his usual self." Bryan offers up and I nod my understanding. With what I heard him say, the way he referred to Isaac, he's being a total dick, which for Randy *is* his usual way.

"I know what I fucking saw."

"Someone wanna enlighten me to what the hell you supposedly saw?"

Bryan's face twists and I second the sentiment. He has no idea that I'm only playing dumb and what Randy saw actually did happen, but it twists me up because it's none of their fucking business what I do.

"Since when are they letting queers play ball?"

"Randy, holy shit!" Bryan smacks him before lowering his head and shaking it. "Kane, ignore him. He's a fucking idiot."

"They've been letting them on the team for about four months." I reply, ignoring Bryan completely and turning my full attention to Randy.

Just the way I expect, Bryan's head flies up, his eyes wide in shock and his mouth following suit as it falls open and Randy shoots him a know-it-all smirk. These guys and their attitude is exactly the way the guys in high school used to be. They're nothing but ignorant jerks who wouldn't know something real if it hit them right between the eyes.

"You're not even gonna deny it?" Randy asks snidely, his face leering and making me wanna take a few steps closer so I can knock it off his face completely.

"Nope. I've been denying it long enough."

"Ry, stop fucking around."

"I have stopped. Haven't fucked around for a few weeks now."

I know it's not what he means, but I'm not gonna give these assholes an inch. Bryan's not calling me names, but that's only because he hasn't wrapped his mind around the fact that it's real yet. All he needs is time and he'll be even worse than the douchebag to his right.

"Very funny man."

"Bry, he's fucking admitting to shoving his tongue down Crawford's throat. How can you still be in denial?"

"Because I know him."

Oh hell no. I'm not letting that sit. The only person that can even remotely say that he knows me is Dillon, and he doesn't know nearly as much as he thinks he does.

"You don't know shit. As hard as it is to believe, Randy's right. I'm gay and Isaac and me, we're a thing. If you got a problem, you know what you can do with it."

"Oh yeah, what's that?"

Lifting my middle finger in the air, I grin. "Sit and spin because I really don't give a fuck what you think. My life, my choices."

"No way. I'm taking this to Coach. No way am I staying on the team if he's gonna let a queer play."

If I hear that word one more time, I'm gonna snap and take his damn head off. The last thing I need to do right now is lose my shit and repeat what happened in high school. I might have gotten away with it back then because I was younger, but now, it won't be the same.

I will not fuck this all up over someone like Randy.

"No need. I'm about to go tell him myself, but just so you know, he won't kick me off the team even if he does agree with you guys. He wouldn't want the shit storm it would cause."

"You wouldn't dare fuck with the team. It's your life." Bryan speaks up finally and I just shrug. He's right, a few weeks ago it was my life and if I'm honest, it's still a pretty big part, but not the biggest.

"Try me."

"Did you lose your fucking mind when you got kicked off the team? Do you even hear yourself right now? You're basically giving a big fuck you to your brothers in favor of a fucking fruit."

Fruit is sweet. Isaac being a fruit, at least in my head, it fits even if it's not the way he meant it.

"Yeah, you know, that's exactly what I did." Done with the conversation and remembering again exactly what I'm here to do, I just shoot them both a cocky grin and push past them, the heaviness I'm used to in my chest now significantly lighter.

Telling the truth. Being who I'm really meant to be, it's the right move and my body is letting me know it. For the first time since Gavin died, everything's the way it's supposed to be and I've only got one person to thank for it.

Isaac

Being out of classes for the last couple of weeks in order to focus my attention on Ryder and his weaknesses, it's made me fall behind on the current work. I have no idea when I'm going to be asked to take on another student, so if I want to keep up with the material now, it means cracking down and focusing.

The library is the perfect place for that. It's the one place on campus I never have to worry about seeing any of the meatheads from the football and soccer teams. Even better, its quiet, which means a lot less attention is going to be taken away.

I'm so caught up in the required reading for Biology that I don't hear anyone come up from behind me until they're leaning their body over mine and slamming a paper down onto the table.

"Ha! Eighty-five on a math test. I do believe that means I've got another reward coming."

Picking up the test and studying it, I flip through and smile. He did it exactly the way I knew he would. All the hours I spent forcing him to continue working even when he didn't think he could do it paid off.

Two classes down, one more to go.

Writing across the paper, I twist around in the chair and smile before handing it over.

What do you want this time?

"I am *so* glad you asked that." He winks before coming around and taking the seat across from me, the grin on my face mirrored back to me in his own. "A few hours alone with you in the reference section?"

I'm sure the librarians would love that. Try again. :P

"You can't blame a guy for trying. It's secluded. I mean who in their right mind would dare go back there?"

Holding up two of the texts I grabbed not twenty minutes ago from the very section he's talking about, he catches them and laughs.

"Besides you."

Motioning to the other tables directly to the left of me and the people sitting at them, I point with a smile and he laughs again.

"You're no fun."

Put the pout away, it's not going to work on me. I can resist the Ryder charm.

"I know you can resist it, but do you really want to?"

That's a good question and judging from the cocky grin he's displaying now, he knows he's got me. I can't really resist it when all he has to do is look at me and I turn from solid to liquid.

No, never.

"I didn't think so. I don't ever want you to. It takes all the fun out of it."

Reaching across the table and taking my hand, he leans down and gently kisses it before coming back up and facing me down with his heart stopping smile.

"My reward is the same as the last one. I want another date with you."

You could have gotten another date without it being a reward.

"I know. It's just the last time I did this, it didn't turn out the way I wanted it to."

Considering we're dating now and we kissed multiple times that night, I don't see how it didn't turn out the way he wanted. From what I can see, it turned out even better than any plan would have been.

I don't understand.

"I showed up to get you with the smell of whiskey on my breath. Whiskey that I'm pretty sure you tasted when we kissed. I don't like that. So I want the chance to do it over. A second-first date. So what do you say, tutor boy? Can I have it?"

If the way my heart is hammering in my chest means anything, he can have anything he wants. There's no way even if we weren't together that faced with the softness of his eyes and the warmth in his smile, I could ever say no.

For Ryder it will always be yes.

You can, but when?

"Tomorrow night."

Are you going to teach me how to play pool again?

"As good as that sounds, it's gonna be a no this time."

What do you have in mind?

"I want to take you somewhere I've never taken anyone else."

Where's that?

"If I told you that, I'd have to kill you. State secret and all."

If it's such a secret, won't bringing me there ruin it?

"No, because I could bring you anywhere and the last thing you'll do is ruin it. The truth is, it's very important that you alone, Isaac Crawford agree to come with me because it's the only way the secret location can be made even better."

Ryder Kane is hazardous to my health, I'm sure of it. I've watched enough movies, read enough books and spent a lot of time witnessing with Belle and Kayden what affection and sweetness looks like. I've never been lucky enough to experience it myself outside of the friend zone, but with what Ryder just said, I'm pretty sure his level of sweetness is toxic.

Who knew that when you peeled away all of his layers, this is the guy you were left with?

"So about my earlier idea..."

Don't even think about it.

"Too late. It's all I've been able to think about since I came through the door."

Maybe he's not so sweet after all.

You need to go and I need to study. I've got a lab in the morning and you're distracting.

"No idea what you're talking about. I'm just sitting here trying to have a conversation with my boyfriend. If you really want a distraction, I'm sure I could come up with something that doesn't involve talking at all."

He winks again and I roll my eyes, which just makes him laugh even louder, earning us annoyed looks from the other people around us.

Ryder is definitely a distraction and now it's not just me he's doing it to. It won't be long before he has the entire library under his spell.

"Move along!" he calls out. "Nothing to see here."

Turning his attention back to me and leaning across the table, he flashes those mesmerizing eyes of his at me and smirks again.

"Say yes or it's just going to get worse."

The entire library is staring at us. I don't see how it can get much worse.

"Keep avoiding giving me an answer and it won't take long to find out."

If I say yes, will you leave and let me study?

"Hmmm." He muses, mulling over my question. "I *guess* I can do that."

You guess?

"Do you really want me to leave? Be honest. The idea of us alone in the stacks, you want it as bad as I do."

I am definitely not going there with him. He knows the way I am whenever we're alone together. Asking a question he knows the answer to is pointless and I'm not adding any more fuel to the fire.

I really want you to leave. I need to pass this lab tomorrow if I want to keep tutoring meatheads like you. ;)

"Cheap shot, but fine. Have it your way. For the record, you didn't deny you want it as badly as me. I'm officially taking that as a challenge."

Pushing the chair away from the table and sliding his body out, he makes his way around until he's beside me, not wasting any time leaning in until his face is inches away from me.

"You and me tomorrow night, tutor boy. Make sure your mom knows not to expect you home until late."

With a quick kiss, he backs away and grins one final time before turning and stalking confidently toward the door. As I watch him go, I finally release the breath it feels like I'd been holding since he sat down.

I was right earlier. Ryder is definitely hazardous, but not just to my health. To my heart and body too.

Tomorrow night can't get here fast enough.

Chapter Twenty-Two

Ryder

Anytime I so much as think about going into the city, weird shit happens to me.

When it first started happening, I thought it was because I was still raw from the accident and losing Gavin, but it still happens and it's been two years. It turns me inside out so bad that I've bailed on trips because of it and I'm determined that this time, I won't let that happen.

My head starts feeling like it's lifting about 250 pounds at the gym. It's so weighed down and heavy, I can't think straight, let alone see. The sweating comes next. Images of Gavin's mangled up body, the way it looked when it was being lifted from the car flood me and my breathing is erratic. My heart races so fast it could give NASCAR a run for its money and it takes forever to shut it all down.

After meeting Isaac at the library yesterday and forcing his hand with this date, knowing where I want to take him and why, nothing happened. Where I expected the struggle, nothing came and I thought that maybe it had finally worked the way the therapist said and I was past the worst of it. Time healed the wounds.

Not even close.

Waking up this morning and getting a shower, I felt fine until I wrapped the towel around my waist and walked out. Everything became hazy and just like every other time, it all came at me, only faster and harder. I felt my body crash into the side of the wall near the door and then everything went dark until I heard Dillon yelling.

It's been about an hour since he picked my broken ass off the floor and forced me out into the living room to talk and despite his every attempt at getting shit out of me, I've been as rigid as a stone. If just thinking about taking Isaac to my spot in the city is enough to bring this on, talking about it is only going to make it worse.

Cancelling this date, or at least changing it up so I don't have to go through this would be the right thing to do, but for some stupid reason I can't explain, I need to see this through. I need Isaac to be the first person I allow into my escape.

The one place in the world that Gavin asked me to confide in him about and I denied him at every turn because I didn't want to taint it. When every part of my world was falling apart, it was the one place I could escape to and everything was right again.

It's the same way I am with Isaac, which means if there's anyone that's right to bring there, it's him. He won't taint it. He'll do exactly what I told him he would and make it better.

But if I want him to do that, I've gotta get past this shit now.

"You've done some screwed up shit the last few weeks man, but this, I can't let it go like I did with everything else."

"It's nothing. The steam from the shower made me lightheaded."

"Bullshit."

I've got no clue what to say to that. It is total bullshit.

"What happened to you? And don't tell me nothing because I can list a ton of shit that you've made excuses for that just doesn't add up."

"Nothing happened to me."

"Ry, come on. Can the bullshit."

"If you're gonna call everything I say bullshit, what's the point of saying anything at all?"

"I'm not calling everything bullshit, just what *is* total BS."

"Why is this so important?"

"You bring random girls back here, fuck them and discard them. You drink your body weight in liquor every night for weeks. You have these nightmares that make you physically hurt yourself in your sleep, and you're blacking out when you're awake. You scream out in your sleep a lot, not to mention sleep walk. Why do you think it's important?"

He pays a lot more attention to what's going on than I thought. He's nailed everything and no amount of damage control I attempt right now will end this. I'm caught.

"Why did you move here, Ry?"

"Playing in Toronto wasn't getting me anywhere."

"That's bullshit."

"See what I mean? You're doing it again!"

"I told you. I'll call it as I see it."

"I needed to get away from my parents."

It's not a total lie this time. I did need to get out from under them. After the accident and my continued downward spiral after he died, the pressure from them was too intense. Being what they needed me to be was a lot easier to do when I wasn't around them every day.

"I've got two fucked up parents, so that I can actually believe, but there's more to it."

"Bad breakup."

The same way I do with Isaac, I'm doing with Dillon. Talking about Gavin as if he wasn't killed, and is still alive out there somewhere instead of in a pine box six feet underground.

"Who broke up with who?"

"He left me."

Fake it and lie until you've done it so well that you believe in it yourself.

I'm right back where I was two years ago and it's killing me. It would be so easy right now to just put an end to all the lies and tell the truth. Pour it out no matter how it made him look at me and finally be free of the hold it has, but I don't do easy.

I like it hard in every aspect of my life, even if it makes me a complete douchebag.

"When?"

"A little over two years ago. I stayed in the city for a while after, but couldn't take it. It didn't help that living under my parents thumb was starting to drive me fucking crazy."

"I know all about that. You saw a little of the way my mom was."

He's right, he does know. Between a father that used him to make a buck in an underground fight ring and a mother that was completely off her rocker, he knows dysfunctional better than anyone.

"They wanted to send me to some fucking place that would erase the gay."

Why the fuck did I just admit that?

"For real?"

"Does it look like I would joke about that shit?"

"Did you go?"

"No." I scoff. "You've been around me. Do you really think they would have gotten me in a place like that?"

"Nah man, I don't. But if they didn't get their way, what's up with the girls?"

If I explain what I was doing with the girls, I'm gonna have to explain what brought me to that point and that's something I can't do. If I can't even bring it up with the guy I'm seeing, there's no way in hell I can do it with Dillon.

He can appear to be understanding all he wants, but I know that if he knew everything I've been through, he'd turn into an even bigger dick than Randy and Bryan. It's not me ragging on him, it's just the way guys like him are. They're judgmental pricks and I should know because at one point I was one of them.

Even if all I was doing was faking it.

"Fuck and forgets."

"Okay, let me get this straight." He rubs his forehead before sitting forward on the sofa and turning to face me. "You're totally into guys. Some fucker screwed with your head two years ago, twisting you up so bad you thought the only way to deal was to stick your dick in girls?"

Hearing him refer to Gavin as a fucker makes me wanna reach across and make him eat his words, but I bite my tongue. I can't react to it or he's gonna know that I haven't told him everything. He'll never leave me alone.

It's hard enough dealing with the fact that I collapsed and the reason why. Having Dillon on my ass on top of it is overkill.

"Pretty much."

"So what was that in the hall?"

"The result of not sleeping enough, detoxing off the alcohol and spending too much time with a certain tutor?"

When he laughs, I know I've succeeded in getting him off my back. There's no guarantee it's going to last forever, but even having the smallest reprieve right now is a blessing. With Dillon officially taken care of, I can put my focus where it belongs.

A drive into the city for a date with Isaac.

The past, it can't continue to dominate me. If I want this to work, and judging by the way my body visibly relaxes whenever I so much as think his name, it's obvious that it's exactly what I want, then I've got to take the control back.

I've got to take it back so I can do the one thing I've been forcing myself not to do since the accident.

Let Isaac in.

Isaac

"I've been doing some thinking."

With me reporting to Ryder's teachers every day since I started tutoring him and his progress being enough for us to resume our morning classes, tutoring sessions have been few and far between.

Today is the first time in days we've been able to meet at all and of course the first half of our time together is spent focusing on the subjects he doesn't have a problem in.

Biology and Anatomy.

He definitely doesn't need help with those and with how quickly I made sure our tongues met the second we shut the conference room door, it's obvious his expertise is wearing off on me too.

That's pretty dangerous. Did you at least make sure there were no innocent bystanders around when you did it?

"Very funny, but yes, when I did it I made sure there was no one else around."

He winks and I smack his chest, which only serves to make him laugh and pull me close. It's the complete opposite of the way we need to be right now, but liking the way it feels, there's no way in hell I'm making him stop.

What were you thinking about?

"I'm thinking I should get a new tutor."

Of all the things I expected him to say after the joke he made, this definitely wasn't on the list.

Why?

"If I want back on the team, I need to focus on this," he motions to the papers in front of us. "And not you."

It's easy to understand what he's getting at, especially with the way we just spent the last thirty minutes, but there's no denying that it hurts. The one thing I've been good at since I got here, is my ability to tutor people. If he's thinking about ending that, it feels like I failed.

Okay.

"Hey." He soothes, turning me until I'm facing him and am unable to hide the very real hurt I'm sure is in my eyes. "What did I say?"

Nothing. I mouth and he frowns.

"The look on your face, how dull your eyes are, and the fact that you can't even look directly at me prove that it's not nothing. Please tell me what I said."

I thought this was working. I had no idea I wasn't doing my job right. I promised to get you back on the team and I'm not doing it. I'm sorry I wasn't good enough.

"Stop right there. I never said you weren't good enough or that I wasn't learning with you. You're just a very big distraction."

I'm sorry.

"Isaac. Damnit. Stop saying sorry." The anger in his voice, he must realize how it sounds because he sighs and starts again, his voice lower and more soothing. "You have nothing to be sorry for."

Apparently I do if you need to get another tutor. I need to learn how to compartmentalize better.

"Compart—what?"

Divide things up, separate them better. Boyfriend Isaac can't be here with you when we're in this room. Tutor Isaac has to be."

"And if I said I liked having both?"

Then you wanting another tutor would make no sense.

"Okay, I get what you're saying. It does make no sense, but considering it's me, it's not exactly a surprise."

He's doing it again. Putting himself down. The one thing about him that I absolutely cannot stand. I've let him get away with it a lot because I've chalked it up to it being the way he is, but I can't do it anymore.

Stop saying things like that about yourself. You're not stupid or nonsensical, Ryder.

"I just told my boyfriend that I want to replace him because I'm not getting work done. Pretty sure that's as nonsensical as it gets. You can't be expected to do your job when I keep putting the focus on us."

You're not the only one doing that. Who pushed who against the door when we got here?

With the mention of the way things were, he grins and his hands start moving over my body, the very last thing that needs to happen with the conversation we're in the middle of. This kind of thing is exactly why he's not back on the team already. If we can't keep our hands off each other, nothing is ever going to change.

He's right. He needs another tutor.

Grabbing his roaming hand with my own, I stop it completely, lifting and bringing it back down onto my lap where it belongs. When I'm sure he's not going to start rubbing again, I lean over to the paper in front of us and write out what's gotta happen now, even if it pains me to do it.

Rachel Williamson is the only other tutor I trust. I have her number in my phone, I'll give it to you and you can set something up.

As I go to slide off his lap and into the empty chair beside him, his hands come out and hold me in place.

"I hurt your feelings, didn't I?"

Shaking my head, again attempting to move out of his grip, he holds firm.

"If I didn't hurt you then why are you fighting so hard to get away from me?"

I don't have an answer for him. There's only two ways to hurt me these days. Either physically the way Bryan and Randy did months ago, or attack my tutoring ability. He did hurt me because it feels like I'm not good enough.

"Please sit with me. I like the way it feels having you close."

Looking in his eyes, I struggle with what to do. I can move away and risk hurting his feelings or I can stay and just pretend that nothing's changed when it clearly has. With all the pretending I know he's already done, it should make the choice an easy one, but it doesn't.

I can't.

His hands loosen their hold almost immediately and despite seeing it coming, I'm not at all prepared for the loss that takes place when it happens. I've been completely numb inside before. It happens a lot when I meltdown, but numb isn't what this is. Not having his hands on me, I feel empty.

Sliding into the chair, I immediately grab the paper and start writing. I'm not gonna swallow this down and pretend it doesn't exist. I'm going to tell him everything I'm feeling. The absolute truth, no matter how he reacts.

There's only one thing I know unequivocally that I'm good at. Tutoring. Helping people. When you said you wanted another tutor because being around me was distracting, it hurt. It's the only thing left after everything I've been through with the guys on your team that can really make me feel worthless. I see why you need to have one, I

do, but it still hurts inside. I want to be good enough to get you back on the team. I can't handle failing you.

"Fuck." He mutters, reading everything I said, but not breaking eye contact with the paper. It's almost as if he's reading it over and over, letting the words really sink in.

"That is not what I was trying to do at all. I'm a fucking idiot."

Even though his head is lowered and unable to see it, I shake my head vehemently and don't stop until he finally looks up and catches it.

"Yes, Isaac. I'm a complete fucking idiot. I made you feel worthless. Even if it was only for a second and you can understand my reasoning. It was a second too long. It never should've happened."

It was a misunderstanding. It's fine.

"Your definition of fine is different than mine. There is nothing fine about this. I obviously have no fucking clue what I'm doing here."

What does that mean?

"If I want back on the team so bad, it's up to me to make the effort. Coach has been saying that shit forever and I'm just getting it now. I'm the one that needs to compartmentalize or whatever, not you. The only reason I'm even allowed back in the other two classes is because of you pushing me. You're not worthless, I am."

This is exactly what I was afraid of. Admitting the truth because it's always supposed to be better to do then lie. It's coming back to bite me now. There is nothing right about how twisted up Ryder looks and how he's taking everything on himself.

No you're not. I'm just too soft. Touchy. I also don't know when to keep my mouth shut.

Seeing my words he starts to laugh but stops, his eyes looking up into mine, worried, almost as if him laughing is wrong and he's making sure he's not hurting me again.

It was supposed to be a joke. You can laugh.

"Isaac," he sighs. "I'm screwing this up, aren't I?"

Screwing what up?

"This—us. We're supposed to have this date tonight and I'm doing everything I can before it happens to sabotage it. I have no fucking clue how to do this. It's been too damn long."

You think because you were honest about something and it's been a while, that you're screwing this up? Try being the guy that's never done anything like this before. You're not screwing this up. If anything the way I am is screwing us up.

"The way you are?"

My issues. Not being able to speak and always needing a stupid piece of paper or a text message screen in order to share a conversation. How touchy I am, how easily offended and hurt I get. My inability to control the situation because whenever I'm around you, I lose complete control. My lack of experience. All of it. It's all me.

"Okay, fuck this. I've heard enough."

Lifting himself out of the chair, he pulls mine completely out before picking it up and turning it around until the back is against the desk and he's got easier access to my body. Reaching out and grabbing my hand, he yanks me to my feet and immediately turns and heads for the door.

It's only when we're completely outside that he turns around and goes back into the room again, not coming out until he's got all of our things with him. Handing my bag over, he grips my hand again and starts heading down the steps, not looking back once as he drags me along to parts unknown.

When we finally make it to the parking lot and we're standing in front of a car I don't recognize, he finally turns to me, hands me his phone and fills me in on what the hell has gotten into him.

"I wanted to do this later, but with everything I said in there, then what you said, it can't wait. Our date, it starts now. Get in and buckle up. I'm taking you for a ride."

Chapter Twenty-Three

Ryder

"Is it almost time for me to take this thing off yet?"

Sliding the keycard into the door and being met with the green light and the click as it unlocks, I squeeze his hand and take a few steps into the room, kicking it closed once Gavin has made his way in behind me.

Walking us further into the room until we're closer to the middle and releasing his hand, I come around until I'm standing directly behind him and begin to untie the knot.

"I'm taking it off now."

"On second thought, keep the blindfold on. It's kind of kinky hearing you talk about taking things off and imagining what they might be."

Laughing softly, I untie the second knot and let the bandana I used to shield his eyes fall to the floor and watch as his body moves left to right, taking in where we are.

"Ry...why are we standing in a hotel room?"

Moving closer, sliding my arms through until they're resting comfortably around his chest, I lean my head in, catching his earlobe with my teeth, bringing it into my mouth and sucking on it, choosing to answer him in actions instead of words.

Releasing the hold on his ear, I run my tongue slowly down his jawline until I reach his neck. Pressing my lips to it, a whispered moan of my name escapes and his body goes lax in my arms. I begin sucking, making my way down and all the way around until I'm in front of him, his body leaning completely into mine and my arms are sliding around to his back in order to keep him steady.

"Why do you think?"

"Ry—God," he whispers and the craving in his voice causes my body to react. "Please don't stop."

"Wasn't planning on it."

Gripping the edges of his shirt with my hands, I begin sliding it up, Gavin meeting me halfway by lifting his arms in the air until the shirt is completely off and discarded onto the floor.

Starting at his neck again and working my way down, I run my tongue over his chest, backtracking with my lips and leaving a trail of kisses everywhere my tongue has been, sliding my body down as I go until I'm on my knees in front of him. My eyes land on the belt, his hands now digging into my shoulders, urging me on.

Unbuckling the belt and making quick work of the zipper and button of his jeans, I slide them down, bringing his boxers with them until he's standing completely bare and open in front of me.

I've been craving this moment since the first time I saw him in the hall at school. Having my way with him up against the lockers where anyone could stumble out and catch us. It drove me crazy with need and it's only gotten more intense since then.

"Tell me what you want."

"Your mouth."

"Where, Gavin? Show me where you want me to put my mouth."

Releasing his grip on one of my shoulders, he moves it down slowly until it's wrapped around his dick, the guttural moan that follows the minute he strokes it threatening to completely unravel me.

"I want—it here." He chokes out, his voice cracking under the pleasure of his own hand.

Giving him what he wants, I slide my hand over his and we move together, stroking up and down until Gavin's knees begin to give out and he barks out my name, his voice ragged, his breath catching.

"Please, Ry. I want your mouth."

Sliding myself up from my position on the floor until I'm standing face to face with him again, I capture his lips and begin to suck and lick in repetition, until his lips part completely and give me entrance. Gripping onto his arms tightly, I push my tongue into his mouth and the minute we collide, he moans again and I move.

Gripping onto him and lifting, I don't stop until he's completely flat on the bed and I'm climbing on top of him, settling his body comfortably between my legs, bringing my lips back to his. I start sucking, our tongues tangled together before pulling away to making my way back down his chest.

This time when I slide to my knees on the floor, I don't waste time teasing with my hands. I give him what he wants, wrapping my mouth around the head of his dick and licking a few times before beginning to suck.

Adjusting to his movements, I slide my mouth down deeper, gripping my own hands into his thigh the deeper I take him. My own moans rising to the surface as his fill the room around us.

This was worth the wait.

"Fuck Ryder, if you keep that up," he pauses and I hear the sharp intake of breath as I run my tongue in a circle before taking him even deeper. "I'm gonna explode. It feels…so good."

Fuck Ryder. That's exactly what I've been wanting him to do since I met him and what I'm definitely going to make sure happens here tonight before I take him home. I don't plan on leaving this room until we've done every single thing I've been imagining.

Sliding back up, my tongue licking a path as my mouth moves, I feel his body shift again, pushing even deeper into the back of my throat and causing my own hardness to push ungratefully against my jeans. Aching for its own release.

"Ry—der."

He says my name, but there's something in the way it sounds this time that isn't the same as before. It's softer, more drawn out. Not the sound of someone merely turned on and desperate to have his dick sucked. It's tender. More meaningful.

Hearing him that way, everything changes for me. I slide my body up from the floor and position my body on the bed beside his, knowing he's nowhere near finished, but craving something different. Running my fingers across his face, enjoying the feel of his skin against mine, I kiss him, slower this time. When our *tongues come together this time, when we push deeper into each other, a kaleidoscope of feeling comes with it.*

This isn't just about fucking him. I don't just want to bury myself in Gavin until I get off. I don't even wanna do it until we both get off. The way we're connected, the way my heart feels like it could explode at any given moment, it's got nothing to do with sex.

It's got to do with love.

I want to love him tonight. Every night. For as long as he'll let me.

~*~*~

Roused away from the memory by the sound of the horn, I turn just enough to see Isaac's hand slipping back until it's resting in his lap, his concerned eyes on me and his lips resting downward in a frown.

How long was I out? How many times has he tried to get my attention with no response?

Adjusting my ass in the seat, my attention is taken away as I attempt to hide the effect of the flashback that's extremely noticeable in the center of my jeans.

Shit.

It's one thing to be turned on by the guy in the car with me. Being so close to him that my body just reacts and I'm completely powerless to control it. It's a whole other thing to be in the car, taking the guy on a date, and instead remembering the first time I was with my ex-boyfriend.

I just fucking cheated on my boyfriend with a ghost.

"I'm sorry."

Even to my own ears the words sound pathetic. God only knows how fucking long I was locked in that moment with Gavin, a moment that's well over four years old and has nothing to do with what I'm about to do with Isaac. I don't give a shit how bad I want the guy sitting next to me or if he's a sign from Gavin or not. There's nothing right about what I just did.

What I always do. What I need to bury and forget.

I've never wanted a drink so bad in my life.

Turning as I catch him start to hold the phone out, I take it and prepare myself for whatever's waiting for me on the screen. What I'm sure will be his version of *go fuck yourself.*

What was that? Where did you go just now?

Decision time. Lie through my teeth even though something tells me he's gonna see right through it, or tell him the truth and hope it doesn't make him completely bail on me altogether.

There's no question. I know what I'm gonna do. The decision was made the day he sent me the text and brought me home.

"The past. Sometimes I have these flashes of things that happened before."

Handing back the phone, he starts typing and I'm relieved that it looks like he isn't going to leave the way I expected him to.

What did you see?

"Me and my ex."

Oh, I see.

I'm pretty damn sure he saw a lot, which is why there isn't more than those three words on the screen right now. I've never felt so dirty in my life. Am I really that fucked in the head?

"Isaac," I sigh and his head turns to face me at the exact moment his hand reaches out for the phone and rests on top of mine. "I'm sorry."

Your ex. You loved him right?

"More than anything."

Can I ask you something and have you promise to tell me the truth?

I don't even hesitate, I nod and he returns it with a tiny smile before lowering his head and typing away again. The last time we were like this and he asked permission to ask me something personal, it wasn't anything at all what I was expecting. I can only hope that it's that same way again because the last thing I want to do after promising him the truth is have to lie.

Lying to everyone else is easy. Lying to Isaac is impossible.

Your ex-boyfriend didn't just break up with you and leave, did he?

Fuck. I should have known he would see straight through that. After all the time I've spent with him, there's no way he couldn't. Not being able to speak makes him practically a master at reading someone every other way. I walked right into this.

"No, he didn't."

What happened?

"Gavin," I start, already feeling the pain of the last two years flooding straight up through me.

I don't know if I can do this even though he has every right to know. Fuck, why did I have to come back and start this with him? I could have stayed in Toronto and kept myself numb with booze and distractions. Why the hell couldn't I just stay away from him?

Feeling the tap of the phone on my leg, I look down and see the words on the screen and remember that I left him hanging.

Gavin what?

"He didn't just leave, Isaac. He died."

Isaac

The haunted look in Ryder's eyes when he doesn't realize it. The way he zoned out when we got in the car. The memories or flashbacks he just admitted to me that he has. The way he's always running. The reason he uses women to forget. It all makes perfect sense now.

It's not logical of course. I'm not entirely sure anyone could come up with an explanation that would make any of what he's experiencing the right and logical way to deal with things, but what confused me before, doesn't now. This is how Ryder deals with loss and even if it's not something I would do, it's completely understandable.

When I got in the car and clicked the seatbelt in, I turned to him, figuring that he was gonna peel out pretty quickly with the way he practically dragged me out of the conference room. Seeing his gaze locked straight ahead and his body completely frozen in place, it tipped me off pretty quickly that he wasn't there with me anymore.

Reaching over and honking the horn was my last ditch attempt to pull him out of it. The way I had to drag my entire body all the way over into his personal space, I was super aware of everything, and it didn't take me long to see that whatever he was reliving, it wasn't something innocent. Ryder might have completely checked out, but his body hadn't. He was turned on and this time, it had nothing to do with me.

Being met with a look of shame when he finally heard the horn and came back, it made my heart hurt for him. For whatever reason, his reacting upset him and in that moment, I knew I had to push him, get him to tell me what was really going on because I couldn't stand seeing the look anymore.

This happening also explains his reaction earlier. How easily he beat himself up and took the blame for everything I felt. Whatever happened to Gavin, Ryder blames himself for it.

Where I've been drowning in sadness, depression and inadequacy, he's been drowning too, only his are a whole lot heavier than mine.

Ryder's drowning in loss, regret and shame.

"You got nothing to say to that, huh? I guess I shouldn't be surprised. If the roles were reversed, I'd be pretty damn speechless too."

Very funny. :/

Realizing his mistake, he slams his hand off the steering wheel and throws his body back into the seat with a loud depressing sigh.

"I'm sorry, I didn't...I never think shit through."

Reaching out and placing my hand on his arm, the touch has the desired effect as his head turns until his eyes are level with my own.

Parting my lips and mouthing his name, he exhales another long breath and as his body visibly relaxes, he leans over closer, bridging the gap between us even though we're still not as close as I wish we could be.

"Yeah?"

Will you take me to your secret place now?

Reading my question, his eyes find mine again, widened now, the surprise at my question obvious and instead of pulling them away, he lets them linger.

"You still want to go?"

I slide my hand down his arm until I'm gripping his hand tightly, squeezing it, infusing him in the moment with the two things he needs most right now that I've got an unlimited supply of. Understanding and acceptance.

Yes.

"After what I just did, admitted to and what I'm pretty sure you can see," he motions down toward his pants with a scowl. "Why would you want to go anywhere with me?"

Because it's where the answers are.

"What answers would those be?"

The ones you want to show me so bad we had to leave school early. Now quit stalling. It's time to do what you promised me.

Breaking through his walls, catching the miniscule rise of his lips, settles my heart. It was touch and go there for a while, but it looks like I might be able to bring him back out of this after all.

"And what's that?"

Clipping the seatbelt across my lap again, I turn to him and smile wickedly.

You promised me a ride. So I think it's time you make good and do that, don't you?

Chapter Twenty-Four

Ryder

Six months.

That's how long it was after the accident for me to even look at another car again.

Nine months.

How long it took before I could sit behind the wheel and drive on my own without seeing the accident every second. Hearing the smashing of the glass, the jolt before I hit the windshield, Gavin's strangled cry before his world went dark.

Once.

The exact amount of times I've had another person in the car with me. Well, until now anyway. Against my better judgment, I let Cadence in a couple of months ago, and now Isaac.

There was one time shortly after I started driving again that a friend of mine from school started to get into the passenger side with me so we could head out together. No sooner did he bring his one leg in and prepare to sit then I lost it.

It's embarrassing to think about now, but I yelled at him, my entire body so charged up that it was shaking and my mind was flooded with the accident all over again. The smell of blood, the smoke billowing around the car. Gavin's lifeless body, broken and bruised. The guy got out and avoided me every day after.

Can't exactly say I blame him. Not a lot of people knew about the accident unless they were avid news watchers and because I didn't openly talk about it, no one had a clue. It wasn't until I finally ran from Toronto that I reached out to someone again, but even with him, he was at arm's length.

Dillon was the first person I allowed myself to be friends with because I saw a lot of my own shit in him and it bonded me.

Not enough to open up, but just enough to keep me moving from one point to the other, when all I really wanted to do was end it the same way I ended Gavin.

Having Isaac in the car with me now, I'm super aware of every single thing going on around me. Before I even peeled out of the parking lot at school, I barked out a command not to text or write me until I stopped. He flinched, but nodded and the ride up until this point has been silent.

I've been white knuckling it the entire drive. I pay attention to every car moving in and out of the lanes around me, both through the windshield and the side mirrors. If I took this drive any more seriously, I'm pretty sure I'd put turtles to shame with how slow I'd drive. As it is, I'm running below the limit, but not enough that it shows a noticeable difference to everyone else around me.

This is fucking hard.

I know this was my bright idea. I wanted to take him out of the city and bring him to the one place on earth I feel the most safe, but what it takes for me to get there is almost too much to handle. My mind keeps staring at every turn off on the highway and I have to force myself not to pull off and just park the car somewhere so I can break from the pressure.

It also doesn't help that he has no idea what the fuck is going on with me. I'm pretty sure he can tell how tense I am since I'm not doing a damn thing to hide it, but he hasn't asked and I don't know if I'm grateful for that or sad.

I want to tell him what happened. For the first time in two years, I don't want to fucking pretend that everything is cool and I'm just a screwed up guy because of my parents. Living with this secret is almost as hard as living with that night. I'm losing the damn fight and it won't be long before I break.

Not being able to shake the flashback of me and Gavin at the hotel isn't helping either. Isaac might have taken everything I said easily, his eyes and body language showing no judgment, but he didn't need to. I was doing it enough for the both of us.

I can't erase the feeling that I betrayed this really great guy by having thoughts like that about my ex.

Merging into the right lane, the one that will lead to the turn off I need in order to get us to our destination, I cheat and look over at him. It only lasts a second or two, but the way he's resting in the seat beside me with his eyes closed, a small contented smile on his face, it does what I need it to do and relaxes me.

The way he is doesn't take it all away, but the small bit it does do, it's enough to remind me that what I'm doing here is the right thing. He's the only other person on the planet that when we get where we're going, I'm sure will love and appreciate it as much as I do. He won't taint it.

He'll enhance it.

Isaac

"Don't type or write anything when I'm driving because I won't see it. I need to keep my entire focus on the road."
It doesn't take very long after he's told me that and I've nodded for him to turn back to me with softer eyes and apologize. It only sucks that he pulled out of the parking lot before I could get a response off because he needs to know that I get it.

I've been with my mom and dad enough times to know about the rules of the road and the focus needed in order to prevent accidents from happening. My dad has swerved out of the way enough times over the years for me to see just how quickly everything can change if you're not prepared.

I might not drive, but I definitely get it.

Whenever my family would go for long car rides and they didn't want to turn the radio on, I would focus my attention out the window and count things. It didn't matter what, I was just always counting. One time, I got all the way up to two hundred before we reached our destination. Two hundred evergreen trees between my house and wherever I ended up.

Not being able to talk and Ryder not wanting the distraction, I go ahead and start doing that again, but I don't get past fifty before my eyes grow heavy and everything goes dark.

Tap. Shake. Voice.

That's what I'm met with when I finally open my eyes. It feels like I'd only just closed them, but when I finally turn and look at Ryder after he repeats my name, I can tell that it's been a lot longer than minutes.

"I was wondering if you were gonna wake up."

Moving my hand around the side closest to him, I search for the phone and the longer it takes for my fingers to find it, the more I panic. Mouthing a couple of words is easy, having to do full sentences, no way. There's no way he would be that good of a lip reader.

Brushing his hand on top of mine, I feel the cold metal of the phone and let my heart still.

Thank you.

"You're welcome." He smiles before squeezing my hand and then motioning with the other to where we're now stopped. "We're here."

Rosewood Gardens.

Our date is in a flower garden?

Rubbing at his forehead at the exact moment his cheeks begin to flush, he nods, then laughs softly.

"It's stupid, right?"

No. To be honest, it's pretty close to perfect.

"Now you see why I wanted you to come here."

I don't actually see why, but I'm not going to go back and forth trying to figure it out.

I don't see. Can you explain?

"Flowers, Isaac. The way they make you feel when you come home every day. You're the only person I know that would appreciate this place as much as I do. No one else would get it and I don't think I want them to. Just you."

Ryder had a greenhouse when he lived at home. He spent more time there than he did in his actual house. I remember him telling me that, and when you add it to the way I feel about the flowers I planted outside my house, it's something we have in common. It bonds us.

This being Ryder's safe haven makes perfect sense.

So this is where everything is gonna start making sense?

"Yes." He agrees with another smile. "But in order for that to happen, we need to get out of the car."

Reaching over and pushing the button to release my belt, he does the same with his and before I can even blink, he's got the door open and he's getting out, shutting it and running around to my side. Knocking on the window, he grins and motions down with his hand and I catch on quickly to what he wants.

Unlocking the door for him, he wastes no time pulling it open and sliding his hand in for me to take.

I don't have a whole lot of experience with dating, but being a guy and spending as much time as I have watching them, I know how out of character this is. Opening a car door and helping the person out, I've only seen a handful of guys do that in my life. It's just something that not a lot of us do.

Ryder's being a gentleman and I'm not even sure he's aware he's doing it.

When he's helped me out and the phone is back in my hands, I hold up a finger and start typing quickly. I'm pretty sure I want to get on with this as much, if not more than he does, but not before I say something about what he just did.

Opening car doors? I had no idea you were such a gentleman. :P

The emoticon at the end, it's calculated. I've learned after complimenting him before that he doesn't take them well. If I don't want to completely blow this before I've experienced it, I gotta make sure he doesn't take it too seriously, even if I mean every word.

"Sorry to burst your bubble babe, but a gentleman is the last thing I am."

Oh. You do that for everyone then? :(I thought I was special.

Looking from the words on the screen to my face, he laughs.

"Nicely played, Crawford. Nicely played. What if I told you that my motivation for opening your door wasn't as pure as you believe it is?"

The devious look in his eye, the one that matches his grin isn't lost on me, but he makes no move to act on it, instead tapping his fingers on his arm waiting for me to respond.

I would say that it's not real until you act on it.

Where time seems to have frozen since we got out of the car, it speeds up as he reads my words and does exactly what I said. No sooner does he look at the screen then his body is charging into mine, pushing me back against the car and his hand is gripping my face, his lips smashing down onto mine. The combination of his dry and hard ones mixing with my damp and soft until the only sound around us is the sound of our pounding hearts and ragged breathing.

"Shit."

Coming down from the moment, catching my breath, but not willing to let the moment end, I push him again.

If it was shit, we should do it again until we get it right.

Sucking in a sharp breath of his own, he growls and leans his body into mine, boxing my body in against his car until there's no escape.

"If you keep teasing me like that, I will take you back."

Practice makes perfect, Ryder. ;)

What I never had experience with before is so easy now. I had no idea flirting could feel this good. I'm not even sure it would with anyone else. It only works this well because it's with him.

"You're mean, you know that?"

Typing out another message quickly and turning it around, I grin.

I'm sorry. Please don't take me home.

Leaning his head in until his lips are barely brushing against mine, they lift into a grin of their own.

"I never said I was taking you back to your place, but if you don't stop, I'll definitely be taking you back to mine."

Kissing me softly, he releases a contented sigh and finally pulls away, the only sign left of our connection the feel of our hands locked together.

"Come on, tease. It's time for me to show you my Disneyland."

Ryder

Isaac may not have the experience I do with relationships, but he damn sure learns quick. He's also brilliant at turning the tables until it's the student guiding the teacher.

It's like we're locked in a game of pool all over again. His ability to focus and watch, absorbing everything he sees, makes it easy for him to turn it around and use it to his advantage. He's unlike anyone I've ever met.

My intention bringing him here, what I needed to set right after the bullshit he spouted off at school, for a split second was thrown out the window. All I wanted was to get him in the backseat and finish what he started when he called me a gentleman.

Telling him that if he didn't stop I wanted to take him back to my place, it was supposed to set things back on course, but all it did was intensify the already strong need I have for him.

He's definitely the one teaching me now. He's giving me a crash course in restraint because it damn sure took a hell of a lot of it to back away.

Giving Isaac all of me the way I wanted to the night of our first date, I still want to do it, but it doesn't mean I want to push it at him all at once. When I finally give myself over to him and the way he makes me feel, it's going to be right.

I'm not going to fuck Isaac Crawford. I'm going to worship him, which means taming the fucking beast he's bringing alive in me and focusing on the reason I wanted him to be here.

The one place in the world that not even my past can touch. My personal heaven on earth. The place that even from where we are in the parking lot completely centers me.

Making our way down the path, I'm determined to ignore everything going on around me until I'm where I need us to be. There are so many things I want to show him about this place, but not until I've shown him the most important one.

So when he stops cold when we start making our way through the gazebo that sits in the middle of the path, I'm taken off guard and almost off my feet entirely.

Why are you going so fast? We've got the entire day. We can take our time.

"You're right, we can, but there's one spot I want to show you first."

Understanding dawns in his eyes as he grips my hand tightly and moves forward, which I do with him until we're standing exactly where I need us to be.

Two stones in the center of a gigantic circle, one in the shape of an egg and the other short and flat, water flowing over them until it hits the ground below. The area completely boxed in with shrubs and flower displays.

This is my version of home. My nirvana. My center.

Motioning to the bench directly in front of the waterfall, we make our way over and sit as he pulls the phone out and starts typing.

Wow.

"Exactly. Now you see why I didn't want to waste time walking around?"

Yeah. How is that even possible? Where is the water coming from and how is it not leaking out all over the ground?

The questions and the wonder I can see in his eyes, it heightens my own excitement at being here again. Right now, it's as if I'm experiencing this for the first time. It's amazing.

The first time I came here, was for a charity event my parents were the chairpersons for. They held it in the wide open field behind us and while they were busy droning on about things I didn't give a shit about, I made my way over here and for ten years after the fact, I never left. I always found a way to come back.

I questioned the way the water seemed to come out of the rock the same way Isaac did and after searching it for signs of a hose or other device that would make the water flow and not finding any, I chalked it up to magic. It's the only thing that made sense then, and it's the only thing that makes sense now.

"It's magic."

It's perfect.

"I wasn't so sure about that before, but now I think you're right."

Why?

"It was missing something. It's not anymore."

Lifting my arm and laying it across the back of the bench, Isaac looks from me to the phone before scooting his body across and resting it on mine. Bringing my arm down and around him the second he's comfortable, he lifts the phone and shows me what he was typing as I just enjoy the feel of having him this close.

What was missing?

"You."

The way the answer just comes so easily, combined with getting to witness the very instant his dark eyes go soft, it really is the way Isaac said. Its perfection or as close to it as I'm ever going to get.

My response, what I feel inside and out, it's monumental. My words affecting someone so much, it's never happened. Not even with Gavin. I believe they meant something, but not at all the way it appears to be with Isaac. I'm used to seeing his brown eyes reflecting the hurt and pain of the things he's been through, but right here in this moment, it's not there.

He's completely at peace and it's because of me.

This is the best decision I ever made.

Thank you for sharing this with me.

"I should be the one thanking you for that."

Why?

"I basically kidnapped you from school to bring you here and you had no idea where I was even going to take you. Thank you for trusting me and wanting to share this with me."

My pleasure. So is this where you give me answers?"

"Depends. What's the question?"

Why did you really want to bring me here? Why was it so important?

Now that we're here and he's seen and experienced what this place means to me, it only makes sense that we get down to the reason why I yanked him out of the conference room.

"I'm not good with feelings. I haven't felt anything but numb for two years, and for a long time I liked it that way. Being around you, all I do is feel and it scares the fucking hell out of me. Hearing you say that the way you are is screwing us up, I couldn't stand it because it's a lie. I could have sat there and muddled my way around finding the right words to prove that to you, but I thought showing you would be better."

How does bringing me here show me that what I said is a lie?

"I'm pretty sure you could have found this place on your own eventually, but because of the way I feel about it, what it does for me being here, I like to think of it as mine. I've never brought anyone here, not even Gavin. It never felt right."

And now it feels right?

"Yeah. When it involves you, it always feels that way."

Ryder.

"Too much?"

Not at all.

"Bringing you to a place I never want anyone else to find or know about, it's me letting you in. If the way you are, your issues or inexperience or whatever else you blamed this on was true at all, we wouldn't be here now because I don't do this."

You don't do what?

"Feelings, opening up. Letting someone behind the curtain."

But I am here.

"Yeah, you are. You're right where I want you to be. The same way you were when I ran. The way I figure you're always going to be, which means you're not screwing this up."

Well if I'm not, you're not either.

"I'm not so sure about that. It is early after all. I've got plenty of time to ruin this."

You won't though.

"How can you be so sure? Is two weeks with someone enough time for you to draw conclusions about the future?"

In most cases, no. In this case, yes. Trust me, there's no way you could screw this up.

I know of one way I can most definitely screw it up and with as open as we're being, me even going so far as to admit that bringing him here was my way of letting him in, I know it's time to do what I've been avoiding since I met him.

What I've been avoiding since it happened.

I've gotta tell him what really happened to Gavin. Why I ended up in Wexfield and why I'm here with him in my arms now.

Restraint isn't the only thing Isaac's been teaching me since I walked into that conference room two weeks ago.

He's teaching me what love looks like. What it sounds like, which right now is the buzz of our bodies being connected and our hearts beating in their own rhythm.

Thank you for letting me in, Ryder.

Shit. He's thanking me. I can't let him do it.

"Don't thank me. I don't deserve it."

Why would you believe something like that?

Attempting to lift his body up and away from mine, my arm feeling the strain as he moves backwards and hating it, I pull him back into me. I know he's only moving because he wants to look at me when I answer, but I can't let it happen.

I'll let him go, but not yet. I still need him right now.

"I need to tell you something."

Okay. I'm listening.

"When I told you Gavin died earlier, I lied. He didn't just die, Isaac. I killed him."

Chapter Twenty-Five

Isaac

Finally.

I'm pretty sure that if this was anyone else, the first word that they think or even say when they hear what Ryder just told me, wouldn't be what mine was, but that's what sets me apart from everyone else. I don't think or react the same. As much as I've hated my differences over the years, this is one of the ways I don't.

Ryder's revelation should feel like more of a bombshell then it does. It should alter me in some way, but it doesn't. I feel the exact same way I did when we sat here and he opened himself up so I could curl into him.

If anything, the only real change that's happened is I'm relieved. What happened in the car before we got here; the guilt, shame and loss I felt radiating off him, it all makes sense. He's walking around with guilt and shame because not only did he lose someone he loved, he had a hand in it.

Please tell me what you mean.

"I tell you that I killed someone and the first thing you do is ask for an explanation?"

Was I supposed to do something different?

"Run. You're supposed to run as fast and as far away from me as you can get."

Is that what you want me to do?

He falls silent and it's easy to see why. This isn't an easy answer for him. He's so weighed down by the pain of whatever happened to Gavin that he believes my leaving is the right thing. At the same time he's fighting against the selfish part of himself that doesn't want me to go anywhere.

What he said earlier is true and I'm getting to witness it firsthand. He does feel something for me and it's scaring the hell out of him. It's blurring his black and white line of right and wrong. Who he needs to be for everyone else and who he should be for himself.

"No." he sighs heavily. "I don't want you to run. I've done that enough for the both of us."

Good, because I have chicken legs. I don't do running. It's embarrassing.

His lips curve up just slightly, but it's enough for me. With whatever he has to tell me next, I have to make sure he stays above the tide. I can't let the weight of his past pull him under. If the only way to do that is to crack jokes, so be it.

Ryder's been drowning long enough.

"I don't know what I did to deserve someone like you."

You failed a bunch of classes and got kicked off the football team. Come on now, your memory can't be that bad. :)

Two things happen the second I hear his laughter. I finish typing out what I want to know, handing it over before moving in and pressing my lips to his. This kiss different then all the other ones we've shared, but no less important.

This is one of comfort and security. I need Ryder to know that whatever he has to tell me, I'm not running from it. Even if I am new to this and it's a lot to take in, as long as he's trying, I'm staying.

"If that's what it takes to keep you in my life, I'll fail every damn class I have."

The impact his words have on me is huge. He might be afraid of what's happening between us the same way I am, but it doesn't make him pull away. It brings him closer, opening the locked door to his heart wider than I think it's been in a very long time.

He's not alone. My heart is open too.

Finally glancing down at the phone, obviously remembering the message I typed before kissing him, his eyes scan over the screen before he breathes in deeply and releases it heavily, his own way of preparing for what happens next.

Now that we've established that I'm not going anywhere, will you tell me what happened?

"It's a long story." He frowns and rubs his fingers against his temple, sighing. "Are you sure you want to hear it?"

No. I'm not sure I want to hear it, but I am sure you need to tell it.

"Will you promise me something?"

Okay, but there's a condition.

"Name it."

You tell me how they got the water to come out of that rock.

He laughs softly again, this time closer to the way I'm used to, which only serves to make my heart soften more. Nothing will ever compare to the way it feels hearing him react to me this way.

"I told you it was magic. I'm sticking to that."

Fine. Magic it is, but I will get it out of you eventually.

"Isaac, God. I—"

The way he quickly looks away, breaking our connection, his face contorting into a frown, it's obvious that whatever he was about to say is something he's struggling with. I hate how conflicted he is. If opening himself up to me is going to cause this level of conflict in him, I'm not sure I want it to happen at all.

No one should ever struggle this much.

"I have absolutely no fucking right to ask this, but promise me that no matter what I say, you won't react to it the way you think I need you to. Please promise that good or bad, you'll be honest with me. If what I say makes you want to run, changes everything between us, just tell me. I'll deal with it. Take you home, distance myself from you, whatever you need. Just don't hide it from me."

I'm not going anywhere, but since I know you won't believe that right now, okay. I promise to be honest with you and not hide anything.

"I met Gavin in my junior year. I told you about that. It was lust at first sight. A lot like it was with you when we met. It didn't take long for the two of us to connect and when we did, I swear it was like the sun and moon collided. All the years I spent hiding away, believing I was wrong because of who I am inside, Gavin saw past it all until I didn't want to hide anymore."

"I fell in love with him the first week. He was everything I wasn't and it was impossible not to be drawn to him. We moved so damn quick, but it felt so fucking right that I didn't even care. Up until he showed up, I was closed off from everyone. Hardened. A total dick really because it took so much focus to be who I wasn't that I didn't have time for anything else. I didn't have time to be me. He changed everything."

The Ryder I've been able to see in the rare moments where he's let his guard down, I understand what he's getting at. The way I always thought he was based on the way he acted when he did show up to class, it was the way he was before Gavin. It was such an accustomed routine by the time I met him, all he had to do was flip a switch.

"Gavin made everything easy. I worshipped the ground he walked on the same way he did with me. It was us against the world." He pauses and swipes at his eyes and it's only when I really study what he's doing that I realize what's going on.

He's crying.

Ryder

What's going on? Why does my head feel like its split in half? Why do I smell smoke?

Opening my eyes, forcing the pain down, I attempt to move my body and cry out in agony as the pain shoots straight up through my legs and into my chest, completely paralyzing me.

Scared to push it again, not wanting the pain to repeat, I look around. I see the windshield first, my gaze locked on the small blood droplet that's making its way down in a straight line slowly from the gaping hole in the middle. The place where my head impacted.

Gavin.

Twisting to the side, the pain so intolerable I just want to scream out again, my eyes land on the passenger seat and his body lying still, his neck twisted and limp.

Forcing my body to move, I slide over the armrest between our seats and attempt to yank his seatbelt off.

"Gav! Wake up. I've gotta get us out of here!"

I can smell the smoke now, even stronger than it was when I woke up. It's mixing with the scent of gasoline. My head is fuzzy and in a lot of pain, but I know that those two things aren't a good combination. If there's smoke, there's fire and it won't be long before we become casualties of it.

Finally untangling him, I push my body over and summoning up every bit of strength I have, force his body up until I can get my arms completely around it.

"Come on baby, wake up."

Shaking his shoulders, watching as his head falls limp against me, I notice the gouge in his head, the blood seeping out, and the smell of gas and smoke is replaced with the overwhelming scent of his blood. Focusing my gaze, I look him over and I see two more cuts, not as deep as the one at the top of his hairline, but still big enough to seep their own blood.

The scent and sight of the blood mixes with the haze in my brain and where I had seen his flawless face and smooth tan colored skin seconds before, now all that's left is dark red and tinges of brown.

This isn't real. It's just a dream. He's just sleeping. This can't be happening.

Placing my fingers on his neck, checking for a pulse, I scream out when I can't find one.

No. This can't happen. Gavin has to have a pulse. He has to be breathing.

Bringing my face over his until it's resting over his lips and nose, I attempt to feel his breath on my skin but there is none. Gripping the seat and forcing myself to move, I adjust my body *until it's over the seat and finding the release lever, I yank it and hold onto him as it falls back flat.*

Laying him back, I pry his lips apart, opening his mouth before bringing my hands down and starting compressions on his chest. Every breath of air I force into his lungs, willing him to breathe, physically hurts, my body begging me to collapse, but my head too stubborn to listen.

I can't lose him. It's supposed to be us against the world.

"Don't you dare do this! You hear me, Gav? Don't you dare fucking leave me! Fight baby, please!"

~*~*~

This is exactly what I didn't want to happen.

I'm not in Rosewood Garden anymore. Isaac isn't with me and none of what we just shared together is happening.

It's two years in the past and I'm in my car with Gavin, testing his restraint. Pushing him, even though I know he's freaking because I keep taking my attention off the road. He's giving into me, moaning and aching for me and I'm determined to drive him to the edge.

The scene changes in a flash and I'm swerving the car out of the path of the tractor trailer at the last second and losing control until I hear a crash, feel myself being thrown forward and the world going black.

Waking up and finding Gavin's lifeless body covered in blood and bruises, completely broken and not responding to anything I do. Pounding on his chest, breathing air into his lungs for what feels like hours before my body completely crashes again and everything around me goes silent and dark.

Coming to after I've been rescued, my final glimpse of him as he's being pulled from the mangled mess that used to be my car. A car that I found out a couple of days later exploded shortly after they pulled us free.

An explosion that should have taken me with it.

The sound of shattering glass, Gavin crying out before everything went dark, the overwhelming smell of blood mixed with gas and smoke, the pain insurmountable. It's so real that if I reach out right now, I'm sure I'll feel his blood tinged skin.

Lifting my hand and bringing it out, desperate to make contact, confirm my reality, it makes contact with the softness and in that moment, I experience true nirvana. Inner peace like I've never known before.

It was all a dream. He's still here with me and the electric hum I feel through my entire body the minute I make contact with his skin proves it.

Gavin's alive.

Fingertips brush against my face tenderly and I lean completely into it, aching for more. The simple touch not enough to curb the storm inside me. As I start to adjust to the feel, the touch begins to fade and I'm no longer feeling skin, but hard metal, colder to the touch and not at all what I want.

"Don't pull away."

Again I feel the push of the metal against me and shaking myself, forcing past the haze in my head, it's not Gavin's eyes I see when I finally lift them up and really look at the person beside me.

It's Isaac.

Gavin wasn't real. It wasn't him I was feeling. It wasn't his pulse steady under my hand. It was Isaac's.

Holy shit.

The cold I felt was the phone he was pushing at me to get my attention. He was attempting to do what he did in the car earlier. Save me from myself.

"I—I can't..."

Then don't.

It would be so easy to do what he said. He's giving me the easy out. I don't have to tell him what happened, what I caused because I was reckless and stupid. I can just shake this off and get back to the way things were before I had to stupidly want to admit the truth. He'd let me because that's just the kind of person Isaac is.

He's a better person than me.

"I killed the only person that mattered."

He stares at the phone but makes no move to write anything. I'm not sure there's anything he can say. If the situations were reversed, there would be no words for this. I would just stand up, back away and get the hell away from this crazy train before it dragged me under.

Isaac isn't you. He isn't running. He won't leave.

"I couldn't save him."

Fuck. I'm not making any sense. I need this to make sense. Isaac needs to know what he's getting himself into. What could happen because he's choosing to stay with me. I have to make him understand that he's in danger. Anyone that gets close to me is.

I need to make him leave.

You don't want him to leave.

What I want doesn't matter. I need to stop thinking so selfishly and finally do something right for a change. I have to save him the way I couldn't save Gavin.

"We were together for two years, completely out everywhere but at home. He was, but with the way my parents were, I hadn't gotten there yet. One night I decided it was time to tell my parents the truth. I could be myself everywhere else, so in order to make everything perfect, I had to be able to be myself at home too."

"We used to drink, but nothing too excessive, just doing it at parties and shit. That night, I told them the truth and they argued with me. Admitting I was gay went against everything they believed in. I wasn't the son they raised. They wanted to send me to a place that could fix me. Erase the gay and turn me back into the son they wanted and not the one they were given. I fought against it, ended up knocking my dad on his ass when he tried to get me to comply. I ran. I always run, but that night I ran to the nearest bar and did shot after shot until I couldn't feel anymore."

If what I'm admitting is getting to him, he's not showing it. His head is dipped to the side the way it was when I started talking and he's made no move to change it. His eyes are wide and alert and focused solely on the horror I'm unleashing on him.

Closing my eyes, pushing down the twisted feeling in my gut, I force myself to focus on getting this out before breaking down. I can't let him see me break.

"I had like four shots of whiskey. I thought I was fucking invincible. I left the bar after texting Gavin and drove to his house. I didn't think I was drunk and since I got to the house in one piece, I thought I was good to drive. I explained everything that happened and that I needed to get away from my parents and he came with me. It was us against the world, Isaac. He wouldn't let me go alone. He should have, but he didn't."

"All I could see was the way Gavin made me feel. I was so damn addicted to it, craved it so badly that nothing else could get through. He wanted me to slow down, begged and pleaded with me to keep my attention on the road that night, but I didn't listen. Thinking that nothing could touch me, I started teasing him. I was going to drive him crazy until he stopped pleading and gave in. I always loved it when he gave in to me. He took his eyes off the road for a split second, the way mine already were and we almost crashed into a tractor trailer."

"I swerved out of the way at the last second, seeing the panic in his eyes even though I couldn't hear him screaming at the time. I swerved, but wasn't able to get the car under control. I slammed on the brakes, we skidded and slammed into the pole."

Feeling the pull inside me, the familiar blackness beginning to set in, I shoot my eyes open and focus them on Isaac. I can't succumb to the memories again. Once is enough. I can't go into that night again because if I do, I'm afraid this time will be the one time I don't come back out.

Reaching his hand across until it's wrapped around mine, he squeezes and just like I did when he tried bringing me back out of the memory, I relax into it, leaning my body into his until our heads are resting together.

Looking down to where our hands are, I see the phone and his words on the screen, new ones that weren't there the last time and at a complete loss as to when he wrote them. Admitting to everything, the first time I've ever spoken out about that night, it's like I'm locked in two places at once.

I'm here in the moment with Isaac; my reality, but also in the past with Gavin.

It's a tug of war between the past and the present and I have no idea which side is going to be the victor.

It's not your fault.

"You promised you wouldn't do that!" I yell accusingly and he flinches, our hands breaking apart as his body slides away from mine. The intense pain in my chest the minute he separates is more than I can stand. I knew it would happen this way, expected it, but I didn't prepare myself for exactly what it would feel like when it actually did.

I hate this. I need him to come back. I need him to help me breathe again.

"I'm—sorry." I choke out through a sob, stretching my hand out in order to connect and bring him back. Flinching again at my touch, he starts typing manically and doesn't even look up and acknowledge my existence again until he's done.

I promised that I wouldn't tell you what you wanted to hear. I promised I wouldn't lie to you. I didn't do either. I told you the truth. It is not your fault. You made some seriously bad choices that night, Ryder, but you were 18 years old and your parents treated you like you were a broken toy that needed to be fixed. Drowning in alcohol is stupid, but it makes sense. Going to Gavin that night makes sense. The way you acted in the car, ignoring his pleas for you to pay attention was reckless, but also understandable. You weren't thinking clearly or in your right mind. It was a mistake. A horribly tragic mistake, but not your fault. You wanted the truth, there it is.

Reading what he wrote, he's not the only one who flinches. I accused him of trying to tell me what I wanted to hear because hearing it wasn't my fault is like music to my ears, but that wasn't what he was doing at all.

I'm the world's biggest dick bag.

"How can you believe that?"

I wasn't there. I'm not as close to it as you are. Gavin didn't have to get in the car with you that night. You could have left on your own and maybe nothing would have happened. He made a decision to do it, the same way you did. You're guilty of making bad choices, but you didn't kill Gavin.

I want to argue this. I'm the one that got behind the wheel drunk, even if I didn't think I was at the time. I'm the one that needed to pay attention to what my dick wanted and not what Gavin plainly wanted me to see. I caused the accident. Gavin's death. Me. I did it all.

"You're wrong. I did kill him. Those bad choices you said I made, they did it."

No, Ryder, they didn't. They lead to it, but they were not what killed him.

He makes no fucking sense. I wish he would just spit it out already so I can show him how wrong he is and we can move on. He can separate himself even more and leave the way I want him to.

The way he should.

"What the fuck does that even mean?"

The accident killed Gavin. Not you.

I can't stand this. Even before I got to the accident and admitting what I caused, I felt them coming. A buildup in my eyes until it was hard as hell to see, and now with Isaac laying everything out in as cold a way as he can, completely detached from me and the entire thing, it's hurting so bad they're coming again.

I don't cry. I don't break. No one's allowed to know about this part of me. How soft I really am buried underneath all the shit I've been living with, but I can't stop it. The secret's out.

There's no more strength left to fight and there's still so much that he needs to know. Bringing him here and doing this was a mistake. It's going to change everything. It's not my safe place anymore. I just made it a part of my ongoing nightmare.

I really do ruin everything I even remotely care about. People. Places. Things. I kill it all.

"Well," I start, barking out a dry laugh at how pathetic I'm starting to sound. "Since I managed to ruin the day like I said I would, I suppose I might as well spit out the rest. If you don't already hate my guts, you will by the time I'm done."

I don't hate you.

"Give it time. You will."

Rolling his eyes and shaking his head, he places the phone down on the bench and slides it across, making sure the entire time that there's no way we can touch. Keeping his eyes level with his legs, not daring to raise them even a little to make eye contact just rips the hole in my chest open even wider.

"I was banned from going to his funeral. I still went, but I was hidden the entire time and only visited him once everyone was gone. I made him a promise that day. I did a lot of thinking about it and I finally understood why it all happened and wanted to make it right."

The phone being over by me, there's no way he can respond so I continue. Determined to pour out everything until there's nothing left. It's time for him to get the full effect of the mess I made. The mess I am.

"If I didn't fall in love with him junior year, none of this would have happened. The accident happened because my parents were right. I was fucked up. Confused or whatever. My choice to come out and admit I was gay caused all of this. I stood beside his grave that day and promised that I would never look at another guy again. I would distance myself from all of it. Force myself to be the way my parents wanted me to be. I would be straight, even if it killed me."

"Every night for two years I went to bars, clubs, and raves; basically anywhere there was alcohol to numb the pain and women I could bury my dick in so I could erase the memory of being with Gavin entirely. It worked too. I was dead inside. Completely numb to everything and everybody. I felt nothing for them and they served their purpose. For a little while, I could forget."

"I was keeping my promise to Gavin, everything was the way it should have been. I was getting exactly what I deserved and then I met you and nothing worked anymore."

Catching the movement of his hand before feeling it as it makes contact with my leg in an effort to grab the phone, I bring my own hand down and stop him from pulling away.

With as quickly as he moved, it's obvious something I said affected him and I don't give a shit if it's wrong or not, I need to find out what the hell it is. It's the first reaction he's allowed me to see since I started spilling my guts. There's no way I'm going to ignore it.

"What did I say? Why do you need the phone so bad?"

Finally looking me in the eye, I see a lot more than I'm prepared for. Ignoring the slight shake in his body, I focus solely on his brown eyes and the water pooling in the corners. The damp lines on his cheeks further proof of what's happening. I'm not the only one losing the fight against feeling. He is too.

Attempting to slide his hand out from under mine, I struggle with whether or not to let him. The minute my hand came down on his, it steadied me. Letting him slip away again, I don't think I can handle it. I crave that connection too much.

If you want him to answer your question, you've got to let him go.

Releasing the hold the second reality sets in, I wait for him to recoil back, but he doesn't move. Even though he can move freely, his hand is still resting in the same place, the phone cradled neatly in it.

"It's okay." I whisper as soothingly as I can and when he looks up again, the tears I saw pooling minutes before are now freefalling down his face. "Please talk to me."

What do you mean nothing worked when you met me?

The girl underneath me, screaming for more while I pounded as deep as I could go into her, images of Gavin along with his taste, smell and sound completely overtaking me until I could feel my own release teetering on the edge. Craving it so badly and reaching the peak, my point of no return, and it no longer Gavin I'm seeing but Isaac. His sounds, his smell, his taste.

His name escaping over and over as I surrender.

The night is so clear in my head, but not because of the way it ended or the pleasure and pain I experienced having my first real orgasm in years to thoughts of my tutor. It's so clear because it's the night that my heart crashed into my head and demanded something more.

It's the night everything changed.

"I thought you were straight and the attraction I felt for you was wrong. I was fighting against it because if I gave in, it meant I was betraying the promise to Gavin. I went out, picked up a girl, brought her home and fucked her, but it didn't work. Nothing worked that day. I should have been drunk enough not to feel, but all I did was feel, Isaac. I felt you."

What do you mean you felt me?

"When I'm with them, I'm numb. I feel nothing. I can get off and it never means anything. I'm completely disconnected in the moment. That night, I was separated from her, but not from you. I thought about touching, tasting and smelling you. I felt you, Isaac. And then, when I didn't think it could get any more intense, you walked into the apartment."

Realization dawns in his eyes as they widen. He knows everything now, right down to the day everything began for us. My mess completely on display and the weight on my chest significantly lifted. Not erased, but definitely lifted enough to be able to breathe again.

"Getting off, my release or whatever, it wasn't mechanical that day. It should have been, but it wasn't and even the girl knew it. Called me on it. It wasn't her name on my lips or even Gavin's the way it's been before when I've lost control and slipped. Isaac, it was you. I called out for you."

Isaac

I had one task the entire time Ryder was opening up. I had to sit here and take it all and not react. One seemingly simple task, a way I've been so many times in the past that it should have been as easy as breathing to me, but it was anything but easy.

It had to be this way because I didn't want to say something, have him see something in my eyes or body language that would make him shut down again. As much as he struggled with everything he had to tell me, crying, hurting when I pulled away from him, the last thing he needed was to close himself off before he was able to get everything out.

He's been doing that for long enough. This had to be the moment it ended.

He hasn't said anything for a few minutes, but it's easy to see even with the distance between our bodies that what he has gotten out is helping him.

Ryder's body language is always guarded. He is always on edge even when he has no reason to be and a lot of that comes from everything he's been keeping bottled inside. It's not the same way anymore. What was guarded is now broken completely open.

I have so much I want to say, things I need to do that are almost as important as taking my next breath, but I can't do any of them until I know for sure that he's gotten everything out. I need to know if he's done.

Is there anything else you need to tell me?

There's a flash of something in his eyes, but it's gone before I can make sense of it. He wipes at his eyes again and just like that the moment is gone. Whatever that was, what he's still holding back from me, I've got to put it out of my mind right now. Pushing him will just do more harm than good.

He's admitted more than enough as it is and now I've got to respond to it. Make him understand that not one thing he told me is going to make me walk away. If anything, all he did do telling me all of this is bond me to him even more.

Before I can tell him all of this, there's something much more important that I need to do first.

Close the distance between us.

Nothing I say will mean a damn thing if I don't fix that first. So sliding back across the bench, I reach out and place my hand gently on his leg. When he looks down and sees what I've done, his eyes rise and meet mine. The hardened blue I'd grown accustomed to while he relived the horror of the last two years, is now a soft light blue, every emotion he's kept bottled now on full display for only me to see.

"Can I hold you?"

Silently answering him with a squeeze on his leg, his arm comes out and I glide into his arms easily, my body buzzing the instant we connect again and only settling when his arm comes around to rest over me, pulling me even closer into him.

"Isaac, I need to know something."

What?

"When I take you home tonight, am I going to see you again?"

This is most definitely not the same guy I sat down with a little over an hour ago. He's wide open, no longer guarded, but with that also comes the fear. He's still worried that after everything he's said, I'm going to leave. If I can't find the words for anything else, I have to find them for this.

Do you want to see me again?

"Of course I do, but I'd understand if you didn't."

I'm not leaving you, Ryder. No matter how hard you push or try to make me run, I'm not going anywhere.

"What I told you..."

What you told me only makes me want to stay more.

"You can't mean that. It just hasn't set in yet. When it does," he sighs. "When you realize how messed up I am, the shit I caused, you'll bail."

No. That's what you expect me to do. It's what you think I should do, and it might even be what you want me to do, but it's not what I'm going to do. I heard every word you said and I'm not going anywhere.

"Why not?"

I don't care if it's quick. He is not going to be the only one that opens up and admits the truth tonight. It's time I did the same thing, even if what I'm about to tell him is riskier than all of the things he told me combined.

My heart won't let me.

"Do you always do what your heart tells you?"

Yes, when it's right I do.

"And your heart not wanting you to walk away, that's it being right?

That's my heart never being more right.

"Isaac?"

Yes?

"My heart doesn't want to let your heart walk away either."

Chapter Twenty-Six

Ryder

It's a dick move. Something born completely out of selfishness, but I can't stop it once it's started.

The best thing for everyone is to let this guy go. Let the reality sink in around him and when he bails, which considering how smart he is; he will, not chasing after him.

When he admits that his heart won't let him leave, though, the best thing flies right out the window and all I'm left with is the selfishness. My need to keep him close. Never let him go because I like the person I am when he's near.

Isaac doesn't see the train wreck. He sees me and I want to enjoy that for as long as it lasts because I meant what I said. My heart can't let him walk away.

This level of calm, serenity and happiness, it's the last thing I deserve after everything I caused, but even if I could get up right now and do right by him, I won't. I also can't keep thinking about this because if I do, he's going to sense it and pull away again and now that he's back in my arms, it's where I want him to stay.

Yeah. I'm definitely a selfish bastard.

If that's true, then you know what you've got to do next right?

Damn. Every word he says is like a jolt straight to my heart. Dropping my guard, letting him in, I've left myself wide open and what was penetrating my walls before, has broken all the way through now. What I was numb to is all I can feel.

"Not sure. I might need someone to explain it. You know anyone willing to help with that?"

For the first time since we sat here, he smiles and the sight of it is like jumper cables on a car battery, the paddles of a defibrillator kick starting a flat lining heart. His smile breathes new life into me.

I think that can be arranged ;) If your heart doesn't want to let mine go, what you need to do is simple. Don't let it go.

"Wasn't planning on it." I whisper before pressing my lips tenderly to the side of his forehead. Another simple movement that is infused with nothing but feeling.

I am *never* giving this up.

If he wasn't mine before, he definitely is now and the way one small kiss affects me, making me ache for another just proves it. Isaac owns me.

"Do you want to take that walk now?"

When we got here, I was so determined to get him to this spot that focusing on anything else was impossible. Now that I've done that and we've gotten to experience it together, I'm ready to enjoy what comes next.

You mean I'm going to get to see the rest of the garden?

"You say that like I planned on keeping you here the entire time."

Didn't you?

"Maybe." I laugh softly. "But you can't really blame me. Once I got you here, nothing else seemed to matter. We were where the magic happens."

It's not the place that creates the magic, Ryder. It's the person. The magic is wherever you are.

How he can admit that; believe in it after everything he knows, I've got no clue, but the way I grasp onto the words, I don't even care. I just want him to keep saying them.

"We, Isaac. It's wherever *we* are."

Sliding my arm around and bringing it down until it's resting comfortably on top of his, I shift my body inward and when he looks up, all I can do is grin and stare.

I might be a selfish bastard, but I'm a damn lucky one. He's still here and with the way he's looking at me right now, there's nowhere else in the world he wants to be.

The fear is still there, but it's dulled. What I thought would ruin this place for me, has done the opposite. Isaac really has made Rosewood mean more than it did when we got here.

He made it better.

If enjoying this, appreciating every second of it and being so addicted that I want more moments just like it is wrong, I don't want to be right.

It might have been a really long time since I've felt anything like it, but I would recognize it anywhere. Right here and now, on this bench in one of the most beautiful places on the planet, with one of the most beautiful people on it, it's undeniable.

I'm falling in love with Isaac Crawford and no matter how scary it is, how strong the urge is to run, it doesn't change it.

He's in danger.

We both are.

If we fall in love, nothing will ever be the same again and I'm not so sure I want it to be. I want different. I want Isaac. I want it all.

"Come on, tutor boy." I announce, slipping my fingers through his and getting to my feet. "Our second-first date officially starts now."

Isaac

When Ryder finally pulls me up off the bench and we leave the safety of his special place and end up back on the path, it's like a bubble has been popped and I'm seeing a completely different side to the guy that I'm falling for.

One of the advantages of not being able to speak and needing breaks in order to use paper or a phone to converse, is that I can spend a lot of time watching people and the way they interact. Not only how they interact with other people, but also how they interact with the world around them.

Back on the bench in front of the waterfall, Ryder was locked in the past, his posture tight until the moment he allowed himself to relax. His eyes were haunted, his voice drained under the weight of everything he was carrying around, and now that we're no longer there, it's like he's a completely different person.

Strolling along the path, him slowing down only to point out different floral arrangements and trees, sometimes even showing me the epitaphs written on the various benches spread around, he's lighter. More confident. I'm getting to see what Ryder looks like when he's really living and not just going through the motions.

The way he is right now, it's contagious. Walking along with him, I'm more confident, meeting every smile he flashes my way with one of my own, his excitement, the glowing brightness in his eyes when he points out something he thinks I'll love as much as he does, reflecting back on to me. I don't need a mirror to know this. It's just something I can feel all the way through.

Ryder isn't the only one living in the moment.

"Oh, we *so* have to do this! I can't believe I didn't think of it sooner."

Slipping his hand out of mine, he veers off the path, picking up speed until he's jogging, not stopping until he reaches his destination. A very large tree in a wide open grassy area.

Making my way over, the phone gripped tightly in my hand, more than prepared to ask exactly what he means, he grins before lifting his leg and digging it into the bark, quickly following it up by lifting his other leg and proceeding to climb all the way up to the first level set of branches.

"Your turn, babe. Put the phone in your pocket and get your ass up here!"

The last time I climbed a tree, I was eight and thinking I was invincible, decided to push myself until I had climbed all the way to the top. Not realizing until too late that there was no real way of getting down without help.

It's not something I'm looking to repeat, but the way he is right now, it's impossible to say no to.

With his smile guiding me, I mirror his movements until I'm beside him, sliding my legs over the side and looking down to the ground below. His hand finding its way to mine before he slides his body down.

"Do you have protection?"

Turning, not understanding what he means, my eyebrows furrowing in confusion, he laughs and his grin grows even bigger.

"Isaac, I need to know if you have protection."

Protection. Condoms. Why would he be asking me that while we sitting in a tree? Shaking my head, because even if we weren't in a tree, I don't have anything with me, he frowns and pouts.

"I want to kiss you, but I know that once I do, we're going to skip a bunch of steps and be saddled with a baby carriage. I want to prevent that because that's honestly more of a third date thing. In order to do that, we need protection."

His attempt at a straight face fails as his eyes crinkle and he laughs and it all starts to make sense. Belle's song, Kayden's joke and exactly why he wanted to climb the tree to begin with.

Leaning into him, placing my hand on his thigh, his body responding almost immediately by inching even closer and turning into me, a sigh escapes as I slide the phone out of my back pocket and say what I need to say as quickly as possible.

I say we take our chances.

"Mmm, I was hoping you'd say that."

Moving his head until it's resting against mine, he turns and leans in until our lips are touching again, the steady hum of our connection more alive in the moment then it's ever been. Moving from one corner of my mouth to the other, he places one soft kiss after another until I stop him, capturing his bottom lip with my own and focusing all of my attention on tasting it.

Sucking on his lips, feeling his hot breath on my face just adds fuel to my already burning fire. My hand, as if it's got a mind of its own, comes around to rest on the back of his head and I'm pulling him into me until his tongue forces its way past my now parted lips and plunges deeper.

Running my tongue over his, gripping it and beginning to suck, he moans and the sound, mixed with the vibration it creates between us threatens to undo me. The heat I felt the minute our kiss intensified, it's even hotter now as it makes its way through my body until every part of me feels like I'm scorching.

Using his own hand and gripping my leg, he scoots my body closer until we're pressed so tightly together, it's as if we've been crazy glued. His other hand comes up around the back of my head, before running down over my ear, along my jawline, and all the way down to my neck, the ache matching the one in my pants until I'm unable to control it and shiver.

Coming up for air, but keeping his lips dangerously close, he continues to run his fingers in circles over my neck, moving down slowly until his hand reaches the bottom of my shirt and he slides it under, setting my chest on fire the minute his fingers make contact with my skin.

"The way you respond to me when I touch you. Fuck, Isaac. We *really* need protection."

What happened at school earlier, what we talked about when we got here; the struggle I had watching Ryder reliving his past and seemingly falling apart in front of me, it's all gone now. All that's left is the feel of his hands on my body and the way it turns me on and makes me crave more.

Aware of my hand still resting on his thigh, I press it deeper into him, gripping it through his jeans, rubbing and massaging, moving my hand up slowly and repeating the same motion until I hear the sharp intake of breath he makes before exhaling it across my skin.

He's right. With as bold as I am right now, my hand dangerously close to pushing him over the edge, one small movement enough to ignite him, we definitely need protection from the need threatening to spill out and drown us.

From ourselves.

Capturing my lip with his teeth as I slide my hand over the large bulge in the center of his jeans, he growls and bites down, a curse word falling along with another sharp breath and an involuntary shiver of his body.

Knowing that what I'm doing to him is the reason for his reaction, it's intense. Empowering. I'm controlling Ryder's pleasure and loving every second of it. I want more of him and of his reactions. I want it badly.

"We need—to stop." He forces out, his words breaking up as I deepen the grip of my hand of him, no longer massaging, but stroking. Releasing his hold on my lip and attempting to back away, I press my lips to his again, not willing to comply with what he wants and needing to deepen the connection.

Fighting for control, his breathing as erratic as mine when he finally breaks free, I open my eyes and find his intense stare glaring back at me, giving away the conflict he's experiencing.

He wants to stop almost as much as he wants to keep going.

"This is definitely to be continued, but not in a fucking tree. It's too dangerous."

Focusing on the phone gripped tightly between my legs, I slip it out, brushing his hand as I do, the electric pull the second we touch again rejuvenating my need and making me want to reach out and push it even further.

I want to push him to the point of no return.

"Stop looking at the phone like that. I'm getting jealous."

How am I looking at it?

"Like you want to do bad things to it."

Pulling my attention away from the phone and meeting his gaze as soon as I lift my head, I reach out and run my finger across his lips, and he responds with a quiet moan.

"That's better." He murmurs. "Now you're doing it right."

What's so right about it?

"Now you want to do bad things to me."

Do you want me to do bad things to you?"

"Like you wouldn't believe."

Kayden was right.

Sliding his hand off my leg until it's resting over my hand, he links our fingers together and lifts it up until they're resting in a much safer place on his knee.

"Yes he was, which is exactly why we need to get down. Corrupting nature doesn't seem very nice. Fun. Definitely hot, but not very nice."

Leaning over and pressing his lips to mine softly, he lingers for a few seconds before backing away and turning his body straight again.

"I'm gonna jump down and when I'm level I want you to do the same."

If I jump I'm going to break my legs. For that matter, so will you.

"No you won't. Trust me. I'll make sure nothing happens."

Before I can slide my fingers across the screen in order to type out a reply, he's doing what he said and leaping from his spot. After a few seconds of hearing no sound but the rustling of the leaves, I hear the sound of his feet landing and looking down am met with him standing completely upright with a smile playing on his lips.

"Told you! I might not have climbed a lot of trees, but I have done a lot of strength training." He calls up before opening his arms wide, situating his body in proportion to my place on the tree so he can make good on what he said before he jumped off.

He's going to catch me.

If I wasn't sure about how I feel, what he's doing here would definitely prove it beyond a shadow of doubt.

"Okay, babe. I'm ready. Jump!"

Looking over the edge, seeing how perfectly aligned he is with where I'm sitting, I swallow down the fear and do exactly what he said. For a few seconds, the rush of the air around me as I make my descent blocks me from the reality of what I'm doing. It's only when I feel a pair of steady yet strong arms around me, my feet again firmly planted on the ground that it all slams into me.

I just jumped from a tree where I was at least fifteen feet high and I'm absolutely fine. I can feel my legs, I'm standing steady, completely safe and it's all because of him.

"Are you okay?"

I'm great. Ready to do it again?

"Hmmm, which part exactly? The one where I almost took advantage of you in a tree or catching you when you jumped?"

Who says we have to choose? I vote for both. ;)

Nipping my nose with his teeth, he chuckles and pulls me tighter into him.

"You're going to be the death of me. Death by restraint is what's going to be written on my headstone."

There are worse ways to go.

"You might be right about that."

Thank you for making sure I didn't fall.

"I'll never let you fall, Isaac. I promise."

I don't have the heart to tell him that what he just promised me, he'll never be able to keep. That it's too late.

I've already fallen.

Ryder

"Can I ask you something?"

We've been out of the tree for at least fifteen minutes, and no matter how far away from it I drag us, or how many different images I bring to mind in order to block out the very real one I experienced when we were up there together, nothing works. I'm still as hard as a rock.

My joke earlier about what was gonna be written on my headstone, it's not a lie. Being conflicted is a natural state of mind for me, but I've got no experience with this kind. My body wants me to find the most secluded area in here and have my way with him while my head fights against it, restraining me.

The only thing left to do in order to relieve the insane pressure in my pants is to completely change the subject to something that has no way of getting me in trouble.

You can ask me anything.

I've been meaning to ask him about this for a while now, but the timing never seemed right and then with him admitting that he's touchy, the last thing I wanted to do was upset him. With as open as we've been today though, I'm not worried about any of that anymore.

"Not being able to talk, has it always been that way?"

Shaking his head, he slows to a crawl and starts typing.

No. When I was younger I could speak a little. Not well, obviously, but I could do it.

"Can I ask what happened?"

You can ask me anything, Ryder. Anything you want to know, I'll tell you. No secrets.

"You really mean that, don't you?"

Nodding, he starts typing again and touching his arm gently, I motion up the path about two or three feet away to where a bench sits unoccupied. If we're going to get into this, it would be probably be a lot easier to be sitting instead of walking and stopping every few seconds.

Holding his finger in the air, he continues writing and only starts moving once he's done and passed the phone over. Following along, I sit down beside him, bringing my body as close as possible to his and start reading what he's written.

You know when you're a baby and you have all these milestones that doctors expect you to reach? I was right on target, pretty much nailing them all right on schedule, but right after my second birthday, it was like I forgot them. I went from walking to crawling, saying words to doing nothing more than grunting and then making no sound at all. I was drinking out of cups and suddenly I was a baby again and all I would take was bottles.

"What does that mean? How is that even possible?"

He shrugs, but starts typing again, obviously having at least some insight that betrays his shrug.

I'm not sure how it happens. I wish I did because then I might be able to fix it. For the most part you can see that a lot of the other things were fixed over time, but the speech thing never was. My mom took me to the doctor pretty soon after I started reverting back to the way things were. At the time she thought it was because of us moving and me not adapting well. Turns out she was wrong.

What he's talking about, what his mom thought was going on, I know about it. My cousin had something like that happen with him. He was getting ready to start kindergarten and even though it had taken him an extra year to get it, he was finally

249 | P a g e

potty trained and ready to go. He started school and within a couple of days of being there, it was like he hadn't learned how to go at all. He reverted back to the way he was before and it had taken almost the entire year to get him back on track.

I remember my mom explaining it to me once, saying that the doctor said it was normal when there was a big change. What I don't get now is, if it wasn't a big change that did this to Isaac, what else could it be?

"If it wasn't what your mom thought, what was it?"

I was diagnosed pretty quickly. The doctor called me low functioning autistic. Apparently regression is the first noticeable thing. As it turns out, the diagnosis didn't last. A few years later, even though I still wasn't talking or making any discernable sounds, they classified me as high functioning. It just means I learn and experience things differently than you.

"What's the difference between low and high?"

Honestly, I don't know. For me it has to do with severity. With my level of regression, I needed almost twenty-four hour, around the clock care. I couldn't eat on my own, dress myself, walk without falling or talk. As I got older, it changed and I don't really get how or why. I'm still dependent obviously, I live at home for a reason, but not nearly the way I was before.

This is mind blowing. I'm the first to admit that before he agreed to tutor me, I didn't give him the time of day. I didn't give Isaac a whole lot of thought period. Having spent the last two weeks around him, I never would have guessed that he had been through all of this. Other than not being able to speak, he seems to be exactly like the rest of us.

Fuck. That doesn't sound right. He's different, but a good kind of different. Smart, funny, amazing, extremely sexy, an amazing kisser—no. I need to stop this. I can't go there again or I'm gonna be right back where I was when we were in the tree.

Breathe Ryder.

"Since it's obvious that you can walk, eat, dress yourself and all of that, why can't you talk?"

I don't realize how insensitive it sounds until it's out and before he can start typing, I reach out and stop him in order to start doing damage control.

"That came out wrong. I'm an idiot. What I mean is, did they ever give you an explanation for why everything else came back, but that didn't?"

It didn't come out wrong at all. I understood what you meant. There were a lot of things the doctors came up with to try and explain this, but nothing ever fit. They tried every therapy known to man to try and get me to speak again, but those never worked and eventually I got tired of trying. I would rather not speak then spend the rest of my life back and forth at hospitals, therapy places and doctor's offices.

I might not understand what he's dealing with, but I do understand what he's getting at. If you're spending more time in those places then out experiencing the world, it's not much of a life you're living. No one gets being completely shut away from the world better than me.

"Not speaking. It doesn't bother you?"

For a long time it did. Sometimes, it still does. Especially since we got together. I want to be able to speak to you, Ryder. I want you to hear me the same way I hear you. I want

"You want what?"

Please don't take this the wrong way, but the way I feel about you, there's going to come a time where I'm going to want to tell you how much I care and I want you to be able to hear me say it.

He wants me to hear him say he loves me. It doesn't take a whole lot of brain power to get that. What he doesn't get is that whether he says the words out loud or not, I would hear them. Hear him.

"If the time ever comes where you want to say those words to me, Isaac, I would hear them whether they come from your mouth or they're written with a pen. It's the meaning behind them, the feelings they encompass, not the sound that matters."

If the time ever comes?

"Don't take it wrong. I don't deal in absolutes anymore. I want to be able to tell you *when*, but I can't because when isn't a guarantee. Especially after today."

You still think I'm going to leave.

Not wanting to say yes and have it hurt him, I just nod and his eyes lower and look away.

"I'm sorry."

Don't be sorry. You feeling that way just means I get to have fun proving you wrong. :)

"Is it bad that you proving me wrong would be fun for me too?"

No. It's sweet. It means you want me to do it as badly as I do.

I can't argue with that because he's right. I want him to prove me wrong and stay. I've never wanted something so badly in my life, even if there's still a part of me that thinks I'm being selfish.

"So other than wanting to talk to me, you've adapted to not being able to?"

Yeah, I told you. It used to bother me a lot, especially when people don't even try to understand, choosing instead to judge and make fun of me for it. It's not the same anymore. Ever since I met Belle, I look at it all differently.

"Different how?"

I can weed out the meathead assholes from the good people easier. Belle calls it my bullshit detector. The people I want to have in my life, they'll be okay with me not talking and they'll support me no matter what. The ones that I don't want to have in my life, they'll be like Randy and Bryan and won't matter.

God. I didn't think he could be more amazing than he was, but he's proving me wrong. I'm the luckiest person in the world, having this guy care about me and want to be with me. No question or doubt about it.

"Am I one of the good ones?"

No Ryder, you're not.

What the fuck?

Placing his hand on top of mine, pulling my attention back to him and out of my head before it can head down a path I don't want it going down, he smiles and holds up the phone.

You're not one of the good ones. You're the best one.

Chapter Twenty-Seven

Isaac

"Are you sure you're alright with this?"

This is the fifth time he's asked me this since he pulled up in front of my house this morning. He asked me twice before we left for school, once on the drive there, even though I didn't even dignify that one with a response because he was driving. We've been sitting in the car waiting for Rachel to get here for at least twenty minutes and he's asked twice more.

We've been over this. It's okay. I understand.

"Why don't I believe you?"

Because it will take at least another twenty times of me telling you before it sinks in?

It's been two days since our date to Rosewood. Two days that he's spent waiting for the other shoe to drop only to find out that it won't. I'm not going anywhere and at least as far as that goes, he seems to believe me. Now if only I could get him to believe that meeting with Rachel for tutoring doesn't hurt me, I'd be set.

"I'm not that bad."

Sorry to burst your bubble, but yes, you are that bad. All that worry is going to give you wrinkles.

"Very funny."

Thanks. :)

"Anyone ever tell you that you're a ball buster?"

Yeah. This annoying football player that enjoys repeating the same questions even though the answers never change.

"Comments like that will get you spanked."

Ryder, stop threatening me with a good time.

"She's not supposed to meet me until nine. The way I see it, I've got twenty minutes to do more than threaten you. Are you sure you want to keep pushing me?"

Yes. I am *absolutely positive* I want to keep pushing him. It's been exactly forty minutes since his lips were on mine. That means it's been forty minutes too long.

With the way everything happened when he drove me home after our date, how quickly he climbed across the seat, pressing himself into me until we were a tangled mess of hands and lips anywhere and everywhere, it's hard not to want to push him. Test the limits to his restraint and maybe even my own.

Turning in the seat, stretching my body across, watching as he sucks in a breath the minute my hands make contact with his leg, I grin and continue moving across until I'm pulling the lever and his seat is flying back, his body jolted and moving with it.

"Don't say I didn't warn you." He says before lifting his body up and wrapping his arms around my waist, gripping me tight and pulling me all the way over until my body is resting on top of his, the phone falling into the backseat and my lips landing roughly on his.

Ryder's intensity when we're alone used to scare me, but the more he shows me, the more I want of it. Ryder when he's unleashed is unlike anything or anyone I've ever experienced, and he awakens sensations in me I didn't even think were possible.

Like the way my body melts when he runs his hands down my back, the electric sparks that appear when he slides his tongue out of my mouth and runs it along my neck. The overwhelming desire I have to completely rip off every piece of clothing I'm wearing because I'm overheated and constricted when he arches his body into mine, teasing me with his arousal.

Twenty minutes is not going to be enough time.

"Fuck!" he growls, leaning up on the seat and pushing my butt into the steering column, the horn going off and my entire body freezing before I flush red. "Isaac, you need to move before I take this into the backseat."

Doesn't he get that the backseat is exactly what I want? With as easily as I felt the rub of his arousal against my own, I can't understand how what I want isn't completely obvious.

"Don't do that. Don't read into it."

What does he expect me to do? I can't handle this. I'm starting to think that there's something wrong with me. I want to be with him, my entire body, including my head, seems to scream for it every time I'm anywhere near him, but with him putting on the brakes so much, I'm starting to think it's wrong to want it.

That I'm wrong.

"Please look at me." He pleads, his hand coming up and cupping my cheek, my eyes locked on the way it looks, how soft it is against my skin even though the rest of him is so hard. The way a simple touch from him means so much and can get me to do anything he wants me to.

When I've finally lifted my eyes away from his hand and focused them completely on his, he sighs.

"I am not going to have our first time be in a fucking car. I want more than that. You deserve a hell of a lot more than that. It does not mean I don't want you. It's not you at all."

Leaning over him until I can feel the cold plastic of the phone in my grip, I lift it up and proceed to slide myself back over into the seat, making sure to keep my body closer to the door than him. If he doesn't want this happening, then the best thing for us right now is to keep our distance, even if it physically hurts me to do it.

It sure as hell feels like it's me.

"It. Is. Not. You." He spells out and the way he sounds turns my stomach. I'm not an idiot and him spelling everything out and treating me like I am makes me want to leave the car altogether.

Okay. Got it. You don't need to spell it out. I'm not an idiot.

"Wow. You really have no fucking clue, do you?"

Obviously not. Why don't you go ahead and spell it out for me?

"Isaac, I'm not going to say this again. You sit here and accuse me of being the one that has to ask the same fucking thing a million times before it sinks in, but you're doing the same damn thing right now."

It's not the same thing.

"Yes it is." He argues and I just roll my eyes which only aggravates him more. "You wanna know why I spelled it out? Because I'm trying to control myself. It's taking every single bit of strength and restraint I've got not to throw you down on the backseat and fuck you. I don't make love, Isaac. I fuck. I haven't done anything like this in years, but for you, I damn sure want to try."

Who said anything about love?

His face collapses once he catches the words on the screen and it twists me up inside. There is something seriously wrong with me right now. This is not me and now I'm making him pay for it.

"Well, if all you want is a quick fuck, strip and get in the back seat. The windows are tinted, no one will see us."

His voice is robotic, completely devoid of all feeling. I've heard him a lot of different ways during our time together, but never like this. I don't want what he's offering. I don't want it like that. I need to take back what I said. I need to erase the vacant and cold look in his eyes. It's too much.

I don't want that.

"Exactly." He whispers. "And I don't either. You are not a fuck and forget, Isaac. Stop trying to turn yourself into one."

That's not what I'm trying to do. I don't understand what's going on with me. I'm sorry.

"What's going on is, you want me and I get that. I want you too. I haven't had meaningful sex with someone in over two fucking years. I've spent the last two weeks having to get myself off every night, multiple times even, because of the intensity of what's going on here. No one understands what's going on with you better than me. I'm right there with you."

I'm sorry, Ryder.

"Don't apologize for wanting to be with me. It's crazy. That's the last thing you ever need to be sorry for. I just need you to understand that I want our first time to be special."

I do understand.

"Good, because Rachel's going to be here any minute. So before she gets here and I've got to go spend the next few hours learning shit I could care less about, can I kiss you? I'm not going to be able to leave this car until I do."

You shouldn't ask questions that you already have the answers to.

"That's a very smart thing to say and exactly why you're all the tutor I'm ever going to need."

Leaning across the seat, he keeps his eyes trained on me, making no effort to close them as his lips lower to mine softly. After a few seconds of our lips laying completely still, our eyes completely entranced with each other, he pushes himself back and points out the window behind me.

Turning and seeing Rachel standing a few feet back from the car, I frown. After the misunderstanding we just had and the way it was starting to feel coming down from it, the last thing I want to happen is for him to leave and me to go to class.

"I'll see you in a few hours." He whispers into my ear before brushing his lips against mine in another short yet tender kiss before turning and getting out of the car.

It's only when he's out and making his way over to where I see Rachel standing that my words from earlier and his pained expression come back to haunt me. I hurt him when I brought love into our misunderstanding and if I really want to make things right, I need to find a way to fix it.

Even if there's no way to fix it because my feelings are already carved in stone.

Ryder

Well, I can't say that's ever happened before.

Of all the things I've fought with people about, I can honestly say sex has never been one of them. It's also pretty unheard of that I was the one talking someone down from having it, when it's all my brain has been able to think about for days.

I'm torn up over this and I don't want to be. It's supposed to be easy. I want him. He wants me. We give in to the wanting and enjoy ourselves. Pretty simple right?

Not simple at all.

For two years I earned the nickname of campus whore, both here and in Toronto. I think there was even a part of me that sought it out. I'd gotten tired of giving into my impulses and fucking myself until I couldn't feel and started using women to do it. Release without feelings. It was perfect.

It's not perfect anymore. I want more. I need more, and for the first time since Gavin died, I think I can achieve it. I want to achieve it. I just don't think after what happened in the car, it's going to be possible.

Isaac's been living inside himself his entire life. He knew he was gay, but never acted on it because for a lot of us, acting on it means speaking or at least stepping out of a comfort zone long enough to put yourself out there and he didn't. So for years it's just been building inside him. What I could release with Gavin, he held onto until the dam finally broke and it all spilled out.

Being with me has changed him and now there's no holding back even when it takes him completely off guard and he has no idea how to adapt or control it. I understand because I've been there. It's exactly how it felt four years ago. I had absolutely no impulse control. I couldn't resist the urges. The temptation Gavin presented.

I'm Isaac's temptation and I'm getting tired of slamming on the fucking brakes. Maybe perfect for us is in the backseat of a car. What the hell do I know? I've been fucking to forget for the last two years. I have no idea what perfect even is.

No. I can't go there. I meant what I said to him. This needs to happen differently. He will not become like one of the girls to me. He won't even become Gavin. He needs to be the exception. He *is* the exception.

He's the one I want to change everything for.

"You don't really need me."

Right. I'm not alone. Rachel's here. Son of a bitch. Changing tutors didn't do shit. If anything I'm caught up in him more.

"What makes you say that?"

"Isaac gave me the work you've been doing with him. I'm looking over the test he gave you, and this is good work, Ryder. Whatever you had going on with Isaac was working. I don't need to be here."

She's right. She doesn't. He does, but I stupidly had to open my mouth so this is the situation I'm left with.

"Good enough to get back on the team, you think?"

"I'm not sure because I don't know how far behind you are. But based on the test Isaac gave you, I think it should be enough."

Hearing that there's a chance I could be back on the team based on the work she's looking at, it should make me happy. It's what I've been working toward this entire time, but I'm not happy at all.

I'm fucking empty.

The team, the games, even the guys, I don't give two shits about any of it.

All I care about is him.

"So what you're saying is that we're wasting our time here?"

"Pretty much."

That's all I need to hear. I tried changing things up. It doesn't work. If what she's saying is right and I'm pretty damn sure it is, then I need to end this.

I need to find my boyfriend and deal with all this internal shit before I lose my mind. Starting with the question he asked me that I can't get out of my head no matter how hard I try.

"So—uh, we're done here right?"

Nodding as she begins sliding her books back into her bag, I pick mine off the table and sling it across my back before mumbling a pathetic goodbye and ducking out of the room.

My place was never in that room with her. It was with him. The way we were in the car this morning before everything blew to shit, that's what I need. His humor, the playfulness; even his damn sarcastic undertone. All of it. All of him.

My tutor boy. My Isaac.

I just need him and it's about damn time I showed him how much.

Isaac

"Just the mute faggot we're looking for."

I can't say I didn't see this coming. Going from spending all of my time with Belle to appearing everywhere with Ryder, it was only a matter of time before people started talking.

Before the hate started spewing.

"Don't know why you even bother talking to him, Randy. You know he's not gonna answer." Bryan snickers and I resist the urge to roll my eyes.

Oh I'm answering you, jackass. I'm just not doing it in a way you can hear.

Turning away and attempting to get past them, not wanting any part of this or recreating what happened the last time they got me alone, I'm shaken when a hand comes out across my chest and pushes me back.

Guess I'm not going to get away after all.

"What is it about you, man? First, you manage to nail one of the hottest girls in class and now you've got Ryder so fucked up, he doesn't even know what team he's playing on anymore."

The way Bryan refers to me nailing Belle makes me sick. They're so ignorant that they've blinded themselves to reality. They really are meatheads. There's nothing upstairs at all. Brains have left the building.

It slips out before I can stop it and Randy reacts. Instead of standing in the middle of the hall the way I had been, I'm pushed hard up against the wall and there's a fist crashing into my ribs.

Bending over, my hands reacting to the violation by coming up over my chest, I hear them both start in again and it just twists me up even more than their physical response to my inadvertent smile did.

"Look Bry, the little faggot is bending over for you!"

"Fuck off, Randy." he snaps before turning his attention back to me. His shadow falling over my hunched position against the wall, his sick smirk all I'm able to see when I finally get the strength to look up. "This perverse little game you're playing with Ryder's head, it ends now. You hear me?"

Oh, I hear him loud and clear. His hate and ignorance is so strong it blocks everything else out. It's all I've been able to hear for the last four years. I'm just not going to let my fear of it and him win this time.

Shaking my head, making sure he knows beyond a shadow of a doubt what my answer to his question is, I attempt to lift my body back up, but am met with resistance in the form of hands slamming into me, keeping me locked in position as another fist slams into them, the only protection my stomach has from taking another hit.

Resisting the urge to crumple and feeling the blood rushing straight to my head, my own anger about to rise and get the better of me, I move my body forward, shoving it into them hard, hoping that the adrenaline running through me is enough to get me out of here.

Knocking Bryan back, taking him off guard with the sudden movement, I attempt to make use of the small sliver of space that's been afforded to me in order to run.

Stepping in my path, catching on to my movements before I've even had the chance to make them, Randy steps forward, a sick grin rising before his hand comes out and grips my neck, both of us moving until just like before, he's got me completely boxed in against the wall. His grip tightens, constricting the flow of air and blood to my head and where he had been clear a few seconds before, now all I can see is a hazy outline.

"Stay the fuck away from Kane. You want a dick in your ass so bad, I'm sure there's a million other faggots on campus that would be willing to give it to you. He's off limits."

Releasing the hold around my neck, he shoves his knee into my now uncovered stomach and I crumple to the floor, the only sound I hear Randy's nasally labored breaths and the loud thumping in my head as it connects with the wall.

The entire hall now nothing more than a sped up carousel, spinning faster and faster with no sign of stopping, I close my eyes as the nausea sets in and that's when I hear it.

A voice that even though it's angry sounds familiar.

The sounds of a scuffle block out the pounding of my heart and head. Focusing on the sound, needing to know if the voice I heard is really here and not just a figment of my imagination, I crack my eyes open.

Just out of reach on the other side of the hall, I can make out Randy, his body now looking a lot like mine, crumpled and broken on the floor with a very large imposing body standing over him.

It's not a figment. He's really here.

"If you ever," he pauses before leveling Randy with another kick to his stomach. "So much as look at him sideways or put your fucking hands on him again, a beating will be the least of your problems. You hear me, asshole?"

Another kick follows and I flinch, the sight of Randy's body being beaten the same way mine was more than I can take.

Backing off his teammate, he turns and his eyes find mine. In the time it takes me to blink, he's on top of me, wrapping his arms around my body, somehow sensing where the damage had been done and lifting me without putting pressure, all the while whispering the same two sentences, five words in total, over and over until they're all I can hear.

"I've got you. You're safe."

Chapter Twenty-Eight

Ryder

This is happening because of me. They're making him pay because I'm not who they thought I was.

This is all my fault.

They're beating on him the same way they did to Gavin.

He made the mistake of falling for me and it's costing him everything.

It won't be long now before it's Isaac lifeless in the car beside me.

I can't take much more of this. My mind is a mess. The back and forth blame game I'm playing strong enough to make the bile rise in my throat. It's also preventing me from looking at the other person in the car because I'm afraid of what I'm going to see when I do.

He has to know that this happened because of me. If I had never made a fucking move on him, this wouldn't be happening now. Those assholes might make fun of him the same way they always do, but they wouldn't be assaulting him.

"I'm taking you home."

Turning as I see him start to shake his head, our eyes finally connect and the look I see in them confuses me. He looks angry and frantic at the same time. Pulling out my phone even though he's got his backpack and could easily pull out paper, I slide it over and wait while he unlocks the screen and starts typing.

Please don't take me home. I don't want my mom to see me like this.

"If you don't wanna go home, where do you want to go?"

Back to class.

"Not happening. I'm not letting you go back in there. I caught a little of what Randy did. I should take you to the hospital."

Again he shakes his head and it frustrates me. This is not the time for him to be stubborn. The way Randy's hands were around his neck, it was fucking crazy. I know how strong he is, so there's no telling what kind of damage he did before I got there and ended it.

"Isaac, you're hurt."

I've been hurt before. It's fine.

"There was nothing about what I just walked in on that was fine."

Okay. It's not fine, but I don't want to go home and I don't need to go to the hospital.

"I'm taking you back to the apartment then. If you won't get yourself looked at, I at least wanna grab a couple of ice packs for your head, maybe even your ribs."

My head is fine.

"Humor me please?"

Fine.

When he looks up again, the frantic way he looked is gone, but the anger is still there. His eyes are hard and with the way he's been responding to me since I got him in the car, there's no other explanation for it. He's never been this clipped with me. This damn disconnected.

This isn't the Isaac I know at all.

"Isaac, talk to me."

I am talking to you.

"That's not what I mean and you know it. Tell me what's going on in your head. Why you look like you're gonna rip my head off any second. Tell me anything, just stop treating me like I'm one of the assholes that hurt you."

Something I said gets through as his eyes lower and soften. When he finally looks up again after a few seconds of his gaze being locked on the floor, all traces of the anger I saw are gone and he's acting like himself again.

I'm sorry. It's not you.

"I figured as much considering I didn't do anything."

When I'm in situations like that, boxed in with no way out; unable to speak, I lose control. I'm filled with so much anger that I can't even see straight. I'm sorry you had to see that.

"I'm not."

You're not?

"No Isaac, I'm not. I want to know everything about you, which includes the things you don't want me to see."

I don't want anyone seeing that side of me.

"I get that, but it's too late now. I've seen it and I can handle it, but promise me something?"

Anything.

"If it happens again, don't shut me out. Talk to me about it. Let me help you. It screwed me up enough seeing you on the floor. The last thing I want is you shutting me out."

I promise.

"Good."

Leaning over him, I push the release for his seat until it's far enough back for him to stretch out comfortably. Bringing myself back up, I pull his seatbelt over him, locking it in place before moving in closer and kissing him softly.

"Do me another favor?"

Sure.

"Lay back and rest while I drive us back to my place?"

Slipping the phone into my outstretched hand, he gives me all the answer I need when he turns his head away and allows his eyes to close. It's nothing major, but the way he does what I ask so easily finally gives my heart the reprieve it's been craving.

I might have gotten there too late to stop him from getting hurt, but having him here now, about to bring him back to my apartment where I'm going to spend the next few hours taking care of him, it's helping to erase the guilt I feel inside.

What I told him before, I meant it. He's safe with me. I'm going to do whatever it takes to make sure that what happened today never happens again.

No one touches someone I care about and gets out alive. No one.

Isaac

There are times in your life where your ability to remember is a curse. This is one of those times.

The last time I was here, Dillon brought me along on his search for Ryder. At the time I thought he was doing it because he felt bad for me. With everything that's happened since, I see it for what it really was. Dillon saw what Ryder and I didn't. What we couldn't because we were too blinded by our already made up minds.

We walked in and caught Ryder with a girl. The image of them both, the stunned yet shame filled expression on his face and the satisfied smirk on hers, it's the first thing I see when I walk in after him now.

I've never wanted to curse my memory more. Most people would have been able to get over this, but not me. I've got a memory for detail and for putting those details together visually until it creates a complete picture, and the picture I'm seeing now, I'm haunted by.

"Isaac, are you alright?"

Hearing the question, acutely aware of the concern laced through it, I nod, which judging from the way he spins around, grabs my face and pulls it up until there's nowhere to look but straight at him, he doesn't believe for a second.

"I don't believe you, but because I want to get you resting on the sofa with an ice pack, I'm gonna give you a chance to come up with a better answer. Come on."

Grabbing my hand and leading me into the living room, I make it about halfway in before the pressure is too much. The images I have of the last time I was here and exactly what happened on the sofa are too vivid. I can't take another step.

"Okay, maybe we're not curbing this until later." Slipping his phone out and handing it over, he releases my hand and crosses his arms across his chest while he waits for me to tell him why I'm acting like a crazy person.

I can't sit there.

"Okay. You wanna explain why?"

The last time I was here. I just...I can't sit there.

Realization dawns and I'm thankful. If he's catching on this soon it means I won't have to physically go through the motions of bringing the visuals in my head to life.

"Fuck, I forgot. Yeah, um—I don't want you sitting there either."

Pulling away and heading into the kitchen, he opens the freezer, grabs out two ice packs and comes back, handing them over to me before he motions in the direction of the hall.

"My bed. You can rest there."

This is how my mind works. With the visuals I have of the things he was doing on the sofa before Dillon and I walked in that day, it's not a far stretch for me to come up with even worse ones about the things he did to these girls in his own bed. Maybe being here wasn't such a good idea after all because with the way my mind is working, there isn't a place in here I'm going to find safe to lay down.

Have you taken girls in there before?

"Yeah," he sighs as he lowers his head and his shoulders begin to slump, his eyes even though I can't see them, I'm sure filled with shame and regret. "I have. I'm sorry."

I can't let him feel bad for this. It isn't his fault. It's mine. If the sofa is good enough for Dillon and Ryder to sit on even after everything that happened, then it has to be good enough for me. I need to let this go. He's my boyfriend now. That's what's important. What he did before me, it's none of my business.

Please don't be. Can I ask you for a favor?

"Name it."

Could I maybe get a blanket?

Leaning down and brushing his lips against my nose before rendering me speechless with one of his heart melting smiles, he turns and heads for the hallway closet, leaning in until he finds what he's looking for and is holding it up in the air in triumph.

"I can do you one better. I can give you *the best* blanket."

Moving around me, unfolding a sheet and laying it down across the cushion, he motions for me to lay down and when I do, he covers me with what he's referred to as the best blanket, taking a seat on the edge of the coffee table once he's content that I'm covered.

So why is this the best blanket?

"When I was six, I got really sick. I couldn't get out of bed for days, it was disgusting. My parents didn't seem to think it was anything serious, but my grandma was visiting at the time and she wouldn't leave my side. About three days into what I like to call Puke Fest 2001, she sat down on my bed and made me this blanket. I've kept it ever since."

I know the way Ryder feels about his parents, but the way he talks about his grandma, his entire face lighting up more vibrant then I think I've ever seen it, it's obvious he doesn't feel at all the same about her.

Did you puke on it?

Laughing as he catches me wiggling my eye between him and the blanket, he reaches over the space between us and rests his hand on mine.

"As a matter of fact, I didn't, but even if I did, it's been fourteen years. Pretty sure the puke would've been washed out by now."

Wanting to write him, but against moving my hand from under his in order to do it, I slide my left hand across the screen slowly until the question I want to ask is ready and waiting.

Will you lie with me?"

"Are you sure that's a good idea? Won't it be too tight a fit?"

His cheeks flush the minute it's out and I can't help grinning.

I'm not sure if it's a good idea. I've never done it before, but there's only one way to find out if I'm a fan of tight fits. ;)

"You are fucking amazing. Have I told you that lately?" he laughs before motioning with his hand for me to scoot over.

I think you just did. :P

Moving my body even closer to the inside and turning on my side, he slips his body down onto the sofa slowly before bringing his arm around me and pulling me into his chest, my head coming to rest on his heart, which I can feel is completely at peace since the beats are slow and steady.

"So are you a fan?"

I am. A *really big* fan. ;)

He laughs and the way it feels is kind of amazing. His entire chest shakes, but it's what's happening inside his chest that hits me the most. There's a low rumble as the laugh builds and it's almost as if there's a thunderstorm taking place inside him.

Ryder is the most fascinating person I've ever known.

"I really don't wanna be a buzzkill, but I need to ask this before I go out of my mind."

There's only one way he could ruin the moment, and I knew it was only a matter of time before it happened. He wants to know what happened before he got there.

Oh! Let me guess what you wanna ask. I'll even make it into a wager.

"We still have a bet on the table, Isaac. Are you sure you want to add another one to it?"

Absolutely.

"Name it."

If I'm right, you have to make one wish of mine come true.

"And if you're wrong?"

I have to do the same for you.

"You've got yourself a wager, tutor boy. What's your guess?"

You want to know what happened between Randy, Bryan and me before you got there. What they said, what they did, and how bad I'm hurt.

"That's not fair. The minute I said buzzkill you had to know it was about that!"

You might be right, but you still made the bet, which means you need to fulfill one wish of mine.

"Fine, but first you're going to tell me exactly what happened and don't try and sugarcoat it. I wanna know it all, even if you think it's nothing."

They cornered me outside of class. Called me some names. Same as usual, except this time because they know

about us, there were new ones added to it. They shoved me, punched me in the ribs and stomach and then threatened me about you. I think you know the rest.

He sucks in a breath once he's gotten through everything I've written and I can see his eyes going hard. He's not happy about what happened.

"I need to look at your ribs. They might need more than ice."

They're fine, Ryder. I'm okay, I promise. It hurts a lot less than last time.

"The last time?"

Why did I mention that? Now he's just going to get even angrier.

A few months ago they cornered me outside of class and said some things about Belle and me. They like her or want to get into her pants. Anyway, we fought.

"What do you mean you fought?"

I mean, I wasn't going to let them get the better of me. I don't like to fight, but I fought back. I might have gotten really hurt, but they didn't walk away easily.

"Son of a bitch! I swear to God, that's not going to happen anymore. It's done, even if I have to finish it myself."

It's okay. It's in the past. It's all in the past, even the stuff today. Can we please stop talking about it now?

"We can, but on one condition."

Name it.

"After you're done telling me your wish and I'm done making it come true, you're letting me take care of your ribs and not just with a piece of shit ice pack."

I'll meet your condition, Dr. Kane :)

"Doctor huh? Does that mean you approve of my bedside manner?"

I approve of it so much, I don't want to share it with anyone else.

Gripping onto me, keeping me in place as he shifts his body enough to be able to look at me, he brings his hand up under my chin and turns it until our gazes are focused solely on each other.

"You're never going to have to share any part of me that you don't want to. The same way that you're mine, I'm yours, Isaac. All yours."

Sliding his hand down until it's resting on my arm, he pulls it around his body before bringing his lips down on mine. The kiss is soft at first, until the sigh of breath escapes, and that's when he deepens it, sliding his tongue over my lips before slipping it inside, searching and probing until he coaxes my own tongue out of hiding.

It's the same kiss we shared on my own sofa right down to the overzealous heartbeat and the fire it brings to life in every pore of my body. The only difference is, this kiss, though intense, isn't filled with hunger. I was wrong before. He wasn't making love to my mouth when he kissed me that day.

He's doing it now.

"Tell me what your wish is." he whispers before pulling my lips into his again.

Pressing his body closer into mine at the exact moment I gravitate toward his in order to do the same, I inhale sharply at the unwanted pain that shoots through my chest and Ryder pulls back.

"Are you alright?"

Nodding and using the hand still delicately wrapped around his back to pull him back into me, I slide my other one out from where it's nestled between both of our bodies and slide it down until I'm gripping his thigh, putting enough pressure to make his body arch even more into me as a rough moan escapes.

"Isaac...your wish. I *need* to know."

His leg now sliding over mine, the bend in his knee running up and down in slow movements, causing me to move into him and making him feel the full effect of what he's doing to me, elicits another moan, this time more tortured.

Sliding his hand down my side until I feel him brush ever so softly across the outside of my leg, he doesn't stop. He continues to move it down, his hands no longer stroking gently, but massaging until I can feel his fingers brushing against my erection, bringing all of the heat that's filling my body rushing down until it's all pooling around the place where his hand lingers.

Our lips connected, our tongues continuing to push and taste in an intense tug of war, we continue to feel with our hands until we're no longer kissing, but panting against each other, his own bulge now being rubbed and stroked and massaged by my hand.

"Fuck—Isaac, I can't." he pauses, pulling his lips away from mine and burying his face completely into my neck, pulling on my skin with his teeth before beginning to suck, a noise that sounds like a strangled moan escaping through my own lips the harder he sucks.

"I don't want to stop, but you're hurt." He whispers hoarsely. "We need to stop."

Shaking my head, I hear what sounds like a groan mixed with a sigh and I feel his hand slide off of my body, the pool of heat being pulled away with him, moving it around until it finds what it's searching for and he's bringing it up in front of us.

"Tell me what your wish is before I completely lose what's left of my self-control and take you right here."

With my hands trembling under the intensity of his stare, I unlock the screen and begin to type.

My wish, it's you.

I want to be with you, Ryder. I'm ready.

"Fuck." He swears through clenched teeth before tossing the phone over his shoulder onto the table behind us and sliding his hand back down to my body until he's rubbing me again. As both of our bodies start to grind into each other, our breathing rapid, our lips crashing into each other as the hunger finally takes over, he completely penetrates me with his tongue before pulling back long enough to bring those lips around until they're resting next to my ear.

"Your wish is my command."

Chapter Twenty-Nine

Ryder

I want to be with you, Ryder. I'm ready.

Every fuck and forget, all of the running, the pull I felt from the moment I looked at him from the door of the conference room, all of it has been leading me to this moment.

It was always meant to be him. Always Isaac.

"I know what I said out there, but you still have time to change your mind. I'll wait as long as you need me to. All you have to do is say the word."

I'm saying this more for me than him. After what he endured earlier, and the pain he's in, I'm still not sure this is right. He can tell me that he's ready all he wants. That he can handle what's about to happen here, but he has no clue.

I want this to be perfect for him, but the way I want him right now, the absolutely earth shattering need inside of me to take him, fill him, I can't promise perfection. All I can promise is everything I have.

"Are you sure?"

The rise and fall of his head, assuring me with a nod that this is exactly what he wants doesn't even get a chance to finish before my hands are on his face, my body pressing tightly to his, our lips crashing together. Isaac's meeting mine stroke for stroke as my hands find their way around to his back, gripping him tightly, allowing myself the selfish pleasure of feeling him.

His touch, the way his hands feel when they finally make contact with my body, sliding from their place around my neck until they're much lower on my back, it's tentative, nervous, but still unlike anything I've ever experienced before. Each brush of his hand across the back of my shirt as he pulls it away from its snug place in my jeans, is electrifying.

The same way I heard him the night we kissed at his house is happening again as the faintest trace of a sigh escapes the minute my shirt is freed and his hands have finally gotten their reward as they run across my bare skin.

I need to get him on the bed, off of his feet and as comfortable as possible. I can't respond to this the way my body wants me to, or what's about to happen will only end in pain.

"Bed, Isaac. I need to get you on the bed."

Understanding my request, he begins to move backward, fully prepared to lower himself down, but before he can do it, I reach out and grab the ends of his shirt and start lifting until it's rising completely over his head and falling to the floor.

Getting the briefest feel of his skin under my fingertips before he lowers himself down, is pure torture for me. I need more than a second. I need minutes, hours and days of feeling his skin.

Moving closer to where he's seated, I attempt to push him back gently, but he blocks me before I can. His inexperience no longer an issue as he pulls at my shirt the same way I did with his, lifting it off until it's lying on top of his on the floor.

Sliding his hand down my chest slowly, he hooks one finger into the belt loop of my jeans and pulls me to him, our bodies crashing together until he's falling back onto the bed, me coming with him until the entire weight of my body is pressed down on top of him. Shifting his body, flinching, I immediately move off and search his eyes.

"Are you okay? Did I hurt you?"

He nods and then shakes his head, answering both questions and I don't hide my relief, thanking God under my breath, which earns me a crooked little grin before his hands lift up from their place on the bed and find their way to the button of my jeans again.

"Easy, tutor boy. We'll get there, I promise. We will *so* get there, but right now I want to focus on you."

I can tell he's confused and I want to ease it, but I'm not sure anything I say will do it. I'm going to have to show him.

Lifting my body completely off of his, I motion backward with a smile. "Scoot back on the bed until your head is on my pillow. Close your eyes and trust me."

Sliding his body back slowly until his head is resting exactly where I want it, I watch as his eyelids lower completely and the faint outline of a smile appears on his lips, letting me know he's still with me.

Sliding myself up beside him, my face level with his chest, I begin kissing. Starting at the left and kissing over to the right, tracing every inch of his bare skin with the feel of my lips, savoring the taste of his heated skin on my tongue as I run swirls all the way down until my chin brushes up against the tip of his pants. Resting one hand on his thigh while I focus attention on slipping the button from its hole and pulling his zipper down, I hear his breath catch.

Stopping long enough for my eyes to find his face, I keep my gaze centered on his closed eyes and relaxed features as I put my hands back on task, sliding them into his waistband, slipping them down slowly, his body moving with mine, lifting into the air until I've gotten them all the way down to their resting place on the floor.

Repeating the same motion with his boxers until they linger around his ankles, I hook my foot in them and pull them the rest of the way off, sliding my body back up onto the bed and running my eyes from his face all the way down, my gaze lingering on his very hard reaction to my hands on his body. Mesmerized by the way it moves with every breath he takes, calling out to me with every involuntary twitch to be taken.

He's fucking beautiful.

Bringing my eyes back up to his face, reaching out and cupping his cheek, I lean over and kiss the edge of his lips before his head turns to mine.

"Baby?"

The name sounds foreign, almost awkward as it's spoken, but when his eyes flitter open and they find mine, their brightness matching the smile now playing on his lips, what was foreign becomes right.

"Keep your eyes open. I want you to see everything I'm doing. I want you to see me make love to you."

His lips part and he mouths one word with a dip of his head, showing me without a sound that he's asking a question.

He's questioning my use of the word love.

"Yes, baby." Repeating the name and again being surrounded by an overwhelming sense of rightness. "I'm going to make *love* to you. I want to use my mouth to *love* you."

He smiles wistfully and it threatens to shatter my heart. He's affected by what I've said and it's almost as powerful as what we're about to experience together.

His mouth opens again and this time, two words are formed and seeing them, I'm completely lost.

Love me.

I don't want to read into this. He could just be asking me to make love to him the way I intend to, but I can't help it. Right here in this moment I want him to mean them the way my heart believes.

He wants me to love him. Not his body, not his sex. Him.

"I do, Isaac." My voice wavers and cracks from the weight of the truth as three more words rise to the surface and fall. "I love you."

Isaac

Ryder loves me.

No. That can't be right. I had to have heard that wrong. He's just talking about sex, using a nicer word for it. He can't mean it the way it sounds. He just can't.

Not when there's no way I can say it back. Not when I wanted to be the one to say it first.

I'm lightheaded. I need to breathe. I don't think I've taken a breath since he said it. Since those six words burrowed their way into my head first until they spread all the way down to my heart, completely taking it over.

He's giving me exactly what I wanted. Making this experience about love and not about the physical attraction. He's making my first time special, delivering on his promise of making it perfect.

I want to tell him this so bad. I need to tell him. Make him understand what this means to me. What he means to me. I need to tell him I love him. That I think my heart has been in love with his since the second his eyes met mine the day we met.

I've never wanted to talk so badly before. It's so intense, this need to get the words out that I can feel the tears building in the corners of my eyes, the frustration I have at not being able to do the simplest thing making my chest physically hurt.

"Isaac, was that too much?"

Oh God. It's getting worse now. I can hear the sad undertone in his voice, the one that's mixed with concern because he can totally see the tears threatening to fall. I can't let it happen this way. It's going to ruin everything.

Lifting my hand, motioning him to come closer, my entire body buzzing from the frantic need I have for him to be as close as possible, he does as I ask until his face is lying directly in front of mine.

"What is it? Do we need to stop?"

Shaking my head, determined to make him understand that us stopping is the very last thing I want, I reach my hand out until it's resting directly over his heart. With his eyes still trained on me, I open my mouth again, mouthing the words as I draw them at the same time across his heart.

I love you too.

They're falling now, my tears, but I don't do a thing to stop them. The relief that washes over me once I've gotten them out is so intense it's what causes them to fall and struggling to see through the wetness, I'm shocked to see that I'm not the only one.

There's a lone tear falling from Ryder's eyes too.

"I told you I would be able to hear you when you said it. Now I just need you to say it again."

Retracing the same movements over his chest, his body goes completely lax under my touch, moving closer until every part of us seems to be connected.

As his hand comes over mine, pressing it even more into his chest, I feel the erratic beat of his heart and lifting my eyes to his again, I see the reason for it. This is too much for him. Love is the one thing in the world that has the ability to break Ryder Kane.

He's given me the ability to break him.

"You did it."

Needing answers, but not sure how to ask for them, I trace a question mark on his chest and I'm rewarded when he laughs softly. Reaching out and running his hand along my face, he leans in and kisses me tenderly before speaking again and stopping my heart completely.

"You put me back together, Isaac. The untouched created the unbroken."

Ryder

I've thought about how this would happen a lot since our first date.

In the beginning, it was hard, passionate and raw. All I wanted was to bury myself inside him and fuck him until I couldn't feel anymore. Not because he was someone I wanted to fuck and forget, but because the need was too strong.

Over time, the way I wanted him changed, even though the intensity didn't. It was still so raw and needy in my head, but it wasn't rough anymore. I wanted my hands all over him, squeezing, massaging and rubbing every part of him. Softening him up before I gave myself to him completely.

It's the same way now. It's still all about him. What I want to give to him, not what I want to take.

Do I want to feel those perfect lips sliding over my dick as he coats me in wetness? Yes. I want it to so bad my body reacts to it even though it hasn't even happened yet. I crave the feel of his mouth on me almost as much as I do tasting him. I just don't need it as much as I thought I did in the beginning.

When I said I wanted him to see me make love to him, I meant it. Me giving him everything I have, especially after what we just admitted. How we feel about each other. I don't want to take, I just want to give, but he won't let me.

Instead of me being the one to make the first move, shift my body on top of his, start at his lips and work my way down, tasting and feeling every inch of him, he moves. It's slow at first, his body still feeling the effects of what happened earlier, but that quickly changes as he pushes his weight into me and I'm the one flat on my back.

His hands are the ones on my jeans now, making quick work of the button, sliding them down the same way I had done to him before, until he has me just the way he wants me and I'm completely bared to him.

I've spent this entire time wanting to take my time, savor the moment even though the hunger I have whenever I'm around him is as strong as ever. Being guided by it, seeing the way he's looking at me now, everything I feel reflected back at me in his desire filled eyes is earth shattering.

It's also hot. So fucking hot.

His tongue runs over his lips as he smiles, but not one like all his others. This one is playful yet devious and when he bites down on his bottom lip, his eyes rolling up into his head from the sheer pleasure the move gives him, I come completely unglued.

His hand reaches my dick first and even though he's never done it before, the way he wraps his hand around it tight, before using his other hand to rub over my balls, it's as if he's done this a million times before. The friction from his hand as he begins to rub up and down, the smile still playing across his features, it burns and the control I've been trying to keep, the restraint, it crumbles and I cry out.

Hearing my cry, he speeds up the movement of his hands, pushing me even farther while my body quakes and spasms underneath him. Shifting my body up, adding to what he's doing, craving more of the head to toe fire that's now burning its way through my body, he adds his mouth into the equation.

Softly at first, his wetness captures my head and after a few strokes of his tongue around the tip he pushes himself down further, his hand and his lips meeting in the middle and driving me absolutely crazy.

I want to stop him, because it was never supposed to be my pleasure forsaking his, but he won't let me. He just pushes himself even deeper until all I can feel is the wetness of his mouth and the strength of his hand.

It's been too long since I've been intimate with someone like this. I know it won't last long, and from the way his soft and trepid movements turn harder and more determined, I know that he doesn't want me to last long either.

He's stripping away every fucking layer I have, leaving me open before he begins to take those layers and put them back together, creating something new. He's showing me how he loves me in actions and it won't be long now before he feels the result of that love.

"Don't—stop. God, Isaac, don't stop."

I feel a vibration, like a low hum as he slides his mouth back up, his hand still moving in perfect sync with it, and it doesn't take long to realize the sound is from him. My silent love, the one I can hear without a word being spoken is as affected by this as I am. Tightening his hold, he pulls, brushing me with his teeth and making it better with strokes of his tongue until I can't take it anymore.

The fullness in my fucking balls is making them so damn tight and my dick so damn hard it feels like stone. I can't take it anymore, I need to give in.

Wrapping my hands around his head and arching my pelvis into him, I push my way deeper inside, thrusting over and over until I'm the one coating him. His mouth, his tongue. Giving him the only part of me he hasn't already stolen or completely owned.

My release.

Isaac

Intensity by definition is a high or extreme degree of a particular emotion or experience. Desire, a strong feeling of wanting or wishing to have something.

When these two things are put together, they create what has been happening between me and Ryder for weeks. An intense desire which seems to switch gears until it's no longer a want but a life altering, earth shattering need.

It's that need that makes it impossible for me to play by his rules. What started out as me wanting to let him control the situation changes after what he revealed, what the words meant for him and the way they impact me.

I had to have him even if I didn't have the first clue what I was doing. Needed to feel his flesh under my hands, be surrounded by the sounds of his pleasure as I taste him. It was supposed to be awkward, my hands not knowing where to go, what to touch first, how to taste him properly, but it wasn't like that at all.

He was guiding me even if he wasn't aware of it. The movements his body would make with each touch of my hand and stroke of my tongue, they fed into my need until I was lost in my own arousal at being able to pleasure him this way. Being able to release what's been pushed down, pent up and avoided for weeks. It gave me a confidence I didn't even know I had.

Controlling someone's emotional and physical response is intoxicating and it has the ability to push every other thought into the background in favor of having the entire focus placed on it alone.

For the first time, I took control and he didn't fight me. He let me make love to him.

"Baby, come here. I want you close."

His voice is weightless, which plays well against the curved position of his lips and the glazed over, almost drunk and sated look of his crystalized eyes. Ryder has never looked more enticing or more beautiful than he does right now.

Watching as his body moves rhythmically up on the bed, his legs spread apart, his arms coming out the same way, more than ready to welcome me into them, I waste no time crawling back up until they're wrapping around me, his hands on my skin still having the ability to scald me.

Resting his legs over me, his ankles trapping me in place, he pulls me back into his chest as his hands begin their slow descent down my arms, until they're glazing over my hands. Hooking his pinky around mine, he lets it linger for a moment before sliding it out and moving his hands down until they're lingering on the inside of my thigh.

His breath hot on my ear as he tightens his hold, kneading his hands as if I'm a piece of clay he's attempting to mold into shape, I lean back even more into his body as the sound of his words completely fills me.

"You don't know how badly I've wanted to be this way with you. How long I've craved it. I want to make you feel my love."

Rubbing into him as he continues to massage my thigh. He moans, biting back a curse as I match the speed of my body's movements with the ones of his hands.

"Isaac..."

Even now when he wants to be the one in control, making me feel the same level of pleasure I had given him, I can't let him. I still have to push myself, experience everything I've only been able to dream about in my most private moments over the last seven years.

His hand moves so quickly, wrapping itself around my throbbing hardness that the shock makes me inhale sharply, which only seems to push him even more.

As he begins to stroke me with both of his hands, one moving up as the other one around the head moves down, he attempts to speak, his struggle enhancing the pleasure I'm experiencing and making me relinquish the control as I give in to the way it feels.

"For days—weeks even, I've had these visions of what this moment would feel like. What it would feel like being buried tight and deep inside you. I've only got my hands on you and what I envisioned will never compare. This is so much better than any vision could ever be."

Leaning his body back onto the bed, cradling me closer, his hands move again and it feels as though I can feel him everywhere all at once. His one hand begins to stroke my hardness, while his other one moves and rubs itself over my body, starting with my inner thighs and moving up slowly until I can feel the rush of his touch on my stomach, chest and arms until it finally seems to rest on my neck, inches from where his lips are devouring me, the sting from his sucking and the pleasurable pain overpowering.

Seconds turn into minutes and the only sound able to break through my desire is Ryder's erratic breathing when his lips finally come up for air, focusing his attention on my pleasure by pumping his hand faster and then pausing, going slow and driving me crazy by continuing again at the same quickened pace.

The way this feels, I can't take it. It's too much. My body, it's pushing into his hand now, I'm bucking, using my body to plead with him for more. Answering the call, tightening the hold and moving even faster, my lips part and I feel the heavy vibrating hum of moan after moan as they pour out of my mouth, the first sound I've been able to voice in years.

"Yes, baby. Give in to what you're feeling."

What I'm feeling. Head to toe burning, a vice grip hold on my balls, the pressure of his hand on me so intense it's making it hard to think straight, let alone breathe. I need… I don't even know what I need, I just want the pressure to stop.

"I love you, Isaac."

The tender way he tells me he loves me, along with the now slowing pace of his hand, takes my body over the edge until all I can feel is overwhelming release, the bucking of my body finally slowing and evening out even though my heartbeat still threatens to break completely free of its place in my chest.

He continues to stroke me, his now damp hand sliding smoothly over me, the wetness my own. The result of his words, his touch and his love.

"Isaac—shit."

Moving and turning my body into his, the need for closeness almost as powerful as the pressure seconds before, he meets me halfway, his arms holding me tight, keeping me still, calming the racing in my heart as I burrow my face into his neck, not wanting to kiss or feel, just inhale the scent of him.

The scent of us.

"It's never—I've never…"

Ryder unable to find the words makes my heart swell. He's as affected by what we just shared as I am, and he's had more time to come down from the high I'm experiencing. It's almost as though with the way he's reacting, he's right there with me, step for step.

Tracing my fingers across his chest, this time on the opposite side as my head is now resting comfortably on his heart, I spell out the words I have never been so desperate to vocalize. His arms, relaxing, a sigh escaping the minute I'm done and he's felt them.

"I've never made love like that before."

That makes two of us. It makes what we just experienced that much more meaningful, finding out that even though Ryder has been with someone and isn't completely new to the experience of sex, he still feels as though this was a first.

It may even make me love him more.

"And, I love you too. I—It…" he pauses and lifting my head, catching the look in his eyes, it puts me at ease. Whatever he's struggling with telling me, it's nothing bad. His eyes are drowning in feeling. "It heals. Loving you, it's healing."

Pressing his lips into the top of my head, my eyes closing and reveling in the full impact of everything we've shared, there's only one thing in the moment that I wish could tell him that I can't.

Loving him is healing me too.

Chapter Thirty

Ryder

I'm back on the team.

English, Math and Political Science marks improved so much over the period Coach gave me that my exile from the team is officially over.

This should be celebration time, but because two little girls had to run their mouths about what I did to them, celebrating is the last thing I'm going to be doing.

"I'm going to be honest, Kane. I thought the next time I had you in this office, it would be because I needed to slam some sense into you again. I never thought it would be for this."

A few months ago I would have said the same thing. Taking out two of my teammates wasn't even on my radar, but that's because a few months ago I wasn't right in the head. I wasn't seeing the reality of the shit going on around me and even when I did see it, I didn't care. I also didn't see Isaac.

I definitely see him now and after what happened between us, what we shared and the way we feel, he's the only damn thing I want to see. Who I love is the reason I'm standing here now.

"You know how I feel about aggression off the field."

He's right. I do and until I walked in and saw those two beating on Isaac, I was the same way, but it's not like that anymore. You mess with what's mine and I'm going to come back harder and end you.

"Should I even bother explaining or have you already made up your mind?"

"I wouldn't have called you in if I didn't want to hear your side of things."

"Remember when you told me to find a tutor? Show up and keep showing up until someone paid enough attention to want to help me? Well, I did that."

"I'm well aware that you took our conversation to heart, Kane, but what does that have to do with took place between you and Davidson?"

"They attacked the person helping me. An innocent. I ended it."

"Come again?"

"Isaac Crawford is my tutor—well, he was."

"Does this have something to do with what we spoke about a few days ago?"

He grimaces when I nod.

"We're together. Not sure why the fuck I'm telling you that, but if you wanna know what really happened, you gotta know it all. My sexual orientation isn't a problem, you made that perfectly clear, but the guys don't feel the same and they made sure they drove the point home. They hurt Isaac to get to me."

When we're on the field, it's not uncommon for the older man to curse at us while we're running plays. Hearing it off the field though, it's practically unheard of. At least it was until now.

"How is he holding up?"

"He's fine, but if I didn't show up when I did, I would be telling you something different. Coach, I know how you feel about fighting, but that shit, I can't let it fly."

"Of course not."

When I got here, his face was warm, proud even, as he told me that my focus and hard work paid off and I was back on the team, but now it's different. I'm at risk of being kicked off again because I broke the rules in order to do the right thing.

"Do I need to clean out my locker?"

"No. I'm not happy about this, but if what you're telling me is the truth, you were justified doing what you did. You were defending someone. If I kicked you off the team for that, I might as well resign."

"What happens now?"

"I deal with O'Halloran and Davidson."

I know how I want to deal with them, but I get the feeling that's not what he's getting at. As much as I feel a solidarity to these guys because of the way we work together on the field, I can't help wishing that when Coach deals with them, he does it in a way that erases them forever.

After spending the night together, listening as he broke down and told me everything he's been through with them, Isaac needs them to be erased. He should know what it feels like to not look over his shoulder every other second.

Be free.

"Dealing with them is gonna be a hit to the team."

"I'm well aware, but that's not something you need to concern yourself with. All you need to do is be here for practice tomorrow and be prepared to play your ass off. I'll worry about the rest."

"I can definitely do that."

"It's good to have you back, Kane. The team was shit without you."

There was a time right after he booted my ass to the bench where I would have said I was shit without them too, but that's all changed. Being back, getting to play again, even after everything that happened with Bryan and Randy should put me over the fucking moon, but it doesn't.

Getting back on the team in the beginning was supposed to be the thing that fixed me. Made all the torn up shit inside me right. Gave me an outlet for all of the things I'd been running from. I'm right again, settled and even, but it's not because of the team or excitement at playing that did it.

It's all Isaac and with the way Coach calls out to me when I've turned to leave, it becomes pretty obvious that I'm not the only one who sees it.

"Kane, I know it's not my place to say this, but what you did for that boy, it was the right move. It says a lot about the kind of person you are. Your character. I just want to be sure moving ahead that you don't lose sight of that."

It might not be his place to say it, but it doesn't mean that I don't enjoy hearing it. Spending so much time believing I was a liability to everyone around me, it's nice to hear different. It's nice to hear I'm an asset.

"It might mean shit coming from an old codger like me, but you can't help who you love. No matter what happens next, how bad this gets, don't let it change that truth."

You can't help who you love.

He has no idea how right he is. How hard I fought against loving because all it ever brings is pain. How badly I still want to run because I know it's only a matter of time before history repeats itself and loving someone comes back to haunt me. How much I wish I could stop it, but can't because it just is.

"You? A codger? Never would have thought that about you."

"Wipe that shit eating grin off your face, boy, and respect your elders." He responds with a laugh before turning serious again. "It's nice to have you back, Ryder."

"What do you mean? I never left."

"You were here, but you weren't here. You get me? The version of you standing here, it's nice to finally meet him."

Well there's no confusion about what he's getting at now. There's also no denying it because he's right again. The guy that's been playing for him since he got here, it's what becomes of someone when they die. The person standing in the office now is what you get when you live.

"Yeah, I was thinking of keeping him around for a while."

"You do that." He laughs before coming out around the desk and patting me on the back. "Just make sure he doesn't take out any more of my players before Friday's game, would ya?"

Isaac

"So, I've got a very important question for my tutor." Ryder says as his hands brush gingerly across the back of my neck before he slides his body down on to the ground beside me.

Depending on the question, I might have an answer.

"I've also got one for my boyfriend, but the answers to both are going to have to wait because it's been way too long since I've done this."

Pushing his body closer into mine, he kisses me, parting my lips and sliding his tongue in effortlessly, a rough moan escaping from deep inside him as we connect, both of us needy and hungry and no longer trying to tame it.

If it's possible, the way we kiss since we admitted our feelings and slept together has intensified even more. Finally giving into the attraction and emotion between us is heightened instead of calmed, the way one expects when they surrender.

The separation, at least for me, is unbearable, making the moments when his lips are on mine even more significant.

"Mmm yes, that's much better." He sighs, his words so serene, they almost sound as though they're being purred instead of spoken.

It will be even better when we're alone and not surrounded by a campus full of people.

"You may be right about that, but the anticipation for that moment makes the struggle getting there worth it. I can be good—for now."

The way Ryder doesn't entirely back away from me, his face staying close and rubbing against my neck, his breath on my skin both tickling me and driving me crazy, centers my nervousness about being so public with our affection. His presence so powerful it envelopes me, making me feel safe and protected.

What if I said I didn't want you to be good?

"I'd suggest we blow off the rest of our classes and head back to my place. Finish what we started before I brought you home."

Any reminder of the way things were last night before he insisted on bringing me home turns my insides to liquid, the rush of it all landing squarely in one place, making his suggestion very tempting and almost impossible to resist.

Agreeing when Ryder insisted that we needed to take our time and not dive straight into anything more than just the feel of our hands and mouths on each other was hard. He's made mention a few times about picturing himself being buried inside me and with the way I can feed into his words, making the image come alive in my head; it makes me want to push for more. Until we've experienced everything together and made love in every way.

There you go, threatening me with a good time again.

"Only this time, I'll deliver." He whispers seductively before nipping my ear with his teeth.

It would be so easy right now to get off the grass and drag him across campus until we're in the backseat of his car, but I can't do that. We've already left enough since we got together. If we keep things going the way they have been, academic probation will be the least of our concerns.

What was your question for your tutor?

The struggle inside me changing the subject is as intense as the contact between us. My body is fighting a battle with my head, desperate to get its way and disappear with him instead of staying and doing things logically.

"Is the reward system still in effect?"

If you're going to ask for another date, No. That's something you ask your boyfriend, not your tutor.

"In that case, the answer's a yes because I'm not asking for a date."

Then what are you asking for?

"I need to know what kind of reward is given when I get back on the team."

Ryder back on the football team was always the end game here. I didn't want to admit it before, but I thought that when he accomplished that, he'd be gone. I never believed for a second he would be sitting here now asking me what reward he's earned by doing what I knew he always would from the start.

This is the moment I assumed I would wake up from the dream that the last few weeks have been, not continue it.

Anything you want. Your wish is my command.

"If you keep saying things like that, I won't *ask* you to come back to my place. I'll just take you there."

Promises, Promises.

"Keep that up and I'm not against taking you in the backseat of my car."

The stir that awakens inside, the absolute ache in my groin because of the visual his words create, I want nothing more than to act on it. Turn into him, push him back onto the grass and crawl on top of him, the rest of the world and the people that will see be damned.

Everything has definitely become more intense since last night. The nervous, shy and inexperienced Isaac no longer exists. In his place is an animal whose sole focus is when he will get to feed next. Ryder has no idea what he's created.

"Isaac, if you keep looking at the ground like that, we're not going to make it to the car. We'll be having another first together because I will take you right here for the world to see."

Breathe Isaac. Think logically. That can't happen.

What do you want for getting back on the team?

"I lied. I want a date, but it's a very specific date."

You've piqued my interest. What did you have in mind?

"The Roxy is playing a movie tonight and considering which one it is and what it means to me, it's important that we go together."

Before the bigger theaters moved in and stripped its business away to barely anything, the Roxy Theater was the place to be. I can bring up a lot of memories of being there with my family, but to have the chance to create new memories with Ryder makes it even better.

What's the movie?

"Iron Man."

If the idea was to switch gears so that I didn't focus on the things I want to do with him, it's failing. Knowing what Iron Man means to him, only makes the restraint I'm trying to exert, completely fall apart.

"Before you say yes, there's something else I want that goes with it."

Name it.

"I want to take you out for dinner first. Not some random casual fast food thing either. I don't want to take you to the mall and wine and dine you. I'm talking full on restaurant, with waiters and everything."

Dinner and a movie? Ryder, are you trying to seduce me?

"Yes. That is *exactly* what I'm doing. Is it working?"

It is.

"Good because there's more, but this isn't something you have to say yes to. I just really want you to."

The answer is already a yes, but because I'm curious, what else did you have in mind?

"Spend the entire night with me."

Let me refer you to my previous answer.

The rise to his lips is quick and vanishes in an instant, but not fast enough for me to miss it.

"This morning when I woke up, nothing felt right. I don't do lonely. I don't need a warm body in my bed in order to get through the night. I know I did a lot of stupid shit in that bed with people that didn't mean anything, but I didn't ever need them to stick around."

You don't need to explain. It's a yes, Ryder.

"I know I don't need to. I want to." Gripping my face in his hands, bringing his face as close as possible, he sighs. "I woke up to a cold empty bed this morning and there was this huge gaping piece of me missing. I don't want you staying the night because of sex. I want you to do it because when you do, you'll put the missing piece back together. It will make me whole."

The heart he's been keeping under strict lock and key, not allowing the world to catch even the slightest glimpse of, it's opening even more. The feeling of numbness that he coated himself in so that he could cope with everything he'd been through, it's defrosting. The Ryder that could only deal in the physical is as gone as the version of me.

We're both changing, but in the best way.

I'll do it on one condition.

"I thought you said it was a yes?" he laughs as he cocks his eyebrow up at me. "Your first answer is the one that counts. No conditions allowed."

Even if I can guarantee you'll like my condition?
"When you put it that way, name your condition, tutor boy."
Can the night begin now?

Ryder

Where the hell is he?

I knew I should have insisted on picking him up. If I had just put my foot down, made up some excuse about wanting to have my way with him before we went into the theater, I wouldn't be standing here like a chump now.

Texting him earlier, explaining that the only showing of the movie was earlier in the night then I thought and dinner would have to happen afterwards, he'd responded, letting me know it was okay and said he couldn't wait to see me. The time on that final message hours ago now.

This isn't like Isaac. He's always on time, if not early. The only time I managed to beat him to one of our sessions was when I slept like shit in the beginning and left to meet him. Otherwise he's always been there before me, waiting and ready.

The opposite of what's going on now.

I've been here for thirty minutes and even though I've seen a bunch of different people walking past the marquee, none of them have come anywhere near it and none of them have been him.

Isaac, where the hell are you?

After about twenty minutes of rocking back and forth against the wall while I waited for him to get here, I texted him, but that's not wielding the results I want either. It's like when I walked with him to class earlier, he completely vanished into thin air.

I've been trying to ignore the knot in my gut, the one that's been there ever since the accident with Gavin. It's the same as Isaac's bullshit detector, only mine ties me up when something is wrong. In the beginning I never paid it much attention, but after two years, it's hard to ignore how right it always is.

Something's not right.

Isaac not being here, it being so out of character for him, it means something's wrong.

I've never done this, never having a reason to, but I can't continue standing here like an idiot when one call could put an end to everything.

It hadn't happened at first, but not long after we got together, he gave me his home number. His reasoning at the time was that he didn't use his cell much so he had a habit of putting it down and forgetting where it was. If I wanted to reach him and the cell was getting me nowhere, I could call his house and his mom could let him know to text me.

It's what I've gotta do now. Fifteen minutes late I could easily ignore considering he had to take the bus to get here, but thirty, no way. I need answers.

Pulling out my phone, finding the number and pressing talk, I send up a silent prayer that the feeling in my gut is nothing and I'll find out he's just running late. There's also a part of me that wishes he would be the voice on the other end of the line even though I know it's impossible.

I'd give anything to hear Isaac speak, even if it was through a crappy telephone connection.

"Hello?"

"Mrs. Crawford? It's Ryder. Is Isaac there?"

"Ryder! No, he left about forty-five minutes ago to meet you. He told me not to expect him back tonight. Is he not there yet?"

The lump in my throat and the sickening knot in my stomach, it's ten times worse now.

"No. I've been here about thirty minutes, the movies about to start any second and he's nowhere to be found."

"I'm sure it's nothing, dear. It wouldn't be the first time he got on the bus and became so lost in what was going on around him that he missed his stop."

I wish I could look at it the same way as her, but with the shit I've been through, all I do is live on the worst case scenario. He didn't miss his stop.

Something bad happened.

"Yeah, that's probably it. Sorry for calling."

"Don't be sorry. It's nice to see someone that cares about Isaac as much as I do."

She has no idea just how much I care about him. She also has no idea how many sick scenarios I have running through my head about why he's not here. I need to fucking end this and find him.

"If you do hear from him, please tell him to text me."

"I have a feeling that he'll reach out to you first, but if he does contact me, I'll pass the message along."

Thanking her, ending the call and feeling like a supreme asshole for making the call to begin with when it's probably just going to make her worry, I toss it back in my pocket before giving the theater doors one final look.

The disappointment I expect to feel at not being able to recreate a pretty monumental moment in my life with him doesn't come. My brain won't let it. All I can focus on is the sick feeling inside. The one that says something is seriously fucking wrong.

I need to find him. I won't be okay until I do.

Chapter Thirty-One

Isaac

Someone slammed their hand down on the fast forward button of my life and they aren't letting up for anything. I need them to pull back, slow things down until they're normal speed because it's all happening so quickly, I can't keep up.

It didn't start out that way. The day started out perfect, especially the part where I made plans with Ryder for a date night that would last well into the morning. Everything was on regular speed then. Time moved the way it always does, even if I did feel that it was a little too slow this time around.

Coming home from school, spending time outside with the flowers I planted, allowing them to calm me the way they always do before heading inside to get ready, it was all very routine. Even explaining to my mom that Ryder wanted me to spend the night at his place and not to expect me back until the end of classes tomorrow went over the way I expected.

I packed a bag, made sure I had my phone and money for the bus and walked from the house with a confidence I'd always wished for, but had never been able to have. I had one solitary focus that left me unaware of everything else that might be going on around me.

Get to Ryder, be alone with him, let things go wherever they would lead and enjoy myself. Be like every other person on the planet and just live life in the moment instead of worrying about every little thing that might be hiding around the bend.

I never should have lost my focus.

I'm paying for it now.

Even now, I can still make out the bus stop, the plexi-glass shelter that would become my resting ground for the twenty plus minutes it would take for the bus to show up and take me to Ryder. The sky a mixture of sun and gray clouds above me, a combination of light and dark, rain and sun, fire and ice. The perfect manifestation of my emotional relationship with the college football player with the tainted past.

That's when someone hit fast forward, because every instance after that is a blur. One minute, I'm amazed at the cloud cover above me and the next all I see is darkness. The kind that filters into a bedroom without lights or windows at night. An almost suffocating blackness that if I had closed my eyes would have taken me under.

Voices come next. Five of them, two I recognize. All of them yelling things back and forth to each other before unleashing their words on me, informing me just what they have planned for me next.

Line after line, each one more sickening then the last, making my now overworked heart almost beat itself straight out of my chest.

"Get him into the van, Teddy. Quick, before we have company."

"Bry, he's a fucking toothpick! Just grab his legs and let's go!"

"He's a lot stronger than he looks, asshole! The fucker won't keep his legs still."

"Little mute faggot. You thought you were so smart."

"You're gonna pay for getting us kicked off the team."

"Consider this our gift to Kane. He won't be able to penetrate that ass for weeks after we're through with you."

I drown their words out, both with the tears that flow from my eyes and the focus I put into exactly what this is they're doing. What the payback to Ryder is supposed to be. The material rubbing into the skin on my arms, the friction is creates as they try and manipulate my body into the van they're talking about, I know it. It's wool.

My hands not trapped yet, I'm able to feel it and it doesn't take me long to figure out it's not clothes, but a blanket. Even though they have to realize I recognize their voices, they're still trying to hide themselves.

They really are as brainless as I thought.

One of the people with them, his name is Ted. He's another player on the team, but not one I know a lot about. Another mistake I made. I should have paid more attention to the people that were making my life hell. Maybe I could have seen this coming and prevented it.

I'm fighting back, struggling against the blanket, something they definitely don't like because fists pound into the small of my back, making me stumble, tripping on the ground below me. I can't let the pain stop me. I need to keep fighting. If I can struggle enough to get out from under this blanket, I might have a chance to end this.

The second hit to my back comes, followed up by a third and a fourth until not only do I feel the blanket over me, but the asphalt below me. I'm completely on the ground now, at their mercy and none of them waste a second.

There's the sound of a door sliding across and hands seemingly everywhere on me and before I can adapt, shove them off, somehow fight whatever's about to come next, I'm being lifted into the air until a few seconds later when it's falling hard onto what feels like carpet.

Rubber, followed up by what feels like hard metal slams into my legs, my back and my arms, repeating over and over in a cycle so quickly that trying to figure out what direction it's going to come from is pointless.

I'm trapped. They've got me right where they want me and along with their physical assault, they just keep repeating the same sickening lines about Ryder and what we share together.

There's rough movement in my throat, a groan or a moan, I'm not sure which and completely out of my control as my body just continues to react. My face is soaked and I want to lift my hands to wipe at my eyes, but I can't, their position under my now flat body making any movement impossible.

My vision is hazy and I know it's only a matter of time before the pounding in my head, and the pain spreading through my body as it's continuously assaulted by boots makes me pass out.

The forced darkness turning into a very real darkness.

Here in this van, separated from the people that love me and want to keep me protected, I'm almost positive I'm going to breathe my last breath. They're going to take it all from me until I'm nothing but a shell.

Until I'm dead.

"Since you were too fucking stupid to hear us the first time, maybe this will teach you. Stay the fuck away from Kane."

"You're a fucking stain on the world and we're here to erase it."

More kicks. More punches.

Wetness under my cheek. Vomit, not tears. I've thrown up from their brutality. They need to stop. I need this to slow down before it's a whole lot more than puke on the carpet of this van.

"He sounds like a deformed fucking animal. You hear that shit?" One of the voices I don't recognize says before cackling in laughter.

"I always knew he was faking."

"Hear that, you little fruit? We know your game now. You might be able to fool Kane and even that little slut Isabelle, but we know the truth. You're nothing but a fake."

They've lost their minds. How does my body reacting to an assault mean I'm a liar?

The haziness in my head, it's more powerful now. The voices are becoming muffled, making it hard to place who is saying what or even if they're saying anything to me at all. I can see spots in front of my eyes, growing bigger with every breath I take.

I need to sleep. Just close my eyes and sleep. Block this out completely. Let them finish with me until they cast me aside somewhere and I can figure out a way home. A way to move. A way to even breathe again if their plan is to leave me alive.

This is bad. I'm used to their words, what they believe about me, especially now that they know I'm gay, but it's never been this bad. Even the beating Randy and Bryan leveled on me because of Belle months ago was better than this.

I didn't feel like I was going to die then. I wanted to die, go home and never come out of my house again, but that was all internal. This time, it's all them and it's all physical. I'm fighting for my life and I'm losing.

"Do the world a fucking favor, Crawford. Just give up and die."

With the sounds of their grunting and laughing around me, along with the feel of their feet, knees and fists marking my entire body, I do exactly what they want me to do. I close my eyes, succumb to the darkness and give up.

Ryder

This not knowing. I can't take this shit.

It's been three hours since he was supposed to meet me at the Roxy and despite going everywhere both on campus and off trying to find him, I've got nothing.

I don't even know why the fuck I came back here. I just know I had to. If there was anywhere he would come if something happened, it was here. My apartment. My bedroom. Our oasis.

Except it's not much of an oasis now. It feels like a tight space where the walls are closing in and breathing is next to impossible. Empty and cold and completely devoid of the color he brought to it when he came here yesterday.

It feels the way it has every single day since we moved in. It's a place I can throw my body down at the end of every day and nothing more. A means to an end. A location on a map.

Fuck! I don't want it to feel like this. I want it to feel as alive as he makes me when we're together.

I need to find him. He needs to come back. He has to be okay. I don't know what I'm going to do if he's not.

"Have you called his mom back? Let her know that he still hasn't shown up anywhere?"

"Yeah, of course. I've been calling her nonstop for the last three hours. She's as freaked as I am now. Maybe even more. This isn't like him at all. Something fucking happened, Dill. I can feel it."

"Don't you dare do this! You hear me, Gav? Don't you dare leave me!"

It's happening again. I'm right back in the fucking car again, only it's not Gavin I'm begging not to leave. It's Isaac. It's happening just like I said it would and nothing anyone can say right now to make me see different will change it.

Isaac. My physically intoxicating, tender hearted tutor boy is out there somewhere, with god knows who, paying for my fucking selfishness.

Paying because I couldn't resist and had to give in. Want something I lost the right to deserve years ago. Out there missing, hurt, cold and alone. Somewhere I can't find him in order to help.

I'm completely fucking useless and he's paying the price for it.

"I know you're worried, but Ry, you need to calm down."

Confused, I throw him a look and follow as he motions to my body. He's right. I do need to calm down. I'm shaking. It's more than just the physical reaction, though. I need to chill out because I know what this means. It won't be long now before I completely check out and the past pulls me under.

"If for some reason I'm taken away from you, promise me you'll move on, Ry. That you won't feel the way I do right now. Mike not being here feels like someone has ripped a part of me away. I don't want that for you."

I feel myself crumble, my body falling, the sharp measure of pain that comes when my body finally makes contact with what I assume is the floor. Dillon yelling to me, saying what I think is my name, but the drum solo going off inside my head so intense that I can barely make it out.

The promise I made to Gavin the day of his funeral, it was the right one all along. The one he got me to make after losing his cousin, that's the one that was wrong. The one I never should have made.

Moving on and living again, it didn't stop what Gavin was trying to prevent for me. It only made it worse. Loving Isaac, allowing him to alter my perception, change my world and soften my heart, it's all wrong. It never should have happened.

"Jesus Christ, Ry!"

The shake in my body, it's full on convulsions now. I can feel the spasms, the movements no doubt exactly what Dillon is so freaked about as his hands grip my shoulders and he adds a shake of his own, attempting with everything he has to snap me out of it.

He's going to fail because this is worse than the other times. I'm not going to come out of it this time. Isaac not being here, Gavin being six feet under, it's all I can see. All I can feel. They're different, yet exactly the same because I caused them both. I'm the reason for all of this.

I don't want to come back from this. Maybe this time, I really can just slip away the way I've wanted to for the last two years. Make the world a better place by pulling myself out of it. Let the darkness finally do what it should have done in the car that night.

Kill me.

"Oh no you don't!" Dillon yells again, this time his hands no longer on my shoulders, but on my face. "You're not gonna do this shit again."

Even if I could speak, with the way his hands are gripping my face he's making it physically impossible, but the effort he's making, the force he's using to try and break me out of this, I want to grasp on to it. I just can't. The minute I do, he'll become another casualty.

There can't be any more of those.

"Ry," he sighs, the hardness to his voice gone as he sees my body begin to go lax under him. "Tell me what to do here because I have no fucking idea what I'm doing."

"You can't." I bark out the minute he releases his hold on my face, resting on his knees about a foot away from my slumped position on the floor. "You can't do anything. No one can."

"Where did you go?"

I'm going to tell him. I can't keep holding on to this shit the way I have been. It's not helping the way it did before. It's only making everything worse and now Dillon's catching the end result.

"The past. Always the past. Isaac is missing because of me. Gavin is dead because of me. It's all because of me!"

"You're losing me. Who is Gavin?"

"Someone I love. He died. I caused it. I cause everything. The blood, it's on my hands. It's always on my hands and no matter how hard I scrub, it never comes off."

I'm digging into my flesh. The friction from my hands as they rub together combined with my thoughts creating a physical response that I can't control. No amount of rubbing stops the pain.

I need him. I need Isaac. He's the only one that can break through this. Make it all stop. He's the only one that can heal the broken before the shards completely destroy me. I need Isaac to come back, be okay and say he'll never leave me again.

The way I wished Gavin would.

"It's off now, see?" Dillon says as he lifts my hands. "You got it all off. It's all clean, I promise."

The shakiness in his voice, the result of the confusion he has over what the hell is going on with me, it's all there crystal clear. Even though he has no idea what the fuck is going on, he's doing whatever he can in the moment to break through.

He's being a friend.

"Isaac..."

"We'll find him, Ry, I swear, but first I need to get you off the fucking floor. You're no use to him this way. You're gonna be no use to anyone."

Maneuvering his body around me and pulling with everything he's got, I use the small amount of strength I've got and move with him until I'm no longer on the floor, but on the sofa, his body crashing down onto the soft cushions beside me.

He's right. I'm no use to anyone. I haven't been useful to anyone for a really long time, but there was a point I'd gotten to over the last few days where I thought that maybe I was.

"Where did you look before you came here?"

"The library, Kayden and Belle's place, the bar I took him to on our first date. I even went to the park that his mom told me he likes to go for walks in. He wasn't there. He's nowhere. I'm starting to think I made him up."

"I can safely say that he's not a figment of your imagination, Ry. If he is then I'm just as fucked up as you are." He laughs and despite the emptiness inside me, I laugh too, only the sound of mine is forced and hollow because I don't feel it.

"His mom said he left around four to head to the bus. He insisted on meeting me at the theater instead of letting me pick him up the way I wanted to. I didn't push it. Dill, I should've pushed it."

"No man, you shouldn't have. Take it from someone who knows. If you forced it on him, it would have come back and bit you later on. You're focusing on his issues when you do that shit, not on the person he really is."

"It has nothing to do with his issues."

"Yeah man, it does. You know the shit that he's been through because he can't speak and you're worried sick. You want to protect him, but you can't. Not every second. At some point you have to let him live."

"Look what letting him live caused. He's gone, D. No one can find him."

There's no way he can argue. All I've done is state facts. Isaac is missing and just like it did this morning when I woke up, everything just feels empty without him. Not knowing anything, believing my boyfriend vanished into thin air or one of the other dozen scenarios that flash through my mind every few seconds, it's going to be the thing that kills me.

I want to let it, but not until I find him. Not until he's back and even if he's hurt, I know he's okay. He's still alive. I won't break, I won't let this kill me until that happens. I won't leave until I know he's safe.

Feeling the walls of the apartment shake, the heavy weight of something being dropped in the hallway so powerful it makes the floor under both of our feet vibrate, Dillon's attention goes right to the door before mine quickly follows.

We've heard a lot of different noises at all hours here since we moved in, but something about this one isn't like the other times. With the way Dillon jumps off the sofa and heads for the door, it's easy to see I'm not the only one thinking there's something not right about it.

"Jim say anything about someone new moving in next door?" I throw out as he reaches the door, laying his hand on the knob but turning his focus back on me in order to answer.

"No, but he did tell me he rented it out. Maybe they're getting a jump on shit and moving in early."

Hearing the crack of the door as Dillon pulls it open, I hear his sharp intake of breath first before it's quickly followed up with a string of curse words, ending only when he yells out louder than I've ever heard him.

One word. My name, and before I can even adjust my body to get off the sofa in order to find out what the fuck is going on, he does it again. Repeatedly yelling my name until I've made it all the way over to where he's kneeled and I see exactly what all the yelling was about.

Wrapped in a faded brown blanket, his head barely recognizable with the way the blanket blocks his face, the ends where his feet should be, tied together with what looks like some kind of fishing rope and his hands nowhere to be found, is Isaac.

Unable to take my eyes off his still form, Dillon now bending over in order to check on him, it happens again.

My entire world shatters and falls apart.

Chapter Thirty-Two

Ryder

A fucking blanket party.

Isaac didn't make our date because the pieces of shit I play ball with thought it would be funny to beat the ever living shit out of him with a hazing tactic even the military is sickened by.

It's never happened to me, but I know about it. A few of the guys put some of the freshman through it on my old team in Toronto. They ended up getting arrested for it, that's how fucked up it is.

Taking someone off guard, throwing a blanket over them, restraining their hands and legs so they can't mount a defense or do much of anything at all but take the punishment dished out.

It's a dickhead move, but it's not supposed to be life threatening. The way Isaac looked when we finally got him on my bed, stripping him of the blanket and restraints that were tightly bound around his legs, there was nothing mild about what he went through.

The guys in Toronto, they didn't look like him. They had noticeable marks, sure, but nothing remotely close to the way Isaac looked before I called his mom and Dillon took him to the hospital.

His body was so discolored, a mixture of purple from the bruising and red from the welts that were noticeable from his knees all the way down to his ankles. I was able to make out his normal skin tone, but the tender patches of peach were few and far between.

Isaac was completely destroyed. Broken.

Those assholes whipped and stomped him because of me. They didn't do it for initiation, a drunken thrill or some other equally stupid reason. They took all of their rage, hate and ignorance and put it on the one person in the world that didn't deserve it, all because of who he chose to love.

I don't care what Dillon said before he rode with Isaac to the hospital. I am going to make them pay for it. Before I leave tonight, distancing myself from Isaac and the horror I brought into his life by falling for him, I will end this. Once and for all.

~*~*~

"I know what you wanna do, but you need to stop and think about it, Ry."

There's nothing to fucking think about. I need to end them. Period. I warned Randy when I caught him with his hand around Isaac's throat. If he ever so much as looked at him again, I would end him. It's time to make that happen.

"They need to pay."

"Yeah, they do, but not like this. We need to go to the cops."

Is he kidding right now? What the hell are the cops going to do? I haven't even been here all that long and I know how this damn town works. All those assholes have to do is alibi each other and it will be their word against Isaac's. Not fucking happening.

"You go ahead and do that. In the meantime, I'm ending this."

"Ry, if you go off on them, it won't be them paying for this shit. It will be you."

"Don't care. This happened because of me. It's going to end because of me."

"You really think that's what Isaac wants?"

I damn well know it's not what he's going to want, but it's what has to happen. I don't give a shit what happens to me. As long as those dickheads get what they deserve, I'll take whatever I have coming.

It's about damn time I paid anyway.

"Come to the hospital, Ry. Be with him."

Dillon doesn't get it. He'll never get it because he doesn't know the truth. He doesn't know that the last place in the world I need to be right now is with Isaac. The farther away I am, the safer he is.

He'll stay alive, which is more than Gavin ever got.
For once, I'm going to do the right thing by someone.
"Not until I finish this."

~*~*~

My agreeing to be there ended the conversation. Dillon knew he wasn't going to be able to talk me out of what had to happen next so he didn't say another word until right before he left.

"Be careful."

The time for being careful and ignoring what's clearly going on around me, is over. The blinders are off. My goal is clear and nothing is going to stop me.

Randy and Bryan wanted Isaac to pay, well I want them to and I won't stop until one or both of them is so completely destroyed they'll never be able to hurt anyone else again.

Until they're as dead as I am. Inside and out.

Isaac

Every part of my body is in pain. Then there's darkness. Being lifted in the air and carried. A blank slate. More pain as my body hits the ground. More darkness. Dillon. Ryder.

A soft touch. Caring hands. Lips on my skin.

Ryder's, not Dillon's. The room spinning and then the loss of more time.

Bright flashing lights. An ambulance. Mention of a hospital. Another blank slate.

Opening my eyes. People talking around me. Words stringing together to make complete sentences that I can't decipher because everything hurts too much.

Ryder. I want Ryder.

I don't get him.

I get Dillon instead.

"It would be really fucking great if you people would stop doing this shit to me."

I have no idea what shit he's referring to, but right now I don't even care. All I want to do is push past this language barrier and ask him where Ryder is. Why his crystal blue eyes aren't the ones I'm waking up to.

I want those eyes. They'll stop the storm that's coming. The tears that are like rain, wanting to pour from my eyes as I relive what happened to me. The beating of my heart like thunder, crashing so loud and hard into my chest it makes breathing hard.

All I need is Ryder.

More voices. My mom, followed up by my dad and an unknown voice with a rough edge. White coat. Doctor. Right. I'm in the hospital.

Randy, Bryan, a guy named Teddy and two other people I don't know beat me so bad I ended up here.

"The x-rays show bruising to his ribs, which judging from the way it presents, had to have happened in the last twenty-four to forty-eight hours, but no other internal damage from the beating he suffered. I would like to keep him overnight for observation, but barring any complications, he's free to go in the morning."

The more time that passes, the more aware I become of exactly what's going on around me and the doctor's words set in. The attack at school, the one I went home and never talked to my parents about, it's not a secret anymore.

"Where the hell are the police?"

It's been a week since I saw my dad. With him always out of town for work, I've started forgetting the way he sounds. The stress in his voice is undeniable, as is the toll it's taking on his body. In the last two minutes alone he's run his hand through his hair a total of fifteen times, sometimes letting it linger and pulling on it.

He's the one that called the cops. I know it. He wants to make them all pay.

"Wayne, we've called them. They will get here when they get here. Until then, I think it's best if we try and remain calm. Isaac doesn't need to suffer any more than he already has."

The way they're standing around talking, it's like they don't even realize I'm wide awake and can hear every word. It's like I'm not even in the room at all. A painting on the wall. Insignificant.

Why can't they just stop talking about what happened to me and tell me what I really want to know.

Where the heck is Ryder?

Gripping the light blue sheet resting over me. I ball it up until I'm strangling it with my hands. Every breath I take pulls on those bruised ribs the doctor was talking about until I can hear the grunts building and escaping through my cracked and dry lips. The noise enough to get their attention off each other and back on me.

"It's okay, baby. We're here. You can relax now."

Her hand slips over mine, pulling at my fingers until the stranglehold I've got on the sheet is gone and my grip is now tightly wrapped up in hers.

"Wayne, get him some paper and a pen."

My dad disappears and even though I know it's pointless because Dillon won't understand my unspoken communication, I turn to him anyway, pleading with my eyes for answers that I know only he can give me.

I remember being in their apartment. Feeling Ryder's lips on my forehead and then on my lips, his voice low as he tried to soothe me while I dipped in and out of consciousness. Dillon was the one that carried me in. If anyone knows where Ryder is, he does and I need him to tell me.

I need it badly.

"He'll be here. He just needed to deal with something first."

Deal with something.

Even through the haze in my head I know what he means. He's telling me in the only way he can that Ryder isn't here because he's dealing with the people that did this.

He's going to hurt them. Make them pay.

The rain of tears, they're falling now, I can feel their streaks of wetness on my face as they trickle down, but make no move to stop them. I'm not crying for me or for anything I went through today. These tears are for Ryder.

Dillon doesn't need to be here. He needs to be wherever Ryder is right now. Stopping this. Making sure that he doesn't do something he's going to regret and end up taken away from me forever. If my dad would get back here with the damn paper, I'd be able to tell him that.

"What could possibly be more important than being here?"

The answer to that question is so simple, but it's not one Dillon or I want to answer. Even if I could speak, I wouldn't answer this because it would just make everything worse. I'm not going to get Ryder in any more trouble. He's going to do that enough on his own with what he thinks he has to do for me.

Avenge me.

Iron Man. Avenger. Protector. Fighter.

Oh god. I'm going to be sick.

Where is my dad with the paper?

Almost as if he's heard my silent cry, he comes through the door and beelines straight for the side of the bed closest to where Dillon is standing, hard as a stone, his face matching his body and giving away nothing.

The second my hand reaches out for the pen, I push past the pain I feel as I lift it and start writing across the page, bending it just enough so that my words, ones that I want only Dillon to see, aren't visible to my very overprotective parents.

I know what he's dealing with. You need to find them first. Stop him. Don't let him do this, Dillon.

Folding the paper up when he's done reading, he nods and slips it in his pocket. His understanding of what I need loud and clear.

"I'm gonna head outside and try calling Ryder again." He says to my parents before leaning down to me and speaking. "I won't come back until I've got him."

Turning to leave, his promise hanging in the air between us, I finally release the hold on my mom's hand and lean back onto the bed. With me being stuck here, Dillon's my only hope. I just have to rest now and hope that he finds Ryder before something really bad happens.

The untouched created the unbroken.

I need to make his revelation real. I can't let Ryder break again.

The guys on his team might have thought they broke me and what they did would keep me away, but they're wrong. I'm beaten down, but I'm not broken and if I have my way, when I get out of here, neither one of us will ever be broken again.

Ryder

Bruises. Tons of them. Cuts and other abrasions litter his body, a limp visible in his leg when he turns away from the door to let me in and his arm dangling at his side, like it's made out of rubber.

But none of that is what demands my focus. Calls to me so forcefully that I can't ignore it.

The blood does that.

Gavin is bleeding from his left eye.

"They got the jump on me. I didn't see them coming. Not even a sense that something was gonna happen until they landed the first hit into my spine."

The 'they' he's referring to are the guys on the team. My friends. People I thought I could trust. The ones I thought had my back.

We'd been dealing with the threats and sickening pictures for weeks. I'd had my clothes stolen, my tires slashed, my car spray painted with fucked up words, but until now, there hadn't been one move physically. Until now I thought the lack of physical altercation meant that they were just fucking with us.

I was wrong.

This wasn't the ignorant assholes on the basketball team that did this. It was my teammates. It's been them all along, but I was too blinded to see it. I can't believe what a fucking idiot I've been.

"You sure it was them?"

Even now I can't make my mind believe it.

"Yes, I'm sure. Adam, Ryan, Grant and Steven. They've spent a lot of time around us. I'd know their voices anywhere."

"Who cut you?" I demand, switching gears and getting down to what I really need answers for. I'll make all of those douchebags pay, but not before dealing with the one that marked his face.

"Adam. He said something about wanting to leave his mark behind. That when you saw it, you'd know that I was his bitch and be done with me."

He doesn't realize it, but Adam is a dead man walking. When I'm done with him, he's going to be the bitch. Mine. No one does what he did to Gavin and gets away with it.

No one touches what's mine.

"I'm taking you to the hospital."

He starts to argue and I shake my head, not willing to listen. It's a first for me, shutting down on Gavin this way, but I'm done hearing this shit. The time for listening is over. It's time to act.

"You need to be taken care of, Gav, and as much as I love your parents, that's not going to happen here. They can't treat this. You can barely fucking walk."

"It's fine. I just wanna lie down. Close my eyes and sleep."

"Not happening. You wanna sleep, you can do it there just as easily as here."

"Ryder."

"No, Gavin. I know you're acting like this because you don't want me to lose it, but this is a big fucking deal. So let's go. I'm taking you in."

"You're gonna go after them aren't you?"

Gripping his hand tight, walking him slowly out of the house and to my waiting car, I don't even wanna bother dignifying his question with a response, but because it's Gavin, I give him all I've got.

It's not an admission, but it is the truth and says everything that with the way the rage is building in me, needs to be said. I've made my point.

"They took it too far. They hurt what I love."

~*~*~

There's a form of static in my brain, like a snowy TV screen when the cable goes out, and as the remnants of my vision of Gavin fade away completely, it comes in vivid and bright again, only this time, it's Isaac I see and what happened to him, complete with surround sound.

The marks on his body, the brutality he suffered at the hands of another set of guys I didn't give enough credit to. I knew they were assholes, but I just never knew how big until now.

Randy, just like Bryan and the other guys on the team, they're creatures of habit. Routine. When they aren't on the field or blowing off classes, they're at the bar.

Getting wasted is almost like a rite of passage in Wexfield. It's what makes the boys into men. When there's nothing else to do, you do what you're presented with. I should know. I did it for months. Years if you count what happened before I left Toronto.

I've been outside this dingy hell hole for an hour now, watching from the window while the group of them get their party on like they didn't just fucking destroy an innocent person a few hours before. I bide my time while the anger stews inside, waiting for the moment when Randy takes his drunk ass off the bar stool and walks out through the doors I'm waiting on the side of.

To the moment when I'll make him feel exactly what Isaac feels.

The last time I was in a place like this, I had come across Adam and unloaded with my fists first before tiring myself out and moving to the full power of my legs until the guy couldn't even stand, much less walk.

If what happened to Adam was me taking things too far, I'm going straight to hell for what I'm planning to do to Randy.

Five on one is what Isaac had to deal with. It's what I have waiting for me, which means I'm bringing an equalizer. They might end up taking me out, but not before I take a few of them with me first.

Not trusting myself to drive meant that I had to walk and along the way, I found more than enough items littered across the side of the road. One in particular stood out and it's the feel of the steel in my hand now that guides me.

"I swear to you, man! With the way the fucker was grunting, you'd think we were pounding his ass or something. Fucking hilarious!"

Randy, just the way I want him. Moving his body through the doors without a care in the world, a sinister grin on his face, talking to someone, yet nobody standing beside him.

He's on the phone. He's alone.

The knowledge hits repeat in my brain and I lunge forward when the door finally slams shut, throwing the full weight of my body into his until I've tackled him to the ground.

Shifting my hands around when he starts to struggle, I bring his arms together and push the weight of my body down on his, forcing him to look straight up at me. Realize just who the fuck it is that's trapping him in.

The face of the last person he's ever going to see.

"Kane?"

The shock in the way he says my name makes me sick. He's going to act like he doesn't know why the hell I'm here.

Idiot.

Bucking his legs, attempting to throw me off, I push down harder, keeping one hand gripped around his hands while moving the other one up to his neck, laying pressure until I hear his struggle for breath.

Isaac's face might not have been hurt, but the breath sure had been beaten out of him with every punch and kick they leveled him with. It's time for him to get a clear view of what that feels like.

"You stupid—piece—of—shit." I snarl, my voice feral, my eyes no longer seeing Randy, but flashes of Isaac's broken body surrounded by a sea of red.

He's choking now, gasping for air and I don't bend. I just push down harder and watch as his eyes start to roll back into his head. The minute they start to shut, I release the hold and back off, not stopping until I'm standing and hovering over him.

I want him to stand. I want him to get the fuck up and come at me. Give me a reason to use the pipe I discarded at his side when I took him down, so I can beat him to hell and back with it.

I need it like an addict needs their next fix.

Running my hands up and down the piece of steel, my focus floats between Randy's body as he struggles to get back to his feet and the way my hands move smoothly up and down, simmering the blinding rage flowing through me.

When he finally gets to his feet, I'm on him again, first with a crack to the back of his spine, and when he crumples back to the dirt below, kicking him before bringing the pipe back up again and leveling him with hit after hit.

I attack every part of his body that even brushed against Isaac's, his injuries flooding my mind on a loop until Randy's cough breaks through and I see the dark stain flowing from his lips down to the ground.

A pool of crimson.

His blood.

Adam's blood.

Gavin's blood.

Isaac's blood.

The rustic smell mixes with the faint traces of car exhaust permeating the air around me, flowing into each other, tangling themselves around my rage until everything is such a blur, I can't tell where I end and Randy begins.

Lifting my leg, I repeatedly stomp my steel toed boot down into his back before moving over and doing the same to his chest, the pipe still in my hand, whispering its need to be used again.

Bringing it up and over my head, more than happy to give it exactly what it wants, I'm pulled backward by the tight grip of arms around my midsection. A hold so tight that no amount of struggle I mount can release it.

"Enough Ryder!"

Dillon.

What the hell is he doing here? Why isn't he at the hospital with Isaac? When did he get here? Has he been here the entire time? Is he in on this with them?

"Let me go!"

I can tell from the rumble in my throat that it's me screaming, but the sound of it is not me at all. It fluctuates between high and low, hard and soft and torn apart.

"Not on your fucking life. No one's going to jail today!"

Releasing the hold when he feels my body start to steady, he moves around me, making his way toward Randy's broken frame, but obviously thinking better of it turns back until he's facing me again.

"Don't fucking move, Ryder."

I hear his words, but I don't listen. I can't. The need inside me to see this asshole pay is too strong. I lunge forward again, but this time it's not Randy I take down. It's Dillon. If I want to finish what I started, and there's no doubt that I *have* to finish it, I can't do it with him in the way.

He's preventing me from ending this.

Where Randy hadn't seen it coming, there's something about the way Dillon hits the ground that tells me he did. He moves differently, and before I can subdue him, he's on top of me, leveling me with his own set of punches, some of which hit their mark when I can't get my body to shift fast enough.

"You had to make me do it again, you stupid, selfish, son of a bitch!"

"Get the fuck off me!"

When any attempt to move my legs to buck him off fails, my hands trapped under the weight of his position on top of me, I use the only tool I've got left. I slam my head forward until it knocks clear into his and sends him backwards.

"You shouldn't be here. You don't want to be involved. Get the fuck out of here!" I yell even though with the force of the head-butt I gave him, I have no idea if he's even coherent enough to hear me.

I mean it. He shouldn't be here. The only one that needs to pay for what I plan on doing to Randy is me. The way I should have paid two years ago.

The more things change, the more they stay the same.

With his hand on his head, Dillon struggles to his feet and the same rage inside me, it's all over his face now. His lips are curled into a snarl, his eyes are cold and vacant. He's no longer my roommate or best friend. He's an animal.

Just like me.

"Six years I spent going head to head with people even bigger and stronger than you. I'm not afraid to do it again. You want a fight so fucking badly, you've got one!"

Dillon's past. What he's spent the last almost two years trying to escape from and rise above, I'm pushing him right back into it now because I can't stop the turmoil inside me.

I want to take him out almost as badly as I do Randy and I know for a fact he didn't do shit, but talk me off the edge and save Isaac's life.

His fist connects with my face first and as I stumble backward, he comes at me again even harder than before, knocking the breath straight out of my body as he connects with my stomach.

"I promised your fucking boyfriend I'd bring you back to the hospital. It's your choice if it's on your own two feet or in a body bag!"

My boyfriend.

Isaac.

God. Even thinking his name hurts. I'm out here beating on Randy so hard that he's choking on his own blood, and going to head to head with someone I consider my best friend all because of what happened to him.

I'm going after the wrong people. They aren't the ones that need to pay for this.

I do.

Watching as Dillon bends over, his hands no longer balled into fists, but completely spread out over his knee, massaging it as he mutters curse words under his tongue, unaware that he's still loud enough for me to hear, it hits me.

It wasn't just Isaac that was in danger from me. Dillon was too. The damage I just did to his leg, knowing exactly what happened and what it cost him, proves it.

I need to get the fuck out of here. Away from him before I do something I'll never be able to take back. Moving forward, shoving into his shoulder as I pass, I hear him call out, but ignore it.

Turning and acknowledging him isn't an option anymore. If I want to do the right thing by everyone, it's gotta mean walking away. Going back to the scene of the crime. The place I never should have left to begin with.

It's time for me to go home.

Chapter Thirty-Three

Isaac

It's happening again.

Dillon's back, but Ryder is gone.

I didn't even need him to tell me, I felt it long before Dillon came back to the hospital that night. I think I've always known it would end this way. Even after he told me everything about his past, he was still running.

The difference between this time and all of the times he's done it before is, he didn't run alone.

He took my heart with him.

Where it used to rest is empty. Nothing more than a shell. A pumping organ with no beat. I've become nothing.

"I'm sorry, man. I tried. He came at me and I still tried to get through. Show him where he needed to be. He just wouldn't listen."

Of course he wouldn't listen. The wrong person was telling him. It wasn't supposed to come from Dillon. I thought his friend would have a better shot at the time because of his strength, his sheer determination and overwhelming need to do the right thing by the people he cares about. He was the best person because of what he had already lived through.

I was wrong. It was never meant to be Dillon that made Ryder see what's right. The truth. His very real purpose.

It was me.

Forty-eight hours have passed since Ryder walked away from Dillon outside some bar on the outskirts of town, headed for parts unknown. There hasn't been so much as one word spoken, either in text or a call to let any of us know he's alright.

There's just been me and Dillon putting our heads together and figuring him out.

When Ryder runs, it's always to one place.

Toronto.

It didn't take long after putting that together for us to find out that we were right, but that he wasn't just holed up somewhere drowning in himself. He was back home with his parents, attempting to again be the person they want him to be and not the person he's truly meant to be.

The person he was when he was with me.

I've seen Ryder alive. The way the light touches his eyes and he's surrounded by so much brightness it looks like he's soaring. That's the Ryder the world needs to see and with what I'm about to do now, I'm going to make sure before I'm done that they see it.

They see him.

It's my fault. I never should have sent you.

"You wanted me to stop him from doing something he would spend the rest of his life paying for. None of this is your fault. I'm just sorry I couldn't keep my promise."

It wasn't a promise you could keep. No one can control Ryder, but Ryder. I knew this. I'm glad that you stopped him, but what's gotta happen next, it has to come from me.

"Tell me what you need me to do."

Take me to his parents' house.

The look I get when he reads what I've written is exactly what I expect. Going to Ryder's parents, it's going to cause problems. It's just too bad that I don't care about the trouble it's going to cause because it's something that needs to be done.

The last time he ran, I swore that I wouldn't take it if he did it again and we weren't even together at the time. As much as I want to stick to that, I can't. He might not want to see me, distancing himself because he thinks it's the right thing to do, but that's not right. What's best for me is the way I feel when I'm with him. What we share. He can run and hide away from that all he wants, but I'm not going to.

I'm going to show him what it really means to fight for something.

"You do know what going there is going to do, right?"

I know and I don't care. I spent half the night working out what I wanted to say to him. I'm not walking away from this. It needs to happen.

"Well, damn. Guess there's not a whole lot I can say to talk you out of it."

There's nothing you can say. I'm tired of him running and I think deep down you are too.

"Understatement."

So will you take me?

"You know I will. All you gotta do is say when."

When.

Ryder

When you're cold and empty inside, some would say the worst place in the world for you is any physical location that mirrors it. Some people aren't me. There's no better place for me with the way I feel then here. The one house in the world completely absent of all feeling and emotion.

From the white coat of paint on the walls, to the perfectly placed paintings and other auction items my father indulged in for my mother, this house is nothing more than bricks on a shitty foundation in the ground. It's not a home or a safe place to land.

It's cold, empty and broken. Exactly like me.

In the months since I left, it might have been turned even more into a mausoleum. A place filled with nothing of substance or meaning, like the two people that live here.

Diane and Richard Kane are nothing more than wax figurines, their every expression painted on perfectly, with no margin for error.

I fucking hate this.

Being here never felt right when I was growing up, but it's even worse now. The location might be exactly what I need to feed what's going on inside me, but the people definitely aren't.

Especially when it's like no time has passed at all and the conversation I had with my old man six months ago is happening again, almost verbatim.

"I knew it was only a matter of time before you came back with your tail between your legs. How many times are you going to have to do this nonsense before the truth finally sticks?"

The truth.

My sexual orientation. How wrong it is.

I don't even fucking know how he figured it out, but with Richard Kane, it's always best not to question it. He just knows shit and there's no sense denying it. Maybe the destroyed look on my face did it. Maybe it was the disheveled and dirty look of my clothes when I landed here two days ago. Whatever it is, he knows and now he's going to make sure I'm aware of his beliefs on the subject.

How he believes me to be wrong.

A fuck up.

Nothing more than a stain on the roadmap of his life.

I wanted this when I got here. I came in expecting it. I almost craved it because it felt like in a way I was paying for all of the havoc I caused. Both in the past and now.

The difference this time, is that when he attacks me for being with another guy, he's attacking Isaac and that's something I can't let him do. I might have fucked up and he can attack me all he wants, but no way am I letting him do the same to him.

Isaac is innocent. Isaac is fucking everything.

"Not sure, Dad. I was thinking I might do it a few more times so I can see if the speech changes."

"It's apparent that you've been spending entirely too much time with the wrong kind of people. You know how I feel about that smart mouth."

Yeah. Okay. The reason I'm so combative is because I hang out with *'shady characters'* and the *'wrong kind of people'*. It has nothing at all to do with the robot that raised me. Well him and the stepford wife I got stuck with as my mother.

"Did you not learn anything from what happened with Gavin?"

Oh hell no. He's not going there. If Isaac is off limits, so is Gavin.

"Considering I spent the better part of two fucking years doing exactly what you taught me, I think you already have the answer to that."

"And what is it that you believe I taught you?"

"Besides what it feels like to be raised by people that aren't even your family, how about how to dip my stick in something that doesn't belong to me?"

"You watch your tongue, boy."

"Why, Dad? Did I hit a nerve? Too close to home for you? Does Mom even know what you do when you tell her you're working late?"

He's been doing this shit for years. It's half the reason fuck and forgets were so easy for me. I learned it all from him. Catching him in the pastor's office six years ago, the treasurer bent over with her skirt around her ankles, was a real eye opener.

Richard feels absolutely nothing for anyone. The pounding he gave that woman while he grunted and got off on top of her, like she was a useless piece of garbage he had to take out, drove the point home.

"You have no idea what you're talking about and this conversation isn't about your mother and me. It's about you."

Right. I need to stay on point because the God fearing man in front of me, the one that believes the sick shit he does is all in the name of the higher power, needs to remind me what a piece of shit I am because I fell in love with a guy.

"You need help, Ryder and this time, you're not leaving until you get it."

Fuck. We're definitely back in the same recycled conversation. He's bringing up conversion therapy again.

Because you know, reprogramming my brain will fix all of his problems.

"You couldn't force that shit on me two years ago. What makes you think you can now?"

"Because the minute you stepped through the door I placed a call."

Swallowing the anger and scanning around me, not sure what I'm expecting, but wanting to be prepared for whatever he's got planned for me next, my eyes fall on him as he does something I haven't seen him do since I was six.

The fucker is smiling at me. He thinks he's won.

Over my dead body. I don't care what call he made. I might be fucked in the head over what happened, still believing that me loving Gavin caused his death, but I'm not that far gone.

I don't want to jam my dick up in some girl in order to escape and be something I'm not anymore. I don't want to think about my dick at all. I just want a place to be so that I can wallow and die alone.

No therapy needed. No therapists telling me they want to help solve my issue so that I can be a productive member of society again. People painting me pretty pictures of a wife and kids instead of the very real image of one person in particular that I have filtering through my head.

The one person that despite running from him, still won't let me rest.

Turning as the door to the study opens, I see three bodies make their way in. Two male and one female and that's when I feel my dad's grip on my arm, stronger than it's ever been, scalding me with his need to see me changed. The hatred he has for who I am.

As the shadows move toward me, I shove into him until he's falling backward onto the leather sofa, and my body shifts in order to fight what I know is coming with the two closing in on me now.

No one is going to take me anywhere. I'll finish what I started on Randy if they even try.

Ducking out of the way of one while shoving the full weight of my body into the other, I race for the door, more than ready to shove past my own mother in order to get the fuck out of here.

It's only when I hear my dad call out for my mom to stop me and her voice screaming back at him that I freeze in place. The little stepford wife apparently has a backbone after all.

"Richard, I'm done! I've sat by and let you behave like an ignorant jackass for long enough!"

Turning to me, her eyes soft, she motions toward the door, her blue eyes showing an onslaught of emotions I never thought were possible for her.

"Go. Get out of here. I'll settle him down and make sure he doesn't follow. But Ryder, don't come back. This isn't your place anymore. It never was."

Isaac

This is a lot to take in.

Ryder never hid the fact that he came from money. The gifts he bought me the night of our first date spoke to it, but standing here now, looking up and seeing just how high in the air his childhood home goes, it doesn't even seem real.

Three times the size of my house, it reminds me of something you would see in Hollywood, not in a city like Toronto. I don't feel like I'm standing on the doorstep of an ordinary person, but a celebrity, and it just makes the doubts that were creeping in on the way here stronger.

Will I get lucky and Ryder will be the one answering the door, or am I going to get stuck trying to explain myself to his mom or dad?

I planned ahead of course. Made up a couple of note cards with explanations of who I was and what I was doing there, but standing here now, I'm wondering if it's going to be enough. As badly as I want to find him and bring him home, maybe I should have done it a different way.

Dillon is right. This is a very big risk that could end up causing more trouble for Ryder in the end.

Lifting my shaky hand and pressing the doorbell, lingering a few seconds longer than I intended and hearing the bell go off inside the house three times in succession, I slip back down off the top step and try to gain control of my breathing before the door swings open and the reality of my situation hits.

You can do this. Just focus on what he means to you. You'll be fine.

Focusing so intently on the pep talk I'm giving myself, repeating it over and over until it's no longer a pep talk but a mantra, I don't hear the door crack and open until the shadow of a person falls over me.

A woman, but not just any woman. One with the same crystalized blue eyes as the man I love.

Ryder's mother.

Holding up the card high enough so that she'll be able to read every word, even with the shaking in my hands getting worse, I step forward and wait her out, studying her expression as she reads.

Hello. My name is Isaac. I'm a friend of Ryder's from school. He was supposed to meet for a tutoring session this morning but didn't show up. I've talked to his Coach and some of his other friends and they haven't been able to locate him either. I was wondering if he was here and if so, may I have a few minutes to speak with him?

Her expression changes a total of three times as she reads my words. At first she displays confusion, obviously not understanding who the strange person on her doorstep is, but that quickly turns to understanding once her eyes have scanned over the first few lines. It's only when she reaches the end that they turn soft, reminding me of her son and when she raises them to look at me, they're knowing. Accepting.

She knows the truth and she wastes no time letting me know it.

"You're the one."

Nodding, she smiles weakly before taking a step toward me and shutting the door securely behind her.

"We'll be able to speak more freely out here."

There's a fear in her eyes, and it doesn't take me long to figure out why. What I'm unable to pick up on myself, she fills in the blanks for. The fear, it's not about Ryder. She's out on the step with me now because of the other person inside.

Her husband. Ryder's dad.

"He's not here. He left about thirty minutes ago. I wish I could tell you where he went, but I have no idea. I assume he is probably making his way back to school. There was an incident between him and my husband earlier. I felt it best that he leave."

Reaching up into my breast pocket and pulling out a pen, turning one of the cards over and leaning it over my knee, I start writing, hoping at the same time that when I'm done, she's still as open as she is right now and will tell me what I want to know.

What kind of incident? Is everything okay? Are you alright?

"I'm alright. It's not the first time this has happened and I'm sure it won't be the last. What's important is that Ryder not be the one experiencing it."

Pointing to my original question she sighs and my heart hurts. Whatever she's going to tell me, I know I'm not going to like it. It's something that hurt him, which means I'm hurting too.

"Ryder came home two days ago. After spending a couple of days sleeping off whatever it was that brought him here, he got into it with my husband. A phone call was placed and a fight ensued."

A fight. A phone call.

They wanted to erase the gay. Erase me.

His dad tried to send him away. Force his will on him and Ryder left again. I know for a fact that he didn't head back to school. If he wanted to be there, he never would have left in the first place, but it didn't leave me with a lot of places that he could be.

Where would he go in the city?

My mind instantly goes to Rosewood Gardens, but as quickly as it comes, I throw it out because with everything we shared there, the last place he's going to want to go is to a place that reminds him of what he's trying so desperately to forget.

"He isn't aware that I know, but before he moved to Wexfield, he spent a lot of time at Gavin's grave." She pauses and her eyes study me, I assume trying to figure out just how close Ryder and I are and if I know about Gavin. "I can take you there."

I don't mean any disrespect, Mrs. Kane, but with everything Ryder has said about you, why would you want to help me?

"Two years ago I watched my son die. He was still here walking and talking, but make no mistake, he was dead. The man I saw tonight, the determination in his eyes not to fall victim to his father the same way he had done in the past; the way we have both done, it wasn't at all the same. Isaac, he was alive and I think that has a lot to do with you. I saw it in your eyes the minute I opened the door."

Saw what?

"Your love for my son." Gripping my hand tightly in hers, she moves in closer, lowering her voice and squeezing. "I wasn't willing to see it before. I believed in everything his father said. I truly believed that the way Ryder was would end up costing him everything. When he walked away six months ago, I finally saw what he'd been fighting to tell me that night. He wasn't wrong, he was just different and I've spent every day since wishing he would come home so I could tell him how wrong I was."

"Isaac, I can't lose my son again."

Well that makes both of us. I can't lose her son either.

If I'm going to get through to Ryder, not only do I need the guy sitting in the car down the street, but I also need his mom. For the first time in two years, Ryder is finally going to see that what he's believed all this time is wrong. He's not alone and if I have my way, he never will be again.

You really want to help me find him?

"Yes, but I have one small condition."

What is it?

"When we leave here tonight, Ryder can't be the only one that never comes back. I need to do it too. It's time for things to change. Will you help me?"

If I can.

"Isaac, something tells me that you're the only one that can. You're the first person in two years that's cared enough to try."

Are you sure you want to do this?

I need to know before we take another step that her decision is final. If her admitting that she wants to reconnect with Ryder is real and not just a play in order to get him to come back so that they can trap him into something he doesn't want. Something he doesn't deserve.

"If it's a choice between my son and the monster on the other side of that door, it's always going to be Ryder. So yes, I'm sure. I want to bring my son home."

What she wants, it's the same thing I do. I want to bring Ryder home. To me. To Wexfield. To the family he should have had from the start.

I just hope we can do it before it's too late.

Ryder

Everything is exactly the way it was that night.

I've had exactly four shots of whiskey, the distant burn welcoming me back with open arms, missing me almost as much as I missed it during our time apart. I've got the perfect buzz now, giving me the ability to finally block what happened with Randy and my time with Isaac out of my head altogether. Well not really, but it is blocking it enough that when I do think about it, I feel nothing but numb.

Women move around me, running their hands over me as they pass, whispering the magic words that in the past would have had me off the stool and buried away in a bed with them, but now do nothing.

I'm not here for the women. I'm here to drink just enough so I can get behind the wheel of my car, drive past Gavin's house and make the day end the way it should have that night two years ago.

Wrapped around a telephone pole. My blood seeping out and falling on my hands. My broken neck. My end.

This is my gift to the world. I'm finally going to pay for the nightmare I created. I'm going to rid myself of the survivor's guilt once and for all. Join Gavin the way I was meant to. Free Isaac of the burden of being with someone like me. A person that destroys everything he touches. Everything he loves.

I'm going to give the world and everyone in it what they deserve.

Sliding off the stool, slapping the money down on the bar, the sum total plus a twenty dollar tip, I head for the door and what lies just behind it.

My death.

Chapter Thirty-Four

Ryder

I couldn't do it.

One fucking objective and I'm such a piece of shit screw-up, I couldn't even get that right.

Leaving the bar, I was supposed to get into my car and head for the same stretch of road that had cost me everything before. I was going to pretend that he was in the car with me, and I was teasing him the same way I did then. End up in the wrong lane, swerve at the last second and end up wrapped around the telephone pole.

Only this time, it wasn't going to be me staying alive. I was going to be the one dead.

I followed everything the same way as I did before, but when I swerved back out of the lane, I was able to right the car and now instead of being wrapped around the pole, I'm leaning up against it.

Still alive.

After the accident, a lot of people came around. They told my parents what a miracle it was that I had survived when Gavin hadn't been so lucky. They also spouted off a lot of bullshit about how it was God's plan. It was in those times that I started believing that this God everyone believes in was as fake as the Easter bunny or Santa Claus. It had to be that way because no real God would let me live and take the light away.

Miracles, luck and the power of prayer are all illusions. Pictures painted in an effort to keep the demons at bay. As long as people are believing in that, they can't focus on the reality of how shitty life really is.

They don't have to be me.

I haven't been in this exact spot since the night they air lifted both me and Gavin out of here. I found other ways to get where I was going if I had to pass this spot, sometimes even taking the long way around just because if I thought Gavin's grave was hard, this was worse.

Two ribbons are tied around the pole. I can also see that it's not even the same one anymore. It was replaced somewhere along the way, as what was brown in the past is now a light colored gray. The city is like me. They want the reminder of what happened here to die the same way I do.

Slap a fresh coat of paint on it and it will appear as though it never existed, and with me gone, I was pretty sure that's how it was. Until I saw the damn ribbons.

One blue and one white.

Memoriam colors, but also Gavin's favorites. Whoever has been out to this spot obviously misses him as much as I do. They don't want to forget. It also means they probably wish that I hadn't backed out on what I came here to do because maybe if I'm taken, Gavin can be brought back.

In a perfect world he would be.

Why me? Why did I have to be the one that wasn't like everyone else? Why couldn't I hold that girls hand when we were kids and fall in love the way the rest of the world does? Date different girls until finally finding the right one and settling down with a house and two point five kids? Why did I have to choose Gavin?

Why, even after everything that's happened, do I want to get in my car and drive back to Wexfield, break down whatever doors are in my way and just be with Isaac?

The accident killed Gavin. Not you.

"If for some reason I'm taken away from you, promise me you'll move on, Ry."

I'm so sick of making promises. I promised Gavin I would move on if something ever happened to him and then when it did, I promised him again that I wouldn't. I couldn't move on because when he died he took the best parts of me with him. I promised to be the kid my parents wanted, be the *right* fucking way and again, it all blew to shit.

All because of a boy that to the rest of the fucking world can't speak, but to me is louder than life.

Every single promise I've ever made, I've screwed up. I don't even know which one is the right one anymore. I don't know anything.

Cars have been moving past me the entire time I've been sitting here, but the one thing I've felt secure in is that none of them have stopped. They just keep moving forward to their destination, while I sit here stuck.

Except for one.

I hear it pull up, I can even make out the bumper as it pulls in closer and comes to a full stop. This car isn't moving and hearing a door open from my bent over position with my head in my knees, it closes and I can make out the faint trace of footsteps.

It's only when I look up, expecting to come face to face with a passerby that assumes I had car trouble or even a cop wanting me to move and finding neither that it all starts to make sense in my shredded and torn brain.

Another sign. One that this time tells me which promise is right and giving me the answer to the earlier question of why I wanted to head back to Wexfield, when I know that I'm better off where I am.

Isaac's here.

As another body moves from their place by the vehicle and comes to stand beside the guy I'm pretty sure is a figment of my imagination, my heart sinks. He's not alone, but the person he's with makes me wish he had never come at all.

Isaac

The entire ride to Toronto, Dillon didn't ask questions. He drove silently, every once in a while asking the odd question, but never pushing me to learn anything else. It became obvious quickly that while Ryder had opened up to him a bit, there were still a lot of blanks, but it wasn't going to be up to me to fill him in.

When Ryder's mom got in the car and we explained where we needed to go, he wasn't going to sit back and accept the scrapings of information we'd been giving him anymore. He wanted to know it all and fueled by my desire to find him, I told Dillon everything that I knew.

He's the reason we're standing here now. Dillon could think like Ryder better than I could. Put himself in my boyfriend's shoes and tell me with certainty where he though Ryder might have gone. With his mom's help, we located the accident site and sure enough, Dillon's little mind trick paid off.

Ryder's here and he's okay.

Pulling up and seeing his car so close to the pole made me sick inside. I know what happened here and I know the crippling hold it's had on him since. With as close as he's parked, barely any space at all between the front bumper and the pole, it's pretty obvious what he wanted to happen.

He came here to finish the job. What he thinks he started two years ago and there's only more evidence of that when I step close enough to breathe him in and smell nothing but alcohol.

I'm glad I wasn't too late.

"What the fuck is she doing here?"

Paper. I need paper if I'm going to be able to answer him. He knows this, but judging by the half smirk on his face, he doesn't care.

"Leave. Now."

Armed with something I can respond to, I shake my head and he leans forward before picking himself off the ground and standing, bridging the gap between us by taking one step, followed up by another until we're face to face.

His blue against my brown.

Darkness and light.

Relief versus shame and self-loathing.

"I know you're not deaf, but since you sure seem to want to act like it, let me say it again. Get the fuck out of here and take her with you. I don't want you here. I don't want you at all."

His words sting, but not enough to get me to back down. He's reacting to his mom being here, that's all. I know their relationship and I knew that it wouldn't be easy when they did come face to face again. I just need to push past the way my heart wants to react to his anger and finish what I started coming here.

Bringing him home.

"Ryder—"

"No. I'm not talking to you. I'm talking to him."

Remembering another method I can use to speak to him, I slip my phone out of my pocket and start typing. Getting out of the car, I left the pen and the notecards inside without a second thought. If it wasn't for this piece of metal I never cared much about before, I'd be screwed.

I'm not going anywhere, no matter what you say.

He grins and for the first time since I've known him, I'm scared. It's not a smile I've seen him give before. It's not even the one he had the day he took out Randy at school. It's like it's not even him at all.

"I was weak. I gave in and fucked you, but babe, you gotta move on. Run on back to Wexfield and live your pathetic little life. I gave you what you wanted. I'm done."

You're right.

"I know. So leave."

You are weak, but we are not done. You want to call me a fuck and forget, go ahead. Why not call me retarded, deaf mute or faggot while you're at it? It's not like I haven't heard them all, especially the last couple of weeks. Do it if it makes you feel better, but I'm not going anywhere.

The wall he's putting up. The cold *'you're nothing but a piece of shit'* attitude that he's trying to maintain in order to get his mom and me go away, it's pretty strong, but not as strong as me. With everything I've endured over the last few years, he could slam me into multiple walls and it wouldn't stop me.

There's a flicker in his eyes, one that gives me hope as he reads what I've said. He can think that the way he's acting is going to work, but he's going to be in for a rude awakening. It's two years in the making and nothing's going to stop me from delivering it.

Ryder needs a wakeup call.

Looking between the two of us, our stances tense, almost as if we're ready to go to battle, his mom turns to me, moving closer until she's squeezing my shoulder, calling my attention away from Ryder.

"I'm going to wait by the car. I think you'll have better luck if I'm not standing here. His issues are with me, not you."

There's no argument I can give for that because it's true. Had it been me alone that stepped from the car, I have a feeling the response wouldn't have been as cruel, but because it didn't happen that way, I was paying the price. She's right, I need to get him alone.

Nodding my acceptance, she walks away and I turn back to Ryder. The flicker from before, it's there again as his eyes are no longer cold and hard. They're softer, but still not the way I want them to be. He's still lost.

"You can't—be here."

Why not?

He's struggling. I can easily tell he doesn't mean the words, at least not in a way that is meant to hurt, but this spot for him is sacred. It's where he lost his first love. I'm invading a spot that I have no business being a part of and he's trying to warn me.

"Why are you with her?"

When I came to see you, she answered the door.

"Did she tell you how wrong I am?"

Shaking my head at the same time as I start typing a message, I don't stop doing it until I'm holding the phone out and he's facing the truth down.

No and even if she had told me that, I wouldn't have believed it. She told me how right you are and how wrong she's been for not seeing it. But I'm not here to talk about her.

"Then why are you here?"

I love you.

"Got a death wish, huh?"

What's that supposed to mean?

"You're standing in the very spot I killed the only other person I loved and you have to ask me that?"

You didn't kill Gavin, Ryder.

"He loved me. He knew I was a fucking mess and loved me anyway and how did I repay him? I made sure he was buried six feet under. You loved me the same fucking way and look what happened!"

I got hurt because of ignorance. Not because of you.

"Lies! It's all fucking lies. They beat the fucking hell out of you, threw you a god damned blanket party because of me!"

No. They did all of that because they don't understand differences. All they see is what they perceive as normal and anything that isn't that way deserves to be broken down until it changes or dies. They used YOU as the excuse for it. You were never the reason. Just the excuse.

"It doesn't change anything. I still destroy everything I fucking touch."

Now who's the liar? That's the pain talking, not you. If you destroyed everything you touch, then how am I standing here? How is Dillon driving me here in order to bring you home? The only person you're destroying is you and I can't let you do it anymore.

"Why do you care?"

I refer you to my earlier statement. I love you, Ryder. It doesn't shut off because you run away. It doesn't die because you want it to in order to protect me. You think you're destroying me, but loving you strengthens me. Heals the broken.

The untouched created the unbroken.

What he said to me the night we made love, it works both ways. He was as untouched as I was. He didn't let anyone get close, only taking what he needed and distancing himself again.

It might mean different things for us, but it doesn't make it any less true.

He created the unbroken the same way he believes I did that night. The way I need him to believe in again.

"Isaac..."

Ryder, I understand now. Please come back. Come home.

His eyes widen and he looks away, but not to the side or to me the way I expect. He looks up to the sky, his gaze lingering for a few minutes before he closes them and takes a deep breath. When he opens them again, they're on me, completely transfixed, lighter than they've ever been.

"What happens when you get hurt again?"

When that happens, I'll just tell my boyfriend and he'll beat the hell out of whoever it is that hurt me. :)

The response I want when I answer, he rewards me with as his mouth cracks open and lifts. Laughing and smiling at the same time.

"What happens if he's the reason for it?"

Then I threaten him with a good time. I know from experience that makes everything better.

"It really doesn't scare you, does it?

Lots of things scare me, but no, this doesn't because it's not real.

"What is real?"

We are. What I feel.

"What do you feel?"

I thought I already told you this.

"Humor me. I want to hear you say it again."

I love you, Ryder Kane.

"I love you too, but it scares me."

Because of what happened here? I write, motioning around, the place that was once a scene of horror, but is now glowing with brightness, lighting our way. A sign if there ever was one about just how right this is.

"Yeah. I don't want to lose you."

You won't.

"You can't say that. There's no guarantee and with my track record…"

Maybe you're right. Nothing is a guarantee, but as long as you're with me and we're in this together, both of us in one place, not running, I can guarantee I'm never leaving.

Your track record was erased the day I met you. It's time to write a new one and this time, make it permanent.

"You want to make this permanent?"

This. Us. We're already permanent. We've been that way before we even got together. He's been it for me from the moment he walked into our first tutoring session. The physical gripped me tightly, pulled me to him and his heart did the rest.

For me you already are.

"Why is my mom here, Isaac?"

She needs to start over too.

"How do you do it?"

Do what?

"See past all the bullshit. I run away every chance I get and you're here fighting to bring me home, loving me; even walking into the lion's den to do it. You spend a few minutes with her and believe in her. I just don't get how you do that. Why you don't cut your losses and give up."

I already told you the answer to that question before.

"Okay boyfriend, I think it's time you bring out my tutor boy, because I don't remember asking this and I definitely don't remember an answer."

You asked me when we met what I thought you deserved. The reason I don't cut my losses and walk away is the same as that.

"You said I deserved everything."

I did. But I also said something else. Do you remember or would you like me to remind you?

"Remind me."

If I give up and walk away, I'll never see if you get it.

"This new track record, the one you want me to make permanent, it's dependent on me getting everything. I don't want you to walk away, Isaac, because if you do then it won't happen at all."

Why do you say that?

"Because you are everything. That's what's so fucking scary. I want everything so bad. I want permanent. I want it all, but the last time I wanted something this bad, it was taken from me. I lost it. I can't lose it again, Isaac. I can't lose *everything*."

You won't. I promise.

His eyes close again and he takes another breath, but there's something different about him this time that wasn't there before. He's at peace. My promise, it's offered up the one thing in the moment that Ryder needs more than anything. Relief.

"Will you do a couple of things for me?"

Anything.

"Stay with me while I talk to my mom?"

Of course.

"There's something else. When I'm done talking to her, no matter what way it goes, I need you to come with me somewhere. It's another place that no one else has ever been, but one I think it's time I bring you to."

I'll go anywhere with you, Ryder.

"You have no idea how badly I wanted to hear you say that."

Where do you want to take me?

"There's someone I need to introduce you to."

He's being cryptic and it's confusing, but not in a stressful way. Whoever he wants to introduce me to, with the way he reaches out and pulls me into him, his heart beating in perfect sync with mine, it's obviously important to him.

I meant what I said, whoever it is, wherever it is, I'm with him. I'm all in.

Who?

"Gavin."

Chapter Thirty-Five

Ryder

Money changed my entire life.

It wasn't always like that. I never used to believe that before, but sitting with Isaac and listening to my mom open up about her life and the way it was before money came into it, well, I'm pretty sure that's when everything went to shit.

I like to think my dad would have been an asshole whether we were rich or poor, but because I didn't know him before the point where money and status became his entire life, it's something I'll never know. I'm never going to go back and ask.

My mom was right. I can't go back again. The only direction now is forward.

~*~*~

We've been sitting in this piece of shit coffee shop for twenty minutes and if it's possible, it's even more awkward then it was when we first walked in. I know what I promised Isaac before Dillon drove us all here, but I've got serious issues with this.

She's been the same damn way for twenty years, so her sudden change of heart, I can't believe in it.

The reassuring squeeze to my hand under the table as I face my mother down, though, that's what keeps my ass firmly planted here instead of back out in my car driving away.

I expect her to cut to chase. Explain to me what that shit earlier today was about, first stepping up for me with my dad and then doing whatever she could to help Isaac find me, but that's not at all what I get.

"I don't know how much you remember about the way things were when you were little, but it wasn't always like this. I was different. Even your father—Richard," she switches gears for the guy sitting to my right. *"Was different."*

We've been living in the same house in the same cookie cutter neighborhood for years, so what part of my childhood she's getting at is a mystery to me.

"When you were two, we lived in this two bedroom apartment in a really shady part of the city. We were both working. I had you sitting with a babysitter during the day, but no matter what we did, we could never get on solid ground. The power got shut off, bills were never paid on time and we even went a few months behind in our rent because making sure you had what you needed mattered more than the roof over our head."

This happening when I was two explains why I don't remember any of it. If things were as shitty as she's making them seem, I'm kind of glad I don't have the memories she does. I'm not a big fan of the money, but damn, maybe that change was a good one.

"When Richard finally brought up wanting to patent his idea and then ended up selling it, it was as if all of our hard work and prayers had been answered. We were out of the bad neighborhood with more money than we knew what to do with, and at the time I didn't see it, but that's when everything changed."

"Changed how?"

"Your dad started working longer hours and the decision was made that I stay home with you. Those hours turned into one affair after the other, but I didn't even care because all I cared about was the disconnection that seemed to take place between me and you. All those babysitters when I was working and then the staff we hired, that's where your loyalty was and somewhere along the way I stopped caring enough to try."

"When he was home, your father was angry, as disconnected from me as I was from you and everything started falling apart. It went on like that for years until we found the church."

The fucking church. Yeah. I know all about it. She made me go there for years until I finally told them I had enough and stopped *going. I had no issue with God, but I wasn't in the mood to spend an entire Sunday morning having someone else's belief system crammed down my throat. Not wanting to go though, it didn't change a damn thing with them.*

My parents became fanatical about it.

"He stopped the affairs, seemed more dedicated to me, and with their help we got involved with a lot of charities and organizations that pulled us both even farther away from where we should have been. With you. That was another mistake in a long list I was making at the time."

"Why are you telling me all this? What difference does it make now?"

"It makes a difference because I need you to understand the way things were. As much as you want me to understand and accept you, it's gotta work both ways."

If Isaac's hand squeezing mine as the tension rolls through me is any indication, he believes the same thing. I'm just not sure I can handle this walk down memory lane shit she's spewing. It doesn't go back and fix anything so I don't see a point.

"I became accustomed to a certain kind of life. Between the money and the prestige that came with being with a man like your father, I became lost in it and blind to everything going on around me. I knew the day you met Gavin that you were gay, I might have even known it before then, but because of what it would mean to our situation; the way everything would change, I remained silent."

"Yeah, until you told me that I was wrong and needed to be fixed. You sure weren't silent then."

She lowers her head to the table and having been down this road before, living with it for the last two years, I can spot what's going on with her a mile away. My mom is filled with guilt and shame.

"You weren't the one that needed to be fixed. That was me, but you're right. I wasn't silent about it. When your father said he knew people that could set you right and we wouldn't have to deal with the fallout that you coming out would bring, I followed him blindly."

"It really was all about your social status then?"

She nods and my stomach rolls. This is all shit I knew. It's not exactly like either one of them hid the way they were from me. It's also why I was closer to the staff than I was to her. Her loyalty was always to my asshole father.

"I'm not going to sit here and make excuses, Ryder, but a lot of my choices were centered on standing by your father because of what being by his side would mean for me in the long run. I didn't want to end up back in that apartment barely living."

"A cardboard box on the sidewalk would have been a better home then the one you gave me."

"I agree. It's too late for me to go back and change what happened, but I can sit here now and tell you that I want to make what happens next different. It's twenty years too late, but something's got to change."

"Change how?"

"What I said to you earlier, I meant it. I don't want you coming back to that house. At some point I'm going to have to in order to get what's needed to truly break free of Richard and his controlling ways, but I definitely don't want you there. You were right when you called it a mausoleum."

That's exactly what living there was like and my dad was the damn crypt keeper.

"So how does this sudden need to change involve me?"

"It doesn't, at least not in the way you seem to think. I just want to do what I should have done from the start. I want to put you and your happiness first. Even if it's at the expense of my own."

"Didn't figure you for a martyr, Mom."

Feeling the brush against my arm, I lower my eyes down to the phone laid out in the space between Isaac and me. His words on the screen, ones that he knows to be the truth, but my mom in all of the time she spent here storytelling never bothered to bring up.

I heard fighting when I got to your house earlier. She doesn't know I heard it, only that I saw what the fighting caused. Your dad is exactly like Randy.

A bully.

Isaac's telling me that my father has been using my mother as a punching bag. I knew he had the ability to act like a complete jackass when he didn't get his way, but knowing that he's been taking his frustration and disappointment about me out on her doesn't sit right with me. I don't want to have any sympathy for her, but seeing this, it's breaking me down.

"How long has he been taking his shit out on you?"

"Since you admitted you were gay. Richard has always thrived on one thing and in the beginning of our life together, I let him have it because it was easier. He needs the control, Ryder and when you went against his plan for you, he lost it."

"So he took it out on the only person that he still could control?"

"Exactly." She nods before lowering her head again. "If it kept him away from you, I would have let him do whatever he wanted to me. You can think that I didn't care, and for a lot of it, you're right, but that might have been the one damn thing I did get right. I kept you safe from it."

"If I hadn't run that night, would you have stopped him from sending me away?"

"Yes. As it turns out you made the decision for me, and again, I just fell back in to old routines. Especially when it seemed like after the accident, you became the exact same way as him."

"I am nothing like him."

"You were back then. I know it hurts to hear, but you were definitely his son during that time period, but for different reasons. Your father was that way by choice. Yours was the result of losing the only person that cared. It's only when I saw the two of you face to face today, and then Isaac showed up to bring you back that I saw the truth."

"Which is?"

"That Gavin wasn't the only one that cared about you anymore. When you stood face to face with your father, it wasn't just your will that made you stronger. It was love. What we tried to take away, you took it back."

~*~*~

I don't know where things will go with me and my mom. The way shit went down was wrong and even if I did feel bad for her at points while she recounted the past, there's still a hell of a lot of resentment inside and until I can resolve that, moving forward with my life won't involve her.

It's time for her to be the same afterthought I was.

What I'm about to do now, though, it's another thing that she can't be a part of. In order to go home again, start living and experiencing what it feels like to be healed instead of broken, it's got to happen this way.

Isaac has to meet Gavin.

Isaac

I've read about these things.

You start dating someone and eventually you run into their ex and there's this whole awkward exchange and usually you walk away wondering if the person you love is thinking about what they lost instead of what they have.

When I read about that happening, there was never anything written about what to do when the ex you're going to see isn't even alive anymore. Ryder needs this and I think in a way I do to, but it doesn't mean I'm not completely stuck.

How do you talk to a dead person when you can't even talk?

What's the proper etiquette here? Do I walk up to his grave, type out a message on Ryder's phone and somehow the signal from the phone will reach Heaven and Gavin will know how I feel about him?

I really need to stop watching so many movies.

After talking with his mom, he asked Dillon to drop her off at a hotel after he dropped us off here and we've been stuck at the gate ever since. Neither one of us knows what to do. It should bring me some comfort knowing that he's just as awkward about this whole thing as I am, but it doesn't. He's not the one that's got to stand in front of a gravestone and basically say *'hey I'm the guy that's sleeping with the love of your life'.*

"This was a stupid idea. I don't know what I was thinking. We don't have to do this. We can go."

His body turns, but before he can make it all the way around, I reach out to stop him. I'm not sure why he feels this is what we need to do, but I do know that if he walks away now, I'll never find out.

"Coming here, wanting you to meet Gavin, it's crazy right?"

You're crazy maybe, but the idea isn't.

"I'm crazy, huh?" he smirks. "Anything else you wanna get off your chest while you're at it?"

I want crazy.

The smirk turns into a full on smile and in a movement so quick I have little to no time to process it, his lips are on mine and the rest of the world fades away.

"Good, because even if you didn't want crazy, resistance against it is futile. You're stuck with it."

Is resisting the crazy the same as resisting private time with you in the library?

"Yes. You can try to fight me on it, but I know for a fact that it's going to happen." The light in his eyes dims as his face turns pensive and he turns away from me to look out over all of the markers in front of us. People who have passed, some old, some new and some that never should have left at all.

"Do you think you can give me a couple of minutes alone with him?"

The pain on his face asking me that hurts. He's trying so hard to appear normal and show me that he's alright and not as affected by his past as he was a few hours ago, but he's failing. Ryder is struggling with this and taking my feelings into account is only making it harder for him.

It needs to stop.

Take as much time as you want. I'll wait.

"I love you."

I know.

"Wanting to do this alone, it's not about me not wanting you there or hiding things. I just—"

I don't have the luxury of cutting him off in ways other people would, so I reach out and touch him instead. It gives me exactly what I want as the touch of my hand across his jaw is enough to freeze him in place, his eyes rising until they're locked on me.

It's about you needing time alone with Gavin. Just the two of you. I understand, Ryder. It's okay to love us both.

This is what it's all about. The guilt and shame he had when he was hiding himself away, the thoughts he had about me ripping him apart at the seams because it was a betrayal in his mind of how he felt about Gavin, it all has to do with him believing he can't care about us both.

Another thing he needs to stop because it's wrong.

Ryder is going to love Gavin for the rest of his life. Maybe it won't be in the same way it was when he was alive, but it's never going to die, and I won't be the person that tries to make it happen. I will not be his father. He's had that for long enough. Ryder doesn't need to feel bad or change for me.

"It's not fair to you."

It may not be fair, but it's not unfair either. Whatever you feel, don't bury it because you think it's what I need you to do. You'd be doing it for the wrong reasons. What I need from you, you've already given me by standing here with me right now.

"Isaac..."

Talk to Gavin, Ryder. Tell him whatever you need to say. Get it out and when you're ready, I'll be here.

With a quick brush of his lips against mine, he turns, finally releasing the hold he's had on my hand since we got here and begins the slow descent that will take him to his first love. It's only when he's made it about twenty feet away and comes to a stop that I realize exactly what I have to do while I've got the time to myself.

Ryder isn't the only one that needs to talk to Gavin.

I might not be able to physically voice the words to the stone with his name on it, or even to the sky so that he'll hear me, but I can still have a voice. Make my words mean something.

The note cards from earlier. The ones I wanted to use in order to speak to Ryder's mom, they're still in my back pocket. If I want to make this moment count, I need to use them.

It's time for me to use my voice.

Ryder

"Two visits in less than a couple of weeks. If I keep this up, I'm pretty sure you're gonna get sick of me."

Reaching out and touching the familiar gravestone, chuckling softly, I run my fingers along the grooves in the letters of his name, along with the date of birth and death. It's not the same as it was the last time I was here. Everything has changed now. I finally see what he's been trying to get me to see from the day he met me.

What happened that night could have been handled differently, I could have made better choices, but he doesn't hold it against me. He's forgiven me and still believes in what he did when we were dating.

I deserve to be happy. Deserve to live.

It also helps that I'm not here empty handed. His gift is with me.

"This was almost a different kind of visit, Gav. I was seconds away from fucking everything up again, but like usual, you couldn't let that happen. You wouldn't let me self-destruct. He came for me just the way you planned. He saved me."

Admitting how close I was to the edge, how badly I needed to escape, it's brutal, but I have to do it. I've never hidden how I feel from Gavin before and I'm not going to start now. He needs to know how bad things are now, the same way he did then.

He also needs to know the truth about Isaac even though it creates this huge gaping wound in my soul to admit that there's a possibility he might be replaced. That I might let him go.

It's okay to love us both.

There's not a damn thing about this that's okay. Gavin is gone. Isaac is here, yet it's like I'm betraying both caring about the other. I'm in a tug of war and I don't want there to be a clear winner. I want to love them both. If I believe Isaac, I can do that. I have the best of both worlds even though my world stopped being here a long time ago.

"Gav," I whisper, the emotion I feel just using the shortened version of his name, causing my voice to crack under the weight. "I love him. He's different. I wish you could meet him because I think you'd probably love him even more than I do. He's not afraid to bust my balls or call me out on my shit..."

Referring to him as *he* instead of saying his name, it's more proof of how torn up I am. The minute I say his name, it makes it all real. I want it to be real, I just don't know if I can handle any more pressure.

I need to find the words. Isaac deserves it.

"His name is Isaac, but I figure you know that since it's because of you that he's in my life at all. He started out as my tutor, but I swear, the more time I spend with him, it's not the course work that I'm learning. He's teaching me how to breathe again. I understand the meaning behind a smile now. He's shown me the meaning behind a heartbeat. How it really can beat for another person."

"It's not really any of that stuff that matters though. It's what he's showing me being here today. Isaac makes me believe that forgiveness might be attainable. As guilty as I feel for what happened to you, maybe in time, I can forgive myself the way you already have. For the first time since you died, I don't want to run anymore."

How many can say that they had their life altered by two of the most beautiful people in the world? How they both in different ways touched a part of me I wasn't even aware existed?

I got to experience what living really meant the day I met Gavin and even though I lost him and myself in the process, Isaac found me and brought me home.

He gave me something to live for. Something to fight for.

Something to believe in. A reason to breathe.

To live.

"I wanted to bring him here because I think it's time you see what I see. A promise being fulfilled. I promised you I would move on and now I am. But moving on doesn't mean I'm going to forget. I can never forget you. I just think it's time I did a little bit of living for the both of us."

Sliding up from my place on the ground, I turn back toward where I left Isaac and my heart drops when I see that he's not there. Panic rises in my chest and as I take steps forward, ready to go find him and bring him back, I hear a rustling from behind me.

Turning, I see him and the soft smile on his lips before he motions with his head to the gravestone and slides down to his knees. Placing the phone on the ground to his right, I head back and fall down beside him, reading the message he has waiting for me while he starts to dig at the ground with his hands.

I couldn't wait anymore.

"What are you doing?"

Studying him while he continues to dig at Gavin's plot, his eyes never deviating away from whatever it is he's trying to accomplish, I notice the paper resting on the ground by his knees.

"Isaac..."

Reaching out and touching him, he breaks away from the ground momentarily and grips my hand, his lips parting and mouthing words to me slowly.

I'm talking to Gavin.

Turning back and focusing again, he pulls pieces of the ground up, creating a small hole just big enough for him to slide what I can now see is white note cards into it. They're all bent in half, but there has to be at least four or five of them. Whatever it is Isaac has to say, it's obvious he's found a way for Gavin to hear.

"What are you talking to him about?"

Moving the pieces of the ground back over the plot, grabbing the phone with one hand while he uses the other to even out the ground, he types slowly and after a few minutes pass, hands it over.

I can't tell you what I said, but Ryder, it's not bad. I just wanted to thank him.

"Thank him for what?"

For you.

Is it possible that I'm not the only one that believes Isaac was a gift from Gavin? Does Isaac know and believe it too?

I know how crazy it sounds, believing that my dead ex could have a hand in what's happening here, but with his eagerness to bury whatever it is he had to say and his need to thank him for me, it makes me believe in something that I haven't since I was a kid.

The magic I told Isaac about at Rosewood.

It's real and we're living proof.

Epilogue

Three Months Later

Ryder

"Put it down over there. We'll figure out what to do with it later."

I've been doing the same shit all day. Movers bring the furniture in and I direct them to whatever room in order to dump it off and send them back down for more. It might seem like the world's most tedious chore, but I fucking love it.

It's something solid. Real. A tangible piece of life that I can hold on to and never let go of. Isaac is moving in with me and becoming part of the new and improved script of my life.

Everything changed the night I took him to Gavin's grave and he wrote my ex-boyfriend a letter.

I never did get to read it. I'll always wonder what was so important that he had to dig up the ground a bit in order to bury it, but knowing Isaac, it's more of the same stuff he's been doing with me for the last four months.

Have I wanted to go back to Toronto and dig up that spot in order to find out? Damn right, but I don't because I don't think Gavin would want it that way. He got to see me happy for the first time since he died and that's the way I want my angel to remember me.

Happy. Brought back to life. Complete. Keeping his promises. *The right ones.*

Content that I've got a few minutes before the moving guys invade the space again, I head down the hall until I hit the bedroom.

Our bedroom.

All it took was one night with Isaac to know that I didn't want to go another day without the feel of him next to me.

He altered my life that night and even though I ran from it more times than I stayed, it didn't lessen it. He was with me everywhere, every second and in every possible way. The truth is, I didn't run myself into that pole three months ago because I wasn't the one in control of the wheel.

He was.

Isaac has been saving my life for four months and for the first time since we met, I can't wait to start that life. Which means getting my sexy as fuck boyfriend alone in our bedroom for a few minutes before we're interrupted.

Pushing the door open and walking in, I expect to see him placing things, making the room as much his as it is mine, but he's not up and moving around at all. He's sitting on the bed, his eyes staring off into space, his face indifferent.

When I asked him to do this a couple of days after what happened in Toronto, it wasn't easy. He wanted to be with me, he made sure I knew that, but he was afraid that living with me was a little too much. He had needs and after spending so much time living at home with his parents, he wasn't sure I was going to be able to handle them.

He has no fucking idea.

I don't care what his differences are, or how hard or easy it will be living with him. What I do know is that I love him, and no matter what life wants to throw at us, whether in the form of his diagnosis or otherwise, I want to face it together instead of apart.

His place is here with me and it always will be.

"Baby," I say, making sure to call attention to myself so I don't spook him. "Is everything okay?"

His nod is immediate, but so is the notebook that appears in his lap, along with a pen. Apparently my coming in here wasn't as big a surprise as I thought.

Sitting beside him, but making no move to reach out the way my heart is screaming at me to, I wait patiently for whatever his response is going to be.

Are you sure this is what you want?

"Absolutely." Reaching out and laying my hand on his, I slide my fingers around his hand and give it a reassuring squeeze. "I've never wanted anything more, but you asking that, does it mean you aren't?"

I want this, Ryder. I want to be with you.

"So what's with the sad eyes?"

They're not sad. There's nothing sad about what we're doing. It's just a lot to take in. I still can't believe I'm really here.

I can take what he's saying a couple of ways. I'm pretty surprised I'm here right now too. If you asked me a few months ago where I thought I would end up in the future, I would be the first to tell you that there wasn't a future for me. I wanted to die. Be buried six feet under the same way as Gavin. The world deserved to have me be that way.

Isaac changed all of that and I thought with the way he opened himself up and gave himself completely over to me that he felt the same way. We were both broken and in need of something. At the time, neither of us knew what, but with all the time that's passed, we know it now.

We needed each other.

What was once broken has been put back together.

"Here with me or something else?"

Here with you. Our apartment. Our life together. I didn't think that would ever happen for me. I gave up hope a long time ago.

Another way we're alike. The situations aren't, but the end result is. He thought he was doomed to be alone the rest of his life and I resigned myself to the fact that it's what I deserved.

We were so fucking wrong.

"You didn't give up hope, Isaac. If you did we wouldn't be sitting here now."

When things are too much and I freak out and pull away. When I need to be on my own because being around you or anyone else is going to cause me physical pain I wouldn't be

able to tolerate, are you going to be able to handle that? Will you be able to handle me?

This isn't my Isaac talking. It's the years of abuse he suffered for being different. If people had just come at him the way I did, saw what was inside before the rest of it, he wouldn't be the way he is now. It also means that we wouldn't be together because some guy out there would have seen his fucking awesomeness way before now and snagged him before I could.

I can't let him keep going down this road. I know it's huge; us living together, but as big as it is, it's also right. I need him to remember that.

"Can I ask you something?"

He nods and when he doesn't make a move to write anything on the paper, I take it as a cue to continue.

"At the end of every day, when you close your eyes, where do you see yourself?"

His answer is a whole lot quicker than I expect it to be. It's also singlehandedly the most important thing besides I love you that he's ever said to me.

In this room with you. I want my day to begin and end with you, Ryder.

"What happens when I want to be alone? When I've driven you so nuts with all the stupid shit I do that we can't even stand to look at each other?"

I still want to be here with you.

"Then you have your answer. I know this isn't going to be easy. I'm not a moron. We've both got issues. We're also both in therapy for those issues so we can figure out the right way to make this work. As long as this is where we end up at the end of every day, then I'll handle whatever you throw at me."

About a month after the shit with Randy, I made an appointment to talk to someone. After the initial appointment and then the few that came after it, what was going on with me finally had a name attached to it.

The nightmares, the episodes I had where I would lose track of space and time, combined with the way I relived the accident any chance I got and acted out with women and alcohol, it had a name.

PTSD.

What I thought was survivor's guilt because it was what the doctors at the time assumed my problem was, turned out to be something a lot heavier and with the right treatment could be handled. I'm not cured—not by a long shot—but seeing a therapist three days a week, along with talking openly with Isaac, my mom and Dillon, it's helped. What threatened to kill me before, is being handled now.

About a week after I started therapy, Isaac said we needed to talk. At the time, with us being so new, I expected to hear the break up speech. I shut down again, but in true Isaac fashion he made sure that didn't last long.

He wanted to look into therapies too. What he told me that day in Rosewood, he wanted to go back on it. He knew there was no guarantee that he would ever speak, but he wasn't willing to rest until he was sure he had exhausted every available option.

It easily became another reason in the forever growing list of why I love him.

Would it be amazing if he spoke to me? Of course, but what he's learning, the same way I am is that sound is not all it's cracked up to be. I can hear him loud and clear and he doesn't have to say a word.

That's what love is. A vibration or frequency that only two hearts can hear.

Hearing without a sound.

Why is it that the rest of the apartment looks like a tornado blew through it, but this room looks perfect?

He thinks he's being funny, redirecting the conversation away from what I admitted, but the way his body responds when I wrap my arm around him and bring him close, it says so much more than any words on the paper ever could.

"Even with our issues, a move like this is huge. When I got here yesterday, I wanted to make sure that there was one place where that wasn't a problem. So I stayed up half the night in order to make it happen."

When Dillon talked to me about moving out, explaining his situation with Cadence and how life was about to take a pretty big turn for him, it all came together and I went and talked to my mother.

Keeping true to her word, she'd left my dad and was determined to start a new life. One that included me and making sure that what I'm doing now could happen. It wasn't perfect, but it was a good place to start.

It's like my therapist keeps telling me. Baby steps. I have to take these miniscule little steps in order to get to a place where the accident and everything that happened afterward doesn't haunt me, and I've got to do the same with her.

Why do I get the feeling there's more you're not telling me?

"Not following."

You had an ulterior motive for the room, didn't you?

Even with all the time that's passed it never ceases to amaze me how easily he sees through me. How he never truly takes anything at face value. Isaac has one of the most analytical minds I know, and what he doesn't piece together with facts himself, he observes until the real motivations are known.

He knows why I focused my attention on the bedroom and now all he needs is for me to confirm it.

"Let's say you're right and I do have another motive. Is that a bad thing?"

Yes Ryder. It's a *very* bad thing.

One of the easiest ways for me to tell if he's joking or teasing is the faces he'll draw on the paper or type out when he's got my phone. For the first few weeks together it was the only way I could gauge his mood, but now, he's been trying to be less obvious. There's only one problem with what he's trying to do. He forgets that when he teases me, his eyes dance.

"Maybe bad was what I was going for."

His body shifts in my arms and where I expect him to pull away, aware as I am that we're not alone in the apartment, he turns just enough to press the front of his body into mine, the weight of him pushing me back on the bed.

The movement continues as he shifts his body over mine until his legs are pressed into the outside of my thighs and his lips are pressing down on mine in a kiss. The attraction between us manifesting itself in urgent need as his tongue slips out and pushes against my lips until they're separated and he's deepening the kiss, his hands continuing to move over every part of skin he can reach.

Searing me.

"Isaac—movers." I breathe out as our lips momentarily separate. He needs to know I want this as badly as he does, maybe even more, but not with an audience.

Holding up a hand, he slides his body off of mine, lingering for a few seconds before pulling himself off the bed, making quick work of the steps it takes to get to the door. Watching as he pushes the door closed and hearing the lock click into place, in the time it takes me to blink he's back on me again.

Gone is the shy inexperienced guy I met months ago, and in his place is the result of what happens whenever we get within a few feet of each other. As his lips touch the skin of my neck, his tongue darting out and licking before he begins to suck, all thoughts of the move, the guys we have helping, and all of the work we're gonna have to do later fades into oblivion until all I can feel is him.

He wins.

Isaac can be in control, just as long as he doesn't ever stop doing what he's doing right now. He's bringing me to life and I'm going to enjoy every god damned second of it.

Isaac

These are the moments I enjoy most.

Some people call them the calm before the storm, but when you've been through everything that Ryder and I have, there is no storm. You're just left with the calm and it's so simple that it's perfect.

Every sense is heightening lying here like this. I can feel the rise and fall of his chest as I've finally allowed him to come up for air after the assault my lips leveled on him. The beat of his heart as it attempts to regulate itself. The barely there scent of our lovemaking mixed with the sweat of our bodies, connecting us more than just emotionally.

The time where desire and need have been sated and all that's left is the aftermath.

Love. Adoration. Peace and Acceptance.

A sense of belonging.

When I'm with Ryder, I'm home.

"I never get tired of feeling that."

What he's feeling, it's got nothing at all to do with what we just shared. The way it felt tasting him or the way it feels every time he's inside me. It's what I do afterward.

Tracing my feelings into the fine hairs of his chest as I lay with him. Repeating the same three words while adding other ones that after the last few months together, he's learned to pick up on easily.

I'm the first to admit that when I thought about how this would feel the first time, being intimate with someone and not having the ability to voice the words to express everything I felt, it scared me. I always assumed that even if it did happen, it wouldn't last because there wouldn't be a person alive willing to get past the language barrier.

I would end up alone.

Ryder changed all of that. He heard me. Or as he likes to tell me every chance he gets; he feels me.

"We need to get out there and get this finished, but before I shift my body and totally ruin this moment, I need you to do something for me."

Tracing the okay in the center of his chest and hearing the soft chuckle I'm rewarded with, I feel his hand move until it's over mine and he's bringing it up to rest over his heart.

"Isaac, you know what I want."

I do know. Whenever we're alone this way and we know that we have places we need to be, he always asks for the same thing.

It's his way of staying connected and one I'm more than happy to give him because it does the same thing for me.

"Mark me."

The first time we made love, how focused he was on making it perfect, I did this and ever since he's referred to it as a mark. When I tell him that I love him, running my fingers slowly over the place where his heart resides, I am marking it and now it's a routine we both need and want.

One that we never want to change.

I love you.

"Maybe getting you to do that wasn't such a good thing after all."

Laughing the minute I trace the question mark on his skin, he lowers his head and tips mine up until we're focused solely on each other.

"I don't want to move. Staying here and having you mark me, is a hell of a lot more fun than telling overgrown meatheads where to put our shit."

He captures my lips the minute the smile causes them to lift and instead of focusing on the way it feels whenever we're together like this, I think about just how far we've both come since the first time we kissed.

Ryder on the road to self-destruction and me wrapped up tightly in my bubble. Both of us attempting to just get through each day, survive in the only way we knew how. How we fought the attraction first and the feelings second because it was just never something either one of us thought we deserved.

Flashing forward to months later and what we're about to embark on now.

Living together, going to school, completely committed to being better than we were and giving something back to the world we thought had taken everything from us. Ryder losing Gavin and me losing my voice and being labelled with a diagnosis that made me feel like less instead of more.

Broken open. No longer running from what we feel. Instead embracing it even though it's still just as scary as it ever was.

We've come such a long way from that first kiss, but no matter how hard it was, I wouldn't change a second of it. In order to have this moment now, I would walk through fire if it's what was needed.

"Okay. Yes. I'm definitely getting up because kissing me like that isn't playing fair."

Not even attempting to hide my grin as I move, I slide to the end of the bed, picking my clothes off the floor and as I'm about to stand in order to slide back into my pants, his arms reaches out, grasping mine and stopping me cold.

"I'm gonna finish this. We're going to get something to eat and then I'm bringing you back here and we're not leaving again until the morning. Think you can handle that, tutor boy?"

Leaning over the bed until my forehead is pressed gently to his, I smile before nodding slowly, kissing him again, eliciting another growl as he reacts and again fights to control the situation. Content that I've teased him enough, I pull away but not before hearing the desire filled moan and exhale of breath he releases the minute I've let him go.

"Thank you."

Sliding the phone off the nightstand, I type out the question and turn it toward him.

For pulling away?

"No. I didn't want you to do that, even though we need to."

So what are you thanking me for?

"For choosing me and for not pulling away when I kept giving you every reason to. I love you, Isaac."

I love you more, Ryder.

Before he can respond, there's a bang from the front of the apartment and the feelings we've been acting on, what we've spent the last few minutes completely engrossed in finally settles as reality sets in.

Slipping his body off the other side of the bed away from me, sliding into his pants so quickly it's hard to imagine he'd even had them off, he makes his way around until he's picking up his shirt and sliding it over his head. Kissing me softly, he slips the phone out of my hands and reads what I've left for him.

Do you think they heard us?

Grinning, he hands the phone back and runs his fingers along my jaw.

"With as loud as you made me, I damn sure hope they heard. I want the whole world to know how fucking hot my tutor boy makes me." Pulling back and turning his body toward the door, he grips his hand around mine, prepared to finally head out to what's waiting for us.

"Now let's go. The sooner we get these guys out of here, the sooner we can get started on christening the rest of the apartment."

Ryder

It's the strangest fucking thing, but standing in the doorway to the kitchen and watching as Isaac makes something as basic as a peanut butter sandwich, it stirs things in me. Some familiar and others new, but all of them welcomed.

I wonder what it would be like to take him on that counter he's working so diligently over, but it's something far sweeter that dominates me.

It's the way he just fits so easily into the picture of my life. Having him in the kitchen making us dinner, even if it is the cheapest thing on the planet, is the most natural thing in the world. What's stirring in me is the knowledge that this is what I want. It's what I've always wanted and now, with this amazing guy that just sees past all my bullshit, I get to have it.

I have it all.

When the movers brought the last box up, I made them hide it away in the bedroom. It wasn't like all the others. What I put in there when I started packing up the things in my old apartment, it couldn't be seen until the time was right.

The time is now.

Unpacking it the minute the guys left, making sure that it had made the trip in one piece, I wrapped it back up in the towel that it had been packed with and ended up out here.

"Babe, do you think I can steal you away from that for a second?"

When he turns, the familiar flash in his dark eyes telling me without words exactly what he wants rejuvenates my earlier thought about the counter and it takes everything in me to swallow it. Isaac is insatiable and while I plan on delivering on exactly what it is he wants, it has to wait until later.

What I'm about to do now matters more.

"That look in your eye is a to-be-continued. I want to show you something."

Meeting me at the doorway, he slips his hand easily in mine and I guide him into the bedroom again, a move that judging by the way his eyes go wide is not lost on him.

"Relax boyfriend, this is not what you think. Like I said, it's to-be-continued." With a squeeze to his hand I slip mine out and head over to the bed, being extra careful not to disturb what's underneath the towel as I pick it up and make my way back over to him.

When I first put this together weeks ago, I had this plan in my head that I was going to blindfold him and make it a whole big surprise, but with as eager as I am for him to see this and for me to explain to him what it really means, drawing it out is definitely not going to happen.

Slipping my phone out of his back pocket, he types a message out and turns the screen toward me.

You wanted to show me an old towel?

"No, smartass." I laugh. "I wanted to show you what's underneath the towel."

With a grin of his own he flips the phone around again and proves to me just how insatiable he is.

Unless it's you naked under that towel, I'm not interested ;)

"Focus baby. I'll make that wish come true later too, but only if you stop trying to distract me by turning me on."

Sliding my one hand off the surprise, I motion for him to give me the phone and when he does, I hold the gift out. It's time for him to take this now. Once he slips the towel off and sees what it is, he can have the phone back, but until then, this is where I want his focus to be.

"When you agreed to move in with me, I put this together. It's not a lot, but I wanted you to be able to see something every day that would remind you of what you mean to me. How much I love you."

Taking it from my hands, both of us reacting to the jolt that flows through us the second our fingers touch, he looks down at it before looking back at up at me, the water already beginning to pool in the corner of his eyes.

"You can unwrap the towel now, babe."

Moving over toward the bed, sitting down and placing the surprise in his lap, he makes quick work of the towel until all that's left is all I have to give since he already owns the rest.

A mahogany square picture frame, but not filled with a picture the way I'm sure he was expecting when he first pulled it out. What's inside this frame says everything that a picture can't.

It's a single flower, but not just any flower. A bright yellow dandelion. One I picked the night we went to Rosewood and set to work encasing in the frame so that it could create the one thing that he wanted as a kid, but could never have.

A dandelion that will never die.

The tears that I could see building when he first took the frame are falling now, but he doesn't make a move to stop them. Sliding onto the bed beside him, wanting to capture more of this moment than standing a few feet away can give me, he lifts his head from the frame and levels me with his soft gaze.

With the frame secure in his lap, his hands begin moving and unlike the last time he did this, I don't reach out to stop him. It's another thing we've been working on since we got together, even enlisting Cadence and Dillon to help.

He signed to me the day I kissed him on the side of the road. A way for him to say what he couldn't get the words out for and it ate at me for weeks afterwards because while I knew basic sign, I didn't know enough to express my feelings back to him, something that now, I can do.

"You're welcome and I love you too."

Handing the phone back, he wastes no time responding and holding it up for me to see.

Why?

"Why do I love you or why did I do this?"

Why did you do this?

"You told me before that dandelions make you sad because they die. I never really gave it much thought before, but like the rose color was symbolic to me and to us, so is this."

How so?

"What you're holding in your hand is a flower that will never die. It's what the rest of the world cares little about, just a weed in the ground that over time will wither and fade into nothingness. Until I met you, I was that weed, but just like the dandelion in the frame, I'm not dead. I do exist and it's all because of you and the way you love me."

You're not a weed, Ryder.

"I know and before you argue with me and say that you are, let's just agree that you aren't either. This dandelion, though, it's more important than just what it symbolized for me personally. It's what it means for us."

Which is what?

"It's me wanting to deal in absolutes. Instead of saying *if* that happens, it's now *when.* That flower, it's vibrant and alive and it's the perfect way to show you how I feel when we're together. Isaac, it means that what I have with you, as long as I'm breathing, won't ever die."

I don't know what to say…

"Who says you have to say anything? Your eyes tell me how this makes you feel and what it means to you. That's more than enough for me. You are more than enough."

Moving his body closer to mine on the bed, he places the frame down softly onto the blanket and leans into my willing and waiting arms. After a few minutes of enjoying the quiet; the absolute calm that comes from being with him this way, the clicking sound of his fingers across the phone screen brings me back to reality.

I think I know what I want to say now.

Typing quickly across the screen, he lays it across my lap and bring his hands up to my chest, right beside the spot where his head rests, and the same way he did earlier when we made love, he traces the familiar words across my heart.

Reveling in the feeling of his fingers as they graze my skin, I let my eyes fall to the message written on the phone. The one that in the moment I had forgotten completely about.

Us against the world.

"You're wrong." I whisper and as he looks up, I smile softly. "It's not us against the world anymore because what we have *is* the world."

I love you.

His fingers begin their trail again and just like earlier, the rest of the world fades away as the words come alive on my skin, burning a path straight through the shirt I'm wearing, onto the skin below until it penetrates and marks the very part of me that he owns so completely.

My soul.

The untouched has created the unbroken...

The End.

Isaac's Letter to Gavin

Gavin,

Thank you.
For as long as I can remember, I've wanted two things in my life. One was to have a friend. To have just one person in the world that I could turn to when nothing else seemed to make sense and know that they were there for me and with me. I got to experience that for the first time months ago and now because of you I'm getting the other thing I want.

Love.
With Ryder.
Thank you for loving him. If you hadn't done that, I wouldn't get to experience what it feels like to be loved and accepted by him now. I've had a taste of how that feels even though he's still holding back and I can't imagine living the rest of my life without it.

Your life and even your death doesn't just have meaning and purpose for Ryder. Because of what you gave me that day a little over a month ago, you also mean something to me. Wherever you are right now, I hope that you can see or sense these words and know that I mean every one of them.

Thank you, Gavin. Not only for giving me the chance to love Ryder the way he deserves, but for trusting me enough to keep him safe and bring him back to life the same way you did when you met him in high school.

If nothing else I've said means anything, I hope this last sentence does.

I won't let you down.
Ryder will never be broken again.
As long as we have each other and we stand together, we'll be what we were meant to be right from start.

Unbroken.

Unbroken Playlist

Solitary by Faber Drive
Creep by Radiohead
Unbroken by Black Veil Brides
Castle Of Glass by Linkin Park
The Memory by Mayday Parade
I Am Machine by Three Days Grace
Stormy by Hedley
Welcome To My Life by Simple Plan
Easier To Run by Linkin Park
Underneath by Adam Lambert
Crash by Seether
Painkiller by Three Days Grace
Outlaws Of Love by Adam Lambert
Wicked Game by Chris Isaak
Book Of Me And You by The Maine
Chalk Outline by Three Days Grace
The Last Night by Skillet
Runnin' by Adam Lambert
Fire And Fury by Skillet
Broken Open by Adam Lambert
The Mess I Made by Parachute
They Don't Need To Understand by Andy Black
Write It Down by Framing Hanley
Something Worth Defending by Enation
Better Than Me by Hinder
Be Yourself by Audioslave

Acknowledgements

To my amazing beta readers that have been with me on this journey for the last three books and never wavered once in all that time. Lisa and Pamela. Your tireless efforts to help me bring this book to life in the best possible way are tremendous and I love both of your faces so hard for it. Unbroken is what it is because of the time you spent working right along with me, letting me have it when things didn't add up and picking me back up when I wondered what the hell I was even doing taking this on at all. You mean the absolute world to me and you always will.

To the Hummel to my Berry. Thank you for your ongoing support of everything I do and for being a sounding board when I told you this book was coming to life. I love you, Hummel, more and more every day. One day, I hope to be along on your crazy ride as you take this journey with me.

Joey. As much as I acknowledge you in these books, you'd think I'd run out of things to say. Best friend, left arm, superhero, beta-reader and even part time writer (Dillon Murphy forever), I love you and it's an always and forever kind of thing. Thank you for being who you are and for leaving your mark on my world.

My kids. Caleb, Noah, Raine and Isabella. I love you more than words can say and I'm so blessed that I was the one you chose to be your mother. No matter where you go from here, the highs and the lows, one thing will never change, and that is my love and adoration for all of you.

To each and every person that picks up a book of mine. I appreciate each and every one of you. I wouldn't be able to do what I'm doing if it wasn't for readers like you, so from me and every other author on the planet, thank you so much for reading. It means the absolute world to me and to us all.

About The Author

Melyssa Winchester is a mother of four from Toronto, Ontario, Canada. When she's not knee deep in adolescent awesomeness, she's falling in love, one book boyfriend and girlfriend at a time. She is a lover of all things romance and will forever believe in a real and true happily ever after.

When she's not off being a mom or writing you can find her doing one of two things. Reading or buried under the covers watching Supernatural, Sons of Anarchy, The Flash or Veronica Mars.

Melyssa is currently working on **Take My Hand** (The ending to the Count On Me series) as well as the standalone new adult contemporary romance **Remembering Sunday**.

You can find her on the web, either at her personal site, Facebook (which she just might have an obsession with) or Twitter (@WinchesterBooks) where she talks incessantly about her kids, her writing and all things book boyfriend related.

Other Works by Melyssa Winchester

Love United Series

Holding On To Heaven
My Heaven (HOTH Alternate Ending)
No Surrender
Wanted
Stairway To Heaven
A Light In The Dark

Count On Me Series
(Can Be Read Standalone)

Count On Me
Hear Me Now
Take Me With You
All My Heart
Here & Now
Unbroken
Take My Hand (Coming Soon)

www.ingramcontent.com/pod-product-compliance
Lightning Source LLC
Chambersburg PA
CBHW071206250626
47159CB00001B/217